Oaklade

by

J. M. Nydam

Oaklade

Copyright © 2014 by Jacqueline Nydam

ISBN: 978-09912256-0-6

Printed in the United States of America

Paperback edition / January 2014

Cover Design: AlarmEighteen/Jack Tuckwell

In loving memory of

Nik Townend

A brief, but intense spark
in the light of the world.

Prologue

I am old now. Even though the elves blessed me with a very long life, I am way past my time to be gone from here.

My Order tried to stop me telling this story, but I don't think it matters now. Most of the elders are gone. Just about all of the elves and elviron that were involved in this tale have also gone. Only the youngest connected to any part of this remain, and they are unaware of the events that took place.

I would like to remain anonymous, but you may recognize me, as I played some part in this.

It all began when the elves in the Realm of Kimadrian and the elviron in the Realm of Distardrian shared a prophesy.

The prophesy said that from a liaison between a human, and either an elf or an elviron, an offspring would be born to save both realms, thus restoring peace.

The written information about the prophesy, was sketchy at best. All who knew about it couldn't remember when it was made. As time passed it became just a story.

Then one day everything changed.

Grymlons *n.*(grimlon) set of five glass spheres
protected by the elves.

Part One

Chapter One
Two Years Ago

Charles Ghenestone was navigating the car through darkness and heavy rain. Audrey, his wife was in the passenger seat beside him. Jesse, their twelve year old son sat in the back. He stared out of the window, watching as the rain spattered onto the glass, exploding into small silvery blobs.

"Well, I thought the play was very good," Charles commented.

"So did I," said Audrey. "You were very good as Puck, Jesse."

"It was just a silly school play," Jesse muttered.

"Did you enjoy playing the part of Puck?" Charles asked, peering into the darkness.

"Yes," Jesse answered, making a wobbly line with his index finger through the condensation on the window.

"Well then, that's an added bonus," Charles said, pulling his sleeve over his right palm, wiping the fog from his side of the windscreen. "All in all, a good play with some very good actors."

"I agree," Audrey chipped in.

"It would have been nice if Liz and Grandma Rose had been able to come," said Jesse.

Audrey turned, looking at him. "Your gran had a Women's Institute meeting tonight, and Liz had already made arrangements to stay with Meg."

Charles leaned forward, squinting at the glare on the windshield. "This weather is atrocious."

Audrey noticed headlights coming straight at them. "Charles, is that car on the wrong side of the road?"

"There may be something in the way, Aud. There, see? He's moved over."

"CHARLES, LOOK OUT!" Audrey shouted, too late.

The car speeding towards them suddenly veered over to their side of the road again. The impact of the cars hitting head on, shattered Charles Ghenestone's ankles, shoving his feet three inches up his legs. The steering wheel pushed his ribs into his heart, killing him instantly.

Blood and grey matter flew around the inside of the car, as though shot from a cannon, when the front of Audrey Ghenestone's head hit the windshield. She died without regaining consciousness at the local hospital a few hours later.

Jesse Ghenestone was pronounced dead at the scene from head injuries.

The driver of the other car was nowhere to be found.

Chapter Two

It was midnight when the police arrived at the Reese residence.

Lillian Reese woke to the doorbell ringing. She glanced at the clock on the wall, as she pulled on her robe and hurried down the stairs.

"The persistence of that doorbell can only mean trouble," she thought.

She opened the door to find two police constables standing on the step.

"Good evening, madam. I am Constable Woolford and this is Constable Wilkins," announced the older of the two. "We're sorry to wake you, madam, but we understand that you have a young lady by the name of Elizabeth Ghenestone staying with you."

Lillian peered around them, noticing Rose Humphries, Elizabeth's grandmother standing off to the side.

"Rose?"

Rose stepped forward. "We need to talk to Elizabeth."

"Of course, come in. All of you, come in," Lillian said, stepping aside.

The three of them entered the hallway. Lillian closed the door. She shuffled passed them, leading the way to the living room, where everyone found a place to sit.

Lillian Reese sat next to Elizabeth's grandma, noticing Rose's tear stained face.

"Lillian, something horrible has happened," Rose said, "Audrey, Charles and Jesse were killed in a car crash earlier this evening."

Lillian suddenly felt heat radiate through her core, causing a slight sensation of nausea. "Oh my god, Rose! I'm so sorry. Can I make you a cup of tea, or perhaps something stronger?"

"A cup of tea would be nice," Rose said, hoping the tea would quell the feeling in the pit of her stomach.

"I think a nice cup of tea would do us all the world of good," said Constable Wilkins.

Lillian stood. "I'll go and wake Elizabeth and ask her to come down, then I'll put the kettle on."

Megan Reese had jumped out of bed when she heard the police car pull into the driveway. She crept to the door, and opened it just enough to see out. She closed it quickly when she realized her mother was coming up the stairs, and turned to Elizabeth who had sat up, disturbed by Megan's movement. "I think your gran is downstairs, and she's not alone."

Elizabeth yawned. "Are my mum and dad here too?"

"Someone's here with her, but I don't think it's your parents, Liz. My mum is coming up the stairs," Megan said, jumping into bed.

Lillian pushed open the bedroom door. "Good, you're both awake. Elizabeth, your gran is here to see you."

Elizabeth glanced at Megan, then at Lillian Reese. "But it's almost one o'clock in the morning."

"Yes dear. Please put your dressing gown on and come down with me. Megan, I want you to stay here."

"But mum, why can't I come down with you?"

"Meg, do as I ask please, and stay here. I'll come and get you in a minute."

Elizabeth followed Lillian down the stairs. As she entered the living room, both of the Constables and Rose Humphries stood.

"I'll be in the kitchen," Lillian said, closing the living room door behind her.

Elizabeth looked at the three of them looking back at her. "Gran, what are you doing here?"

Rose Humphries sat back down on the couch and moved over to make room for her. "Why don't you sit down, dear."

Elizabeth stared at the empty cushion next to her grandma. A dull humming sensation began to fill her head. "I don't want to sit down."

"Please miss, sit down," said Constable Wilkins.

Elizabeth took the seat offered.

Rose Humphries turned to her granddaughter. "Elizabeth, there has been an accident."

"What sort of an accident?" Elizabeth asked, swallowing down the bitter taste in her mouth.

"Your mum and dad and Jesse were in a car crash tonight," Rose's voice broke as she heard the sound of her own words.

The dull humming between Elizabeth's ears turned into a loud rushing sound.

"And?"

"They were hit head on by a car. They are all, well..."

"Dead?" said Elizabeth, feeling her throat constrict.

"Yes dear," Rose Humphries answered, unable to hold back the tears any longer.

Elizabeth stood. "Gran," was all she said, before she collapsed to the floor.

"Elizabeth!"

Rose Humphries dropped to her knees beside her.

Constable Wilkins was already on his radio asking for an ambulance. He knelt down and took Elizabeth's pulse.

"I think she has fainted ma'am," he said.

"If you will excuse me," Rose Humphries said. She left the room, breaking into a run for the toilet. She locked the door, fell to her knees and vomited violently into the toilet bowl.

"Rose. Are you all right?" Lillian inquired from the other side of the door.

Rose Humphries stood. She looked into the mirror over the sink, noticing dark circles under her eyes. "Yes, I'll be out in a minute," she said, as she wiped her mouth and flushed the toilet.

The ambulance was arriving just as she was returning to the living room.

Two paramedics entered, and one of them examined the still unconscious Elizabeth.

"What happened here?" one of them asked.

"She has just been told that her parents and brother are dead." Constable Woolford answered.

"She is in severe shock," the paramedic said, reaching for the radio on his left shoulder. "We'll have to take her to hospital straight away."

"Can I come with you?" Rose asked. "I'm her gran. She'll need a familiar face if she wakes."

"I'll give you a lift, Rose," said Lillian. "Let me just go and tell the children where I'm going."

Lillian Reese went back up the stairs. Andre, Megan's brother had joined her in her bedroom by now. They were both looking out of the window when their mother walked in.

Andre turned to his mother. "What's happened, mum?"

"I have to take Grandma Rose to hospital with Elizabeth."

"What's wrong with Elizabeth?" said Megan.

"She's just found out that her mum and dad and Jesse have been killed in a car accident. When Elizabeth was told, she fainted and we have to take her to make sure she is all right."

"Bloody hell!"

Lillian's head shot around to her son. "ANDRE! I'll have none of that sort of talk in this house. Do you understand?"

"Yes, mum. Sorry, mum."

"I've spoken to dad on his cell, and he'll be home in about an hour. If you can't sleep, you can go downstairs until he get's here."

Andre put a hand on his mother's shoulder. "Don't you worry about us, mum. We'll be all right here. Won't we, Meg."

"Absolutely," Megan said.

Lillian Reese hurried back down the stairs and grabbed her coat. Rose Humphries was waiting by the door.

"You all right, Rose? Can I get you anything before we go?"

"No thanks, Lillian. I just want to get to the hospital. I've lost enough family tonight. I'm worried to death about Elizabeth."

Lillian and Rose followed the ambulance out of the driveway. Megan and Andre watched from the living room window as they disappeared from sight.

"Bloody hell. How awful!" said Andre. "Do you think she'll be all right?"

Megan turned away from the window. "Don't swear, Andre. You know how mum and dad hate it when you swear. How would you feel if you lost mum and dad both in one night!"

"I wish dad was here," said Andre.

Megan turned on the television. "He should be home soon, so we'll just sit up and wait for him."

***

Rose Humphries and Lillian Reese waited for three hours before the doctor appeared.

He took a seat beside Rose and patted her arm reassuringly. "Elizabeth is conscious, but she is unable to move her legs."

"Why?" asked Rose.

"Sometimes when a person has experienced severe shock, it can manifest itself in other parts of the body," he explained. "We can't find anything physically wrong with Elizabeth's legs. Very rarely do these situations become permanent, but only time will tell."

Part Two

Chapter One
Present Day

In the village of Kimadria, a slightly overweight elf sat at the bar of the Three Fishes Inn. His name was Brondly Blakely. His red hair dropped down in front of his eyes, refusing to be combed into any sort of neatness.

Until recently, he had been employed as a King's guard at the castle in Kimadrian.

Brondly looked around him, watching the hustle and bustle of the customers talking and moving around.

"I'm going to get drunk and to hell with everyone and everything," he thought.

The Inn wasn't the nicest place in town. It smelled of stale beer. The floors didn't look as though they had been cleaned in months, but it had a reputation for cheap drinks.

"Uh, I'd like another ale here, please?" Brondly said, raising his empty glass for the innkeeper to see.

The innkeeper put a glass of amber liquid in front of him. Brondly lifted the glass to his lips and was about to take a drink, when one of the guards who worked at the castle came in. As the guard sat at the bar, Brondly noticed that he was still in uniform.

"You're not supposed to be in uniform when you are off duty," Brondly said, not looking at the guard.

The guard bridled at Brondly's remark. "You can't order me around <u>sir</u>. You don't work at the castle anymore."

Brondly faced the guard, staring him up and down. "I don't care if I work there or not. You should not be in uniform away from the castle, if you are not on duty."

"I don't think the way I'm dressed is any of your business," said the guard. "Besides, it didn't seem to bother you much when you were still employed there."

"It's Jolen isn't it?" said Brondly, beginning to feel slightly irritated. "What's that supposed to mean, Jolen?"

Jolen stood. "Well we all know why you don't wear this uniform anymore, don't we," he said, pointing to his chest and looking around at the other customers.

"And why is that?" said Brondly, pushing his stool back.

Jolen grinned. "Because you're a drunk, Brondly. We all know it. That's why no one will give you a job. Look at you. You can't even stand up straight."

Brondly stepped forward. He was about to punch Jolen in the face, when someone from behind caught his arm in mid-swing.

Brondly turned to see Gredly, another off duty guard standing behind him. Gredly was out of uniform, and had been watching the situation unfold from a table by the door. He kept his hold on Brondly, as he looked at Jolen and shook his head. Jolen sat back down and took a swig from his drink.

Gredly stood between the two of them. "Why don't you go home sir, take a bit of a nap. Jolen here, he don't mean no harm. Do you Jolen."

Jolen muttered something under his breath and took another drink.

Brondly pulled his arm away. "I don't need a babysitter, thank you."

Momentum overtook Brondly as he turned. He lost his balance and landed squarely on his bottom on the flagstone floor.

A hushed snickering reverberated around the room, as Brondly stood, brushing off the pants of his tunic.

"You think that's funny, do you?" he said, shaking his fist at the room. "I could take on any one of you lot with one arm tied behind my back," he shouted, staggering to the door.

"Hey, Brondly. You haven't paid your bill!" the innkeeper shouted.

"I'll pay it," said Gredly, putting elven coins on the bar.

Brondly lurched out of the Inn and onto the street. "I've never been so embarrassed in my life! I don't understand. I wasn't that bad. I've worked all those years, just to be tossed out like a piece of old rubbish, and now I'm running out of money. What am I going to do?"

Elves were staring at him as they passed by.

"What are you all looking at?" he shouted, feeling anger stir in him again, as he staggered down the street towards his house.

"Everyone is talking about me as though I'm some sort of criminal," he continued to mutter as he walked. "They are saying I'm a drunk and that I'm unreliable. Well I'm not a drunk! I like a drink once in a while, but I'm a good worker. My nephew, Bindyl will be the first to tell you that I'm a good elf,"

"Bindyl's a fine young elf, he is. Makes good money at the castle as an aid to Prince Gideon. I wish I had a job!"

Elves were now crossing over to the other side of the street to avoid him.

When Brondly reached home, he made a cup of strong hot elven tea.

"Fegler told me that there might be work at the feed store. I'll sober up a bit, change my clothes and go into Kimadria," he thought.

After half a dozen more cups of elven tea, Brondly walked back to Kimadria. He made his way along the cobbled stone streets, heading for Blackburr's Farm Supply Shop.

"I have known Narius since we were children," thought Brondly. I'm sure once he knows I need a job he will employ me."

When he reached the shop, Brondly noticed that the help wanted sign was still in the window.

It read.

'Wanted, a reliable elf to stock shelves, load carts and other various duties. Apply within.'

Brondly licked his fingers and ran them through his hair, straightened out the top half of his tunic and walked in through the front door.

"May I help you sir?" asked the man behind the counter.

"Hello Narius. I am here about the job in the window. I have a strong back and I'm willing to work hard."

Narius did not look up, as he wrapped a customer's package. "Uh, I'm afraid that position has been filled."

"But the sign is still in the window," said Brondly.

Narius hurried over to the window. He pulled the sign down and put it under the counter. "I'm sorry Brondly."

Brondly looked around the shop. "Then where is your new employee?"

Narius turned red as he faced Brondly. "I don't think that is any of your business. Now if you will excuse me, Brondly. I have customers."

Brondly knew it was useless to argue. He left the shop and continued around the corner. Once out of sight, he peered around the building he had just walked behind and looked back at the shop. He was just in time to see Narius putting the 'Help Wanted' sign back in the window.

Brondly stood for a moment. "I'll never find a job at this rate. I need a drink and I know just the place."

He turned away from the shop and went down a back alley to the Skeletons Head Pub. He stepped through the door and went to the bar, taking a seat with the locals.

"Hello Brondly," said one of the elves, already sitting at the bar. "Haven't seen you in a while."

"I'm not working at the castle anymore," said Brondly. "They accused me of drinking on the job. It was a lie of course. Just an excuse to get rid of me."

"Well, I'm sorry to hear that," said the elf. "If there's anything I can do for you, let me know. I'm here most nights, so you'll know where to find me."

Brondly smiled at his drinking partner. "Thanks. If you hear of anyone who is looking for help, I really need a job. I'll be running out of money soon."

"I'm being portrayed as a lazy drunk," Brondly said to the barkeeper, who nodded in an understanding manner.

"My only sin is not being understood by my employer. I worked at the castle for years. Worked my way up the ranks I did, but that didn't seem to matter. When it suited them, I was out on my ear."

An old elf was sitting at a table in the corner of the room. His grey hair rested just above his shoulders. The skin on his face was wrinkled and his teeth were long and discoloured. His chicken claw hand reached out and lifted his drink to his mouth.

He watched Brondly and smiled. "My patience and searching has paid off. I think I've found the perfect person for my little plan," he thought.

The old elf stood and hobbled over to Brondly.

"I could not help but hear you, as I was sitting over there," he said, pointing to his table. "I was wondering if perhaps you would allow me to buy you a drink?"

Brondly eyed the old elf, who stood a little too close. He smelt musty, like old stale hay.

"Are you from around here?" asked Brondly.

"Actually no. I have a small farm over by the Kimadrian-Distardrian border. I don't come into town much, unless I need some supplies. Would you like a drink?"

"I don't suppose it could hurt," said Brondly, "but I can't return the favour. I don't have a lot of money to spare these days, now I'm unemployed."

The old elf smiled, revealing his missing teeth. "As I said, I have been listening to you. Come on, come and sit down. We will drink ale and have some good conversation."

"I didn't catch your name," said Brondly.

The old elf ignored him.

Brondly followed him to his table. On his way across the room he tripped.

"Oops, I'm sorry," Brondly said, to the elf whose foot he had fallen over.

"Look where you're going, stubby," the injured elf said, rubbing his foot.

Brondly turned back towards the offended elf. "Watch your mouth!"

The old elf took Brondly's arm, leading him away. "He's not worth it."

"I suppose you're right," said Brondly, staring balefully at his abuser, as he took a seat opposite the old elf.

"Barkeep, may we have two more drinks over here please?" the old elf shouted.

The barkeeper nodded, arriving a few moments later, with two flagons of elven ale.

The old elf handed the barkeep some coins. "Keep the change."

"Thank you sir. If you need anything else, just give a shout."

The old elf nodded, picked up his drink and took a sip.

He turned to Brondly. "You must be very upset with the king, and understandably so."

Brondly took a swig of beer and wiped his lips with the back of his hand.

"Would you like to seek some revenge for your wrong doing?" asked the old elf.

Brondly turned, facing his new friend. "And just how might I do that?"

"All I ask is that you procure some items for me."

"Just what are you getting at?" said Brondly.

The old elf grinned again. "Allow me to refill your drink."

The old elf ordered another round of ale. He watched as Brondly promptly drained half his glass. "Could you perhaps take the Grymlons from the castle and give them to me? I would pay you handsomely for your efforts. I assure you, no one would come to any harm."

Brondly looked at the old elf and laughed, but he quickly realized that the old timer was not joking.

"That's treason!"

The old elf looked Brondly in the eye. "Please keep your voice down, sir. It would be wise not to draw attention to our conversation."

"I would be hung in the castle courtyard for all to see if I were caught," Brondly whispered, beginning to slur his words. "Besides, no one can get into the castle without being seen."

"I thought I heard you say that you were part of the elite guard. That means you know where they are and how to get to them. Am I right?"

"One of my duties was to guard the door to the room where the Grymlons are kept, but I'm not even allowed inside of the castle anymore."

The old elf leaned forward again, looking into Brondly's eyes. Brondly could smell stale beer on his breath. "What if you could get in without being seen?"

"I think the only way you could get me into the castle, is if you were an informant or something," Brondly whispered, returning the old elf's gaze. "For all I know you could be setting me up to get arrested. I wouldn't be a bit surprised. I think the king has it in for me."

Brondly closed one eye in an attempt to look intimidating as he spoke, but he couldn't focus on the old elf's face.

The old elf let out an exasperated sigh. "Look, I have been searching for someone to do this for weeks. There is a great deal of money in it for you, if you want the job. I am not in the employ of the King of Kimadrian. I am however, in the employ of another King. If you're too scared to do it, just say so and I will find someone else."

"I could turn you in," said Brondly.

"And I could follow you home and have you killed," the old elf hissed.

Brondly slammed his mug down on the table and stood to leave.

A few customers looked their way, disturbed by the noise.

"Now don't be so hasty," said the old elf. "When I said I could get you into the castle, I meant that I have the means to use magic. I could get you in and out undetected."

Brondly sat back down. "Just how much money would this little adventure be worth?"

"One hundred and fifty elven coins," the old elf replied.

"Ha!" said Brondly. "Looking for a little cheap labour, are we?"

"Each coin being of one thousand elven pounds in value," the old elf added.

Brondly stared back at him. "Phew, that's a lot of money! Are you sure the magic works?"

"Absolutely certain," the old elf grinned.

"The Grymlons are checked twice a day. I know the times, so I would be able to get into the castle if I were not seen, but I would not be able to get them all."

"Why not?" asked the old elf.

"Because they sometimes hum really loud. Why do you want them anyway?"

"They hum? Why do they do that?" asked the old elf.

"How the hell should I know! I was just paid to be a guard, and I asked you why you want them?"

"I don't," said the old elf. "The elviron want them, but if you can only get one of them, I may be able to get the others some other way."

"The elviron! I'm not sure I like the idea of the elviron getting their hands on the Grymlons," said Brondly. "They just don't look right with their big ugly eyes. And that soul stealing thing they do, ugh!"

The old elf smiled again. "I find them rather enchanting."

"Haven't they been after the elven set of Grymlons for some time?" said Brondly.

The old elf sighed. "What does it matter who has the Grymlons? As long as they are well looked after."

"The money sounds really good, but to steal the Grymlons? To be a traitor? No, I can't do it."

"Very well. Good night to you," the old elf said, standing.

He left Brondly and exited the bar.

Brondly shrugged, finished his beer and staggered home. He fell into bed fully clothed, asleep within seconds.

Chapter Two

Brondly dreamt he heard a knocking sound off in the distance. As his brain slowly surfaced from sleep, he realized that someone was banging on his front door.

He looked at his clock and sat up. "Oh my, it's three in the afternoon. I didn't mean to sleep that late."

"Bindyl, can you get that?" he shouted, holding his pounding head.

There was silence in the house.

"Must be at work," Brondly said to himself. "Oh my aching head. I shouldn't have drank so much."

The banging continued.

"All right, all right. I'm coming!" he shouted, wincing at the loudness of his own voice. He opened the door to see Fordly, his landlord, standing on the doorstep.

"Are you going to make me stand in the street, Brondly?"

"No, no come in," Brondly said, turning away and walking into the kitchen. He filled a kettle full of water and put it on the stove to boil.

"Would you like some tea?" Brondly asked.

"No thank you. I have other business to attend to, but I think you know why I'm here."

"I know, I know. You want the rent." said Brondly.

Fordly stood by the kitchen table. "It's a week late, Brondly. I told you not to worry, but time is getting on. I will need payment within the next two days or you will have to leave."

"But I've lived here for years and never once been late paying. Can't you at least try to understand my situation?"

"Does Bindyl know you are behind in your rent? Perhaps he can help you out a bit."

"No," said Brondly. "He gave me his half and I… well, I sort of borrowed it."

Fordly turned his back on Brondly and opened the front door to leave. "I'll come back in two days. I mean it Brondly. Pay or you're out."

"I'll have it for you somehow."

"Business is business," Fordly said, closing the door behind him.

As the front door closed, Brondly took his tea and made his way back to his bedroom. He was dozing off again, when he heard someone else knocking.

Brondly covered his head with a pillow. When it was obvious that whoever it was, would not go away, he sat up and slid off the bed.

"I'm coming!" he shouted, making his way back through the kitchen.

As Brondly put his hand on the door knob and turned it, the door was shoved open from the other side. He was pushed back with such force, he fell backwards onto the floor.

"Didn't think we'd find you, did you?" said the shadow standing in the doorway.

Brondly put his hand over his eyes, shielding them from the light. "Oh no," he said, under his breath.

A small, well dressed, pudgy elf walked into the kitchen, followed by two very shady looking elves. One of them closed the door.

"Nice place. Must cost a lot in rent. How many rooms do you have?" the pudgy elf asked, inspecting his surroundings.

Brondly stood, brushing off his pants for the second time in twenty-four hours. "What do you want Gavin?"

"You know what I want. My money of course," Gavin replied, with a perky smile. "I thought we had a deal. I let you borrow the money, you pay me back within two weeks, or we cut off one of your fingers. Don't you remember?"

"Well, I don't have it at the moment, but I will very soon," Brondly said, beginning to sweat. "It's taking me longer than I expected to find a job."

"We had a deal," said Gavin, motioning for his two henchelves to step forward. "Now I'm hearing that no one will give you work because you can't stay sober. I'm not an unreasonable elf. So just to show you I can be nice, my fellow elves here will only break one of your fingers for now. You know, a little encouragement perhaps, to give you some incentive to find a way to pay me what you owe."

Brondly began to visibly shake. "Wait just a minute, Gavin. I said I would get you the money and I will."

Gavin picked at his manicured nails. "I don't know Brondly? Can I trust you?"

Brondly put his hands together in a gesture of good faith. "I will definitely have the money within two days."

"Two days it is then," said Gavin with the ever perky smile. "Mind you now Brondly. Don't try to run. I will find you."

"You have my word," said Brondly.

Gavin turned to leave, his henchelves following. "I will be back in two days and you had better be here," he said, closing the door behind him.

Brondly sat down at the kitchen table and put his head in his hands. "I hope that old elf is still in Kimadria."

He went to his bedroom and tidied himself up a bit. Then went back into the kitchen and drank a few more cups of strong elven tea.

Chapter Three

When Brondly reached the Skeletons Head Pub, he took a seat at the bar and ordered a mug of elven ale.

He stopped the barkeeper as he passed by. "I was here last night and I met an old elf. He didn't give me his name. I was wondering if he was staying here?"

"I know the elf you mean," said the barkeeper. "No, he isn't staying here, but he has been coming in every night for the past few nights. He might come in again tonight."

"What time does he usually come in?" asked Brondly.

"He's been coming in just after dark."

"In that case," said Brondly, "I'll have another ale."

Not long after nightfall, the old elf entered the Pub.

He approached the bar, holding up his hand to get the barkeepers attention. "Could I have an ale, and some of your best bread and cheese, please?"

"If you would like to take a seat, sir. I will have my waiter come over in just a minute," the barkeeper said.

The old elf ignored Brondly and took a seat at the same table as the night before.

Brondly picked up his drink and walked over to him. "Do you mind if I sit down?" he asked.

The old elf looked up. "You again?"

Brondly took a seat opposite the old elf. "I've changed my mind about the job we were talking about last night. I'll do it."

"Good, be here tomorrow night. I will give you instructions and a potion to make you invisible, so that you can get in and out of the castle."

The waiter brought the food and drink for the old elf, who immediately began to eat.

"You didn't look surprised to see me," said Brondly.

"I wasn't," said the old elf, between bites of food. "You are having some money troubles I gather."

"How do you know that?"

"At this point I don't think it matters, do you?" The old elf replied with a grin.

"Just who are you?" said Brondly.

The old elf motioned for the barkeeper to bring him another drink, then turned his gaze to Brondly. "Do you want the job or not? This is your last chance."

"The uh, object we are talking about. It won't lose its power will it? I mean the elviron will look after it, won't they?"

"Of course. Why would I... a, they destroy it?" said the old elf.

"Very well then, I'll do it."

After the two of them shook hands, Brondly had an overwhelming urge to wipe his right hand on something. The old elf had by now finished his supper. He got up from his seat and threw down some elven money.

"Be sure to give the barkeep a tip. You can keep the rest for yourself," he said, turning to leave.

"A gentle elf to be sure," Brondly said, walking to the bar.

***

The old elf stood for a moment in the darkness of the street. He bowed his head, taking a couple of deep breaths. As he did so, he changed.

His back straightened and his face lost its old, withered look. His beard disappeared and his stature became smaller. The old elf was now a strange looking teenage girl.

Once the transformation was complete, the girl smiled.

"At last! I was beginning to think I was never going to find anyone stupid enough to help me with my plan."

She looked around to make sure no one was watching, chanted a spell and vanished.

Chapter Four

Brondly made his way home and fell into bed. His dreamless stupor took him into the night and through most of the next day. He finally surfaced as the sun went down. He bathed in an effort to clear the dull ache from his head. He tried to eat, but had little appetite.

"A nice big mug of beer and I will be just fine. Hair of the dog, I think the humans call it," he thought.

Brondly walked to Kimadria and once again made his way to the Skeletons Head Pub.

"A large mug of elven ale please," he said to the barkeeper, as he took a seat at the bar.

"You're starting to become a regular around here," the barkeeper said, handing him his drink.

Brondly picked up his mug, found and vacant table, and waited.

When the old elf finally entered the pub, he waved to Brondly, ordered a drink and joined him. The old elf took a couple of sips from his drink then produced a piece of paper and handed it to Brondly. "Here is a list of instructions. Follow them carefully."

"When do I get paid?" said Brondly.

"When you have delivered the orb," the old elf replied, handing him a small bag. "You will need to drink these potions. The instructions will tell you how to use them, and when and where to deliver the orb. Then you shall come back here to Kimadria. You will meet with an assistant of mine on Candle Street, which is not far from here. The directions to the meeting point are also on that piece of paper."

"My assistant will pay you. You will no longer be needed after that."

"Will we meet again?" said Brondly.

"No. No need."

Brondly drained his mug. "It's goodbye then," he said.

"Yes, yes. Goodbye, Brondly and good luck," the old elf said, dismissively.

Brondly stood and held out his hand for a handshake, but the old elf was already heading towards the bar.

Relieved at not having to hold onto the old elf's bony hand again, Brondly quickly pulled his hand back and left the pub.

When he reached home, he put the two bottles on the kitchen table. The bottle with the red potion was labelled 'Invisible'. The bottle with the green potion was labelled 'Visible'.

He made himself a cup of elven tea, then sat down and read the instructions twice, to make sure he knew what to do.

***

The next evening, Brondly was ready to leave for the castle. He picked up the bottle of invisibility potion and uncorked the top.

"I hope this works long enough for me to get in and out of the castle, or I'm in a lot of trouble," he thought, swallowing the contents.

Brondly noticed a slight metallic taste, as the red liquid passed over his tongue. A few seconds later, he experienced a mild bloating feeling and burped loudly.

"Oh my! I hope that goes away before I get to the castle."

He went to his bedroom and opened the door to his closet. He stood in front of it a full length mirror, but all he could see was the room behind him.

Brondly burped again. He returned to the kitchen and headed for the front door. He put his hand on the door knob and stopped.

"What if I do this and I doom all of Kimadrian!" he said aloud, suddenly feeling a stab of fear hit his chest. "But the old elf assured me that no one would be harmed. It will be all right."

Brondly stepped out of his front door and began walking towards the castle. He had only gone a few paces when someone bumped into him.

"Do you mind?" Brondly said, rather loudly.

The elf looked around, startled. "Who is there?"

"Oh dear!" Brondly said, under his breath. "I forgot. No one can see me!"

He walked a little farther.

"Buuuurp, excuse me," Brondly said, quietly, as he sidestepped an elf walking towards him.

The elf turned to another elf behind Brondly, staring at him accusingly.

"Some of us have no manners!" the elf remarked, as he continued along the street.

When Brondly reached the castle, he passed the guards at the front gate and walked in through the front doors, undetected.

His tummy rumbled slightly.

"Buuurrp," he uttered again, looking around him.

He continued through the castle, until he reached the door that led up to the tower, and waited.

At precisely 10:00 p.m. Captain Hadley Allynberry appeared. He approached the door, opened it and began to climb the steps. Brondly followed close behind.

They were half way up, when Brondly could no longer hold in the burp that had been threatening to surface. His hand shot up to his mouth too late, and he let out a long, low gurgling sound. The Captain stopped and turned. "Who's there?" he shouted, listening, as his voice echoed down the stone steps.

Seeing no one, he headed back up, shaking his head. "I've got to stop telling the children scary bed time stories. I'm frightening myself more than them."

The Captain continued up to the top of the tower where two sentries stood guard at a door. He returned their salutes as he approached.

"Step aside," he commanded.

The guards parted, giving him access.

Captain Allynberry used the combination on the front of the door as he had many times before. He turned the embedded circles in the middle this way and that, until the door clicked open. He entered the room, closely followed by Brondly.

The room was a large circle with light brown stone walls and a purple carpet on the floor. There were five windows at regular intervals around the room. In front of each window was a small round table. On each table was a pedestal that resembled the bottom half of an hourglass. Sitting snugly on the top of each pedestal, was a small clear orb.

The Captain looked around the room, counting the orbs and making sure the room looked as it should. He stopped each of the tables, looking behind them and out of each window down to the courtyard below. Brondly stood next to the Grymlon nearest the door.

Captain Allynberry was half way around the room, when Brondly's stomach growled. As the sound gently reverberated around the bare stone walls, Brondly held his stomach. He pursed his lips together, desperately trying to quell another burp making its way up into his throat.

The Captain walked out into the hallway. "Did you hear that?" he asked the guards.

"What?" they both said at the same time.

The Captain shook his head. "Never mind."

He re-entered the room and made one more round. Assured that nothing was amiss, he exited the room.

As Brondly followed the Captain out of the room, he swept the orb closest to the door off its stand and put it under his cloak. He followed the Captain down the steps, through the castle and out of the front doors.

Brondly reached the street and doubled over. A long, low whistling sound escaped from his backside. "Oh my, that's better! I thought I might explode back there."

When he reached home, Brondly rushed to the bedroom and picked up the bottle with the potion to make him visible. He stood in front of his mirror. "Oh please let this one be a bit gentler on my stomach," he thought, as he swallowed the green liquid.

Brondly watched his reflection slowly re-appear. "That's better. My stomach doesn't feel as though it's going to erupt anymore! Time for phase two."

He went to the kitchen and opened the cupboard where he kept his wine. He took a bottle his best red wine from one of the shelves and poured it into a flask.

Brondly entered his bathroom, took a key from the pocket of his tunic and opened a drawer under the sink. Inside were a few small bottles and jars. One of them contained some medicine he had bought from the apothecary a few days ago, to help him sleep. He picked up the bottle examining its contents. "Nothing like a good skinfull of ale to knock you out when the need arises, but today, this will do nicely."

He put a few drops of the sleep medicine into the flask with the wine, and put the flask in one of the pockets of his cloak. He went back into the kitchen and found three small cups, and put them in his other pocket.

Brondly left his house and walked through the streets of Kimadria. He ordered a horse coach to take him to Humadria.

Twenty minutes later, the carriage pulled up to a pair of large doors embedded into a rock-face. Brondly exited the carriage and paid the coachman. A guard was standing at a smaller door to the right of the large ones.

Brondly approached the guard with a friendly smile. "Good evening Morgly."

"Hello Brondly."

"I have some business in Humadria."

"Will you be returning this evening?" Morgly asked.

"I most certainly will," said Brondly, trying to maintain a careless grin.

"You have no business in the Human Realm?" asked Morgly.

"No, no. Why would I want to go up there?"

"If you would kindly sign the book. Please state where you are going," said Morgly, pointing to a large book on a podium.

Brondly signed his name and wrote Humadria.

"Have a good evening sir," said Morgly, opening the door.

"You too," replied Brondly, as the guard closed the door behind him.

Once on the other side, Brondly stopped smiling and wiped the sweat from his forehead. "I just know I'm going to get caught," he muttered, under his breath.

He stood for a moment, letting his eyes get used to the dimness of the lamps that lit the enclosed street burrowed into the rock. He looked around, hoping no one would recognize him, then headed upwards.

The street branched off a half a mile up. To the right, it levelled off to some houses hewn into the rock. To the left, it narrowed and went to the roots of the Willow tree by the river in Oaklade.

When Brondly reached the tree's base, there were two sentries standing guard by the opening. Three feet to the right of them, was a wall of rock about six feet high. It ended abruptly into a dirt ceiling. The dirt wall constantly bled tiny trickles of water from the river behind it. The water was drained away through small channels that led downward, ending in a scenic waterfall where the street forked.

"Now all I have to do is get past these guards," Brondly thought, as he approached them.

"Brondly! What are you doing here?" asked Lockly, the youngest of the two.

"Well, I assume you both know that I've been sacked?" said Brondly.

The two guards nodded.

"I started thinking about you both, and thought I might come up here and have a farewell drink with you."

The guards looked at each other.

Myer, the other guard, eyed Brondly. "We are on duty. You know we are not supposed to drink when we are working."

"It's the last shift of the day for you two isn't it?" said Brondly. "As I remember, this is one of the most boring guard duties. No one comes up here. Not many elves go through that tree do they? Come on lads, who is going to know?"

Lockly and Myer looked at each other and shrugged.

"I suppose it would be all right just this once," said Myer.

The three of them sat by the roots of the tree as Brondly poured them a drink from his flask. He poured himself a drink too, but only pretended to sip it while he watched his former colleagues drain their cups.

Brondly refilled them and raised his in a toast. "I will miss you two. You are such good elves. You always obeyed your orders and never questioned my judgement. Here's to you both."

He watched as the two guards drank down their wine for a second time.

Brondly sat reminiscing about past events. The guards dozed off after about five minutes of conversation. When he was sure that they were both asleep, he moved around them, entering the interior of the tree trunk.

He pushed on a knot in the wood and the tree split open. He stepped out of the trunk, into the darkness and through the branches to the Human Realm.

Brondly made his way along the riverbank, until he came to where the river narrowed slightly near a small clump of trees.

Standing by one of the trees was an elviron.

As Brondly approached, the elviron turned his gaze to him. "I understand you have something for me," the elviron said, stepping forward.

Brondly stopped a few feet from him. "Don't come any closer.

You'll not be pulling the life out of me! I'll just put the bag on the grass, here, and when I step back you can take it."

Brondly bent down, and placed the bag on the grass, never taking his eyes off the elviron. Then he stepped back.

The elviron ran forward and snatched up the bag. He opened it and put his face inside. When he was sure the contents held the required item, he turned and ran off into the darkness, towards the Willow tree.

"It was nice to make your acquaintance too," Brondly said, following him back along the river.

The elviron ran until he could see the bridge, then he slowed down. He was about to turn and walk over it, when he tripped and fell. The orb dropped out of the bag, rolling into the long grass. The elviron fell to his knees, feeling around in the dark for a few seconds. He looked up suddenly.

"Who's there?" he shouted into the night.

Panicked, he ran over the bridge without retrieving the orb.

He hurried across the lawn of Willow View Cottage, towards the Beech tree in the back corner of the garden.

Brondly neared the Willow tree, and could just barely see the elviron running across the bridge. He didn't stop to see where the elviron went, instead he entered the tree and crept passed the still slumbering guards.

Chapter Five

Myer opened his eyes, suddenly realizing that he had fallen asleep on duty. He turned to see Lockly fast asleep beside him. "Wake up, Lockly!"

"Huh, what? Where are we?"

"Brondly, he drugged us!" said Myer, trying to shake the sleep from his head.

"Why would he do that?" said Lockly, standing up, brushing off his uniform.

"I don't know, but if Captain Allynberry finds out, we are going to get into a lot of trouble."

"Do you think anyone saw us sleeping?" said Lockly.

"Oh I hope not," replied Myer.

"Well, I won't tell, if you won't," said Lockly.

"We'd better keep our mouths shut. Sleeping on the job will get us both thrown in the dungeons," said Myer.

Do you think he drugged us to get us into trouble?" said Lockly.

"You mean because we still have our jobs and he doesn't?" asked Myer.

Lockly thought for a moment. "No. If that were the case, we'd be surrounded by guards by now."

Two guards turned the corner and headed towards them. It was time for the shift change.

"That was close!" said Lockly. "If they had arrived a few minutes early, we would still be asleep."

"Where did Brondly go?" said Myer.

Lockly looked at the fast approaching guards. "I don't know and I don't want to know, Myer. Now shut up, or they'll hear you."

Myer and Lockly were relieved of their watch.

Chapter Six

Brondly made his way downwards and back to Kimadria.

"I'm glad I made it up to the Human Realm and back without getting caught," he thought. "Myer and Lockly won't tell. They'll be too afraid of being punished."

Brondly scurried through the back streets of Kimadria. He passed the pub, tempted to pop in and have a quick drink.

"One beer," he thought to himself, "just to calm me down a bit. I'm still shaking from having to deal with that horrible elviron."

He turned and went back to the Skeleton's Head. He sat at the bar and downed three beers before heading to the address on the instructions.

He stood in the dark alleyway waiting for his rendezvous with the unknown friend of the old elf.

Brondly turned when he heard a rustling sound. A small spindly legged creature stepped out of the shadows. A cloak covering its body.

"Oh rot! Now I'm done for!" Brondly said, under his breath, as he stepped back a few paces. "Don't you come near me! I've heard about you meckits. I know you like to eat us elves."

"You needn't worry, Brondly," the meckit said, in a raspy voice. "I have already eaten tonight, but you're right, you elves do make a tasty meal, had to make do with a small dog tonight, though. My master says I must give you this."

Brondly noticed the meckit's unusually long fingers, as it held out a leather pouch.

The meckit looked up and smiled as Brondly took the pouch, revealing a chalk white face.

"I hope that's not blood on those pointy little teeth of yours," Brondly thought, trying to avoid eye contact.

"My master says to tell you thank you for your help."

Brondly turned his head sideways to avoid the stench of the meckit's nauseating breath. When he turned to look at the meckit, it was gone.

Brondly jiggled the pouch. "It feels heavy. I'll just take a quick peep," he whispered, looking this way and that.

"Oow, there's a lot of coins in here!"

Brondly put his hand in and pulled out a thousand pound elven coin.

"I can't wait to get home and count them," he thought. "This should be enough to set me up for the rest of my life. Yes! A house in the realm, with a little bit of land would do nicely, and all the ale I can drink."

Brondly ran through the streets of Kimadria, until he reached his house. He hurried to his bedroom, locking the door.

"Can't have Bindyl disturbing me now," he said with a grin, as he emptied the pouch onto his bed. He gleefully counted his coins and fell asleep surrounded by them, without one bit of guilt for what he had done.

Chapter Seven

Morning came in Kimadria with the usual hustle and bustle in the castle. At 10:00 a.m. it time for the morning check. Captain Allynberry climbed the steps to the tower where the Grymlons were kept, as he had done twice a day for the last fifteen years.

He opened the door and stepped into the circular room, looking around him as he entered. He strolled around looking out of each window. He paused at one of them to look down onto the royal family's private gardens.

"What a beautiful day," he said, with a smile.

Captain Allynberry was about to turn and leave, when he paused. He looked at the table closest to the door, and felt his heart leap in his chest.

"Where is the Grymlon that sits on this table!" he shouted.

One of the guards ran into the room. "Something wrong, sir?"

Captain Allynberry wheeled around, facing him. "GET OUT! AND DON'T COME BACK IN HERE UNTIL I TELL YOU TO."

The guard backed out of the room.

Captain Allynberry crawled around on the floor. Then he checked the other Grymlons in case there were two on one table. When it was obvious that the Grymlon had gone, he hurried out of the room.

"Go and get the king, now!" he told the guard to his right.

The guard ran down the stairs.

"Anything wrong sir?" The remaining guard dared to ask again.

"Stand to attention and mind your own business, soldier," The Captain the said, pacing back and forth.

The guard became a statue, afraid to move.

A few minutes later, a tall middle aged elf in heavy robes came up the steps. As he approached, the Captain bowed. The king nodded, acknowledging him.

"What seems to be the problem?"

"Would you please come into the tower room with me, your majesty."

The two guards re-took their post, glancing sideways at each other.

The king entered the room. Captain Allynberry followed, pulling the heavy door almost closed.

The king turned to face his senior officer. "What am I looking at?"

"The Grymlon closest to the door, your majesty: it's missing!"

"Where is it?" asked the King.

"It's not here, said the Captain. "I came in here and did my inspection the way I always do. All five were here last night when I checked, but when I counted them this morning, there were only four."

King Morvand pulled the door open and stepped between the two guards. "I want you both to come in here."

The guards entered the room, and stood beside each other.

King Morvand pointed to the Captain. "Search him," he said to both of them.

Neither of the guards wanted to search their commanding officer, so neither of them stepped forward.

"You," the King snapped, impatiently, pointing to one of them, "search him."

The guard approached the Captain. "Sorry sir," he said, as he patted the Captain down. He turned to the king. "He is hiding nothing, your majesty."

The king turned to the Captain. "Search both of these elves."

Captain Allynberry searched each of the guards. "They have nothing on them, your majesty."

"Has anyone been up here besides the guard change?" the King asked.

"No, your majesty," the guards both answered.

"You," King Morvand said, to one of them. "Go and get my son."

The guard ran down the stairs as fast as his legs would carry him.

"And you," the King said, to the other guard, "stand by the door and don't let anyone in. Captain, you and I will stay in this room until the Prince arrives.

A few minutes later, the guard returned with Prince Gideon.

"The guard said you needed to see me urgently, father?"

The king pointed to the empty pedestal. "One of the Grymlons is missing. I am going to take the guards down stairs. I want you to change the lock combination on the door and give it to me."

Gideon nodded. His father, Captain Allynberry and the two guards disappeared down the stairs.

As soon as they were out of sight, Gideon closed the door. He moved the circles on the front of the door, pressing various points within them until he had changed the sequence.

Once finished, he reversed the sequence opening the door. He repeated the process three times. "That should keep anyone out for now," he said, running down the stairs.

At the bottom of the tower, he found Captain Allynberry standing guard by the door. "Where did my father go?"

"He said to let you know that he would meet you in your apartments."

Gideon hurried to his rooms where he found his father with Brondly's nephew, Bindyl.

"I have just been informing Bindyl about our situation with the Grymlons."

"Do you have any suspects, father?" Gideon asked, taking a seat at his desk. He grabbed a pen and a piece of paper and wrote down the new combination.

"It has to be the elviron," said the King. "The two guards guarding the Grymlons are waiting to be briefed about the secrecy of the situation. We must try to keep this to ourselves. If the rest of the realm found out about this, there may be trouble."

"I suspect that the elviron have stolen a Grymlon because they know the orbs can only be regenerated if they are all together. If the Grymlons aren't taken to Avebury for the hundred year regeneration there will be no seasons anymore. I think the elviron are going to use the one they have stolen to get the rest of them."

"But only Elizabeth's family can do the regeneration," said Gideon.

The king paced the room. "There are elviron that can do it. They had their own Grymlons at one time. I know it was a very long time ago, but someone must have been able to do the hundred year regeneration. Either that, or they think they have produced their own chosen one. We know that the chosen one has to have human and elf in their blood. The elviron were elves once. If they get their hands on the remaining Grymlons, they may be able to regenerate the orbs themselves. If they do, they might be able to manipulate the seasons so that they can go up to the Human Realm."

"There are always a few elves that would use this situation to their advantage in some way. You and Bindyl must try to get it back before anyone else finds out.

I suggest you start by going to Distardrian. Ask around and see if there is any gossip by the border."

"If you cannot find out anything there, go up to Willow View Cottage and watch the Beech tree in the back corner of the garden. We know the elviron have an entrance to their realm there. Stay hidden and watch to see if there is any coming or going. It won't be the first time the elviron have tried to negotiate a sale with the humans using the Grymlons. I want you to report back to me as soon as you know something."

Gideon handed the king the new combination.

"We will talk again later," the King said, leaving the room.

Bindyl turned to Gideon as the king closed the door. "What do we do now?"

"We'll go to Distardrian. Do you remember that elviron we pulled out of the river?"

"Yes. A bit overweight, with a bad disposition as I remember."

"Let's try to find him," said Gideon. "If we pay him, he might tell us something. We should start by going to that tavern near the Distardrian border."

Chapter Eight

Gideon and Bindyl sat by the window in the Ogre's Rest Inn, waiting to be served. They both kept their heads covered with cloaks to hide their faces.

Bindyl scanned the room as they waited. "This could take days. I hate being near the elviron. I detest being near elves who rub shoulders with the elviron even more."

The innkeeper put two ales in front of them and Gideon handed him four elven coins.

"Keep the change, sir."

"Why thank ye young master," the Innkeeper said, as he turned and headed back to his work.

"Look," said Gideon, "over there. That's him!"

Sitting at a corner table was a scruffy elviron. His dark wispy hair was dishevelled and his clothes were dirty. His head bobbed from side to side as though he was ready to fall asleep.

"He seems to be a little drunk," said Bindyl.

"I'm going to go over and talk to him," Gideon said, getting out of his seat. "You stay here. I won't be long."

Bindyl looked in the direction of the scruffy elviron. "Be careful Gideon, don't draw attention to yourself."

Gideon went to the innkeeper. "That um, person in the corner over there. What is he drinking?"

The innkeeper looked over to where Gideon was pointing. "Well sir, that customer has a particular taste for elven ale."

Gideon handed the innkeeper more coins. "Then I'll take two, please."

Gideon grabbed the two drinks and headed over to the sleepy elviron. He put the mugs on the table and sat down opposite him.

The elviron squinted at him.

"Do you remember me?" Gideon asked.

"No, but thanks for the ale. Don't suppose you have any fresh meat hidden under that cloak, do you?"

"I'm sorry, no. Do you remember falling in the river about a year ago, not far from here. My friend and I pulled you out?"

The elviron looked a little closer. "Oh yes, I remember you. Didn't recognize you all covered up. What are you doing in these parts?"

Gideon leaned forward. "Actually, I was looking for you. When we saved you from drowning, you said that if we ever needed anything, to find you and you would try to help?"

"Yes, I did say that didn't I. You Kimadrians are too nice. If it had been you in the water, I would have left you to drown. You had a friend with you as I remember."

"Yes, he is over there, see?" Gideon pointed to Bindyl.

Bindyl waved back at them.

"What do you want?" asked the elviron.

"You know, you never did tell us your name," said Gideon.

"Feckle."

"Well, Feckle. I would like to know if there has been anything going on up at the castle in Distardrian lately."

"Like what?" asked Feckle, trying to stay awake.

"You know. Anything about to happen? Like the elviron perhaps trying to steal our Grymlons."

"Nope, haven't heard anything of that nature," Feckle slurred.

Gideon leaned closer to the elviron. He put a pouch of elven coins on the table. "You haven't heard of anyone doing anything out of the ordinary, or anyone going up to the Human Realm for anything?"

Feckle sat for a moment, staring at the money pouch. "Now that you mention it, there was an old elf in here a few nights ago, looking for someone to do a job for him. He wanted someone to go up to the Human Realm and pick something up. He couldn't find anyone, so he left."

"Do you know who the elf was?"

Feckle began to blink and his head began to bob again. "No, never seen him before."

Gideon stood. "Thanks. Enjoy your drink." He dropped the pouch of elven coins on the table. Feckle grabbed the pouch and pulled the strings apart, looked into it, and smiled up at Gideon.

Gideon put his hand on the elviron's grimy shoulder. "Try not to spend it all on ale."

By the time Gideon reached Bindyl, Feckle had put his head down on the table and was fast asleep.

"Let's go home Bindyl," said Gideon, not bothering to sit back down.

Bindyl drained his mug and got up from his chair, following Gideon to the exit. "Did he tell you anything?"

"He mentioned something about an old elf, asking for someone willing to go up to the Human Realm and pick something up."

"That's unusual," said Bindyl.

"Yes," said Gideon, "yes it is."

They left the Inn and hurried back to Kimadrian.

Chapter Nine

King Morvand looked up from his desk by the window when Gideon and Bindyl entered.

"Did you manage to find anything out?"

"Our informant told us about an old elf, trying to find someone to go up to the Human Realm, but we have no idea who he is," said Gideon.

The king sat back in his seat. "This Grymlon theft could not have happened at a worst time. I want to be informed immediately you find something out."

The two elves left the king's office and made their way out of the castle.

"I am going to go up and watch to see if anything happens up there," said Gideon, pointing towards the Human Realm.

"I will go with you," said Bindyl.

Gideon shook his head. "No, I want you to go to that dingy little tavern in the backstreets of Kimadria. You know, the one near Candle Street where all the drunks go for cheap ale. I have heard that some shady deals happen in that hole in the wall. Sit and listen to them. See what you can find out. We will meet back here in a few hours."

"I know the one," said Bindyl. "I am ashamed to admit that my uncle Brondly goes in there on occasion. If we keep visiting these seedy taverns, we will begin to get the reputation my uncle worked so hard for."

"But we will find out more that way," said Gideon.

Bindyl left immediately for Kimadria. Gideon made his way up to the Human Realm.

Chapter Ten

Gideon came out of the Willow tree and climbed up into its branches. "If anything unusual has happened my little friend will alert me," he thought.

He positioned himself so that he had a good view of the cottage from across the river. He whistled, letting his informant know he was there, then settled back against the tree, watching the back corner of the garden where the Beech tree stood, and waited.

Chapter Eleven

Andre Reese ambled across the fields towards Willow View Cottage. He was in no particular hurry. School was over for the day and homework had been done.

Gideon watched him approach. He had seen this young human once or twice before. Andre, Gideon knew, was a friend of the girl named Elizabeth who had moved into the cottage with Rose Humphries.

Just before Andre reached the bridge, something caught his eye.

"What the?" he said, bending over to look into the grass. He picked the object of his interest up, holding it in to the light to get a better look. "I wonder what this is?"

Gideon leaned forward trying to see what Andre was holding. It glittered in the sunlight.

"He has the Grymlon!"

Andre put the orb into his jacket pocket. "I'll show it to Liz. She likes presents," he said, as he walked over the bridge spanning the river. He whistled as he strolled through the gate and along the pathway.

Gideon jumped down from the branches of the tree and disappeared.

When Andre reached the back door of the cottage, he knocked politely, then let himself in, as he always did.

"Anyone home?" he called, as he entered.

Elizabeth was in the kitchen with her gran.

"Andre! How nice to see you," said Grandma Rose.

Andre shot Elizabeth a smile. "I thought I would come and visit Elizabeth for a while. How are you Grandma?"

"I'm well, thank you."

Elizabeth smiled back. "It's nice to see you, Andre."

"Why don't you two go outside and sit in the garden for a while. I will bring you both a cold drink," said Grandma Rose.

Andre held the door open, so that Elizabeth could get her wheelchair through, then followed her.

He thought back to when her parents and brother died. "I wonder if she will ever get over the shock and walk again," he thought. "I miss walking to school with her and taking walks along the river. And she used to look so pretty on a horse."

Elizabeth looked over her shoulder at him, noticing a far away look in his eye. "What are you thinking about?"

Her voice dragged him back to the present.

"Sorry Liz, I was daydreaming," he said, catching up to her. "How are you?"

"Same as usual. I hate being stuck in this wheelchair. I hope this summer is better than last year. I was so bored, I thought I might go nuts."

"I could come over during the summer holiday and we could go for some walks, well, I mean, I could walk and push you. Or we could go to the stables and ride the way we used to."

Elizabeth ignored him. She pushed her wheelchair up to the summer table, and Andre sat down across from her.

Grandma Rose brought out some iced lemonade. She put the tray down on the table and poured a glass for each of them.

"It will be supper time soon, Elizabeth," Grandma said, as she turned and headed back into the house.

Elizabeth was listening to her grandma, but she was looking at Andre, who, she had noticed, was staring at her in an odd way.

"Come on Liz," he said, "you know it will be fun. Mavis said that they have the perfect horse for you. You remember Arthur, the one who does tricks for sugar cubes? He's very gentle. I promise you won't get thrown."

"Why do you stare at me like that, Andre?"

"Like what?" he said, turning a little pink at the jaw line.

"You know, as though you like me."

"I...I wasn't looking at you like that at all! Don't try to change the subject, Liz."

"So you don't like me?" she asked with a grin.

"No! I mean yes, I mean no, I don't. I mean, well, of course I like you. Stop it, Liz. You know that's not what I mean."

Elizabeth laughed, deciding that she had embarrassed him enough.

"I can't go to the stables Andre. I feel awkward. I don't want to be a burden to anyone."

"Being a bit of a baby aren't we?" Andre bit his lip, but it was too late. The words had already dropped out of his mouth.

Elizabeth's expression changed, as she aimed an icy stare at him.

"Nice going, Andre. Now you've ticked her off!" he thought.

"A baby?" she said, looking down her nose at him. "If I ever get out of this wheelchair, Andre Reese, I'll show you just how much of a baby I can be."

"Sorry Liz! I didn't mean to upset you. I just meant. Oh never mind. I can't force you to come to the stables with me. I just miss you, that's all. You had more guts than any of the others. You were more fun to ride with. Nothing scared you. Now I can't get you near a horse, let alone up on one."

"I might change my mind, but for now I don't want to talk about it."

Grandma Rose called Elizabeth from inside of the house.

Andre stood, and put his lemonade glass onto the tray. "I'll come back and see you in a day or two. It's probably time for my supper too. Ta, ta for now."

He patted Elizabeth lightly on the head, as he walked around the table, then began to jog along the side of the cottage.

He ran down the pathway to the gate by the river, and hesitated as he felt the forgotten orb in his pocket. "Oh blast. Oh well, I'll bring it back next time I visit."

He broke into a run again.

Elizabeth watched him as he sprinted across the fields towards home. It was the first week of the month of May, and the days were beginning to warm up.

She closed her blue eyes and turned her face upwards towards the sun. "Sunshine equals freckles. Oh well."

She had just had her fifteenth birthday, and although Elizabeth Ghenestone was unaware of it, events would unfold over the next few days that would change her life forever.

Her long, wavy, red hair cascaded down her back, as she tilted her head. Elizabeth soaked up the sunlight for a few seconds, then turned her chair around and wheeled it into the house for supper.

Chapter Twelve

Grandma placed a plate of food on the dining room table, and went back to the kitchen. Elizabeth wheeled up to the table and waited for Grandma Rose to take her seat.

"It was nice to see Andre. How is Megan, did he say?" Grandma asked, as she sprinkled malt vinegar over her chips.

Elizabeth halted her fork full of food before it reached her mouth. "He came over to try and persuade me to go riding again. He didn't mention Meg, but I'm sure she's fine."

"You don't want to give it a try?" asked Grandma.

Elizabeth stopped eating. "Is this some sort of plot to try and get me back on a horse?"

"No dear," said Grandma, "it's just that you get so bored around here during the summer. I thought perhaps you might like to give horse riding a try. Andre obviously feels the same."

"You used to love it before you were in that wheelchair. I'm surprised that you let the fact that you can't walk defeat you in such a manner. The Elizabeth I know would never have let such a small thing slow her down."

Elizabeth felt tears of frustration well into her eyes. "I don't want to go horse riding, and I don't want to talk about it anymore!"

Grandma Rose visibly jumped at Elizabeth's harsh tone. "Don't be angry, dear. I was only trying to help."

They finished supper in silence. Elizabeth helped with the dishes, then wheeled herself back out to the garden again.

She pulled herself out of her wheelchair and stretched out on the grass. She closed her eyes, listening for noises, unfamiliar noises. "I wonder if the stories they tell around here have any truth to them," she thought, looking up at the sky. "They tell of small beings that used to be seen around the river, mostly at night. Some say they were elves."

Elizabeth put her arms down, stretching out her fingers so she could feel the grass tickle her palms. She breathed deeply, smelling the perfume from the rose bushes that lined the pathway. When it began to get dark, she pulled herself into her wheelchair and went back into the house.

Elizabeth watched the television in the living room with Grandma for a while, before going bed.

She was almost asleep, when she heard a noise coming from the slightly open window. Being used to the sounds of the countryside, she dismissed it.

She was drifting off again, when she heard a voice.

"I think she is asleep now. Come on, I'll help you up onto the window ledge."

At first, Elizabeth froze.

"Someone is trying to break into the house! What should I do?" she thought. "Should I call for help? No, don't do that. They'll hear!"

Elizabeth watched with her heart in her mouth, as two small people climbed in through her bedroom window and onto her dresser.

Too afraid to move, she looked on, as one of them took something from his belt and threw it into the air. A fine dust, like gold rain shimmered for a few seconds, fading into nothing before it hit the floor.

"This invisibility dust will shield us if she wakes," Gideon said. "Can you see it anywhere? It has to be here somewhere. I saw the young male human with it. I heard him say he was going to give it to her."

Elizabeth tried to lie still.

"The blond one must be about my age, and the other one too," she thought. "His accent sounds a bit like Welsh, or could it be Scots? What a strange outfit he's wearing. Are those green tights with a matching shirt? The other one is wearing a similar outfit. What are they looking for?"

Bindyl was running from one side of the dresser to the other, looking around him as he went.

Gideon put his hand on Bindyl's shoulder. "Be quiet! Do you want to wake the whole house?"

"I must stay still," thought Elizabeth. "I don't want to scare them off."

Gideon had got down on his stomach and pulled himself forward. He put his arms down, trying to open the top drawer of Elizabeth's dresser. Bindyl held onto his legs as he hung over the side, but he lost his grip on Gideon's ankles and he slipped forward towards the floor.

"Oh Gideon, I am so sorry!" he shouted.

As Bindyl shouted a panicky apology, Gideon managed to flip himself over so that he wasn't falling head first. His bottom hit the carpet with a dull thud and he bounced up onto his feet. He stood looking at Bindyl, rubbing his rear end and shaking his fist.

Elizabeth, unable to keep quiet any longer, began to laugh. Both of the elves immediately froze. Gideon slowly turned and looked at her.

"Can she see us, Bindyl?" he said, not taking his eyes off her.

"Of course I can see you, why wouldn't I?" Elizabeth said.

She sat up, and watched Gideon leap upward, landing on the dresser. As he ran to the window, he put his hand into a pouch that was tied to his belt. He threw a small bag into the air, took his bow from over his shoulder and shot an arrow into the bag as it travelled upwards. Elizabeth sat back in surprise, as the room filled with sparkles of reds and blues and greens.

"How beautiful!" she said, trying to catch them before they disappeared.

The two elves turned, diving headlong through the opening at the bottom of the window, disappearing into the night.

Elizabeth's bedroom door opened with a rush of air, as Grandma hurried into the room. "I heard your voice. Is anything wrong?"

"No," Elizabeth said. "I think I was having a dream."

"Can I get you anything? Cup of cocoa?"

"No thanks, Gran. I think I can go back to sleep."

"If you need anything come and get me. Goodnight dear."

Grandma Rose turned off the light as she left the room.

Elizabeth put her head back on her pillow.

"I'm so drowsy," she thought, trying to stay awake and think about what had just happened. "I think I've just been visited by elves! They really do wear funny tights and shoes. I hope I remember this in the morning," was her last thought, as her eyes closed.

Chapter Thirteen

Elizabeth sat by the window at the back of the class as Miss Evans began teaching history.

"How many of you can tell me when the Battle of Hastings took place?" she asked, looking around the room. While doing so, she noticed Elizabeth staring out of the window.

"Elizabeth Ghenestone."

"Yes, Miss?" Elizabeth said, turning towards her.

"When you have finished your little daydream, perhaps you could tell us when the Battle of Hastings took place."

"Uh," was all Elizabeth could say.

"1066," another student shouted.

"Yes, 1066," Elizabeth said quickly.

"Too late young lady."

A few minutes later Miss Evans, who had been writing on the blackboard, turned back to the class.

"How many of you can tell me what day in 1066, the battle was fought? Elizabeth Ghenestone?"

Elizabeth had turned back to her window view and didn't hear Miss Evans. A classmate behind her kicked her wheelchair.

"Hey, don't do that!" she said, turning to the offender.

As she did so, the student nodded to the front of the class, where Miss Evans was still waiting for an answer.

"Elizabeth, what day in 1066, was the Battle of Hastings fought?"

Elizabeth began to feel a little irritated. "I don't know."

Miss Evans had walked towards the back of the class and stepped to the side of her desk. "I suggest that you pay attention, or you will be viewing the countryside from the Head Master's office! Anyone else know the answer to this question?"

"14th of October," said the student who had kicked Elizabeth's chair.

"Very good, David."

Elizabeth turned around and stuck her tongue out at a smirking David. He returned the compliment.

Class was dismissed at 10:00 a.m. Everyone headed to the next classroom for English Literature. Miss Evans caught Elizabeth as she was about to wheel herself out of the room.

"Elizabeth, is there something outside that we should know about?"

"I'm sorry, I'll pay attention, Miss Evans," she said, making a hasty retreat to the door.

At 3:45 p.m., school was finished for the day. Elizabeth was about to wheel herself out of the building, when Miss Evans stopped her again.

"Is everything all right, Elizabeth? You seem a little preoccupied."

Elizabeth looked into the teacher's face, noticing her flawless complexion. "How do you tell someone that you had a conversation with two small people, you suspect might be elves? What a good way to get a reputation for being a complete lunatic!" she thought.

"I'm a bit tired, Miss. I haven't been sleeping to well for the past few days. I'm having dreams."

Miss Evans smiled at her. Elizabeth noticed that her teeth were as perfect as her skin. "If there is anything I can do to help, perhaps listen if you need an ear. Please come and see me."

"Thank you. I will," she said, wheeling herself away from anymore questions.

Megan came up behind her in the hallway.

"Ready to go home, Liz?"

"More than ready," said Elizabeth, leading the way to the car.

Chapter Fourteen

After supper, Elizabeth went into the garden. She looked out onto the river, watching as the sunlight danced on the surface of the water.

"I used to look forward to coming here before mum, dad and Jesse died. I never thought I'd end up living here. I like being by the river, but I miss them so much," she thought.

She sat in her chair, letting the sunlight wash over her. As she sat quietly, the sun made her drowsy and she fell into a light sleep.

Over by the Beech tree, to the left of the cottage, in the back corner of the garden, an elviron in his shadow form appeared.

Unseen by Elizabeth, he sidled along the hedge line and ran across the lawn. He stopped for a second at the open gate, turning to look back at her, before running over the bridge.

He hurriedly looked in the grass for the Grymlon he had dropped. He felt pain from the sunlight, as smoke swirled up from his body in hazy spirals. He panicked when he realized it was gone. The sunlight became too much for him and he ran back across the bridge, disappearing behind the Beech tree.

Across the river, up in the Willow tree, Gideon sat watching the elviron. "You are too late, you little monster," he said, turning his gaze back to Elizabeth.

A black and grey tabby cat lay sleeping by Elizabeth's wheelchair. Her name was Charlie. She had appeared not long after Elizabeth's family had been killed, and as cats seem to do so often, she decided to stay.

When the elviron ran along the hedge, Charlie looked up, scanning the garden. She turned her gaze to the corner, suddenly alert. She sat up, turned towards the Willow tree and looked up at Gideon, then turned and looked towards the Beech tree. Gideon nodded to her, to let her know he had also seen the elviron. He jumped down from the Willow tree and vanished.

Charlie settled back down to her nap with Elizabeth, but with one eye on the Beech tree in the corner of the garden.

Chapter Fifteen

Andre came to visit Elizabeth again a couple of days later.

The two sat in the garden as Andre brought Elizabeth up to date on the latest gossip.

"Andrea, Michael and Susan send their regards," he chattered on. "They said that it would be nice to see you at the stables. You don't have to ride, Liz. You could just come and visit."

"Vicky bought a new horse, you know the one I told you about. She went out on a hunt and her horse bolted. She couldn't control him and he overtook the Hunt Master.

Well, as you can imagine, old Hessey was absolutely furious. As you know, no one runs in front of the Hunt Master, no one!

When Vicky finally got control of her horse, Hessey gave her a good telling off and made her cry. I don't think she'll be following the hounds any time soon. At least not on that horse."

"No one is allowed to kill a fox anymore, so why bother with a fox hunt," Elizabeth commented.

Andre ignored her comment and chattered on. Elizabeth noticed he had taken something out of the pocket of his jacket, and was absent mindedly rolling it around in his hands.

"What's that?" she interrupted.

"What?" Andre said, looking down. "Oh this. I don't know. I found it over there by the Willow tree when I was on my way here a couple of days ago. I picked it up and put it in my pocket. I forgot about it until I decided to come and see you. I thought I would bring it back over here. I wondered if you might know what it was."

"Can I please look at it?"

"You can have it if you want," Andre said, handing it to her.

As she grasped it, a bolt of heat ran up her arm and she dropped it. Before it fell, it hung in the air for just a second. The small orb rolled along the grass a couple of inches. It moved a little to the right, then a little to the left, before it came to a complete stop.

"Bloody hell! Did you see that! What did you do to it, Elizabeth?"

"Don't swear Andre! You know how your mum hates it when you swear, and I didn't do anything! It just jumped out of my hand."

"Sorry, Liz. Bit ungentlemanly of me, but that ball moved by itself!"

As Andre stepped forward to pick it up, it rolled a few more inches before stopping. He stepped forward and bent down to grab it, but it rolled away from him again.

Elizabeth wheeled her chair to it. As she leaned over, the orb jumped into her hand.

"Are you sure you don't want it?" she said, holding the ball out to him.

"No thanks, Liz. It's acting a bit too strange for my liking. It seems to like you, though. Keep it, it might bring you luck."

"Besides," he said, getting up from the table, "I have to be getting along now. Dad said I have to help with the chores around the garden this afternoon. I'll drop by to see you in a few days."

He moved around the table to the path. "Bye Liz."

Andre broke into a run, jumped the wall and with a quick turn and wave, was over the bridge and across the field.

Elizabeth looked down at the ball in her hand. She squeezed it and a little bolt of orange ran through the centre.

"It looks like glass, but it's soft and warm to the touch," she thought.

She sat, staring down at it, then looked up shielding her eyes from the sun. "It's getting a bit warm," she said, pulling at the neckline of her dress.

Elizabeth held the ball up, looking at the rainbow of colours running through the middle. "It would be nice if we had a little rain, to water the grass and the flowers," she said, looking over at the roses lining the side wall of the cottage.

Dark clouds rolled in overhead. At first, just a few rain drops fell, then in seconds the heavens opened up. It poured down so hard, the drops stung Elizabeth's bare arms. She dropped the ball into her lap. Grabbing the wheels to her chair, she tried to push herself along the pathway, but her hands were wet and she couldn't grip the wheels enough to move with any speed. "Oh, just stop raining will you!" she shouted with frustration.

As suddenly as the rain had began; it stopped.

In the corner of the garden, an elviron crouched under the bushes, watching her.

"Oh damn it! I'm soaked."

She looked up at the sky and then down to the little ball in her lap. She felt a flutter in her chest, as though she had just experienced something very important.

"Get a hold of yourself!" she thought.

When Elizabeth saw Grandma Rose come out of the cottage and walk along the path towards her, she put the orb into the pocket of her dress.

Grandma Rose smiled as she approached Elizabeth. "I see you got caught in the downpour, young lady. Come in and dry off. I'll make a cup of tea."

"My imagination is going to get me into trouble if I'm not careful," Elizabeth thought, as she followed her gran into the house. "If someone notices my behaviour lately, I might get carted off to the nearest funny farm, and what then?"

Chapter Sixteen

Elizabeth opened her eyes and looked at the clock by her bed. The red numbers glowed 2:30 a.m. in the darkness.

"Something must have woken me," she thought.

It was then she heard a tapping on her bedroom window.

"Elizabeth, it is Gideon. Bindyl is with me. We have something to show you. Please let us in."

She swung her legs to the floor. "Ouch!" she exclaimed, hitting her leg on her wheelchair. Rubbing her shin, she looked out into the darkness.

"What am I looking at?" she asked the two elves, who were now standing on the dresser beside her.

"Look over there, by the Beech tree in the corner of the garden. Look carefully, Elizabeth," Gideon said.

Elizabeth peered into the night. "I think I can see something. Yes, a dark figure by the Beech tree. That's odd. It seems to be transparent. I can see the tree behind it. Is it a ghost?"

Gideon pointed outside. "You are in danger Elizabeth. You must be careful. Do not go outside alone in the garden in the dark. You are safe during the day, in the sunlight, but do not leave your windows open at night.

"Either you have grown to my size, or I have shrunk to yours," she thought. "No, that can't be right. He must be my size or I wouldn't be able to see out of the window.

"There are things outside that want to harm you and Lady Rose. We will try to protect you as much as we can, but we will need your help."

"Lady Rose? Do you mean my gran?"

She looked outside again, just as the shadowy figure moved. It disappeared for a second, then appeared outside of the window. It too was human size. Its transparent body moved in a series of unending waves.

Panic shot through Elizabeth's chest. "What is it!"

"It is an elviron," said Gideon.

Elizabeth heard his voice, but it sounded distant. He seemed to be shrinking, fading away in front of her.

"Wake up! Wake up! Elizabeth, wake up!"

Elizabeth opened her eyes to see Grandma Rose sitting on the side of her bed.

"Oh thank heavens! You gave me such a scare. Are you all right?"

Elizabeth looked towards the window. There were no small people standing on her dresser. No one in the room except her and Grandma Rose.

"I was dreaming!" she thought. "What a horrible nightmare! But it seemed so real!"

She smiled at her grandma. "I'm all right, Gran. I just had a bad dream."

Grandma Rose stood. "If this dream problem keeps happening young lady, a trip to the doctor may be in order. Do you think you can go back to sleep? Or would you like me to make you a hot drink to settle you down a bit?"

"No thanks. Good night, Gran."

By the time Grandma Rose had returned to her bedroom, Elizabeth was fast asleep.

Chapter Seventeen

Elizabeth woke early. She dressed and wheeled her chair to the bedroom window. Down by the side of her dresser, she noticed something lying on the carpet. She bent over and picked up a small arrow. As she turned it over in her hands, her heart leapt.

"So I wasn't dreaming after all! This is the arrow that the one called Gideon shot into the air the other night."

She put it in the drawer with the ball that Andre had given her the day before, wheeled herself out of her bedroom and down the hall towards the kitchen.

Grandma put some scrambled eggs and bacon on a plate and put it in front of her.

"I'm not very hungry, Gran," she said, pushing the plate away.

On the way to school, Elizabeth looked out of the window, lost in thought. "I wish I could get the picture of that creature at my window out of my head! And what was it that the one called Gideon said?"

***

The day began at school as usual. Elizabeth sat in the classroom, constantly looking at the clock above the blackboard.

"Today is dragging!" she thought, as she tried to focus on Miss Evans.

After school, Elizabeth went out into the garden. She sat for a long time, looking at the Beech tree in the corner.

"I have to know," she said, pushing herself over to the tree and putting her hands on the trunk. "It looks and feels like any other tree. Doesn't seem so mysterious in the daylight. All the same, I think I'll close my bedroom window tonight. Pull the curtains closed too."

"Elizabeth? It's time for supper," Grandma Rose called, from the back door.

"Coming Gran."

At bedtime, Elizabeth closed her window, drew her curtains and climbed into bed. She turned on her side and for a few moments watched Charlie, who was asleep on the dresser.

"I wonder where you came from?" she said to the little cat.

She was still staring at Charlie when the cat's head shot up, looking towards the curtains.

"Elizabeth, come to the window and open it… please?" a voice asked from outside.

She looked towards the window, pulling the bedcovers up to her chin.

"Elizabeth, it is Gideon. If you can hear me, please let me in!"

"Oh all right. Wait a minute," she mumbled.

She struggled into her wheelchair and pushed herself to the window. As she pulled back the drapes, she saw Gideon standing outside on the ledge.

He gave her a sheepish grin and shrugged. "I won't harm you. You have been having strange dreams, have you not? I know it's late, but I need to talk with you. I am here to help you, so please let me in."

Elizabeth opened the window. Gideon stepped over the ledge and on to the top of the dresser. Charlie stepped aside, as if to politely let him in. Gideon nodded to the cat, as though he knew her and was saying either thanks or hello. Elizabeth could not quite decide which.

They looked at one another.

"You know, I could have sworn you were in my room a couple of nights ago." Elizabeth said.

"I apologise for the other night. I was looking for something. But I am here again because it seems that you have been chosen to be the new guardian," he said.

Elizabeth glared at him. "I beg your pardon? And just who might you be?"

"You have been chosen as the new guardian of the Grymlons," said Gideon.

"I believe I asked you who you are?"

Gideon dropped down on one knee, bending his head. "Please forgive my forwardness, Lady Elizabeth. I did not mean to insult you."

"Lady Elizabeth? Are you sure you have the right house? I don't know who you are, but in case you hadn't noticed, I'm in a wheelchair.

I can't guard anything, and I have no idea what you are talking about anyway! What are Gremlins?"

"Grymlons," Gideon corrected her, not looking up. "I am here because one of the Grymlons is missing. We have been searching around this area."

"And you think that I have this… Grymlon? You still haven't told me who you are, and what a Grymlon is?"

He looked up making a ball shape with his hands. "Well, it looks sort of like…"

"I was under the impression that the king understood me, when I asked that Elizabeth not be involved with the Grymlons."

Elizabeth's head shot around towards the door.

"Gran!"

Gideon looked up, surprised, "I apologize, Lady Rose. We should have come to you, but, the king, my lady, has told us that Elizabeth is to be the next guardian. There is no other that can perform the task," Gideon said, keeping his head bowed low. "One of the Grymlons is missing. We must find it."

"That still doesn't explain why you are in my granddaughter's room!" said Grandma Rose.

"I…I…" was all Gideon could say.

"Who else knows about the missing Grymlon?" asked Grandma.

"Only the king, me and Bindyl, and of course, now you and Elizabeth," Gideon muttered, nervously. "The king has managed to keep it a secret. He does not want the Elven Realm to know. He fears there may be another war if too many of the elves find out."

Grandma Rose looked down her nose at Gideon. "I'll talk to King Morvand. Go and tell him that I wish to see him as soon as possible. Oh, and don't come into my house without my permission again."

"Yes, Lady Rose. Of course, Lady Rose," Gideon replied, backing towards the window.

When he reached the ledge, he jumped out with the same quiet grace, as he had a couple of nights before.

"Gran?" Elizabeth said, looking from the window to her grandma and back again.

"I'm sure you have questions to ask. Why don't you come into the kitchen. I'll make us a warm drink, and then you and I will talk."

Grandma Rose left the room.

"This should be interesting," Elizabeth thought, following her down the hall. "I wonder if I'll wake up in a minute."

Grandma Rose made hot chocolate for them both.

Elizabeth pulled up to the kitchen table. Grandma Rose took a seat opposite her, and handed Elizabeth her cup.

"I'm going to tell you a story, Elizabeth. A true story and there is no end to it," Grandma began. "The women in our family have been the guardians of the Grymlons for hundreds of years. This house was built for us by the druids, under instruction from the elves. The doors and the beams in this house are of Oak to protect us from evil. Our family has always lived here."

"I was the guardian of the Grymlons for many years, as was my mother before me. When my time passed to protect them, your mother took over the task. This cottage would have passed to your mum and dad when I died, then of course, onto you. Unfortunately, your mum died before it was her time. It seems because you are now of age, King Morvand has passed on the job to you, despite my protests."

"What are the Grymlons, Gran? And who are those small people? Where are they from?"

Grandma Rose held up her hand. "Slow down. You said people. Have other elves visited you besides Gideon before tonight?"

"So they <u>are</u> elves! I was just about to go to sleep a few nights ago, Gideon and Bindyl I think his name is, came in through my window. They were looking for something."

"Yes," Grandma continued. "The stories about the elves are true. They are the keepers of the five Grymlons. The Grymlons are the elements of the earth. They are fire, wind, air, water, and the earth itself.

They are the tools of magic that the elves use. Without them, elves would be seen by all humans and they could not work their magic, to keep nature in balance."

"This means that the seasons would not happen as they should. It would snow in July. There would be a heat wave in December. These are the things that the elves keep in balance for us, but every hundred years, the Grymlons begin to grow tired. At that time, they are transported to Avebury to be regenerated.

Your mother had received the training that was necessary for the renewing of the Grymlons, as this was to happen during the time of her guardianship. Now the responsibility has fallen to you."

"Obviously, this was not supposed to happen. We thought that you would be much older when all this would be passed onto you. It would have been your offspring that would have performed the regeneration.

When your mum and dad and Jesse were killed and the shock caused you to be unable to walk. I asked King Morvand to try and find someone else to do the guardianship. I didn't want to put you in any danger due to your being in a wheelchair."

"He said he would try to resolve the problem and in the meantime, the elves cast a spell on you, so that you wouldn't see them. This was for your own protection. It seems that the old ways are so strong in you, the spell didn't work. I will talk to King Morvand and tell him that he needs to release you from your task."

"Aren't I too young to be of age, Gran? I'm only fifteen."

"Being of age to be the guardian of the five Grymlons, means that at age fifteen, you would have been old enough to begin your training," Grandma explained. "You would not have actually taken over the job, until your mother had reached her late fifties. Your situation should have released you from the task. I was hoping that the king would find some other way to renew the Grymlons."

"Have other families ever been used to protect the Grymlons?" asked Elizabeth.

"No."

"What happens when they have to be renewed?"

As the guardian of the Grymlons, you will cast a spell," Grandma explained, "That spell will bind the Grymlons only to you, until the time of renewal. At the time you say the binding spell, the Grymlons will no longer look like orbs. They will look like ordinary little bits and pieces you would find around any house. You will hide them in a place known only to you and one other elf. You will need some training, including self defence, also some magic that will help you if you were captured.

"I'm supposed to do magic? How will I be able to do that!"

"Elizabeth. This is a dangerous time for both you and the elves. I want you to calm down and pay attention. If the elviron capture you, they may try to trick you into telling them where the Grymlons are. They are good, very good. They will scare you, threaten you. If they find out where the Grymlons are, they will kill you."

"Why do the elviron want them?" asked Elizabeth.

"The elviron used to have their own Grymlons, but they became lost," said Grandma, "If they can get their hands on them at the time of renewal, and they can renew them, then they hold the power."

"They're grotesque looking," said Elizabeth, with a shudder.

"The elviron were once similar to the elves of Kimadrian.

When their Grymlons were lost to them, something happened and they changed. Now the elviron are like vampires. At first they drank each others blood, and eventually they evolved into something else. They developed an uncontrollable urge to eat raw meat, and they possess the ability to steal the essence of another living being. This is how they sustain their shadowy form, but they cannot maintain their form for long in the human world. They can only live in the twilight. The sun burns them. If they become the keepers of the Grymlons, they will control the Elven Realm and the seasons up here."

"The elviron live in a realm called Distardrian. It's never fully daylight there. If they get their hands on the Grymlons, eventually they will become very strong and will be able to stay longer in our world. A human essence is a rare and tasty prize for an elviron. It temporarily gives them great power."

"So not all the elviron can use this shadowy form?"

"No," said Grandma. "Only if they can take a spirit, or essence if you like."

"If the Grymlons control the seasons, did the elviron set do the same?" Elizabeth asked.

"Yes. The elviron set of Grymlons were tied somehow to the elven ones. When the elviron set were lost, it did affect the seasons up here, but the difference was so slight, the only ones to notice were the elves because they monitor the seasons.

"I noticed that the elves spoke with an accent," said Elizabeth.

"Yes, they do have a bit of a lilt when they talk," said Grandma. "I think it is the mixture of Elvish tongue combined with English words that makes them sound that way. Most elves speak Elvish and English. Over the years, the elves started to speak English more and more. I think it's because they have become more exposed to us over time.

You go to bed now, Elizabeth. Get some rest. I'll talk to King Morvand in the morning."

Grandma Rose stood and kissed Elizabeth on the forehead. "Go on with you now. Don't worry, I'll handle all of this tomorrow.

Elizabeth wheeled herself to her room, pulled herself into her bed and cried tears of frustration.

Charlie the cat jumped up onto the bed and sat on Elizabeth's legs.

Elizabeth leaned on her pillow and stroked the back of the little cat's head.

"Oh Charlie, how am I supposed to sleep! I could be going on a great adventure, if only I could walk. I'll never be able to sleep now!"

Charlie jumped down from the bed and leapt up onto the dresser by the window. Elizabeth settled back and closed her eyes.

Then in frustration, she sat up, pulling the covers away from her legs.

"Perhaps if I try really hard and concentrate, my legs will work again."

"Oh, it's no use!" she said, after a minute or two. "They simply won't move."

She pulled the covers back over her and a few minutes later, was fast asleep.

On the floor, between Elizabeth's dresser and the wall, a little figure sat hidden in the darkness with his knees up to his chest.

Unseen by Elizabeth, Gideon had been watching her as she fell asleep. The window had been left open from when she had let him in earlier. Despite Grandma's request, he had sneaked back in when they left the room.

"Should I wake her and tell her to close and lock the window?" he thought. "No, I'll stay until dawn, just in case an elviron tries to get into the house. Next time I'm here, I'll reminder her to keep her window closed."

He stood, jumped up onto the end of her bed and sat cross legged, watching her as she slept.

When dawn came, Gideon slid down from Elizabeth's bed and walked around to her head. He grew to human size and bent over her.

"I have a feeling that you are the key to the future of your world and mine," he whispered. "I promise you this, Elizabeth Ghenestone. I will protect you with my own life, if I have to."

Gideon straightened, pulling a stray lock of long blond hair from his face.

"I can't stop looking at her. She looks so serene when she is asleep," he thought, with a sigh. "Oh well, time to go."

Gideon moved away from her and sat on her dresser. He patted Charlie on the head. She purred, loudly. He shrank back down into his smaller form.

Turning to take one more look at her, he disappeared into the morning light, through the half open window.

Chapter Eighteen

The elviron cowered before King Kalidryd who had been listening to his explanation of failure. "When I returned to the Willow tree to try and get it back, there was a young human walking along the river bank. I watched him pick it up and put it in his pocket. He went to the house and sat with the girl in the chair with the wheels. I think he may have given it to her."

King Kalidryd eyed the elviron with contempt. "My daughter chose you because you are a soldier. Yet here you are acting like a spineless idiot! You will watch for the right moment, and then go into that house and find it. The situation will not go well with you if Princess Verina finds out about this."

"But the house is protected by oak. I will have to endure horrible pain if I go into there!"

The king scowled at the soldier. "The pain you will feel entering that house will be nothing, compared to the pain my daughter will inflict on you, if you do not retrieve the orb. I suggest you rectify the situation as soon as possible."

Yes, your majesty," said the elviron, backing out of the room.

He exited the king's chambers, closing the door behind him.

"Back up to the Human Realm!" he muttered. "I'm still burnt from the last time!"

***

Grandma Rose sat in King Morvand's private apartments losing her argument.

"How can you expect Elizabeth to be the guardian at the time of the regeneration?" Grandma protested. "She can't move her legs. I know I told you that it was supposed to be temporary. At least that was what the doctor told me, but that was two years ago. Goodness knows how long it will take for her to walk again. You know this is a much more dangerous task than the usual guardianship."

"The women in our family have been the guardians for many years. Can't you find someone else just this once?"

"I don't want anyone else," said the King.

"Your father, King Randalph would not have allowed this," said Grandma.

"He was king when you were trained for the guardianship. I am king now, so don't try and make me feel guilty, Rose!"

"Well I won't allow it," said Grandma Rose.

"You have no choice, Rose. I have decided that Elizabeth is the guardian, wheelchair or not. I believe in destiny. I also believe that things will make it possible for her to go on the quest."

"I don't believe there will be any such intervention," Grandma Rose protested.

King Morvand leaned forward in his seat. "She is now of age to be trained, so she will be."

"But this guardianship falls at the time of the renewal. How can you train her in a wheelchair? And we have so little time! She won't be able to do it. You're setting her up to get hurt and to fail in the most important event in your realm."

"I will summon the high elven mage. He may be able to come up with a spell to help Elizabeth walk. You will go now, Lady Rose and bring the girl back down here. So that we might determine just how she will accomplish this task."

"Is there nothing I can say to change your mind?" said Grandma Rose.

"No, Rose. There is nothing you can say or do to make me change my mind. Now go and bring her here. It is time to get things moving along."

Chapter Nineteen

Elizabeth was awake, dressed and eating a bowl of cereal when her grandmother walked in through the back door.

"You are to come with me," Grandma Rose told her.

"Why? Where are we going?"

"You will see, said Grandma. "Now come on. We have to go."

Elizabeth followed her grandmother out of the back door. They travelled along the path, crossed over the bridge to the Willow tree.

As they passed through the drooping branches, the tree split open vertically in the middle. Two elves about twelve inches high, dressed in dark blue uniforms, stood either side of the opening.

"My wheelchair won't fit in there!" said Elizabeth.

"Just trust me and you will see something magical happen," said Grandma.

As they neared the tree, the two of them and Elizabeth's chair shrank down to the size of the elves. Elizabeth pinched the side of her arm.

"What are you doing to yourself?" asked Grandma Rose.

"I'm making sure that I'm not dreaming," said Elizabeth.

"And are you awake, do you think?"

Elizabeth rubbed her arm. "Yes!"

"I remember when your great grandmother brought me into this tree for the first time, said Grandma. "I felt as though I was walking into one of the fairytale stories she used to tell me at bedtime. Your mother said she felt the same way the first time she walked into the tree."

"I know exactly what you mean," Elizabeth said, her heart pounding for the second time in as many days.

As the tree closed behind them, they went downward and were

now under the earth. Grandma led Elizabeth down a slight hill to a fountain where they turned into a tunnel that was also a street.

There were elves walking along a pathway beside the road, all of them going about their daily business.

Elizabeth looked around as Grandma Rose pushed her wheelchair. She noticed stone pillars three feet high with glass domes on the top. They were spaced out at regular intervals all along the road. Inside the domes were large round, flat candles that served as street lights. The flames from the candles flickered with yellows and reds as they lit the pathways. The pillars were intricately carved with beautiful markings.

"Gran is right about this place. The lights look a bit like giant toad stools I've seen in fairytale books," she thought.

Elizabeth peered into windows and doors in the side of the rock that shone light and cast shadows onto the cobbled stone street. Horse drawn carriages travelled back and forth. Some of the doors had signs over them. Among them, a Bakery and a Grocery.

"The sounds from the street are crisp and clear, quite different from above," she thought.

She peered into the shop windows and saw elves shopping for food and clothes, much the same as humans do.

She noticed that all of the elves had the same alabaster skin tone. Although their hair and eye colour differed, they all had the same beautiful almond shaped eyes and a slight point to their ears.

"There are people down here," Elizabeth commented.

"Yes, there are a few humans that work and live down here," said Grandma. "They are also from families that have worked with the elves for hundreds of years. They are sworn to secrecy about this place, just like we are."

"I notice some of the elves carry bows and arrows," said Elizabeth.

"The elves have clans. The Warrior clan usually carry the bows," said Grandma.

"Some of the elven women are carrying bows. Do they fight too?" asked Elizabeth.

"The elven women have the same responsibilities as the men."

"But surely those little bows and arrows can't do much harm up in our world," Elizabeth remarked.

"The arrows can mortally wound another elf," explained Grandma, "and even an elviron. Most of the elves are expert archers and seldom miss their targets. For example, if the elves wanted a human to go to sleep, they would simply throw a bag of sleep dust into the air, and shoot it so that the dust was breathed in. Most humans can't see elves, so they would never know what happened to them."

Grandma thought for a moment. "When Gideon and Bindyl came to visit you, did either of them use their bow?"

"Yes. Just before they left, Gideon shot an arrow through a bag and coloured dust came down all around me. I found the arrow on the floor by my dresser."

"And you have been sleeping well, haven't you," said Grandma.

"Best sleep I've had since... Well, for a long time."

"The sleep dust is used to shield human eyes from the elves, but it is also very beneficial to one's health. Gideon did you a favour," said Grandma.

"I will have to thank him," said Elizabeth.

They continued for about a quarter of a mile, until they came to enormous doors embedded in the rock face.

Grandma Rose approached the doors and knocked. A smaller door opened directly in front of them, and a uniformed elf appeared.

"The king has ordered me to take my granddaughter to the castle. We will need help with her wheelchair."

He looked over her shoulder to Elizabeth.

"Very well, Lady Rose."

Grandma Rose wheeled Elizabeth through the door and stopped.

"Oh my!" said Elizabeth, "but how?"

"It is beautiful, isn't it," said Grandma.

Elizabeth could only nod.

There were trees and grass, and hills as far as the eye could see. There was a blue sky and clouds. The sun shone brightly in the sky.

Little cottages were dotted around the countryside with thatched roofs. Elizabeth could see wisps of smoke rising out of their chimneys.

"Reminds me a bit of Oaklade," she thought.

Off in the distance there was a village. Beyond the village was a castle. It had colourful banners hanging from eight towers. From the largest tower, a huge flag of purple, green and gold fluttered in the wind.

"The castle, it's so beautiful, it doesn't look real," said Elizabeth.

"That's where we are going," said Grandma.

"There?" said Elizabeth.

"It takes about twenty minutes."

A carriage pulled up with four white horses. A guard picked

Elizabeth up and placed her inside. Her wheelchair was folded up and tied to the back. With the crack of a whip, the horses moved into a gallop and they were on their way across the countryside.

"What is this place called, Gran?"

"This is the Realm of Kimadrian. You can see the town of Kimadria over there," said Grandma, pointing to the village Elizabeth had noticed earlier. "Back behind us is the realm of Distardrian."

Elizabeth turned around to see what Grandma was looking at.

Out of the back carriage window Elizabeth saw the blue sky turn to grey.

Chapter Twenty

As their carriage passed through the town of Kimadria, Elizabeth saw elven children playing on the pathways in front of their houses. Some waved to her as the carriage hurried by. She waved back.

"How very unrealistic, but beautiful this all is," she thought. "I feel a bit like 'Alice in Wonderland' I'll wake up any minute now," she thought, turning to her grandma.

"Can we come here and walk through the streets of the village, Gran?"

"Of course we can, but first we must meet with King Morvand. He needs to talk to you. When we've settled a few things, we'll come back to the village and I'll show you around a bit."

A few minutes later, their carriage approached the gates of the castle. The carriage slowed down as the gates swung open and they passed through. It came to a stop in a large courtyard. Elizabeth looked out of the window.

Inside the castle walls there were streets of cobbled stone. Alleyways branched out from the court yard and small shops were spread around the immediate area.

Two guards approached the driver. After exchanging a few words, they saluted Grandma Rose and Elizabeth, then went back to their posts by the gates.

The carriage moved forward through the courtyard, under an archway and over a bridge spanning a deep moat. They continued under another archway that had a large trellis gate hoisted up above. The carriage pulled up to the front of the inner buildings of the castle.

Elizabeth was picked up and placed in her wheelchair. Grandma Rose pushed her inside, where they were ushered into an entryway.

Elizabeth looked around her. The stone walls were covered with hand sewn tapestries. Every now and then there was a painting or a crest with crossed swords and shields.

An elf in a footman's uniform approached them.

"His majesty has asked that you wait in the portrait room. He will be with you in a few minutes," he said, waving a white gloved hand towards a room to the left.

"And where is Alice and the rabbit?" Elizabeth said, under her breath.

"What?" said Grandma, leaning down to hear what Elizabeth had said.

"Oh nothing, Gran. Just talking to myself."

Grandma and Elizabeth entered a room with a large stone fire place on the back wall. Dark blue carpet covered the floor. There were many portraits of elves on the walls.

"Who are these?" Elizabeth asked, looking up at the painted faces.

"They are previous kings and queens, and their children," said Grandma.

Elizabeth looked at the expressions of some of the paintings and let out a little laugh.

"What's funny?" Grandma asked.

"Some of them look a bit ridiculous," said Elizabeth.

"The portraits you are looking at are hundreds of years old," said Grandma. "It was considered proper to pose that way back then. Traditions and trends change here in the elven realm just like everywhere else."

"I like this one," said Elizabeth, pointing to the portrait closest to the door. "He looks like Gideon. Who is he?"

"That is a picture of King Morvand when he first became king."

"Is Gideon, King Morvand's son?"

"Yes he is," said Grandma. "He is a prince and heir to the throne of Kimadrian."

Just as Grandma Rose was about to say something else, a young female elf came into the room.

"I am looking for Gideon. Have either of you seen him?" she asked.

"Sorry no. We have just arrived," said Elizabeth.

"Are you the cripple that I have been hearing so much about?" the female elf asked, with a smirk.

"Are you talking to me?" said Elizabeth.

"Your name is Elizabeth isn't it?"

"Yes," answered Elizabeth.

"Yes, you're definitely the chair jockey I've heard about. Sorry about the human term. I sort of like the way you humans talk, sometimes. You're the one who's mother and father were killed aren't you?" she said, staring Elizabeth up and down. "I was told that you were a beauty. It seems that beauty truly is in the eye of the beholder!"

"Zoe, you will not speak to my granddaughter in that manner!" said Grandma.

The female elf laughed.

Elizabeth looked at her grandma. "You know her?"

Grandma Rose nodded, walking towards the young elf. "You may be nobility young lady, but you're not too special to have your ears boxed!"

Still laughing, the female elf made a hasty retreat towards the door. She passed King Morvand, curtsying quickly, she kept walking. He nodded to her absent mindedly, keeping his eye on Elizabeth.

As the king entered the room, Grandma Rose bowed her head and curtsied. Elizabeth glanced at her grandma and bowed her head to the king.

"So this is the young lady I have been hearing so much about," he said, approaching her.

"I am delighted to meet you at last, Elizabeth," he said, kissing the back of her hand, as he looked into her eyes.

Elizabeth returned his gaze.

King Morvand turned to a guard who had followed him into the room. "Go and request that Vandrayven grace us with his presence."

The guard bowed deeply, turned and left.

The king turned to Grandma. "How are you Lady Rose?"

"I am well, your majesty. How is the queen?"

"She is well. She sends her regards and told me to ask you if you would like to have afternoon tea soon."

"I would enjoy that very much," said Grandma.

Elizabeth, bored with their small talk, wandered around looking at all the portraits on the wall. She turned when she heard a swish and a swoosh of heavy garments being dragged along the floor. A tall, thin man with straight dark hair down to his waist entered the room with a flourish. He was dressed in long, colourful robes. He stamped down his staff as he bowed to the king.

"Vandrayven, thank you for coming. I know you must be busy with your spells and potions," said the King.

Vandrayven nodded briefly to the king as he made a bee line for Elizabeth. "This must be the young female who cannot walk."

When he reached her, Vandrayven held out two thin, boney hands. She took them before she had realized it.

As their hands touched there was an audible crackling sound and a spark flew upwards.

Vandrayven stepped back quickly. "My goodness! This female has mage in her!"

"Calm down. She is one of the chosen humans, remember?" King Morvand said, looking at Grandma Rose and shaking his head.

"Oh yes, of course, how silly of me. You will have to excuse me, young lady. I am getting old," said Vandrayven. "It must have been static, although for a moment I could have sworn... well never mind. Come with me, my child and I will see if I can cast a spell to get you out of that chair."

Vandrayven moved towards the door.

Elizabeth shot her grandma a worried look.

"It's all right. I'll be here when you get back," said Grandma.

Elizabeth followed the magician along the hallway. As they travelled downward, the passageway became dim. After a few minutes they came to a door. The magician wheeled Elizabeth into a well lit room with no windows.

"Is this a library, or a laboratory? Or is it a cluttered mess of both?" thought Elizabeth, as she looked around her.

"I am going to cast a spell, so you will have to keep very still," Vandrayven said.

Elizabeth made herself comfortable.

Despite the disarray, the magician walked around the room picking up various things. Elizabeth looked about her as she waited, trying to make out some of the objects scattered around. She noticed there were vials of different coloured liquids resting on one of the tables. There were strange looking little creatures swimming around inside of the vials.

On another table there was so much stuff, she could barely make out what it all was. Among the mess was the largest hourglass she had ever seen containing multi coloured sand. Elizabeth stared in fascination as the sand in the hourglass changed colours. She closed her eyes and shook her head, not quite sure of what she saw. When she looked back at the hourglass, the sand had turned black. Next to the hourglass was a strange pink and blue bird sitting on a perch. It eyed Elizabeth and cocked its head to one side.

Elizabeth stared back.

"It's not nice to stare," said the bird.

Elizabeth jumped at the sound of its voice.

"Be quiet, Mac," Vandrayven said, not looking at the bird as he spoke.

"I'll speak if I…"

The bird's voice was cut off in mid sentence when Vandrayven waved his hand around and pointed at him. "Sorry Elizabeth. He can be a bit mouthy sometimes."

"I don't mind," Elizabeth said, with a nervous giggle.

With an armload of dried herbs and bottles of strange looking liquids, Vandrayven made his way back to where Elizabeth had been patiently waiting.

He put them all on a table beside her. Picking up the dried herbs, he bound them together until he had a bouquet. He produced a wand from under his robe.

With the herbs in the other hand, he danced around her chanting strange words, moving his arms around furiously.

This went on for about five minutes, then he said, "get up child, and walk!"

Elizabeth sat forward, trying to put her weight in her legs, but nothing happened.

Vandrayven tried again, but with no luck.

"Need something stronger," he muttered to himself.

He turned to Elizabeth. "We're not finished yet. Let's move on to another spell."

Vandrayven made another trip around the room. He picked up three jars and opened them. One was yellow, one was red and the other one was brown. As he dipped the wand into the three different jars of liquid, Elizabeth could smell strawberries, bananas and… coffee?

He held up the wand and began to dance around Elizabeth's chair again: still nothing. Using just about all of the stuff he had gathered, Vandrayven continued to cast spells and chant various chants for almost an hour with no progress. At times, Elizabeth found it hard to stifle a fit of the giggles.

Finally, he gave up. "I cannot help you child. I am at a loss as to what more I can do. I am sorry."

Elizabeth's heart sank. "It's all right. I'm getting used to this chair now anyway."

He rolled her up to the surface and they made their way to the room with the portraits, Elizabeth had found so amusing. When they entered, Grandma turned and looked at Elizabeth, then to the magician.

"Don't feel bad Vandrayven. If it is meant to happen, it will probably do so by itself," she said, trying to console him.

Vandrayven bowed sullenly to Grandma. He turned on his heel and flounced out of the room without bowing to the king as he left.

"I must leave you with King Morvand, Elizabeth," Grandma said. "He needs to tell you things about the Grymlons. I will return in a few minutes."

She curtsied to the king and left.

Elizabeth watched her grandmother disappear down the hallway. King Morvand pulled up a chair and sat down in front of her. She looked into his face.

"He has striking blue eyes," she thought, looking into them. "His hair is greying at the temples, but I can see where Gideon gets his good looks."

The king smiled at her. "Don't be afraid, Elizabeth. The task set before you is very important. But if you do as I say, we will all come out of this splendidly. I am going to tell you some words. They are a spell that you must remember."

The king paused for a moment or two.

"How dramatic he is," thought, Elizabeth.

"When we are finished here," he continued. "You, your grandmother and I will go up to the Grymlons. There are only four of them at this time, but we will do our best to find the one that was stolen."

"When you have said the spell, the Grymlons will be bound to you. You will have to say the same spell to change them back, so I want you to practice often. You must find a place to put them where they will be safe. The Grymlons will for this period of time, be powerful only when you are near them."

"Then what do I do?" asked Elizabeth.

"You will tell Gideon where they are. If anything happens to you, he will bring them back to me," King Morvand replied. "You must not tell him the spell that I am about to teach you. You must protect the orbs and the spell with your life. If you do not, both your world and ours will cease to exist as we know it today. Because you have not had any self defence training, Gideon will accompany you with your task. This is highly irregular, as an elf is supposed to be chosen at random."

"The ceremony to choose the elf will be performed as usual. An elf will be picked from the Choosing Chamber to allay any suspicion, but Vandrayven will arrange for that elf to be Gideon.

You must not tell anyone that you already know who the elf is. Do you understand?"

"I thought Gran knew all of this stuff," said Elizabeth.

"She does, but it is my job to teach the hundred year guardian," said the King.

"If Gideon is your son, and heir to the throne, why can't I tell him the spell?" asked Elizabeth.

"He won't know the spell until he succeeds me," King Morvand explained.

"I don't think I can do it," said Elizabeth, feeling a bit uneasy.

"Will you at least try?" said the King.

"Do I have a choice?" Elizabeth said, looking into the king's eyes.

"No," he answered.

King Morvand spent the next hour coaching Elizabeth. When he was sure she would be able to remember the spell, he went to a writing desk by the door. He wrote down some book titles and handed them to her. "Give this list to Rose. She has all the books at Willow View. You meet with a druid when you begin your journey. He will guide you to the circles once you reach Avebury You will also be making contact with some fairies during your journey. Don't look for them, they will find you."

The king called the sentry on guard into the room.

"Go and find Lady Rose. Ask her to come here."

The guard saluted and left.

A few minutes later, Grandma Rose returned.

"I have given Elizabeth a list of books to read. Please make sure she does so."

"I will do my best, your Majesty, as I did with Audrey."

They all headed up to the tower where the Grymlons were kept.

They came to a door. It had a circle within a circle carved on the front. The smaller circle had engravings intertwined within it.

The two guards stepped aside as King Morvand approached. The king began pressing parts of the inner circle. The door swung open by itself as he touched the last one.

The king turned to the guards. "Please bring Elizabeth in here and put her down. You can both wait outside."

The guards placed Elizabeth on the carpet. She looked around her at the five windows spaced evenly around the room.

She watched as each of the orbs changed into different colours running through at different times.

"I have one of those," she said.

King Morvand and Grandma Rose looked at each other and turned to Elizabeth.

"Where is it?" asked Grandma.

"In my bedside drawer, at home. Andre found it by the Willow tree when he came to visit and gave it to me."

"Who is Andre?" asked King Morvand.

"He's a friend of Elizabeth's. He knows nothing of the elves," said Grandma.

"You must go back up to the Human Realm and get it, immediately!" the king said.

"Wait!" said Grandma, as the he made to leave. "Let Elizabeth say the binding spell, and all the orbs will be unrecognisable until she says it again: even the one at the house."

"Yes, good idea. Elizabeth, say the spell now," said the King.

The guards were dismissed. Grandma and the king stood back out of the way. Elizabeth held up her hands and began to chant the spell.

The four orbs rose into the air. They spun around her head as she said the spell, moving faster and faster until they were a blurred rainbow of colours. When Elizabeth uttered the last word of the spell, the orbs fell into her lap.

All of them now made of a shiny black material. One was a small vase made for a long stemmed rose. One was a picture frame, one was a small spoon, and the fourth was a figurine of a horse. The one that was in the drawer in her bedroom was now a necklace.

King Morvand opened the door.

"You two," he said, pointing to the guards who had carried Elizabeth, "you may come back in."

The king turned to Grandma. "I think we should leave the Grymlons here so they will remain safe, until Elizabeth is ready to leave."

"I agree," replied Grandma.

The king placed one of the Grymlons on each table.

"Please carry Elizabeth back down the stairs and put her into the carriage, and hurry," he said.

The guards stepped forward, picked up Elizabeth's chair, and carried it back down the stairs.

Grandma Rose and Elizabeth hurried out of the castle and into a carriage that took them to the gates of Humadria. One of the guards pushed Elizabeth up to the surface with Grandma Rose close behind.

Chapter Twenty One

The elviron stepped over the windowsill and onto Elizabeth's dresser. A sharp pain promptly installed itself inside of his head as he entered the house.

"I don't know how long I can stand this!" he said, trying to massage the pain in his temples away.

He jumped to the floor, closed his eyes and grew to human size. The pain in his head increased as he grew. He pulled the curtains together, and looked around the room for a moment. As he crouched down to look under the bed, the pain in his head shot down his spine. He took a sharp intake of breath, trying not to scream with pain. He continued his search, looking in the drawers of the dresser under her window, then in the closet.

"If I were a human. Where would I hide things?" he whispered, looking around the room. "But what if I wasn't hiding anything!"

He opened the top drawer of Elizabeth's bedside table. "Yes!" He suddenly stopped and turned, looking towards the bedroom door, listening intently.

"I smell an elf." He shrank back down to his elviron size and slid under the bed.

Chapter Twenty Two

Gideon stood the other side of Elizabeth's bedroom door. He had grown to human size, and had already looked around in the living room and the kitchen.

"I'm glad she is not here," he thought, putting his hand on the door knob. "I made enough noise in the kitchen to wake the dead!"

He pushed open Elizabeth's bedroom door cautiously.

"I shouldn't be in here," he thought, "but I need to know more about her. Besides, I want my arrow back."

Gideon stepped into the room, squinting into the semi darkness. He went to Elizabeth's bedside table and ran his hand over the surface, then opened the drawer the elviron had been looking into, reached in and grasped something.

He didn't hear the elviron as he stood behind him, growing back to the size of a human. He grabbed Gideon by the shoulders, throwing him across the room. The elviron picked Gideon off the floor by his throat. Gideon struggled, shrinking back into his elf form. The elviron did the same, keeping a hold on him.

***

Elizabeth and Grandma Rose came out of the tree, growing into human size as they did so.

Grandma pushed Elizabeth over the bridge, along the path and into the house through the back door.

Elizabeth wheeled herself down the hall. When she reached her bedroom, she pushed the door open.

"I distinctly remember opening my curtains," she thought, hesitating in the doorway.

As she peered into the dimness, she could just make out someone's toes wiggling in the air.

"Gideon!" Elizabeth shouted, as she watched him try to break free from the elviron's clutches.

"The elviron's hand is inside Gideon's chest!" Grandma shouted, trying to get past Elizabeth.

"No, Gran!" Elizabeth said, pushing her back.

Elizabeth stood. She strode into her bedroom, raising her hand as she did so. "GANDRA SHAI, GANDRA BAHEM!"

The elviron dropped Gideon and put his hands over his head, as though Elizabeth had struck him!

"GET OUT OF THIS HOUSE, AND DO NOT RETURN!" she shouted.

The elviron cowered, backing away. He fumbled through the drapes, panicking when he couldn't find a way out. He crashed through the centre of the bedroom window, smashing it as he went.

Grandma Rose hurried to the window, watching the elviron run across the lawn. The air around him shimmered with heat as he disappeared behind the Beech tree.

Elizabeth knelt down and bent over Gideon.

"He's so pale and his lips are blue. Is he dead?" she thought.

"Gideon," she said softly.

Gideon opened his eyes. "I thought I was done for. My whole body feels like ice."

"What are you doing here, Gideon?" said Grandma.

"I... I was looking for the arrow that I left behind the other night. The elviron must have been hiding in the bedroom somewhere before I got here."

It was at that time, Elizabeth noticed she was standing. She turned, looked at her grandma... and fainted.

***

When she opened her eyes, Elizabeth was lying on her bed and Grandma was looking over her. "How are you feeling?"

"A bit woozy, what happened?" Elizabeth asked.

Gideon was sat on the bed at her feet. "You fainted, but before that, you stood up and walked!"

"I remember now."

"Can you get up and walk again?" he asked.

"See if you can stand," said Grandma.

Elizabeth sat up and swung her legs over the side of the bed without having to push them. She put her feet to the ground, and stood.

"Whoa!" she said, swaying a little.

Gideon jumped off the bed and stood behind her. "I'll catch you if you fall."

She took one step, then another, and another. She continued to walk unsteadily, until she reached the broken window.

"My legs feel rubbery and weak, but stronger than I would have thought," said Elizabeth, turning to Grandma who was crying.

"Yes! Yes! By the Grymlons, yes!" Gideon shouted, jumping up and down.

Grandma glared at Gideon. "Stop that!"

Gideon stood still, but couldn't hide a grin. "Sorry. I am very sorry, Lady Rose. I forgot myself. It will not happen again."

Elizabeth turned, hesitated for a moment before walking slowly back to the bed.

"How is she able to do that after spending all this time in a wheelchair?" Grandma thought, watching Elizabeth's feet move across the carpet. "I was told that she would need some extensive physio therapy when her legs got their feeling back."

Elizabeth sat on her bed. "Phew!" she sighed. "That was hard work." She opened the drawer to her bedside table and reached in. "The orb was here. It's gone!"

"Let me take a look," said Grandma, putting both hands inside the drawer. She turned to Gideon.

"I was just looking at it," he said.

"Looking at what?" asked Grandma.

"A black necklace," said Gideon. "I pulled it out of the drawer and as I was looking at it, the elviron snatched it from my hand and grabbed me by the throat."

Gideon dropped his eyes. "You bound the Grymlons didn't you."

"The elviron knew what that necklace was as soon as he saw it," said Grandma. "He would have tried to take it whether you were here or not. It can't be helped now. We will have to find a way to get it back. For now, I think I should make us a cup of tea."

Grandma left Elizabeth's bedroom and headed towards the kitchen.

"Do you humans drink tea _every_ time there is a crisis?" Gideon asked Elizabeth behind his hand, as they followed Grandma down the hall.

Elizabeth giggled. "Pretty much."

"I'm glad you can walk now," said Gideon. "I don't know how my father was expecting you to regenerate the Grymlons in a wheelchair!"

Once in the kitchen, Grandma Rose put a kettle of water on to boil. "Are you sure that you are feeling all right?" she asked Elizabeth, as she put out cups and saucers.

"Yes, Gran. You sound worried."

"I don't want you to be disappointed if you can't walk too well for a while. Sit down you two.

Gideon sat on the table opposite Elizabeth. "She might have a little extra something that the rest of us don't have," he muttered.

"What do you mean?" asked Elizabeth.

Grandma Rose shot Gideon a disapproving look.

"Oh nothing," he replied, looking away.

Grandma poured the boiling water into the teapot and left the tea to brew for a minute.

"Elizabeth, how did you know the words to say in Elvish that would make the elviron let go of Gideon?"

"I didn't even think about it, Gran. I knew I wanted him out of the house, something else seemed to take over from there."

"I think you're the one. The chosen one we have been waiting for these past three or four hundred years," said Gideon.

Grandma Rose looked at him, shaking her head as she did so, trying to shut him up.

"What _is_ he talking about?" asked Elizabeth.

"Gideon is excited about what has just happened. He is referring to a story that the elves tell. I will be back in just a minute. There is a book that I want look for," said Grandma, "in the meantime, I think you two should get to know each other."

Grandma hurried down the hall to her bedroom. She moved her bed away from the wall. Bending down, she ran her hand along the base of the wall, until she found a slight raise just above the carpet. She pressed down on it and a door slid open revealing a hidden room, about the size of her bedroom.

Grandma Rose stood for a moment, peering into the darkness.

Inside, resting on dusty shelves that reached from floor to ceiling, were dozens of books.

"I have been protecting these books for years, as have my family before me," she thought. "Even after all this time my heart still turns over at the thought of what is in them."

She entered the room and turned on the light. Grandma looked for the book that she wanted to show Elizabeth, and found it nestled in a corner. She wiped the dust off the cover and opened it, skimming through the pages.

"There you are," she said, looking at a drawing.

Grandma closed the book. She looked around to make sure nothing was out of the ordinary, before leaving the room.

She reached down, pressing the hidden switch on the wall and watched as the door slid closed.

She put the book on the bed and put the bed back against the wall, careful to place the bed legs back exactly where they were before. She picked the book up and made her way back to the kitchen.

Chapter Twenty Three

Gideon and Elizabeth sat, looking at each other.

"You know, if you are who I think you are, Elizabeth. You will be the most powerful human there is. My father is making the arrangements for me to go with you on the quest with the Grymlons. You must not tell me the words to change them back, even if I beg you. Even if it means to tell me would save my life, you must not say those words in front of me, ever."

Elizabeth looked down her nose at him, then looked out of the window. "I already know that, Gideon. I made a promise to your father."

"First," Gideon continued, "we have to hide the Grymlons somewhere safe: or four of them anyway. That will ensure no one else tries to steal them. We will find a good hiding spot. Then we have to make a plan to go to Distardrian and get the necklace back. It was probably taken straight to the elviron king."

When he noticed the expression on Elizabeth's face, Gideon stopped talking. "I hope she is brave enough to see this to the end. I'm too young to die!" he thought, looking at her.

She turned away from the window and returned his gaze. "The conceited little snot is talking to me as though I'm an idiot. He may soon learn differently," she thought.

When Grandma returned to the kitchen, she was holding a large and beautiful book.

"What's that book for?" Elizabeth asked.

"Gideon, Elizabeth," Grandma said, taking a seat at the table. "This is the book of 'The Elven Prophecy'. It's over five hundred years old. This is one of my remaining tasks until I die, to protect this book and all the others in our possession."

She opened the old book and began flipping through the pages.

"Here we are. Look at this picture," Grandma said, handing Elizabeth the book.

Elizabeth saw an older version of herself looking back at her.

"She looks like me. Who is she?"

"She is your ancestor," said Grandma, "her name was Antelonia. She married an elf and from that marriage there was a children, but none of them possessed special powers as the elves had hoped."

"There was a prophecy: that from an elf and a human there would be a child of great magical power. Either then or somewhere down the family line. The elviron have the same prophesy. It never happened in either realm, and eventually became just a story."

Grandma looked over Elizabeth's shoulder at the picture.

"I don't understand how I could have missed it," she said. "I've been through this book many times during my time as the guardian. I never recognized the resemblance between you and Antelonia."

"I find that a bit hard to believe, Gran. How could an elf and a human have a child. I mean, I know when we are in the Elven Realm, we are all the same size. But up here elves are so much, well, smaller…"

"Gideon, show Elizabeth how tall you can grow."

Gideon jumped down from the kitchen table, closed his eyes and bowed his head. Elizabeth watched as he grew until he was a little taller than her.

She stared at him. "He looks different now, more handsome somehow. Like in my dream," she thought.

Gideon opened his eyes, looked at Elizabeth and took a seat at the kitchen table.

"May I please have a cup of tea, Lady Rose?"

"Of course," said Grandma, reaching for the teapot and looking at Elizabeth, who was staring at Gideon.

"It's rude to stare," Grandma said, as she poured Gideon some tea.

"I'm sorry. Sorry, Gideon. It's just that you look so different now you're not small anymore. How long can you stay like that?"

"Until I have to go back to the realm," Gideon answered, putting spoonful after spoonful of sugar in his tea.

"Why haven't you done that before?" asked Elizabeth.

"I am not invisible to humans when I am this big. I cannot use my magic when I am this tall," he replied, taking a sip of his tea.

"Elizabeth, pay attention," Grandma said. "I need to tell you about this book."

Elizabeth and Gideon both settled down to listen to what Grandma Rose had to say.

"We are not the only family with elven blood in our veins. For over five hundred years, the humans who know of Kimadrian and Distardrian have been waiting for a human child to be born with elven powers.," Grandma explained, looking at Elizabeth. "It has skipped a few generations, but it seems that child may be you."

"Me! I'm just a girl. I don't have any magical powers."

"You chanted a spell to save Gideon," Grandma reminded her. "I've never known anyone speak in Elvish tongue, who has never studied the language. You didn't even know about the elves until yesterday. Yet somehow, you knew what to do."

"You also got up and walked after being in a wheelchair for two years. Even if you could walk after that long, you would still need some help, some physio perhaps, to help strengthen your muscles. That's what Gideon meant when he said you might have a little something extra."

Gideon nodded in agreement.

"Does it say how this person would be recognized?" asked Elizabeth.

"No," answered Grandma.

"So if I'm the one, I'll just know what to do?"

"The druids have some information about who the person might be, or become," said Grandma, "and they are keeping that information to themselves."

"Why?" said Elizabeth.

"The druids are very secretive about a lot of things," Grandma said. "Even if you were to ask one of them, he probably wouldn't tell you."

"We should return to the castle," said Gideon. "Arrangements need to be made."

"But I still have questions," said Elizabeth.

"I'm as curious as you," said Grandma, "but we need to solve the problem of the missing Grymlon and we don't have a lot of time."

The three of them left the cottage and headed for the Willow tree.

Chapter Twenty Four

The carriage stopped in front of the castle entrance, and Gideon jumped out. "I have something I need to do. If you are still here when I am finished, I will find you."

"I think I like him a little more than I would be willing to admit," thought Elizabeth, as she watched him run up the steps and disappear inside.

"We should go to Vandrayven and see what he can do to make you look like an elf," said Grandma.

"Do I have to, Gran? What if he changes me into an elf and can't change me back?"

"Vandrayven is more than a hundred years old, Elizabeth. I have known him most of my life and I have never heard of him doing something he can't undo. I don't somehow think he is going to wait until now to make a mistake."

When Elizabeth and Grandma Rose reached Vandrayven's rooms, he glanced at Elizabeth's legs. "When did this happen?"

"Today," said Grandma.

"So quickly?" he said, watching Elizabeth walk towards Mac, the bird.

"I don't know how it happened either," said Grandma. "We found out that Elizabeth unknowingly had the missing Grymlon.

When we reached the cottage, Gideon was already there and was being attacked by an elviron. I think the shock of seeing him in trouble made her forget her affliction. When she saw Gideon struggling, she got out of the wheelchair and cast a spell on the elviron to stop him. Unfortunately, the elviron escaped with the Grymlon. Now Elizabeth and Gideon are going to Distardrian to try and get it back."

"Oh really," Vandrayven said, eyeing Elizabeth, who by now was having a conversation with the bird.

"Would it be possible for you to make Elizabeth look like an elf?" said Grandma. "If they are going to travel across the countryside, it would be better for them if she could blend in."

"Absolutely," answered Vandrayven.

"Elizabeth, come here and sit down, so that Vandrayven can do his work," said Grandma.

Elizabeth sat down in a chair by the same table Vandrayven had used to put the objects on, when he had tried to make her walk.

"Do you think it will work this time?" Elizabeth asked, looking at Vandrayven out of the corner of her eye.

"Don't be insolent, human. Now sit still."

"I'll leave you to your work," said Grandma. "The king will want to know that Elizabeth can walk."

***

Grandma Rose found the king in his office.

"Rose, how nice to see you. Do you have the Grymlon?" he said, offering her a seat.

"No," said Grandma. "The Grymlon was in Elizabeth's room, but it was stolen by an elviron before we could get to it."

"Well, we must take steps to get it back as soon as possible!" said the King.

"Gideon and Elizabeth have devised a plan to retrieve it," said Grandma.

"Gideon should be in the Choosing Room by now," said the King. "How is he going to get Elizabeth to Distardrian?"

"It was the strangest thing," said Grandma. "She just got out of her wheelchair and walked."

"Elizabeth can walk now? Well, that certainly makes things a bit easier. She won't have a relapse will she?"

"I don't think so," said Grandma. "When she saw Gideon being attacked by the elviron, she didn't hesitate. She stood up and strode forward a few paces, shouting some sort of spell in Elvish."

"Elvish, you say? Do you think she could possibly be…"

"Don't say it your majesty. Let's not tempt fate."

"I think Gideon should go to Distardrian and try to capture one of the elviron guards," said the King. "We can interrogate him and try to find out a little more before they leave."

"I think that's an excellent idea," said Grandma.

"Vandrayven has had his instructions, Rose. He will cast a spell, so that Gideon picks the black stone. When the choosing is finished, he will be escorted here to me as per the ritual. I will instruct him on what I want him to do and he can leave immediately."

"It is unfortunate that we have to go through the motions of the choosing, but I can't afford to let anyone in the realm know what is going on. If anyone finds out that a Grymlon is missing, there could be trouble."

"I will go and see how things are going with Vandrayven and Elizabeth," said Grandma.

She excused herself from the king and made her way back down to the magician's quarters.

Chapter Twenty Five

Vandrayven snapped his fingers and his wand appeared in his hand.

"I remember that," said Elizabeth, "it didn't work last time. Was it broken then?"

"Elizabeth, it seems when your legs began to move, your mouth became broken. Please close it and let me do my work."

Elizabeth laughed.

"If you keep talking," said Vandrayven, "I might make a mistake and turn you into an elviron instead."

He picked up a vial of purple liquid and poured it over her head.

"Hey!" she said, trying to duck away from the sticky fluid.

"Hush!" said Vandrayven.

He stood in front of her, "Calaboon dasto foligro MANDRA!" as he shouted the last word, Elizabeth jumped.

"Now, when I say look up, trust me and look up," Vandrayven said. "I promise no harm will come to you, but you must do as I ask.

Vandrayven took three bottles from the table and threw them into the air. Just before they reached Elizabeth, he swirled his wand in three small circles. The bottles disappeared. Tiny red, yellow and green dots swirled together in a downward spiral.

When they were almost touching Elizabeth's head, Vandrayven shouted, "LOOK UP NOW."

Elizabeth looked up as the coloured dots fell onto her head and face, mingling with the purple liquid.

"Splendid," Vandrayven said to himself.

He seemed happy with his workmanship, as he handed Elizabeth a mirror.

"Amazing!" she said, turning the mirror this way and that to get a better look at herself. Her eyes were now brown and almond shaped. Her hair was dark and short, and she had a slight point to her ears.

Grandma entered the room as Elizabeth was admiring her new look.

Grandma raised an eyebrow. "You look very pretty with those ears."

"Thank you Vandrayven," Elizabeth said with a smile.

"Oh anytime, anytime," Vandrayven said. "Now run along. I have a ceremony to attend, and I am late."

Grandma made her way back to the door. "Come on, Elizabeth. We have some shopping to do. You will need some elven clothing."

"Where are we going, Gran?"

"Into Kimadria, to the elven tailor."

They left Vandrayven and made their way up into the main part of the castle. A carriage took them to Kimadria, and dropped them off in the centre of the village.

On the way to the tailor shop, they passed a large square green lawn with a lake in the middle. Elven children were playing games on the grass, as their parents watched and chatted with each other.

Grandma led Elizabeth to a street just around the corner from the lake. They entered a little shop and were greeted by a female elf.

"Good day to you. My name is Trinia. May I help you?" she asked

"I would like to try on a few outfits please," said Elizabeth.

Grandma Rose took a seat by the door.

The shop assistant turned to her. "Could I interest you in a nice outfit? I have some pretty garments for humans too."

Grandma smiled. "No thank you. This young elf needs only one outfit and please have the king billed for it."

"Of course," said Trinia, bowing to Elizabeth.

A few minutes later, Elizabeth left the shop in a dark green tunic with matching leggings.

Chapter Twenty Six

In a large room close to Vandrayven's quarters, twenty-five elves were gathered. Each had been placed in a circle of cubicles in the centre of the room. None of them could see the others. The top of the cubicles were open.

Vandrayven entered and stood on a high platform, looking down on the elves. Captain Allynberry and a guard were waiting for him.

The cubicles were partitioned off with heavy grey curtains. Apart from the light shining above, the only thing the elves could see was Vandrayven, Captain Allynberry and the guard.

"I apologize for being late," Vandrayven, said to the Captain. "I had a chore to attend to. Let's get to business."

Vandrayven turned, addressing the elves below.

"As you know, you have been called here individually from all over the realm. This happens whenever an elf is required to carry out a task for the king. Please remember that we do this to make it fair on all of you, and to ensure that the same elf is not burdened with all the important tasks in the realm. I thank you in advance, on his majesty's behalf for stepping forward willingly when called."

"I would ask that in keeping with the tradition of this calling, you do not try to find out the identity of any of the elves in this room."

"For those of you who have never been called to the 'Choosing Room' before, I will explain how the process works."

"Captain Allynberry and his guard will walk around to each of you. He will have with him a bag. Inside of the bag there are twenty-five stones, twenty-four of them are white and one is black. All of you will pick a stone from the bag. Please close your hand around the stone before you remove it. Captain Allynberry will close the curtain and you will put the stone in the hole in the wall. You will then wait until the guards come and take you from this room. Before we start, if any of you have any questions, please put your hand in the air and a guard will come and try to answer for you."

"Does anyone have a question?"

No one did.

"Very well. Let us begin," said Vandrayven, nodding to Captain Allynberry.

While the Captain and the guard made their way down to the room, Vandrayven continued to instruct the elves.

"When you have picked a stone, do not open your hand and look at it until I give you permission. If you have the black stone, you must still deposit it in the hole."

Captain Allynberry and the guard began walking around the outside of the cubicles. They stopped at each one and the guard held out the bag. When the last elf had picked a stone, the Captain and the guard left the room.

"You may now look at the stones you are holding deposit them into the wall," Vandrayven instructed the elves below.

A clicking sound could be heard, as each elf dropped his stone into the hole.

One piece of tubing was attached behind the wall of each cubicle. When the stones were dropped into the holes, they travelled down the tubing until all but the black one came to rest in a well. The black one stayed in the tube to indicate who had chosen it.

Gideon dropped the black stone into the hole. "What a gloomy place," he thought, as he looked around him, waiting for the guards to reach him.

When all the stones were deposited, it went quiet.

"Guards, please come and escort the elves out of the room one by one," said Vandrayven.

***

Gideon sat in his father's private apartments in one of the chairs by the window. It overlooked the royal courtyard. He looked down onto the square lawn where he had played so often as a boy.

"I suddenly feel homesick for the days when all I had to do was play with Bindyl," he thought.

"Vandrayven's spell must have worked, or you wouldn't be here," said the King, pulling his son back into the present.

"You always say he is the best magician Kimadrian has ever had," said Gideon.

King Morvand pulled a chair over to Gideon and sat down in front of him. "I want you to go to Distardrian and capture one of the elviron king's guards. Bring him back here and interrogate him. Try to find out where the Grymlon is."

"I'll go to the tavern on the other side of the Kimadrian border," said Gideon. "I will make arrangements for a carriage to meet me. The carriage can bring the elviron guard back here and I will follow it."

"Good, good plan, son. With luck, you and Elizabeth can be on your way quickly to retrieve the Grymlon. I am relying on you to bring her and the Grymlon back here safely."

"I know we agreed that Elizabeth go, but why? I can get the Grymlon back myself. I don't need her help."

"She is the guardian," said the King. "She has already bound the Grymlons to her. We don't know what will happen now that she has performed the spell. You might damage the Grymlon if you touch it."

"If that's the case, won't the Grymlon be damaged if one of the elviron touches it?" said Gideon.

"Who knows?" said the King, "it may already be too late and the Grymlon might be destroyed, but that's a risk we have to take.

Elizabeth must go with you. She must retrieve the Grymlon and keep it with her. Time grows short for the Grymlons to be regenerated. These are unusual times, Gideon. They call for extraordinary measures."

"Can I at least confide in Bindyl?" said Gideon.

"No. Bindyl cannot know of this," the King insisted.

"But father, we have been friends since we were children. I would trust him with my life."

"I am sorry, Gideon. You must help Elizabeth and no one else can know. At least for now."

"It makes me sad that for the first time in my life, I have to have a secret from my best friend," said Gideon.

"It makes me sad that you have to do this," the King said, "but you are of royal blood. There will be things that you may have to do in the future as king that will take great courage. Besides, some instinct is telling me to keep this as secret as possible."

"I will not let you down, father."

"I know you won't, son. Now go and find Elizabeth.

***

Bindyl arrived at the castle and headed to Gideon's quarters.

At the top of the steps he was met by a footman.

"Have you seen Prince Gideon?" he asked.

"You've just missed him sir. He left here a few minutes ago. I think he is with the king."

"Thank you. I'll find him later," Bindyl said, returning back down the steps.

As he was walking out of the main entrance, King Morvand approached him.

"Bindyl, might I have a word?" he asked, taking Bindyl's arm and walking him into one of the reception rooms.

"Is there anything wrong?" asked Bindyl.

"Good gracious me no. Whatever would give you that idea?" said the King.

"We don't usually have private conversations with each other, Your Majesty."

The king motioned for Bindyl to sit. "You will no longer be required to help Gideon find the missing Grymlon."

"Has it been found?" asked Bindyl.

"Yes, in a manner of speaking," the King said.

"I have been looking for Gideon. Have you seen him, Your Majesty?"

"As you know, Gideon will be taking my place one day soon," said the King. "His mother and I have decided that he is to start performing some royal duties. Unfortunately, he will not be available for a while."

"But I am his aid. I am supposed to help him with his duties," said Bindyl.

"Yes, yes, but there are some things a prince has to learn by himself. You are becoming a grown elf too. I would be honoured if you would consider joining my elite guard, at least for the time being. Until Gideon needs you as his aid again."

"I would consider it an honour, Your Majesty."

"Very good, very good. Now I must be getting along. The queen will be wondering where I am."

Bindyl bowed as the king exited the room. He left the castle and went home.

Chapter Twenty Seven

Gideon had been waiting for a while in the library. There were couches and chairs with tables along with the usual stone fireplace on the back wall. He had become bored waiting for Elizabeth and her Grandma, so he skimmed through some of the hundreds of books stacked neatly in the bookcases.

He was unaware of the plan to make Elizabeth look like an elf. So when Grandma Rose and Elizabeth arrived, he stood, hesitating, as though he should know who the stranger was.

Elizabeth looked around her at all of the books on the walls. "Is this the library, Gran?"

"Oh no," said Grandma. "The library is much bigger than this."

"How many rooms are there in this castle?"

"I have no idea," Grandma answered.

As Gideon approached them he held out his hand to introduce himself to the female elf.

"Hello, my name is Gideon," he said, trying to prompt her into telling him who she was.

Elizabeth just looked at him and smiled. When he received no response, he turned to Grandma Rose.

"I have been waiting for quite some time, Lady Rose. Where is Elizabeth?"

"It's me, silly," Elizabeth said, turning a little pink.

"Remarkable!" Gideon exclaimed, circling around her, looking her up and down. "I would never have recognized you."

"I'm sorry, Gideon," said Grandma. "When you and Elizabeth came up with the plan to go to the castle at Distardrian, I had a thought on the way here. It occurred to me that if you and Elizabeth are going to be travelling through Distardrian. It might be better if she didn't draw attention. We went to Vandrayven and he cast a spell on her to make her look like an elf."

"You are a genius, Lady Rose. He certainly did a good job. She looks amazing."

"When do you leave?" asked Grandma Rose.

"I am leaving now," he said, turning his gaze away from Elizabeth. "If all goes well, I will meet you down in the north dungeons at 10:30 tomorrow evening. If I am not back by then, you will need to go to my father and ask for me to be replaced."

"Where are you going?" asked Elizabeth.

Gideon looked into her eyes. Her heart gave a little jump at the intensity of his gaze. "I don't have time to explain now. I have to get going. Lady Rose can tell you about it while I'm gone."

"Time is running out, Gideon," Grandma reminded him.

"We will not fail, Lady Rose," said Gideon, unable to stop looking at the very new and different Elizabeth. "I will see you soon."

He glanced at her one more time before he made for the door. As she returned his gaze, he shot her a smile."

"He has the most amazing smile. Be still my heart!" she thought, hoping Grandma Rose wouldn't notice.

"Where is he going?" she asked.

"To Distardrian," said Grandma. "He's going to do a little investigating before you both set out on your journey. If all goes well, he will return with the elviron who stole the necklace. Are you alright, Elizabeth? You look a bit flushed."

"I'm a bit warm, that's all. That's a bit dangerous isn't it?"

"It's the only way we can find out where the necklace was taken," said Grandma.

Chapter Twenty Eight

Gideon rode out of the castle and headed for Distardrian. He turned off the road just before the Distardrian border and entered the little village of Bregnor. As he approached the blacksmith's shop, he could see the smithy working hard.

The blacksmith was large for an elf. A thick black thatch of dark hair fell over his face as he hammered. His large arms bulged and glistened with sweat, as he lifted the heavy hammer and brought it down onto a long piece of metal. He looked up when he saw Gideon out of the corner of his eye.

"Good day to you, Stanthorn," said Gideon, getting down from his horse.

The blacksmith placed his hammer on the anvil and smiled at the prince. He wiped his hands on his leather apron and they shook hands.

"And a good day to you, young Prince Gideon. How are things with the king and queen?"

"Well, thank you. My father sends his thanks for the good job you did on repairing the combination door for the Grymlons."

"I'm glad to hear it. What can I do for you today, young master?"

Gideon entered Stanthorn's work area. It was dark and uncomfortably hot. Only the flames from the fire pit licking the walls lit the room. "I'm looking for some Bynies," he said.

"Oh, I see. And how many will you be wanting?" Stanthorn asked.

"I think two should do it. I would also like one of those Lead lined sheets that you make so well. You know, the ones that you could wrap around an elviron, to stop it running away."

"Where would you like these Bynies to be with this blanket?" asked Stanthorn.

"At the Grotmouth Inn, in about two or three hours," Gideon said, handing the blacksmith a pouch of elven coins.

Stanthorn put the money on a stone bench near his anvil. "Consider it done young master. The Bynies and the sheet will be at the Grotmouth Inn. They will meet you by the big Oak tree around the side of the Inn."

"That would be perfect. Tell them to stay out of sight until they see me. When I whistle like a Bluetail song bird, they must be prepared to act quickly."

"I'll pass the message on, young master."

"Goodbye to you Stanthorn."

The smithy waved to Gideon, as he rode off into the distance.

Chapter Twenty Nine

Elizabeth and Grandma Rose stayed at the castle that night. Elizabeth was to begin what little training she could, while Gideon was gone.

The self defence instructor to the king and family was summoned to the castle. Elizabeth was escorted to a large room with light brown stone walls that were decorated with swords, spears and other weaponry.

She was greeted by a dark haired elf. "My name is Frimly," he said with a bow. "I am the self defence instructor to the king. I have been ordered to teach you how to use a dagger and a sword."

Elizabeth looked at him observing that he was rather short, but muscular. He handed her an ornate dagger and a sword.

"I thought these would be heavier," she said, moving them around in her hands.

"We have an excellent smithy in a village nearby," Frimly said, choosing his own weapons from the wall.

"I've never done anything like this before," she said.

Frimly stood, looking her up and down. "The basics are easy to learn. It's the practice that makes a difference. Even the little that you learn today, may one day save your life. I don't have much time to teach you, but try to pay attention. Let us begin."

Frimly lunged at her, trying to encourage her to fight back.

Elizabeth jumped to one side.

"I do not have her full her attention. Let's see if she likes the sight of her own blood," thought Frimly.

This time he lunged at her with the grace and speed only an expert swordsman would have, nicking the side of her arm, just above her elbow.

"Ouch!" she shouted, immediately feeling anger well up inside of her. She stopped to look at the damage.

"If you stop every time you are struck, you will not live very long," Frimly said, lunging at her again.

Elizabeth stepped aside as he reached her. Momentum overtook him and he had no choice but to run past her. She poked him in the backside with the hilt of her sword.

Frimly turned. "Good, now we are getting somewhere."

An hour later, the training session was over.

"You did surprisingly well," said Frimly.

Elizabeth handed him the sword and dagger she had been practicing with. Frimly took them and hung them back on the wall.

"Thank you for your help," she said, turning to leave.

"Before you go, miss. I have something for you," Frimly said, going to a glass cabinet on the back wall. He pulled out a dagger in a sheath and a sword in a light weight scabbard. Both bore the royal crest of Kimadria, a dragon holding the sun in one claw and the moon in the other.

He handed them to Elizabeth.

"A gift from Prince Gideon. Here, I'll show you how to wear the sword," he said, taking the scabbard from her and buckling it around her waist. "It is customary to wear the dagger somewhere on your body, known only to you," he said handing her an ornate dagger in a sheath.

"If you would like to come back in a few days, we can continue your training. Go past the kitchen to the room on the left, there is a nurse who sees to our soldiers when they have sparring and fighting accidents. She will tend to your arm."

"Thank you, Frimly. I think I would like to come back and learn a little more."

"As you wish, my lady." Frimly bowed to her and left the room.

Chapter Thirty

Gideon took a seat at a corner table of the Grotmouth in. He ordered a mug of ale and watched a pair of jugglers do their act.

Almost immediately, a particularly drunk and loud elviron caught his attention.

"So Figgis, however did you manage to get the Grymlon?" asked one of the elviron, who had been listening to him tell his story.

"It was so easy," Figgis slurred, "I slipped in through her bedroom window and looked around. That stupid elf found it for me. I can't believe he will rule Kimadrian one day."

The few elviron who were listening to him laughed.

When the jugglers were finished with their performance, they put their props by the door. The two performers sat at the bar, and the innkeeper gave them both free ale and an evening meal.

Gideon sauntered to the door. He picked up one of the juggling balls and slid out of a side door of the inn. He stood by the tree at the side of the inn and whistled. Two Bynies came running from the bushes nearby, carrying the promised lead sheet. Gideon gave the Bynies their instructions and they ran back into the bushes.

Gideon took the brightly coloured ball and attached a piece of string to it. He climbed the Elm tree and hung it from a branch.

A few minutes later, an extremely drunk Figgis stumbled out of the Inn. He fell forward as one of the bynies ran between his legs.

"Come here you little monster," he said, shaking his fist at the Bynie, who promptly disappeared behind the tree.

"Where are you, you little wretch," Figgis slurred, tripping over his own feet.

Gideon jiggled the ball on the end of the string, catching Figgis' eye.

He looked up. "Ooh, what's that?"

He took a swipe at the ball and it moved out of the way. Figgis jumped up to try and grab it. As he did, the two Bynies ran up behind him. They tackled him to the ground, covering him with the blanket.

Gideon jumped down from the tree and hit him hard on the back of the head with a piece of wood. Figgis slumped over and the Bynies tied the blanket tightly around him. They carried him to Gideon's waiting horse and put him on the back, tying him to the saddle.

"Thanks you two," said Gideon, looking down at his little allies.

The Bynies ran off into the night.

Gideon rode towards the border, with Figgis struggling in his bonds behind him.

About ten miles into Kimadrian, a carriage was waiting. Two footmen jumped down from their seat when they saw Gideon. They took the still struggling elviron down from his horse, tying him to the top of the carriage, and took off at a gallop for the castle.

Gideon found a stream near by. He led his horse to it and they both drank. He found a spot near some trees and removed the horse's saddle and bridle. The horse roamed free, grazing. Gideon put a blanket down, stretched out on it and took a much needed rest.

Chapter Thirty One

Elizabeth bathed, and then met Grandma in the main library.

They sat for a while, enjoying each other's company.

"How long do you think Gideon will be gone, Gran?"

"Not too long I hope," said Grandma. "Would you like to go outside of the castle? There's a nice restaurant just a few minutes walk from here."

"Yes, I would enjoy that. Would it be alright with the king?"

"Oh I'm quite sure it would be."

They walked along the corridor, through the main entrance and out of the castle.

Grandma and Elizabeth passed under the large gate, over the moat bridge and into the surrounding streets.

As they strolled along the street, Elizabeth watched the elves going about their daily work. Whenever she and Grandma Rose crossed paths with an elf, he or she would step aside and bow. Even the children bowed their heads to them.

"Do they know who we are?" asked Elizabeth.

"They know who I am," said Grandma, "I have been moving among these elves for many years. They bow to you because you are with me."

"These houses look like the old Elizabethan houses I've seen pictures of in London, during the time of Shakespeare," said Elizabeth.

"Yes, they do. In fact, I believe William Shakespeare was invited down here once," said Grandma, with a grin.

"Really?" said Elizabeth."

"I believe so," said Grandma.

When they reached the restaurant, a doorman ushered them into the dining room. They were shown to a table by a window, and an elven waiter brought them a menu.

"Can I interest you in a glass of wine?" he asked.

"I think we would just like a glass of water, thank you," said Grandma.

The waiter left to get the drinks.

Elizabeth opened the menu. "I can't read this."

Grandma looked up. "I'm surprised. You didn't have any trouble speaking Elvish when you said the spell to help Gideon."

"I know, it's strange, but I can't read a word of this."

"Here, let me translate for you. This item here," Grandma said, pointing to the first dish, "is a sort of pancake made of potatoes with carrots and peas. There are spices added. It's a bit like our bubble and squeak. This one is mixed vegetables with something like a curry sauce…"

Grandma read down the menu until she came to something that Elizabeth thought she might like.

The waiter returned with their water. "May I take your order?"

"I'm not very hungry, said Elizabeth, "but my gran tells me that your mackleberry pie is delicious."

"Indeed it is," said the waiter. "Would you like a piece with sweet cherry cream?"

"Sounds scrumptious," Elizabeth replied.

"I'll have the vegetable medley, with the seven spice sauce," said Grandma.

"Good choice," said the waiter.

He left them and made his way to the kitchen.

"I think after dinner, I'm going to go to my rooms and rest," said Grandma. "You should do the same."

A few minutes later, the waiter returned with their food.

They had just started their meal when Grandma looked towards the door.

"There's Bindyl," she said, "he seems to be looking for someone."

When Bindyl saw Grandma Rose, he waved to her and walked over to them.

"Hello Lady Rose. It is nice to see you. I hope you are enjoying your supper."

"Yes," said Grandma, "we are having a very nice meal thank you. Have you met uh, Jane? She's escorting me around while I am in Kimadrian."

"No, I haven't. It's nice to meet you Jane," said Bindyl, shaking her hand.

"Would you like to join us for supper, Bindyl?" asked Grandma.

"Thank you, but I have already eaten. I must be getting along. I have chores to attend to, but thank you for inviting me."

"Goodbye Bindyl, I hope to see you again soon," said Grandma.

As Bindyl walked away, he looked over his shoulder at 'Jane' and frowned.

"She looks familiar," he thought. "Where have I seen her before? She looks about my age, but I can't seem to place her. Oh well, if she's with Grandma Rose, the king must know her."

He turned and continued on his way.

"Gran! What were you thinking?" Elizabeth said, "What if he had recognized me?"

"Well he didn't, did he. Vandrayven's disguise is working. Bindyl stood only feet away from you and didn't recognize you."

Chapter Thirty Two

Bindyl headed to Kimadria and into the seedier side of town. He looked into some of the bars and inns, searching for his uncle Brondly.

"Jolen told me that my uncle has been spending a lot of money at the Inns around Kimadria," thought Bindyl. It was good of him to let me live at his house when my parents died, but his drinking is becoming quite a problem lately. He's lost his job at the castle, so where is he getting the money to drink? I hope he hasn't been spending the rent money. Come on uncle, where are you?"

Bindyl finally gave up his search and headed home.

"That's funny," he thought as he approached the front door.

"Uncle Brondly never leaves the door open."

Bindyl pushed on the door and entered the house. It was gloomy, almost in darkness. He could just make out a figure sitting still at the kitchen table in the middle of the room.

Bindyl breathed a sigh of relief. "Uncle, I have been looking everywhere for you!"

Suddenly, a bolt of fear suddenly shot through his heart.

"UNCLE!"

Brondly was slumped forward on the table. He had a note pinned to his back. It read, 'TRAITOR'.

Bindyl checked Brondly's pulse. He knew when he picked up his uncle's wrist that he was dead.

"He's a cold as ice," Bindyl said into an empty room.

He took the note from his uncle's back and sat down across from him. He put his face in his hands and cried hard and bitter tears.

"Someone has murdered my uncle! I have to report this to the police," he thought, heading for the front door.

Bindyl made his way into the centre of Kimadria, to the Sheriff's

Station. He entered through heavy wooden doors and walked up to the officer on duty.

An elven Sheriff's officer was sitting at a desk. He was dressed in a dark green uniform, and was concentrating on what he was writing. He looked up as Bindyl approached.

"I want to report a death," said Bindyl.

"Whose death?" asked the officer, reaching for the required form to be filled out.

"My uncle Brondly."

"I know this probably isn't the case, but I have to ask. Were there any suspicious circumstances?" the officer said, as he continued to fill out the form.

"Yes," said Bindyl, "I believe there were."

The officer's head shot up and he looked Bindyl in the eye.

"How suspicious?" he asked.

"I think my uncle has been murdered," Bindyl said, quietly.

"You stay right there, son," said the officer.

He got up from his desk, turned and disappeared through a door directly behind him.

Bindyl paced back and forth for a minute or two. He finally sat down on a bench by the front window.

Two elves, not in uniform came out of the door the officer had entered a few minutes earlier, and approached him.

"My name is Pagely and this is my associate Tion. If you would kindly take us to where your uncle is, we will conduct the necessary investigations."

When they arrived at Brondly's house, Bindyl began to walk inside.

"No, no. You must wait here," said Pagely.

"Why?" asked Bindyl.

"Crime scene," replied Tion, producing a small note book.

"We will be a few minutes. One of us will come and get you," said Pagely.

The two officers entered Brondly's house while Bindyl stood outside and waited.

A few minutes later, Tion poked his head around the door. "You can come in now."

Bindyl entered the house see Brondly still slumped over at the kitchen table. Detective Pagely pulled one of the chairs away from the table and motioned for Bindyl to sit down.

"Was this exactly how you found your uncle?" Pagely asked.

"Yes… well no… not exactly," said Bindyl.

"Explain please?" said Tion, scribbling in his notebook.

"Well, I took the note down from my uncle's back."

"Why did you do that?" asked Pagely.

"I don't know. It just seemed to be the right thing to do."

"Had your uncle been in any trouble lately?" asked Tion.

"I don't think so. Although he had lost his job recently," Bindyl replied.

"Where did he work?" asked Tion.

"He was a royal guard at the castle, but they sacked him," answered Bindyl.

"Why did they sack him?" asked Pagely.

"My uncle had a drinking problem. I think they let him go because of it."

"Did he owe money?" asked Tion.

"I don't know. He might have," answered Bindyl.

"Did you and your uncle ever argue?" asked Pagely.

"If you mean did I kill him? The answer is no," said Bindyl, almost in tears. "My uncle wasn't the best of men, but I loved him and would never want to see him come to any harm."

The two elf detectives looked at each other.

"We will send the undertaker to pick up the body. We are very sorry for your loss," said Tion.

"It looks like your uncle had an enemy. We will look into it, but I doubt we will find the perpetrator," said Pagely.

After the two detectives left, Bindyl waited for the undertaker to arrive. He made some elven tea and sat down to drink it.

An hour later, the undertakers came to take Brondly's body away.

"We usually like to bury the deceased in their own clothes," said one of the undertakers.

"I'll go to his room and find something for you."

He walked into his uncle's bedroom and went to the closet. Bindyl looked through Brondly's wardrobe, found a black tunic and put the outfit over his arm. As he headed for the door, he glanced over at Brondly's bed.

It was then he noticed something shiny at the edge of Brondly's pillow. Bindyl went to the bed and lifted the pillow. Lying on the sheet was a gold coin.

"It's a thousand pound coin!" he said under his breath, holding the coin in his palm. "I wonder why the two detectives didn't find it?"

Bindyl turned. He looked towards the door, making sure no one was there, and stuffed the coin in his pocket. Then he went back out to the undertakers.

"Here," he said, "I hope this will do."

The undertaker held up the outfit. "This will do nicely."

Bindyl and the two undertakers lifted Brondly's body and placed it in the coffin.

"The body will be in the chapel of rest at the Elves Rest Funeral Home, on Mackleberry Street," said the tall undertaker. "I trust you will be able to pay for the burial?"

Bindyl turned the elven coin over in his pocket, as he looked at the elf undertaker.

"Yes," he replied.

"Please come to the funeral home sometime tomorrow and we will help you fill out the necessary paperwork," said the tall undertaker.

Bindyl nodded. He looked on as they carried the coffin out to the carriage waiting by the front door.

He closed the door behind them, sat down at the kitchen table, and took the coin out of his pocket.

His heart leapt in his chest. "What if he stole the missing Grymlon and sold it to the elviron," he thought. "That can't be. He wouldn't be able to get into the castle. He must have come by the money some other way. Although something tells me that uncle Brondly had a hand in this somehow. The more I think about it, the more obvious it becomes. I must try and find a way to make up for my uncle's greed."

Chapter Thirty Three

At 9:00 p.m. the next evening, one of the castle guards found Grandma and Elizabeth in the main library.

"The prince has returned. He asks that you meet him in the dungeons on the north side," he informed them.

Elizabeth and Grandma had just reached the steps to the dungeons when they heard faint screams. They looked at each other and moved faster.

"Phew! What is that smell?" Elizabeth said, putting her sleeve up to her nose.

"I don't know. I never come down here," said Grandma.

Three dungeons down, they could hear Gideon shouting.

"I will turn it on again if you don't talk!"

"I will never tell you, you elven scum!" a raspy voice shot back.

Elizabeth and Grandma entered the dungeon. Gideon was holding what resembled a large torch on the elviron. He turned when they entered. In an instant the elviron lifted his bound hands and brought them down over Gideon's head. Gideon swivelled around in an attempt to get free, dropping the torch. The elviron held him by the throat and pulled him up out of his shoes. Gideon's feet moved back and forth.

"He looks as though he's treading water," Elizabeth thought, watching with morbid fascination as Gideon grabbed the elviron's boney hands in an attempt to pull himself free.

The creature held on to him as he squirmed. He turned his gaze away from Gideon and looked at Elizabeth and her Grandma.

"You again," he hissed. "If you do not free me, I will kill him."

"Who do you think I am?" Elizabeth asked, stepping forward and picking up the torch.

"That disguise does not fool me. You are the witch that was back at the cottage!"

Elizabeth stared at the elviron and pointed her finger at him.

"SHANDAH JEE! PANDENDA JEE!" she said.

The elviron screamed and let go of Gideon. He glared at Elizabeth, backing away from her. She uttered the words again lunging the torch at him. He screamed again, trying to cover his head from the light.

Gideon had staggered away from his capture and propped himself up against the opposite wall.

"I am getting a little tired of being pulled out of my shoes," he said, rubbing his hand back and forth against his throat.

"Stop whining, Gideon. You have experienced much worse," Grandma said, watching Elizabeth.

"Please, I will tell you anything you want. Just stop the light, pleeeease!" the elviron whinged.

"Where is the black necklace that you stole from me?" Elizabeth hissed.

"A little too much drama I think," Grandma observed with a grin.

Elizabeth shone the light full on, in the elviron's face. He screamed again.

"It is in the king's castle at Distardrian," he said, holding his bound hands up to his face.

"Where in the castle?" she demanded.

"I cannot tell! You must kill me! If they find out that I have told, I will be killed anyway," the elviron said.

Elizabeth put down the light and moved closer to the elviron. Gideon began to step between them, but Grandma put her hand on his shoulder. "I don't think she needs your help at the moment."

Elizabeth put her face right up to the elviron's.

"He stinks!" she thought, as she looked into his eyes.

The elviron tried to turn away, but she grabbed his grimy face, turning it back to hers.

He had almost no hair. Little wisps of dark fuzz sprouted out of his head that were long in places, short in others. He had large almond shaped, dark brown eyes with huge pupils, and his skin had a brown pallor. Most of his teeth were rotten. The ones that were still in good condition were long and pointed.

Elizabeth looked directly into his eyes and began to sway from side to side. He began to sway with her, until they were in complete unison. It was as though they were dancing.

"Where is the necklace?" Elizabeth asked.

"It is in the king's bedchamber, in a box under his bed," the elviron said, staring past her, as though he could see something he was intently interested in.

"Thanks," said Elizabeth.

She waved her hand and turned away, but the elviron was still under her spell.

"The pleasure was all mine, oh great princess. I live only to serve you," he said, trying to follow her.

"Get him away from me!" Elizabeth said, visibly shivering at the thought of being touched by him.

Grandma Rose let go of Gideon's arm, he stepped in front of Elizabeth, shoving the elviron to the ground.

He turned glancing at her. "I hope, I nor anyone else in my realm or yours, ever makes you really, really angry," he said, quietly.

"I have no idea what you mean," said Elizabeth.

"Oh, but I think you do," thought Grandma, as she watched Gideon follow Elizabeth out.

A lead box was brought into the dungeon, carried by three jailers and the elviron was placed inside.

"This is the only way we can stop him from escaping," explained Gideon, "if he goes into his shadow form, he could get through the bars of the window.

"He smelled horrible," said Elizabeth.

"That's because they like bloody raw meat," said Gideon. "They lack the means to keep it fresh. So they mostly eat it rotten. They don't seem to mind it that way. They don't wash their food or themselves very often."

The guards closed the box and carried the elviron away.

"Someone needs to teach them how to take a bath!" Elizabeth said.

Gideon led the way out.

"How long are we going to keep him?" Elizabeth asked.

"Until we get the necklace back," said Gideon. "We need to get some rest. We have a very important day ahead tomorrow."

"I agree with Gideon," said Grandma. "I'm a bit tired too."

Elizabeth looked at her grandma. "Are you all right, Gran? You look a bit pale."

Grandma Rose ran her hand across the front of her neck. "I think I'm just tired. I'm going to bed. I'll see you both in the morning."

She left Elizabeth and Gideon and made her way back up into the main part of the castle.

"Can we go for a walk first Gideon?" asked Elizabeth.

"Where do you want to go?"

"Can we go for a walk in the castle grounds?" she asked.

"Yes, I will get you a robe. It is getting a bit cool outside. I will meet you in the portrait room."

Elizabeth walked up to the portrait room and waited for him.

When he returned, he held up a calf length cape. Elizabeth draped it around her shoulders.

"What happened to your arm," Gideon asked, noticing the dressing the nurse had applied to her wound.

"Sparring accident," she replied.

"Then Frimly must have given you my gift," said Gideon.

"Yes, thanks. I've never been given weaponry as a gift before."

"It may save your life one day. Be sure to wear them when we go to Distardrian," said Gideon. "The robe looks nice on you. You could fit in anywhere as an elf."

"Why thank you," Elizabeth said, curtsying. "Grandma and I went out into Kimadria and ate dinner last night. While we were there, we bumped into Bindyl and he didn't recognize me."

They both laughed.

"I wonder what he would say if he knew what was happening," said Gideon.

"I'm a bit surprised that the elviron recognized me. I hope my disguise is good enough.

"The elviron have a very keen sense of smell, Elizabeth. It was your scent he recognized."

Elizabeth shivered slightly. "That's a bit creepy,"

The two of them climbed up to the top of the castle and strolled around the ramparts.

"It's beautiful up here," she said, looking out across the countryside.

"Yes," said Gideon. "I come here sometimes, when I want to sit quietly and be alone."

"I think we should take the Grymlons and hide them in Distardrian," said Elizabeth.

Gideon, who had been a few steps ahead of her, stopped. He turned, staring at her. "Are you out of your mind!"

"We have to take them with us," she continued. "Think about it. Would the elviron look in their own back yard? One of the Grymlons has already been stolen from the tower. Who's to say that while we are gone looking for it, someone doesn't come along and steal the other four. We should hide them in an unlikely place. They'll be looking everywhere but in their own realm."

"She's right," thought Gideon. "The elviron aren't the most intelligent beings. They would be looking everywhere, except were they live."

"Where will we hide them?" he asked.

Elizabeth thought for a moment. "We'll bury them about two miles from the Kimadrian border, where we can find them again easily."

"What if we have to get out of there in a hurry and we can't get back to Kimadrian the same way we left?" he said.

"Then we will go back for them later," she answered.

"What if we die, Elizabeth?"

"Better that the Grymlons never be found, than in the hands of the elviron," she answered.

"Let me think about it," he said. "Come on, let's get back to the castle and get some rest."

A footman was waiting for them when they returned to the main hall.

Elizabeth noticed that he seemed upset.

"Is something wrong," she asked.

"Your grandmother is ill and needs you, my lady. King Morvand is with her."

"Where is she?" Elizabeth asked.

"She is in the north tower," the footman answered, leading the way. "It is quiet up there and she will not be disturbed. The royal physician is with her."

When Elizabeth entered the room, the physician turned to her.

"There you are. Your grandmother has been waiting for you."

Elizabeth looked at King Morvand, who was standing at the foot of Grandma's bed. "It's all right, he knows who you are. He is the only one besides Vandrayven who knows just about everything that goes on here."

Elizabeth sat on the bed. "How are you feeling, Gran?"

"I'm going to be fine. I just felt a little faint that's all."

"If anything happens to you, I'll be completely alone in the world and I'm not ready for that," she thought, looking into her Grandma's face.

"If I might have a word?" the doctor asked Elizabeth.

She stood. "I'll be back in a minute, Gran."

Grandma Rose nodded. Elizabeth followed the doctor out of the room and closed the door behind her.

"I think she has had a slight heart attack," he explained. "I would like you to take her back to your own realm, so that she might be examined by a human doctor. I do not know too much about humans and I am concerned that she may have another bad episode. I will get you some help."

"Thank you," said Elizabeth.

The doctor bowed politely and disappeared down the corridor.

The king stepped up beside Elizabeth. "I have told Gideon that he is to be at your disposal at any time until further notice," he said. "He has willingly agreed to help you and your grandmother in any way he can. If you need any further assistance, just send a message to one of the guards in the Willow tree."

King Morvand turned, following the doctor down the hall.

Gideon was sitting in a chair a few feet away. "You must go to Vandrayven and lose your disguise. I will go with you."

Gideon turned to one of the guards by the door. "Go and get four guards to take Lady Rose to the front entrance and have a carriage ready to leave."

The guard saluted him and left.

Elizabeth went back into her grandma's room. "I'm going to get rid of this disguise." Gideon has arranged for some guards to come and get you. They'll take you down to a carriage and we will get you back up to the cottage. I'll call Dr. Andrews and then I'll call Mrs Reese and ask her to come over for a while."

"Oh, I don't think I need a doctor. I'm already starting to feel better," said Grandma.

"I don't want any argument. It may be nothing, but I think you should be examined to be on the safe side," Elizabeth said.

"Perhaps you're right," said Grandma.

Gideon arrived with the guards to take Grandma to the carriage.

Elizabeth helped her into the small carrier. The guards grabbed onto the four handles and carried her down.

Elizabeth and Gideon hurried to Vandrayven's rooms.

Gideon knocked on the door and entered, Elizabeth following behind him.

"I have to go back up to the Human Realm and I can't look like an elf up there," she told the magician.

"Then let's change you back," said Vandrayven.

The magician cast a spell on Elizabeth. Within seconds, she was herself again. He handed Gideon a small blue bottle with dust in it.

"Sprinkle this on her when she is ready to turn back into her elf disguise," he told Gideon. "Now that the work has been done to make her an elf, the dust will restore the glamour. Throw the dust on her as you say the word 'kajeeka' loudly. This will make her appearance as it was before."

"Thank you Vandrayven," said Gideon.

"Yes, thanks," said Elizabeth.

"Oh, it was no trouble. If you two need anything else, I will be here."

Elizabeth and Gideon made their way to the castle entrance.

"I think we will have to delay this trip for a while," she said.

"I agree, but don't be too long Elizabeth. Time already grows short."

"I won't leave my gran when she's sick."

"And I won't argue with you on that point," said Gideon. "I will help you get her up to the Willow tree. It will be easier with the two of us."

Elizabeth ran down the steps and into the carriage with her Grandma.

Gideon was about to follow Elizabeth down the steps of the castle to join them, when the young elven girl, Elizabeth had met in the portrait room, walked up to him and said something.

Elizabeth listened, but couldn't quite make out what she was saying. As the elf girl was talking, Gideon shook his head, pointing to the carriage. The elf girl said something else, and he shook his head again. The young female elf looked over at Elizabeth and slapped Gideon across the face. Grandma Rose turned and looked out of the carriage window.

"What is going on out there?" she asked, turning back to Elizabeth.

Elizabeth leaned out of the carriage window, trying to listen to their conversation.

The young female elf began to walk away from Gideon, then stopped and turned towards the carriage.

"What are you looking at, bitch!" she shouted, running down the steps and storming off towards the shops surrounding the castle.

"Huh!" said Grandma Rose, turning around again and watching, as the female elf ran off.

"They use the word bitch down here too?" said Elizabeth.

"It would seem so," said Grandma.

With a red face, Gideon stomped down the steps to the carriage.

"Who was that?" asked Elizabeth, as Gideon stepped into the carriage. "She came looking for you when Gran and I were waiting for King Morvand."

"Lady Rose. You didn't tell Elizabeth about Zoe?" Gideon asked.

"I forgot all about her," said Grandma, "too much going on."

"That was Zoe," said Gideon, sullenly. "She is betrothed to me. She thinks because I am helping you and your grandma, that I would prefer to be with you instead of her."

"Did you tell her that you were ordered by your father to help us?" Elizabeth said.

"Yes, but she did not believe me. She thinks that I don't spend enough time with her," he said. "The thing is, she's right. I don't spend as much time with her as I should, but then I don't want to."

"It's a shame you can't tell her what's happening. She might understand a little more," said Grandma.

Gideon glared at Grandma Rose. "I don't care what she thinks!" he blurted out. "There are more important things than pandering to a spoiled brat's wishes!"

"Gideon! You'll be marrying her in a few years!" said Grandma.

"I hate her!" Gideon spat. "She is a brat. She is selfish and mean, and bad tempered. I'm dreading the day I have to marry her."

"That time is a long way off Gideon, and things sometimes change. Don't worry about that now. Please take me home," said Grandma, looking tired and pale.

They hurried to the entrance to the Human Realm.

Chapter Thirty Four

Elizabeth helped Grandma Rose into bed.

"I would like to stay if you don't mind," Gideon said. "Just in case you need me."

"I would appreciate that," said Elizabeth, "but stay out of sight. I'm going to call Megan's mum."

Elizabeth pulled her cell phone out of her pocket and called Lillian Reese's number. "I'm so sorry to bother you Mrs Reese, but my Grandma doesn't feel well. I'm going to call the doctor, but I was wondering if you would come over? Just in case he needs some help."

"Of course my dear. You call Dr. Andrews and I will be there in a few minutes," said Lillian.

Elizabeth hung up, then called the doctor's office. The receptionist put Grandma Rose's name on the list for the doctor to make a house call.

When Gideon heard Lillian Reese knock on the door a few minutes later, he shimmered for a second, then vanished.

Elizabeth opened the back door and smiled at Mrs Reese. Megan was with her. The two of them stood staring at her.

"What's wrong?" asked Elizabeth.

"Where's your wheelchair?" Lillian said, staring at her legs.

Elizabeth looked down. "Yes! We a... forgot to tell you," she said, quickly. I've been working with a physio therapist. The therapy was very successful."

Lillian brushed past Elizabeth and into the kitchen. Megan followed.

"Wasn't Andre here a few days ago?" said Lillian, taking a seat at the kitchen table.

"Yes," Elizabeth said.

"I'm sure I would have remembered if he had told me you were walking," said Lillian.

"I've only been able to walk without help for a day or two."

Megan put her arms around Elizabeth and hugged her. "I'm very happy for you, Liz."

"Me too," said Lillian. "I'll tell Andre the good news."

"Thanks, but I'd like to surprise him. Please don't say anything just yet."

"Good idea," said Megan.

"How is your grandma?" asked Lillian.

"She's asleep at the moment. The doctor should be here soon."

"Well then, we won't disturb her," Lillian said, sitting back in her chair.

"Elizabeth, why don't you make us all a nice cup of tea."

Chapter Thirty Five

Dr. Andrews arrived at the house an hour later. After he had examined Grandma Rose, he made his way to the kitchen.

"Rose has had an esophageal reflux spasm," he informed all present.

He sat down at the kitchen table, and wrote a prescription. He tore it from his pad and handed it to Elizabeth. "You may want to fill this for future use."

"What is it that she has? Is she going to be all right? Is she going to die?" Elizabeth said, frantic with worry.

Dr. Andrews looked at her and smiled. "Your grandmother is suffering from wind pains," he explained. "I have given her some medicine. She'll feel better soon. I have given her one pill to take in the morning and at night for ten days, and they should begin to work almost immediately. If it continues after that, fill the prescription and ask her to make another appointment with me."

"Wind! She had wind! I was worried sick," Elizabeth said, close to tears. "People don't faint when they just have wind do they?

"Has your grandma eaten or drank anything unusual. Perhaps some food that she doesn't normally eat?" asked the doctor.

"Yes," said Elizabeth, trying to think of something to say that would take the place of 'oh yes, we ate elven food!'

"We ate a vegetarian meal the other night with herbs and spices."

"And she doesn't usually eat that sort of food?"

"Not very often."

"Then I would have to assume that is what caused the acid reflux," said Dr. Andrews.

"Occasionally, when a person eats something spicy, or something that they don't normally eat, they can make too much stomach acid," he explained. "Sometimes, it can cause so much discomfort, that it can feel just like a heart attack. With Grandma Rose being a little older now, it could well have been something more serious. You did the right thing by calling me."

"Now I understand," Elizabeth said, feeling relieved.

"I'll be going now," said the doctor. "I have other patients to visit. If your grandma gets any worse, contact my nurse and I will come back. By the way, it's nice to see you on your feet again."

"Thank you doctor," said Elizabeth.

"I will show you out," said Lillian.

When the doctor had gone, Lillian went to Grandma's room. "Can I come in Rose?"

"Of course," a voice said from inside.

Lillian sat on the edge of Grandma's bed.

"If you need anything, anything at all. Either call me, or tell Elizabeth she can call. I mean it. Rose, day or night."

"I'm so very grateful for your help, Lillian."

Lillian Reese patted Grandma's hand. "Megan and I are going to leave. Remember, anything at all."

"I promise I'll ring you if I need you," said Grandma.

After Lillian and Megan left, Elizabeth made a cup of tea and took it to her Grandma.

Grandma took a few sips of the tea and put the cup down. "We will go back to the castle in the morning, so that you and Gideon can be on your way."

"Are you sure you're up to it, Gran? We can wait a day or two. Or I can get someone to come and stay with you if you want."

"I already feel better. I'm tired, but apart from that, the pill Dr. Andrews gave me worked quickly. I'll get a good night's rest and we'll go back down to the elven realm tomorrow. I can rest when we get there if I don't feel well."

"All right then. Good night, Gran," Elizabeth said, closing the bedroom door behind her.

"Gideon. Are you still in here?" She asked when she reached the kitchen.

Gideon appeared. "That was interesting," he said, growing to human size.

We'll go back to the castle tomorrow," Elizabeth said.

"I will come back in the morning and take you to the castle," he said.

"Bye, Gideon," she said as he left by the back door.

Elizabeth went to bed, feeling thankful that nothing bad was going to happen to her grandma.

Chapter Thirty Six

Grandma Rose was already up and placing the breakfast things on the table when Elizabeth entered the kitchen.

"Gran, what are you doing? I got up early so that I could make the breakfast this morning."

"I'm feeling much better, Elizabeth. Now sit down and have a cup of tea and some toast."

Gideon had arrived earlier. He sat at the kitchen table, human size, devouring toast with lots of strawberry jam and a cup of very sweet tea.

"You're here early," said Elizabeth, sitting opposite him.

"How can someone eat that much sugar and not be sick?" she thought, as she watched him sprinkle sugar on the jam he had already spread had on his toast.

"I have come to escort you and Grandma Rose down to the Elven Realm," Gideon mouthed, between bites.

"Hurry up Elizabeth," Grandma said. "We need to be on our way."

Elizabeth ate her toast and marmalade and gulped down her tea.

While she helped clean up the breakfast things, Gideon went out into the garden and was petting Charlie the cat.

Elizabeth watched him from the kitchen window as she dried the dishes. He was bent over talking to the little cat, who sat looking at him as he stroked her fur.

"He must have a way with animals. He seems to have Charlie's full attention." she thought.

Grandma and Elizabeth came out of the cottage. When Gideon saw them coming, he patted Charlie lightly on the head.

"I'll see you soon. Be careful," he told her.

"What an odd thing to say to a cat," Elizabeth thought, as the cat strolled off into the bushes.

The three of them walked to the Willow tree and entered it.

When they reached the gates of Humadria, a carriage was waiting on the other side.

A few minutes later, the carriage pulled up in front of the castle entrance.

Grandma and Elizabeth followed Gideon up into the main hall.

"I am going to the kitchens. We will need food and water for our journey," Gideon said, "and then I will change you back into your elf disguise."

Grandma and Elizabeth went to the banquet room and made themselves busy putting a few supplies into backpacks.

Gideon joined them a few minutes later, with food and two leather flasks containing water. He put the things on a table, and grabbed his backpack. "I'll be back in just a bit. I'm going to see Vandrayven."

King Morvand entered the room. "Good day to you both. Lady Rose. What are you doing here?"

"It was nothing more than a bad case of wind, Your Majesty. The doctor gave me some medicine and I feel quite well now.

"I'm very glad to here it," the King said. "You had us all very worried about you. I will tell Paulina that you are well. Perhaps the two of you can meet for tea later."

"That would be nice, Your Majesty."

King Morvand turned to Elizabeth. "You will need to come with me."

"Where are we going?" she asked.

"To get the Grymlons. The guards won't let you take them without me."

Elizabeth followed the king up to the tower. He opened the door, and allowed her to walk past him. He watched Elizabeth, as she put the Grymlons into her backpack, then the two of them went back to the banquet room where Gideon and Grandma were waiting.

"I think it might be a good idea if we all rested until nightfall. I will have a servant escort you both to the guest quarters," suggested Gideon.

"I feel exhausted, said Grandma.

"You two should try to get some rest," the King said. "I will send a servant for you and Lady Rose in a few hours. I will say goodbye to you now, Gideon. Please find me as soon as you return."

The king embraced his son and left the room.

Elizabeth turned to Gideon. "See you in a little bit?"

"Yes, try to relax for a while," he said, heading to his own rooms.

"You too," she replied.

***

Elizabeth and Gideon met in the portrait room a few hours later. Grandma arrived not long after, to say goodbye.

Elizabeth put her arms around her grandma. "Take care of yourself, Gran. If you need any help or you don't feel well, Mrs Reese said that you could call her any time."

"I don't want you worrying about me," said Grandma. "Just do what is needed to get the Grymlon back and come back here safely."

"I don't want to leave you, Gran." said Elizabeth.

"You have to," said Grandma.

"Why do we have to walk? Why can't we ride to Distardrian?" asked Elizabeth. "There are plenty of horses in the royal stables."

"Believe me, I would much rather ride," said Gideon. "It would cut our travel time in half, but we don't want to draw attention to ourselves."

"Gideon is right," said Grandma. "It'll be harder to hide with horses."

"It will be dark in a few minutes. If we leave now, we can make use of the darkness," said Gideon.

As they walked away from the castle, Elizabeth felt both scared and exhilarated.

"I hope we get through this venture without dying!" Gideon thought, as he took a sideways glance at her.

***

King Morvand stood in the tower where the Grymlons were kept. He watched Elizabeth and Gideon walk across the field and into the forest.

"I have tampered with a tradition spanning hundreds of years. Oh well, too late now." he sighed. "I hope no one saw them leave. May the powers that be, watch over you both."

Only when he could no longer see them, did the king return to the royal chambers to be with his queen.

Chapter Thirty Seven

Zoe stood looking out of the window in the north tower. She watched them disappear into the dusk, then turned and stuffed some belongings into her own backpack.

"Gideon is up to no good and I'm going to find out what," she said. "First he snubs me for that freckle faced human, and now he is wandering off across the countryside with a female elf I've never seen before! I'm going to find out where they are going and I'm going to tell the king."

She went quietly down, then out through the north dungeon… But someone was watching her.

Chapter Thirty Eight

Gideon and Elizabeth crossed the border into Distardrian.

"Perhaps we should start looking for a good place to hide the Grymlons," Elizabeth said.

"How about over there?" said Gideon, pointing to a small thicket of trees.

"Looks good enough to me," she said, walking ahead.

Gideon marked the bark of the tree with a knife. He put his back against the tallest of the trees. He walked ten paces to the south, pulled a small shovel out of his backpack and dug a hole. Elizabeth placed the bag into it and Gideon covered it with earth. He pulled up a few ferns and placed them over the newly disturbed dirt to hide it.

"That should do it," he said. "Let's get going. We still have a long way to go."

Zoe stayed just far enough away from them, so as not to be seen. She watched as they worked. When she was sure they would not see her, she found the spot where they had been digging and dug up the bag. A rustle of leaves disturbed her as she was about to look into it.

"Who's there?" she said, spinning around. She peered into the thicket of trees. "Is anyone there?"

Zoe looked in the direction that Elizabeth and Gideon had headed.

"I must move quickly," she thought. "I don't want to lose them."

She shook the excess dirt from the bag, stuffed it into her backpack and hurried on.

Gideon and Elizabeth entered a forest and had been walking for a while.

"I'm thirsty," said Elizabeth.

"We can stop for a few minutes and drink some water. I'm a bit hungry anyway," said Gideon.

They sat down and Elizabeth pulled the water out for them both, and some bread and cheese.

"How much longer will it take to get there?" she asked.

"We will need to camp perhaps one night each way, but no more than that," said Gideon.

"How long has it been since you were at the elviron castle?"

"Quiet," said Gideon, looking behind him.

"What?" asked Elizabeth.

"Be quiet, Elizabeth!"

He looked around and motioned to her to stay still.

"But," she started to say.

Gideon put his hand over his mouth and pointed to her. She nodded. He disappeared into the forest and returned a few moments later.

"What's wrong?" she whispered.

"I thought we were being followed," said Gideon, "but I couldn't see anyone."

"Did you hear something?" she said, looking around her. "It's not an elviron, is it? I don't think I could handle another one quite so soon."

"I don't know. I just feel as though I'm being watched," said Gideon. "Don't you feel it too?"

"A little bit," she said.

"We must be careful, Elizabeth. We cannot afford to get caught now."

They finished eating, and Elizabeth put the remainder of the food into her backpack.

They pressed, and when daylight came they found a wooded area and slept until dusk.

They continued through the night hours, stopping a few times to drink and eat a small amount of food, to keep their energy up. They walked for a few hours more and at the beginning of dawn, the castle came into view.

"How far away is it," Elizabeth asked.

Gideon stared at the castle for a moment. "Perhaps two miles at the most. We will need to wait until dark before we try to get inside."

He looked around until he saw a few fallen trees.

"There, over there, see? We'll make a shelter and rest there until nightfall."

"Good, I'm so tired. I think I could sleep for a week," she said, yawning.

"You're not used to so much walking, are you," said Gideon.

"No," Elizabeth admitted. "After sitting in a wheelchair for a couple of years, walking like this is wearing me out."

"Put your blanket under those fallen trees and get some rest. I'll keep watch," said Gideon.

"You need to rest too," said Elizabeth.

"I'll be able to doze. I don't feel as though anyone is watching us anymore."

"I won't be able to sleep. I'm worried I'll be captured," Elizabeth, said stifling another yawn.

Gideon smiled at her. "Oh, I think you'll sleep. All you have to do is lie down."

Elizabeth put her blanket in the shelter and Gideon covered her with another. He gathered some fern, and covered her blanket with it.

By the time he was finished, she was asleep. Gideon sat with his back to a tree, close to where she slept, and covered himself with the rest of the fern.

***

Zoe had lost their trail. She looked for signs of them, but finally gave up. Tired and hungry, she found a place to eat and rest.

Off in the distance, a figure in a dark robe had been following all of them. The figure waited until Zoe was asleep, then he took the bag with the Grymlons and stole away into the night.

The figure also found a place to slumber, but he did not rest for long. He passed by Elizabeth and Gideon just before the hazy elviron sun had started to go down. Zoe had disappeared.

Chapter Thirty Nine

Gideon woke Elizabeth just after sunset. "Did you get a good rest?"

"Oh yes," she said, stretching.

"Are you hungry?" Elizabeth asked.

"Starving," Gideon said.

"Me too."

She put a cloth down and put out some food and water.

"Tell me about the elviron king," Elizabeth said, as they ate.

"His name is Kalidryd. He is about the same age as my father. He has no Queen to rule Distardrian with him. I have heard that he has three daughters and one of them is a bit strange. There is a rumour that the girl is part human, although I find that hard to believe. No one has ever seen her, so I doubt she really exists."

"King Kalidryd is evil. He has no compassion or pity. He is like all the other elviron, an animal. My father told me that the elviron used to be different from the way they are now. Something happened to them a long time ago. Some sort of sickness spread through their Realm.

They are cunning, and they have become extremely skilled at capturing elves. An elven soul is very valuable to an elviron. It doubles their life span, and gives them great spiritual power. That power enables them to go into shadow form when they wish to, but they pay a price for their evil. They cannot be in the sunlight, it burns them. King Kalidryd's court wizard works constantly to keep the days in Distardrian dull. The lack of sunlight helps the elviron live comfortably."

"How do you keep them out of Kimadrian?" Elizabeth asked.

"Vandrayven casts a spell to repel the elviron. It travels the entire length of the border between Kimadrian and Distardrian. This magic has been practiced by the magicians at Kimadrian since the war between us and the elviron, yet some of them still manage to get through."

"How?" she asked.

"They get help from elves," said Gideon, "they pay the elves to help them over the border. Some elves are greedy. We have good and bad in the Elven Realm, just like you do.

We need to be on our way," he said, getting to his feet. "You put all the stuff in the backpacks and I'll make sure there is no one around when we leave the forest."

***

They travelled cautiously into the darkness. The outside of the castle looked un-kept and dismal.

"The castle looks like the one in Kimadrian," she said.

"Yes it does," said Gideon, "except this one has not been maintained for many years. The elviron don't care where they live, or how they live."

Elizabeth felt a pang of fear pass over her. She looked up as they grew closer. Ivy climbed the castle walls. Trees and shrubs had grown around the edges. The grass and weeds around the walls were waist high in some places.

"How do we get in?" she asked.

"Bindyl and I have been to the castle once or twice before. We spent some time sneaking around in there."

"You were lucky you were never caught," said Elizabeth.

Gideon grinned. "It was rather fun actually."

"I don't know if that was brave or stupid," said Elizabeth, giving Gideon a sideways glance.

"Didn't anyone ever tell you to know your enemy?"

"I don't think I've ever had an enemy until now," she said.

"This way," he said, leading her around the castle wall.

They came to a side door, which to Elizabeth's surprise was open.

"Don't they lock their doors?" she asked.

"They don't have to. No one wants to go in there. Look."

He took her hand and led her through the door. They immediately came upon a guard room to the right. It was empty.

"This is where the guards rest at night," said Gideon.

"Where are they now?" asked Elizabeth.

"It's still early enough that they will all be on duty for a while... I hope."

They made their way up a spiral staircase with a high ornate bannister at its sides. There were remnants gold of carpet on the steps. Elizabeth almost tripped over more than one of the worn pieces.

At the top of the stairs, Gideon led the way through a long corridor and up more steps.

As Elizabeth followed him, she noticed a suit of armour placed in front of a dusty yellow curtain, hanging from the stone wall. The armour looked as though it was made of gold. She reached out to touch it and one of the metal gloves clanked noisily to the floor. The sound echoed through the hallway.

Gideon turned.

Elizabeth bent down and picked up the glove.

"Put that down!" he hissed.

"Sorry!" she whispered, gently placing the glove on the floor next to the suit of armour.

"How do you know where the king is?" asked Elizabeth, following him along the passageway.

"Bindyl and I have been all over this castle. We found out where the king and everyone else sleeps."

Elizabeth followed him as he made his way through the corridors.

Everything was covered with cobwebs. She looked up into the high ceiling.

"If these cobwebs are huge!" she thought, pushing her fingers into one of them. "How big must the spiders be?"

She pulled her hand back, trying to remove the sticky gossamer from her fingers.

Elizabeth looked up at the pictures as they passed through the halls. Some were of battle scenes, but the faces of the elviron on some of the pictures had been so badly slashed, they were unrecognisable.

"No pictures of elviron," she thought, "only elves."

"We should have seen more guards on the way up here," said Gideon.

He stopped, as the corridor split in two directions.

He peeped around to the right and saw two sentries standing at the king's rooms.

He turned to Elizabeth. "Two guards are standing at the door," he whispered.

"What now?" she asked.

"Well don't you have any ideas?" asked Gideon.

"I could just walk up to them. Do you think they would be very surprised?" she whispered.

"I'd say. How surprised would you be, if an elviron walked up to you and introduced itself?"

Both Gideon and Elizabeth found it hard to stifle a fit of the giggles. After they had settled down, they decided that they would indeed both walk right up to the guards and see what would happen.

Elizabeth turned the corner and approached the guards. Before they could say anything, she waved her hands across one another, and said 'sleep'. The guards dropped where they stood, sound asleep.

"How did you do that?" Gideon asked, stepping up behind her.

"I don't know! I just knew that if I waved my hands," she said, starting to wave them in front of Gideon.

"Don't do it to me!" he said, grabbing her hands. "Or you will be on your own for a while! I hope you get the hang of this magic thing soon." He stepped over them "How long will they sleep?

"How do I know? I'm new at this sort of thing," she huffed with a sigh, as she headed for the door.

She turned the door knob and slowly pushed the door open. Gideon followed her. When they reached the king's bedchamber, Gideon slid past her and peeped in.

In the corner of the room was an odd looking bed. The mattress was thin and high off the ground. The bed had four posters. Each poster twisted its way upward and inward, until they met at the top to form one big gnarled nub.

Dirty bed linens were in a pile on the mattress. On the floor, at the foot of the bed there was another pile of dirty sheets and blankets. Underneath them Elizabeth saw the misshapen head of an elviron.

She tip-toed past the sleeping heap on the floor and knelt down by the bed. There was a box sitting alone underneath. She reached for it, slowly pulling it towards her. Elizabeth opened the box, picked it up the necklace from the inside. She put it around her neck, pulling her tunic up to cover it. She closed the box and pushed it back under the bed.

Elizabeth backed away, motioning for Gideon to start walking. They had reached the door, and Gideon was about to open it, when as quick as a flash, the elviron king was in front of them.

"I have been expecting you," he said, leaning against the door to block their escape. "I knew someone would try to steal the necklace if it were of value."

"I thought this was a little too easy," said Gideon.

"How did you get past my guards?" asked the elviron King.

"Oh, I just did this," said Elizabeth, waving her arms again and saying 'sleep' at the same time.

The king dropped to the floor: out cold.

"How did he know we were coming?" asked Gideon.

"I don't know, but I want to get out of here now!" Elizabeth replied. "I'm getting more nervous by the minute."

They walked through the king's rooms and out to where the guards were sleeping. Gideon and Elizabeth ran down the stairs.

They were heading along the corridor towards the dungeons, when five guards came around the corner. The two of them ducked into the shadows.

An elviron guard ran past where they were hiding. He stopped, turned around and saw them.

"Over here!" he shouted.

Before they knew it a hoard of elviron guards were running towards them.

Gideon turned to Elizabeth.

"Do something!" he shouted.

Elizabeth looked at the oncoming elviron.

"What?" she said.

"I don't know? Wave your hands and say something. You know, that thing that you do!" Gideon replied hurriedly, backing away.

The elviron guards ran at them.

"We're done for," thought Gideon. "There are just too many. Elizabeth can't fight and I can't fend them off all by myself."

Then he turned. "Well I'll be...,"

Elizabeth lifted her fist and knocked one of them out with one blow. Another ran at her and she turned sideways, using her elbow to hit him in the side of the head.

"This is good, very good!" said Gideon, diving into the fray.

In no time at all, the elviron lay unconscious around the floor. Gideon and Elizabeth ran through the castle corridors.

"We'll go out through the dungeons, it's faster," Gideon said, changing direction. Elizabeth followed.

They were almost at the dungeons, when a strange looking girl stepped out in front of them.

"She looks human," thought Elizabeth.

When the girl smiled, Elizabeth saw very un-human teeth.

"Let the body keep its place, but let the mask fall from the face," the girl said, as she pointed to Elizabeth and Gideon.

For just an instant, Elizabeth's elven disguise disappeared and the elviron girl saw the face of a human.

"So there is witchery at work here. I suspected as much," said the elviron girl.

Gideon lunged at her. She back handed him. He hit the wall and landed on the stone floor, stunned.

The elviron girl began walking towards Elizabeth.

Without thinking, Elizabeth held up her hand. The elviron girl stopped in her tracks. She looked down at her feet, unable to move.

The girl closed her eyes, turning into the elviron shadow form. Before Elizabeth could get out of the way, the elviron girl was upon her. She punched Elizabeth in the face.

Elizabeth recoiled with pain.

"You won't do that again," she said, stepping back a few paces and turning to face the elviron girl.

"GRANTOBON! GRANTOBON! DESHYN!" Elizabeth shouted.

The elviron girl flew backwards, hitting the wall. She lay on the floor, a crumpled mess.

Gideon sat up, rubbing the back of his head.

"Quickly, we have to leave now! I don't know how long she will stay unconscious," shouted Elizabeth, breaking into a run down the passage.

"The dungeons are this way," said Gideon, getting to his feet.

They made their way down into the bowels of the castle. They were hurrying along the passageway and past the dungeons to the outside door, when something caught Gideon's eye.

He stopped and backed up a few paces. He gasped, stepping back, putting his hands up to his face, as if to block out a terrible image.

"What's wrong?" Elizabeth asked.

Gideon pointed into the dungeon. The door was wide open, and inside was Zoe. She was hanging by her neck from a rope with her hands tied behind her back.

Elizabeth ran into the dungeon and grabbed Zoe's legs, so that the weight of her body would not rest on her neck, but Gideon stopped her.

"She is dead Elizabeth," he said, looking up at Zoe's lifeless body. Elizabeth turned to Gideon.

"We can't just leave her here!"

"We can't help her now," said Gideon. "We have to leave, Elizabeth. If we try to take her with us, we will be caught."

"She can't be dead," she said, unable to move.

He saw the blood drain out of her face. "Elizabeth, don't you dare faint on me! We have to leave now."

He guided her out of the dungeon and along the passageway.

"I think I'm going to be sick!" she said, wrapping her arms around her waist.

Gideon stopped and wheeled around on her. "You can be sick all you want when we get out of here! But for now you have to be strong or you could get us both killed!"

Elizabeth followed Gideon until they reached the door that led to the outside.

They were almost to the wooded area, when Elizabeth stopped and fell to her knees, and was violently sick.

Gideon waited until she was finished, then helped her up.

"I'm sorry," she said. "I've never seen a dead person before."

He grabbed her hand and they began to run again.

Elizabeth stopped, turned, waved both of her hands and said angrily "You will all crawl around like the pigs you are, until dawn."

She broke into a run, catching up to Gideon.

All of the elviron inside of the castle dropped to their knees. Their noses grew large and round, and their ears became pointed. They began to run around everywhere on all fours, snorting and grunting.

All of them that is, except the girl who had attacked Elizabeth and Gideon. She had regained consciousness and was watching her fellow elviron with great amusement.

When Elizabeth and Gideon had put some distance between them and the castle, they slowed to a steady walk.

"Who was that girl?" Elizabeth asked.

Gideon thought back to her face. "I don't know. She looked like an elviron, but she didn't look like an elviron, if you know what I mean."

"You mean she looked human?" asked Elizabeth.

"Uh, yes, sort of."

"But she can't be human," said Elizabeth.

"Well, she looked elviron too," said Gideon.

"Yes she did," said Elizabeth. "Do you think the stories of the king having a half human daughter are true?"

"It's beginning to look like it," Gideon replied.

They headed south, to Kimadrian.

Chapter Forty

The robed figure stayed out of sight as he watched them leave the castle.

"Thank goodness they are safe," he thought. "I wonder why Gideon is with the female elf I saw with Grandma Rose at the restaurant?"

He followed them, careful to keep his distance.

***

Elizabeth and Gideon walked in silence for a while, making good time to where they slept.

"That's where we rested before," said Gideon, pointing to the wooded area. "We won't make it much further before daylight comes. We may as well wait it out here."

"I feel exhausted," said Elizabeth.

"Let's eat, then you can lie down, get some rest," said Gideon. "I'll keep watch. I don't think we were followed, but just in case."

"What do you think Zoe was doing in Distardrian, Gideon?"

"I don't know," replied Gideon. "I don't really want to think about it at the moment."

"Well, we have to find out what she was doing there," said Elizabeth. "It seems to me that if we were there, and she was there. Zoe may have followed us and told the elviron we were coming, to save her own neck.

I want to know how the elviron knew so much. I want to know what is in front of us. I'm sorry if this upsets you Gideon, but we are going to discuss this before we go any further."

Gideon sighed. "You could be right. She may have followed us."

"Gideon, if Zoe followed us. She may have seen us bury the Grymlons."

Gideon crawled out of the shelter and walked away.

"Where are you going?" Elizabeth shouted after him.

"I need some air. I will be back in a bit," he said, not turning.

"I can't let her see me cry," he thought, as he left the shelter. "Zoe had been a pampered, self centred, brat, but she did not deserve to die for it.

Why had she been at the castle? What if Elizabeth is right? If Zoe had followed us, there was a good chance she saw us bury the Grymlons. We have to get back to them and dig them up as soon as possible. Get out of Distardrian as fast as we can."

Gideon returned to the shelter.

"I'm sorry Elizabeth, I didn't mean to be angry with you. I don't want to have to tell Zoe's parents that she is dead. In all honesty, I cannot say that I will miss her, but I still have to inform Zoe's parents and they doted on her."

"I'm the one who should be apologizing. It was insensitive of me to say anything," Elizabeth muttered.

Gideon forced a smile. "We can't do anything more about this until we get back to Kimadrian. We will probably both feel better when we have had some rest."

He put his blanket down and made himself comfortable. Elizabeth did the same.

As she was falling asleep, she unconsciously put her hand up to her neck and touched the necklace. She fell asleep holding onto it.

***

The robed figure stayed off at a distance. When he was fairly certain Gideon and the female elf were asleep, he slid by them.

He travelled as fast as he could, but after days of little sleep, felt exhausted.

"I'll rest: just for a while," he thought, trying to fight the exhaustion.

He hid himself among some bushes and was asleep within minutes. Dusk came, and then darkness.

Chapter Forty One

It was snowing. Jesse threw a snowball, and it hit Elizabeth squarely in the back.

"You'll pay for that you brat," she said, laughing.

"Like to see you try," Jesse shouted, running behind a tree.

Elizabeth picked up a handful of snow and crunched it into a ball. She ran to the tree and chased Jesse around it.

"Time for hot chocolate," Audrey Ghenestone called.

Jesse and Elizabeth turned to see their mother coming out of the back door with a tray full of cups. Steam rose up from them, as Audrey Ghenestone picked her way along the slippery path. Snowflakes landed in the cups, melting into nothing as they hit the hot liquid.

She was almost to the picnic table when a snowball came flying through the air, missing her by an inch. Audrey put the tray on the table and turned to see who had thrown the projectile. A guiltless Charles Ghenestone stood looking around the corner of the house with a grin on his face.

"Come on, before it gets too cold," shouted Audrey.

Charles and the two children sat at the wet picnic bench.

Elizabeth picked up a cup of hot chocolate and sipped it. She coughed a little as the hot liquid mingled with the cold air and ran down her throat. She looked around the table at everyone. Her heart fluttered in her chest with happiness.

"Life is good!" she thought.

"ELIZABETH! ELIZABETH, WAKE UP!" Gideon was shaking her, trying to wake her.

"What? What is it?" she asked, sleepily.

"Look outside, Elizabeth!"

She sat up and looked outside of their shelter. The whole area was covered in a thin layer of pure white snow.

"Oh, it's beautiful!" she said.

"Elizabeth, it is almost June. It rarely snows in Distardrian when it's winter. So why is it snowing? What did you do?"

"Whatever do you mean?" she said, irritated at his accusation.

Then it occurred to her. She had been dreaming about Christmas day four years ago. It had snowed on that morning and the whole family had gone outside to play.

"I... I was dreaming," she said, "We were playing in the snow. I was so happy then."

She remembered when Andre had given her the Grymlon back at the cottage. She had been holding onto it and thinking about rain. A downpour had soaked her. That Grymlon was now hanging around her neck.

"It was me. I did this!"

"Well stop it, and quickly!" said Gideon. "It might alert the elviron to us."

"I don't know what to do!" she said.

"How did you make it snow?" asked Gideon.

"I dreamed it," she replied.

"Well, think of hot weather and make the snow melt," said Gideon. "Or better still, think about making it rain really hard for a few minutes. That should do it. It rains here a lot."

Elizabeth held onto the necklace.

"Thunder and lightning. Heavy raindrops falling!" she thought.

Thick, dark clouds rolled in. Lightning flashed in the sky and it rained.

"That's not hard enough, Elizabeth. Make it rain harder!" said Gideon, watching the rain fall onto the snow.

She closed her eyes and concentrated a little more. The rain came pouring down.

After a few minutes, all the snow turned to slush and melted down.

"That should do it," said Gideon. "Can you make it stop now?"

"No clouds, no rain," she thought.

The rain stopped.

"Lucky for us it's dark. Perhaps only a few elviron will have seen the snow," said Gideon.

Gideon watched Elizabeth as she looked outside.

"She has just performed magic in her sleep!" he thought. "I wonder how powerful she is going to be in the future? Will she stay a good person? Or will the power she has corrupt her? The dark side of her would be too horrible to imagine. She might have to face that demon one day. I hope if that happens, the good side of her wins, or we will all pay the price!"

"We need to move on," he said, stuffing everything into his bag. "It's dark enough now. It's a pretty good bet that any elviron who saw the snow will know that there is something unusual going on. The king will be informed. We need to get going."

Chapter Forty Two

The elviron in the castle had fallen asleep, exhausted from running around.

This did not include the elviron girl who was about sixteen years old. Her name was Verina. She was looking out at the snow that had fallen. She had watched it fall then watched the torrents of rain that followed. She looked like a human, unless you looked really close. There were the eyes that were slightly too big and round. The head was a little too large for the body, and the already thinning hair.

No one had gone after Elizabeth and Gideon. The spell Elizabeth cast, had affected everyone in the castle except Verina.

"I can wait," said Verina. "I'm going to take the soul of the human girl and be all powerful. It will soon be the day of the solstice, and Grymlons will be mine. All I have to do is bide my time."

A young elf cowered in the corner of the room. The elf child ducked lower, putting his arms above his head to protect himself when Verina viciously kicked out at him..

"This could be fun," Verina said, with a sideways glance at the child as she left the room to find her father.

Chapter Forty Three

The figure in the robe woke. As he scrambled to his feet, his hood fell from his face.

Bindyl looked around to make sure he was alone, pulling the hood back up over his head.

"I have slept too long!" he thought. Now I won't make it to where the bag was buried in time. There is no way I will be able to get there before Gideon and his companion now."

He sat down, pulled some dried fruit and water out of his backpack and began to eat. While he was eating, he took out the contents of the bag he stole from Zoe. He put all of them on the ground.

"A figurine of a horse, a vase, a picture frame and a spoon? They are all made of the same black, shiny substance. Why are they so important?" he said out loud.

Bindyl put them all back in the bag.

"If Gideon and the female elf have taken such steps to conceal them," he said, "then they must be important. I will take them to the king when I return to Kimadrian. It will be impossible to overtake them now."

He thought about Zoe. He had seen the elviron capture her.

"I bet they took her to the castle when they dragged her away. Her warrior training should have helped her escape, but they may still have her. They wouldn't dare harm her, but they will probably make her uncomfortable for a day or two.

Well, if I can't get to where the bag was buried. Should I go back and see if I can rescue Zoe? Perhaps she knows why Gideon buried these objects. If she didn't manage to escape, they will have her in a dungeon. It might not have been a bad thing. It may have even taught her a lesson. I should go back, just in case she is still there."

Bindyl packed up his belongings and set out for the castle at Distardrian once more.

Chapter Forty Four

Elizabeth and Gideon had been travelling for some time when they heard a noise above their heads.

"What is that?" she said looking up.

"That sounds like beating wings," said Gideon, "very large beating wings!"

He looked up and grabbed Elizabeth, pulling her into some trees close by.

"Get down!" he said.

Elizabeth crouched low and looked up. Flying in a circle around the tree tops was an enormous bird.

"I've never seen anything like that before,' Elizabeth said.

"It's a perichron," Gideon said, trying to see where it was. It's similar to your eagle or falcon, but much bigger. A perichron will attack anything that moves. I have never seen one this close. It has a poison in the tip of its beak. It bites and leaves the victim to die from the poison. Then it tracks it and eats it."

"Has it seen us?" she asked. "I can't hear it anymore."

"We'll stay here for a few minutes," Gideon said, watching the tree tops. "I don't think it saw us, but we will stay here for a bit. Just in case."

They ducked down in the dense shrubs and waited.

"I think its safe now," he said, after a minute or two.

They had just cleared the wooded area, when the perichron swooped down and grabbed Gideon's right shoulder with one of its claws. With one swift motion, the bird pecked the top of Gideon's right arm. He screamed with pain as the bird lifted him off his feet.

Elizabeth grabbed Gideon's other arm and tried to pull him away, but Gideon's legs went out from under him as the bird began to drag him.

As Elizabeth witnessed the spectacle in front of her, she suddenly felt her heart pounding in her chest and her hands became clammy.

"GLENLOTH, ELFICHROM, ENFENCHIOM," she chanted, pointing to the perichron.

The bird looked at her and froze. Gideon flopped to the ground as it let go of him. The bird began to move towards her. It struggled, flapping its wings frantically, as though being pulled by an unseen force. When it reached her, Elizabeth flipped her right hand as though to shush it away. It burst into flames, leaving nothing but ash in seconds.

***

When Gideon came to, Elizabeth was on the ground with him, cradling his head.

"Does it hurt very much?" she asked, tears rolling down her cheeks.

She had taken part of a change of clothing and ripped it into a bandage.

"I tried to bind your wound to stop the bleeding, but I don't know very much about first aid."

"You should let my shoulder bleed for a while. It will bleed out some of the poison," he said.

Elizabeth loosened the dressing a little, and could tell by his expression that he was in terrible pain.

"He looks so pale!" she thought. "I have to get him to Kimadrian, but if I try to move him now we might not make it."

She sat beside him and watched as he slept.

"If I could just get him to the border, we could get help."

Chapter Forty Five

Bindyl rested now and then through the daylight hours, but did not sleep. Instead, he hurried towards the castle, careful not to be seen.

The contents of Zoe's bag kept creeping into his head.

"Could this be about the Grymlons somehow?" he thought. "Only the king knows about the workings of them, it's a closely guarded secret. Even my uncle Brondly would never speak of them."

Bindyl hurried on. "I need to get to Zoe. Perhaps she has some answers. If I move quickly, I could be back at the castle in Distardrian in a few hours."

***

Elizabeth had managed to persuade Gideon to walk a little, but he was getting weaker by the hour. She noticed his skin looked an odd shade of grey, and he looked tired and frail.

"I can't go on any farther," he said, finally. "I need to rest. I may feel a bit better if I can lie down, just for a while."

"All right, but only for a little while," said Elizabeth.

She put a blanket down by a tree and Gideon collapsed onto it. He was asleep almost before he hit the ground.

"We are almost to where the Grymlons are buried, but they will have to wait," she thought.

She sat down with her back against the trunk of the tree and watched Gideon sleep.

Elizabeth waited for an hour then put together some food.

"Wake up Gideon, you need to eat, then we have to move on," she told him.

Gideon sat up and rubbed his eyes.

"I'm not hungry," he said, sleepily.

"If you don't eat, you'll get even weaker. You must try, even if it's just a few bites," Elizabeth said.

She handed him some cheese, a little dried fruit and some bread.

He put some bread and cheese into his mouth and chewed for a moment or two, then turned to one side and threw up.

"Here, try a little water," she said, handing him a cup.

 Gideon took small sips. The water seemed to settle in his stomach better than the food. He laid down and immediately fell asleep again.

Elizabeth shoved down the panic she was beginning to feel. "He looks so pale and ill," she thought. "What if he dies?"

She looked into the backpack to see if there was anything magical she could use to help him. There were some bottles of liquid that Vandrayven had given him.

She held one of them up and looked at it, throwing it down.

"I don't know how to use this stuff!" she said with frustration. "I just hope I can get him to Kimadrian in time."

Chapter Forty Six

Bindyl had been travelling for a while, when he came across a group of elviron trying to catch some sort of animal. He hid behind some trees and watched.

"Amazing!" he said.

It was a horse with a small set of wings on all four of its legs, just behind its hooves. One of the elviron had managed to get a rope around its neck to stop it from flying away, but it fought valiantly.

"I've heard of these creatures!" thought Bindyl.

"Stab it! Stab it in the heart!" hissed the elviron, holding onto the rope at the horse's head

Two of the elviron had their knives poised. Every time they lunged at the horse, it managed to raise itself into the air just high enough to get out of reach.

"If we can kill it, it will make a good meal," shouted the elviron at the head of the horse.

"Oh no!" thought Bindyl. "They are going to eat such a magnificent beast?"

He sprang into action. With his sword held high and with the element of surprise, he ran forward, cutting the ropes with two sweeping slashes of his blade.

The elviron were completely taken off guard. When they saw Bindyl's sword slashing the air, they all ran in different directions. But Bindyl's element of surprise did not last. It didn't take long for the elviron to regroup.

They circled around him, moving slowly, almost creeping towards him. Suddenly, one of them ran at him from behind. Bindyl whirled around and ran his sword swiftly through the elviron's middle.

Another elviron ran at him from the side. Bindyl saw him out of the corner of his eye. He pulled his sword out of the slain elviron, and slanted the hilt to one side, dealing the other elviron a glancing blow to the head, killing him instantly.

A third elviron ran at Bindyl from the front. He ducked, forcing the elviron to roll over the top of him. As the elviron hit the ground, Bindyl stabbed him in the heart.

That left one.

Bindyl whirled around to see remaining elviron already running for his life. He turned away from the fleeing elviron, not bothering to chase him.

He turned his attention to the creature, who had not fled, but stood at a distance, watching.

It approached Bindyl, stopping just out of striking distance.

"Thank you," it said, in a clear voice.

Bindyl looked at the creature.

"You can talk?"

"Why would I not be able to talk?" replied the horse.

"You're a horse!" said Bindyl.

"All my kind can talk," said the horse.

"Not the horses at Kimadrian, or in the Human Realm," said Bindyl, eyeing the creature with both surprise and delight.

"We are a different kind of horse," explained the horse. "My breed did a great deed for a one of your sorcerers a long time ago. He changed us so that we could talk and fly, as a gift. I thank you for your kindness. I would have been supper to those nasty little elviron if you had not saved me. Is there anything I can do for you?"

"I heard stories about you when I was young. I thought you were just a legend," said Bindyl.

"We are very private, and try to stay out of sight. It would seem I am very real, since I stand in front of you now," the horse replied. "I owe you a debt and would like to repay it."

Bindyl stared at the creature for a few seconds. "I need to get to the castle at Distardrian. Will you carry me there?"

"What is your business at that dreadful place?" asked the horse.

"I need to get someone out of there. An elf, her name is Zoe," Bindyl replied.

"I will help you," said the horse.

"Do you have a name?" asked Bindyl.

"My name is Pennarius of the Pennar. I am one of the leaders of my herd."

"Well Pennarius. It is nice to meet you. My name is Bindyl. Shall we be on our way?" he asked, eager to get to Zoe.

"Climb up on my back and hold onto my mane. We will be there in no time," said Pennarius.

Bindyl climbed onto the pennar's back.

"Please hold on tight. I would not like it if you fell," said Pennarius.

"Neither would I! Try to be smooth. I have never flown before!" said Bindyl, grabbing a handful of mane.

Pennarius rose into the air and they were away. As they moved forward Bindyl looked down, but it was dark and he couldn't see much.

"I hope I don't fall off. I don't know how high up we are!" he thought.

A few minutes later, Bindyl could make out the castle in the darkness.

Pennarius landed gently onto the ground. Bindyl slid off his back. They moved into the shelter of some trees, so they would not be seen.

"How are you going to get into the castle?" Pennarius asked.

"My friend Gideon and I have been to this castle before. We used to sneak in and look around."

"Ah, you like danger I gather. You were lucky that you were not caught," said Pennarius.

"Gideon and I are of a warrior clan. It was a good part of our training to know our enemy."

"You are a brave elf. I will wait for you and take you back to Kimadrian with your friend, if you wish it," said Pennarius.

"I would be grateful if you could do that for us," replied Bindyl. "I think they have her in the castle. I don't know why, but I will get her out of there."

"When you are ready for me to come and get you, just whisper my name to the ground," said Pennarius. "I will hear you and I will know where you are. Be safe, Bindyl and use much caution."

Bindyl guessed that he had a little more time before Distardrian's murky daylight would appear.

"I will see you soon, friend," said Bindyl, as he set off at a run towards the castle.

Pennarius stepped back into the trees and waited.

Chapter Forty Seven

Gideon slept for two more hours. Elizabeth tried to nap a little, but was too worried to get much rest.

"If I could just wake him and get him to walk a bit more," she thought."

"Perhaps a couple more hours of gentle walking. Then we could rest for a while and be home sooner. If we could just make it to where the Grymlons are buried."

She touched Gideon gently on the shoulder. He stirred, but did not wake.

"Gideon, wake up. Please try to wake up," she said, loudly.

He shrugged her hand off his shoulder. "What is it Elizabeth?" he asked, opening his eyes.

"We must try to get a little farther before daylight comes," she said, helping him to sit up. "Can you get up? You might feel a little better if you try to move around a bit."

"I don't want to get up. Let me lie down again," he complained, slumping back down onto the blanket.

"I have to get him moving," she thought.

"Gideon, get up. Don't be such a baby! I was told you were tough, but it looks to me as though you're giving up."

He turned away. "We have a name for humans like you that a decent elf would not voice," he thought.

His head began to spin as he struggled to his feet.

"I think I'm going to be sick again!" he said.

"Here, drink this," said Elizabeth, offering him some water.

Gideon sipped it. "I feel so weak. I don't know if I'm going to be able to walk at all. Let alone two more hours."

Elizabeth pulled him off the blanket.

"You have to try!" she said, folding the blanket and putting it into her backpack.

Gideon looked at her, irritated at being pulled to his feet by a girl.

"You can be very bossy, Elizabeth Ghenestone!"

"Stop whining, Gideon," she said, trying to sound mad, when she really felt scared.

She gathered the rest of their things and with Gideon holding on to her arm, they set off.

After they began to move, Elizabeth noticed it did seem to get a bit easier for him. It was slow going, but they plodded on.

After about an hour and a half they both spotted where they had hidden the Grymlons.

Elizabeth sat Gideon down and tried to make him comfortable.

"He doesn't look at all well," she thought. "I'm beginning to think he might not make it."

She removed the bandage from his shoulder.

"It's green!" she thought, "and it smells awful!

She took a sideways glance at him. "He's sweating. So it's a good bet he has a fever."

After she had dressed his wound, Elizabeth sat him on a blanket, and he fell asleep immediately.

She pulled a shovel from Gideon's backpack and began to dig. She dug deeper and deeper

Not wanting to believe the bag had gone. Elizabeth dug around the hole, thinking that she may have been off a foot or two. Finally, panic began to rise in her stomach, as she put the shovel down.

"Gideon, wake up! Wake up!" she shouted.

Gideon shot upright. "What? Are we being attacked! What?"

"The Grymlons, they're gone!"

"That can't be! We were the only people who knew where they were hidden," he mumbled.

"Apparently not," said Elizabeth. "I think Zoe dug them up. If she did have the bag, the elviron might have it now. They may have killed her for it."

Gideon rested back on one elbow. "Well if they have the Grymlons, they only have four. The fifth is around your neck, and you said the binding spell, which makes the others useless."

"But what do we do now?" she asked, more to herself than him.

"We must get back to Kimadrian," said Gideon.

"I have to get home. If I die who will help her?" he thought.

"It'll be light soon. We're only a few miles from Kimadrian. If we could just get to the border, I could run for help. Do you think you can try to walk just a little more, Gideon?"

"I don't think I have any other choice. I have to try," he replied wearily.

Chapter Forty Eight

Bindyl entered the castle through the same door as Elizabeth and Gideon.

"I'll work my way up to the main part of the castle," he thought, creeping past a room full of sleeping guards.

Once inside, Bindyl hurried through the dungeons. He was almost to the other side, when he stopped. He and walked back to the dungeon he had just passed. Inside was Zoe, still hanging by the rope. No one had bothered to cut her down.

"This can't be Zoe. It must be another elf who looks like her," he muttered, staring at her lifeless body.

He touched her. Only then did the horror of the situation hit him. This elf he had known all of his life was dead: hanging from a rope in a dirty, smelly elviron dungeon.

Both sorrow and anger welled up inside of him. His eyes filled with tears, as he looked up at her face.

"I will burn this place to the ground!" he thought. "No, no! I will come back. I will come back and make these filthy beasts know the consequences of killing those who are close to me!"

Tears were streaming down his face as he cut Zoe down and carried her towards the exit.

"I must not wake the guards. I have to get her home," he thought, struggling with her dead weight, as he crept past the guard room.

Bindyl managed to carry her outside and put her on the ground without drawing attention.

"So it has come to this," he said, staring at her lifeless body. "There will be another war, like the one my father told me about when I was a boy. Many more elves will die!"

He looked down at the ground and whispered Pennarius' name. Then sat beside Zoe and waited.

Pennarius had been grazing and waiting patiently. Suddenly, his head shot up. He listened intently for about two seconds. Then he was off, away before the grass was aware that his feet were no longer there. He found Bindyl and Zoe just outside the castle walls.

"Please Pennarius, you must hurry. We need to get out of here and to Kimadrian as soon as possible," Bindyl said, as he tried to lift Zoe off the ground.

Pennarius knelt down on all fours, so that he could place her across his back. Bindyl climbed up behind her, holding her to him as tight as he could.

"She is dead, Bindyl. There is nothing you can do," said Pennarius.

"I know that, but I still need to get her home."

"Who was she?" asked Pennarius.

"Zoe was a friend of mine. I have known her since we were children. She was of high noble breeding. She could be a brat sometimes, but I always… well… liked her."

"She was betrothed to Prince Gideon, so I kept my feelings to myself. The elviron have murdered the future Queen of Kimadrian. There will be repercussions for this deed. We must take her home to be buried in the proper manner."

"Very well, hold on," Pennarius said.

They rose off the ground and flew away into the darkness.

Chapter Forty Nine

Gideon struggled to stand. Elizabeth wrapped her arm around his waist, as they walked on into the night. They had not gone far when Gideon fell to the ground. Elizabeth knelt down beside him, lifting his head onto her lap.

"I'm sorry Elizabeth. I just can't go on."

She looked around her. "There are some trees close by. I'm going to try to get you there. I'll go the rest of the way by myself. I'll be able to travel faster alone and I can get help."

Elizabeth made Gideon as comfortable as she could and looked in the direction of Kimadrian. "I hope I have enough strength to run that far."

"But you can't…" Gideon started to say.

"I hope she makes it," was his last conscious thought.

***

Elizabeth had been running and walking by turns for some time when she heard a sound like air rushing above her head.

She looked up, fearful of another perichron, but could see nothing in the night sky.

"It will be light soon," she thought, "I have to run faster."

Chapter Fifty

Elizabeth opened her eyes. She was in a room. There were no windows, just a door. Her shoeless feet felt cold on the flagstone floor.

She was sitting in a comfortable chair and there was another one opposite her that was empty.

"How did I get here?" her voice echoed around the walls of the empty room.

As Elizabeth spoke, the door opened and a woman came in. The woman was dressed in a white robe with a hood. Her head was bowed and she was bathed in a glowing light. Elizabeth could not take her eyes off the woman's beautiful long dark hair, cascading down the front of the robe.

Then Elizabeth recognized her. "But this can't be… You… You're dead," she said, tears springing into her eyes.

"Come here," said the woman.

Elizabeth stood. She went to her mother, and stared at her for a moment. Audrey Ghenestone looked into her daughter's eyes and smiled. Elizabeth smiled back, putting her arms around her.

"I have something I need you to do, Elizabeth. You must listen very carefully as there is not much time."

Audrey took a step back from Elizabeth. Then she leaned forward, kissing her on the forehead.

"You are dead aren't you?" Elizabeth asked, looking into her mother's face.

"If that's what you want to call it," Audrey answered. "I'll never be able to be with you in your world again, but here I am very much alive, and I miss you."

Audrey took hold of Elizabeth's hand.

"But your touch, it's… warm!" said Elizabeth.

"Sit with me and let me explain what is to be done. You must listen carefully, Elizabeth. When you were at the castle in Distardrian, you met a girl. Her name is Verina. Her mother died in childbirth, so she never knew her. Verina did know that her mother was human. The elviron, knowing of the elven prophecy, tried some experimenting of their own. Verina is the outcome.

She is a child of two worlds, a child with great power. Verina is aware of her power and she does not know what it is to be good. She has studied the prophecies of the Elven Realm for years. You and she will do battle soon. Try to remember what I say. Your life may depend on it.

Now, on to Zoe and Gideon.

I know you think Zoe is dead, but she is not. It's not her time to die. At this time, her essence is moving around, trying to get back into her body. You can save her, but for you to be able to do this, Zoe has to perform a selfless act.

By using magic, you can help Zoe to heal Gideon and save his life too. After midnight tonight, Zoe's essence will be lost forever and she will not be able to save Gideon.

You are asleep in the castle in Kimadrian the moment, but this is not a dream. When you wake, both Gideon and Zoe will be in Kimadrian with you."

"But I left Gideon in Distardrian and we saw Zoe while we were there," said Elizabeth. "She was hanging from a noose in a dungeon in Kimadrian."

"I know what you saw," replied Audrey, "but things aren't always as they seem. Zoe is in a funeral home and Gideon is in the infirmary at the castle.

When you wake, you must go to Vandrayven and ask him to make a room ready. The room must be completely clean. Vandrayven knows what to do. He is familiar with the spell that I speak of. Ask your grandma to get a book called 'The Taminatin'. Read the words aloud on pages four to eight only. They are in Elvish, but you'll be able to read and understand them. This should restore Gideon and Zoe."

Elizabeth's mother stood.

"Why am I doing all this?" asked Elizabeth.

"Because Zoe's meddling has changed destiny," replied Audrey.

"How?" asked Elizabeth.

"I can't tell you," said Audrey. "You have to trust what I say. Your future and the future of any children you may have will be changed if you don't bring Zoe back and heal Gideon. Remember Elizabeth, you only have until midnight."

Elizabeth sensed the time with her mother was coming to an end. Her chest felt heavy, and tears streamed down her cheeks.

"I mustn't turn into a whining child, not now," she thought. "Don't beg her to stay."

Elizabeth's mother embraced her for one final time.

Elizabeth opened her mouth to say something, but her mother put a finger to Elizabeth's lips and shook her head.

"You know I can't, Elizabeth. You will need courage for what is ahead for you. Always remember that I love you with all of my heart."

Elizabeth looked on, as Audrey Ghenestone walked to the door. She turned and smiled at her beloved daughter for one last time and was gone.

Chapter Fifty One

Elizabeth woke. She was lying in a large bed. An elven nurse was sitting beside her, reading a book.

Elizabeth vaguely remembered being on a horse. They were flying and Bindyl was there with her.

Suddenly, she sat bolt upright.

"GIDEON! ZOE!" she said.

The nurse stood and put a hand on Elizabeth's shoulder. "Please lie back and rest."

Grandma Rose entered the room. When she saw Elizabeth was awake, she sat at the end of the bed.

"How are you feeling?" she asked.

"Gideon! Gran, where is Gideon? I left him in Distardrian. I said I would get help. Gran he is dying!"

"He's here. He's down in the infirmary," said Grandma.

"I have to get up. I have to help him," said Elizabeth, sitting up again.

"When Bindyl found you, you were unconscious and dehydrated. You must rest, Elizabeth. There is nothing you can do for Gideon."

"Bindyl? How did he find me?"

"I'll explain later," replied Grandma.

"Don't try to stop me. I'm going to Gideon, and I'm going to help him!" Elizabeth said, stepping down from the bed.

"I want my clothes," she said, looking at the nurse.

Grandma Rose turned to the nurse, who nodded and went to a wardrobe standing in the corner of the room. She opened the door, reached in, picked up a pile of neatly folded clothes and handed them to Elizabeth.

"These are my elven clothes!" Elizabeth said.

She went to a mirror on the wall and looked at her reflection.

She turned to her grandma. "I still look like an elf. I want to be changed back to me again. I don't want those clothes. I want my own clothes. Where is Vandrayven?"

"He is in his rooms," Grandma answered.

Grandma Rose handed Elizabeth a robe. She put it on and left the room. She ran down the steps to Vandrayven's rooms, knocking politely on his door.

Vandrayven answered. He stood back to let her in.

"I have been waiting for you," he said.

"I want my face back."

"Sit down and keep still," Vandrayven said.

Five minutes later, Elizabeth no longer looked like an elf.

"Vandrayven, there was a strange looking girl at the castle in Distardrian. Do you know who she is?" Elizabeth asked.

"There have been rumours about one of the elviron king's daughters," he replied, turning a little pale.

"I know who it is," she said.

"Yes," said Vandrayven. "So do I."

"Where is Zoe?" Elizabeth asked.

"She is in the funeral home. Her parents are arranging for her burial," Vandrayven answered.

"I want Gideon and Zoe here as soon as possible," said Elizabeth. "I want you to find a room with no windows and have it cleared of everything. The room must be cleaned. There must be no dirt or dust, just the beds that Zoe and Gideon are in, and one table. Everything must be as clean as possible to avoid contamination."

"Elizabeth, Zoe is dead," said Vandrayven. "There is nothing you can do for her now. Her parents will not allow you to take her anywhere. I think I know what you are about to try and I would strongly advise against it."

"My mother said you would know what was to be done. Is she right?"

"Your mother? But she's dead," said Vandrayven.

"Yes, I spoke with her and she said you would know what I am about to do. What does she mean?"

"A small mistake a couple of hundred years ago. Nothing important, but I would rather you didn't try this. If you insist, I have a room down here that will suffice" replied Vandrayven.

"Did it work for you?" asked Elizabeth.

"No," said Vandrayven. "If truth be told, it turned out to be rather, well… disastrous."

"I have to try, so please help me," said Elizabeth.

As she turned to walk out of the room Elizabeth looked back at Vandrayven. "I'll talk to Zoe's parents and try to get them to let me help her. I'll need to tell the king. Please arrange for Gideon to be placed down here. There isn't much time."

Vandrayven followed her. "Don't worry about the king. I will explain everything to him. You just go and do what is needed."

Elizabeth found her grandmother heading towards Vandrayven's rooms.

"I want you to rest, Elizabeth. You're exhausted."

"I don't have time, Gran. I want you to go to the cottage and get a book called 'The Taminatin'. I'll need some clean clothes, so will you. Please do this as fast as you can. When you get back here, we all need to bathe and change clothes. I have something that I have to do and I only have until midnight."

"What are you going to do, Elizabeth? And how do you know about 'The Taminatin'?"

"I'll explain later. Please Gran, you have to go now!"

Grandma Rose gave Elizabeth a puzzled look and left to go to the cottage.

Elizabeth went to her rooms. She changed into her own clothes. Then headed to King Morvand's private residence.

"I have to go to the funeral home. So I would appreciate it if you could arrange for one of the guards to take me," she said.

"Why do you want to go to there?" asked the King.

"I need to arrange for Zoe to be brought here, and I don't have time to explain. Vandrayven is on his way up to you. He will tell you what I'm going to try to do."

"Very well," said the King, summoning a guard. "I will arrange for a carriage."

Chapter Fifty Two

"Please wait here for me," Elizabeth told the carriage driver, as she stepped down in front of The Elves Rest funeral home in Kimadrian.

"This is beautiful," she thought, as she entered the reception area, "Surprisingly cheery for a place where people come to visit the dead."

The walls were painted white. There was a plush carpet on the floor. Flowers in shades of white and blue were placed in vases all around the room.

A dark haired male elf, dressed in black approached her.

"Are you here to visit a deceased friend or relative?" he asked.

"My name is Elizabeth. I'm here to visit Zoe of Mindar," she replied.

"I'm afraid the parents of Lady Zoe have requested no visitors," he said.

"Are Zoe's parents here now?" she asked.

"Yes, they are," he replied.

"Would you mind terribly asking if I could see them for a few minutes?"

The elf undertaker bowed politely. He disappeared through a door to the right. A few minutes later, he returned with Zoe's mother and father.

"My name is Elizabeth," she said, nervously.

"Yes, our daughter has spoken of you," said Zoe's mother.

Elizabeth turned to the undertaker. "Do you think that we could use a room to talk privately?"

"But of course," replied the undertaker, pointing to the room Zoe's parents had emerged from.

Elizabeth followed Zoe's parents into a room with white washed stone walls. Zoe's mother was of small build with a slight figure and black curly shoulder length hair. She had pale blue eyes. Zoe's father was a little taller, though not by much. He also had dark hair.

They took a seat, waiting for Elizabeth to speak.

"They both look as though someone has ripped out their souls," thought Elizabeth. "The sadness in their faces is almost unbearable to see."

Zoe's mother was the first to speak. "Why are you here? Our daughter made it no secret that she did not like you. Yet you say you are here to help her. She is dead. How can you help the dead? We have already lost our son to the elviron."

Elizabeth eyed Zoe's mother. "Oh great," she thought. "No one told me that the elviron had taken Zoe's brother. Now she grieves for both of her children. I can understand her sadness, but does she have to be so ill mannered? How do I find the right words?"

Everyone turned when the door opened.

Vandrayven entered the room unannounced.

Zoe's parents gasped with surprise. They immediately dropped down on one knee and bowed their heads.

"You may get up," said Vandrayven. "We have no time for these polite gestures. There is work to be done. I want you to listen to what the Lady Elizabeth has to tell you. You must then make a decision, as to whether or not you want her to help your daughter. Proceed with your explanation, Elizabeth.

I will wait outside. If either of you have any questions after Elizabeth has explained everything to you, both Elizabeth and myself will try to answer them for you."

Vandrayven turned on his heel and exited the room, his robes swishing around him.

Elizabeth cleared her throat and began.

"I'm not quite sure how to explain this to you, so I'm just going to tell you what has happened to Zoe and Gideon. Zoe is not dead. Her... essence, if you like, is out there somewhere trying to get back into her body.

This is happening because it was not Zoe's time to die. Gideon was attacked by a perichron and he will die if he doesn't get help. In order for Zoe to get back into her body, she has to perform a selfless act. If I can get her essence to go into Gideon's body and heal him, Zoe's essence will be allowed to go back into her own body.

We will have to move fast or Zoe's essence will move on and she will really die. I need your permission to move her to the castle and put her next to Gideon."

Elizabeth took a breath, relieved at being finished with her explanation. She looked at the two of them, sure they would say no.

"Can we be with Zoe when you do this?" asked Zoe's mother.

"No," replied Elizabeth. "It could be dangerous. There is also the danger of contamination that could make things go terribly wrong."

Zoe's parents looked at one another.

"If it means there is a chance of getting our daughter back, we agree to let you try," said Zoe's father.

"We will take her to the castle," said Zoe's mother.

Zoe's father motioned for Elizabeth to follow them through a different door.

They entered a room with dark blue walls. There were large white candles lit all around. In the middle of the room was a table covered with a white satin cloth. Lying on the cloth was Zoe. She was dressed in a long pale blue robe that started high up on her neck and ended at her ankles. Her arms were down by her sides.

"My word, her skin looks grey as stone! She looks so... dead!" thought Elizabeth. "Don't get spooked. You know she's alive. I wonder why the elviron didn't take her essence. Isn't that what elviron do?"

Elizabeth couldn't take her eyes off Zoe's body.

When Zoe's mother walked up behind her and put her hand on Elizabeth's shoulder. It was all she could do not to jump out of her skin.

"We will leave you alone with her for a few minutes," said Zoe's mother.

"She's a beautiful girl," Elizabeth thought, looking down at her. "I hope I can help her. I wonder how she will feel towards me if I can pull this off. Probably be just as mean spirited as ever. Oh well, I still have to try and save her."

Elizabeth went to the main entrance area where Vandrayven was talking with Zoe's mother and father. She walked past them and out of the front door.

She approached the guard who had escorted her to the mortuary.

"Go and tell the king that Zoe is being transported to the castle," she said. "Tell him that she must be admitted with the utmost secrecy."

The guard saluted her and stepped into the carriage.

Elizabeth watched for a moment as carriage sped off down the street, then went back into the building.

"I'll do my best to help your daughter," she told Zoe's parents.

They both bowed politely to her and went to find the undertaker, to make arrangements for Zoe to be moved to the castle.

Elizabeth turned to Vandrayven.

"We will travel with Zoe," she said.

When they reached the castle, Elizabeth found her way to the infirmary to see Gideon was lying on a bed in one of the private rooms. She sat in a chair beside him and held on to his hand. "His skin is the colour of alabaster, and his lips have a blue tinge to them," she thought.

He opened his eyes. "Zoe is dead," he said.

"I know, Gideon. I was with you when you found her. Don't you remember?"

"He's forgetting some of what has happened, and that's a bad sign," she thought.

"Try to rest," she said. "Someone is coming to take you to Vandrayven in a few minutes. I'm going to try to help you."

"It is my fault that she's dead. I deserve to die too," he said.

"Stop feeling sorry for yourself!" said Elizabeth. "If Zoe had minded her own business and not been so jealous, she would still be alive.

As it is, it seems that it was not her time to die. I think I can help her."

"What do you mean? She is dead! You can't bring her back to life!" said Gideon.

"She is not dead. At least I don't think she is," said Elizabeth. "I think she is lost somewhere and I think I can get her back, but I only have until midnight to make it happen. I think I can help you too, but you have got to stay calm."

"How do you know all of this?" he asked.

"My mother came to me while I was sleeping and told me what to do," she replied.

"You mean your dead mother?" said Gideon.

Elizabeth nodded.

Gideon groaned. "This is a nightmare and I'm going to wake up any minute," he thought, as he lost consciousness.

"Good, you go back to sleep," Elizabeth said. "You may not

believe me, but it doesn't matter at the moment. For now, you need to stay as still as possible, so the poison in you doesn't travel too fast."

Elizabeth kissed him on the forehead.

"Time to prepare and I will need Vandrayven's help," she thought.

Chapter Fifty Three

Elizabeth arrived as the guards were bringing Zoe and Gideon into the room.

"Has everything been done?" she asked.

"Yes," Vandrayven replied. "The room has been thoroughly cleaned. I did it myself."

"Place Zoe up against that wall please, and put Gideon up against that wall," she said, pointing to the wall directly opposite Zoe.

She stood in the middle of the room, and Vandrayven came up beside her. "I do not want you to try this Elizabeth. If anything goes wrong, horrible things could happen to both Gideon and Zoe."

"I have no choice, Vandrayven. I have to try. My mother told me that it was very important to the future of Kimadrian."

Vandrayven bowed, slowly backing away from her.

"I could try to stop her," he thought. "Although, I suspect that things might not go well for me if I did. I wonder if she is the one? Well, if I can't stop her, I may as well help her."

He left, returning a few minutes later with an arm load of assorted bottles, papers and jars.

He put them on a nearby table and sorted them into some kind of order.

A few minutes later, Grandma Rose came in with the book Elizabeth had asked for. She placed it on the table beside Vandrayven's bits and pieces.

While Elizabeth and her grandma went to bathe and change clothes, Vandrayven set about putting various things around the room.

He placed different coloured candles and various herbs along the walls. This was done to keep out intruders that were not of the Elven or Human world.

Some oils and powders were splashed onto the walls. Vandrayven drew strange symbols on the paper he had brought in and placed them on the floor in the corners of the room. This was also to keep out anything else that might get curious and cross over from where you go when you move on.

When Elizabeth returned, she went to the table, picked up 'The Taminatin' and turned it over.

"It's beautiful," she thought, putting it back down.

"That book is not to be toyed with," said Grandma. "It has power beyond anyone's imagination. I'm curious as to how you think you are going to use it. How could you have the knowledge to cast the spells needed from that book to help these two unfortunate children, when you have never studied any kind of magic?"

She looked into Elizabeth's eyes.

Elizabeth did not answer her question. Instead, she returned her grandma's gaze. Elizabeth's eyes turned an orange gold colour for an instant. It was then that Grandma sensed something both wonderful and terrible in her granddaughter.

Elizabeth looked over her shoulder at the two beds.

"What if Vandrayven is right, Gran? What if things go wrong?" she said, suddenly feeling unsure.

"We can stop this anytime you want. Just say the word," said Grandma.

"No. I have to believe I can do this," said Elizabeth.

She picked up the book again. As she opened it, she thought of what her mother had told her. The pages of the book began to turn by themselves. At page four they stopped.

"Well, that was an unexpected bonus," Elizabeth muttered.

She crossed the room until she was standing between the two beds. Positioning herself directly in the middle, so that she was the same distance away from each bed. She held the book high and closed her eyes. The book began to glow. Elizabeth let go of it. It did not drop, but hung in the air. She made a downward motion with her hands, as if to ask the book to come down a little. It did as requested.

When the book was just below Elizabeth's elbows, it tilted downward.

Vandrayven and Grandma stood motionless by the table with the herbs and bottles on it.

Elizabeth began reading from the book. The words were in Elvish, but without thinking, she translated them into English.

"Right the error.

Heal the sick.

Fill this room with wonder.

Strength of spirit come this day.

Put the wrong asunder!"

The room turned cold, and a small grey cloud began to form over Zoe. It turned, and grew, until it completely surrounded the bed. A face appeared in the cloud, then a shoulder, then the rest of a body. Zoe's body arched, as it suddenly dropped down onto her and disappeared inside of her.

Elizabeth continued reading out loud. It was so cold now, she could see her own breath. She pointed to Zoe.

"Light of lights go where they may.

Leave the soul behind this day!"

Zoe's body went limp as the light rose out of her and floated across the room towards Gideon, hovering over his body.

As fast as a flash, the light moved down his body, diving into him and out again, until it had travelled the length of him.

Elizabeth pointed to Gideon, then pointed to Zoe.

"Take the poison from this body.

Stay to heal the harm.

The penance done.

You may return."

The light hovered over Gideon's body for a few seconds. Then it moved back over to Zoe and disappeared into her.

Elizabeth thrust her right hand high into the air, looking upwards.

"I command the light to leave our sight!" she shouted.

A light flashed in front of her. It spread throughout the entire room, blinding everyone.

Then it was gone.

The book closed, and Elizabeth fainted. The book hesitated for a moment, before falling to the floor beside her.

Grandma hurried over to her and propped up her head.

Elizabeth opened her eyes.

"Are you all right?" asked Grandma.

"I feel a bit queasy, but I think I'm okay. Did it work?"

Grandma Rose looked over at Zoe. Her head was moving from side to side, as though she was trying to wake. Gideon was moaning as though he was in pain.

"Yes, I think that you may have saved them both. Gideon's skin tone is definitely better than it was."

"Good," said Elizabeth.

Grandma Rose helped her up and Elizabeth went to Gideon's bedside.

"How are you feeling?" she asked, sliding her fingers into his half clenched hand.

"Better, much better. What did you do?" he asked, looking over at Zoe, who was also trying to sit up.

"I used Zoe's spirit to cleanse your system of the poison. Then I put her spirit back into her body," Elizabeth answered.

"How did you know that it would work?" he asked, looking at her with amazement.

"My mother told me it would, if I used 'The Taminatin' in the proper way."

"But Zoe was dead!" Gideon said, as he looked at Elizabeth and then over at Vandrayven.

"No she wasn't," Elizabeth explained. "Her spirit had left her body, but it was not her time to die. So it sort of hung around, waiting to return. It just needed the right conditions."

"She never lost her heartbeat, although it was inaudible and she never turned completely cold. She was in some kind of deep coma if you like, but she was never quite, well… dead. She would have been eventually. If her spirit had not been able to get back into her body before midnight tonight, it would have moved on.

There is a time limit for the body and spirit to re-unite. After that time, death occurs. Because Zoe was in the wrong place, she had to perform a good deed to get her body back."

"My mother told me I could use 'The Taminatin' to help her, help you. That allowed her to go back to her own body and stay there."

Gideon looked over at Zoe. Still too weak to sit up, she had put her head back onto the pillow and was sleeping peacefully.

"Will she remember any of this?" he asked.

"I don't know. I would imagine it will probably take a few days for her to feel better," Elizabeth replied.

Vandrayven called for the guards to take Gideon and Zoe back up to the infirmary. He also sent word to Zoe and Gideon's parents to say that they were both fine.

"I'm exhausted," said Elizabeth. "I need to rest. I want to go home to Willow View, get into my bed and sleep."

"Why don't you go to your rooms and rest for a while. We can go to the cottage later," suggested Grandma.

"I want to go home now. Do you think it will be all right if we do that?" asked Elizabeth.

"I'm sure it will be fine. Vandrayven, will you please tell the king that we are going back to Willow View for the night?" said Grandma.

"Most certainly," Vandrayven replied.

Grandma picked up 'The Taminatin' and they made their way home.

Chapter Fifty Four

The next morning Elizabeth got out of bed looked outside to see a summer rainstorm in full swing. "I don't think I have ever noticed how colourful the flowers are when they're in bloom. All the colours in the garden look so vivid. Even the grey, blustery look of the river is beautiful!"

"It's so nice to be able to walk again," she thought, glancing down at her feet.

"I wonder what will happen now that the Grymlons are lost. I hope we'll be able to find them in time for the ritual. I don't want to consider the alternative. We'll be going back down to the Elven Realm after breakfast. There will probably be a meeting with me, Gran and the king. I'm sure that a plan will have to be formed to try to find the Grymlons. I feel responsible for them being lost. It was a stupid idea to bury them in Distardrian. If I hadn't suggested it, they may still be around."

She showered, dressed and went to the kitchen where Grandma was making breakfast as usual.

Grandma turned and smiled at her. "Did you sleep well?"

"Yes, thanks, Gran. Did you?"

"Very well, thank you. Now sit down and eat your food. We have to get back to the Realm."

When they arrived at the castle, Ledry, the king's personal assistant was waiting for them.

"The king asked that you go straight to his private chambers when you arrived," he announced.

"Here we go," thought Elizabeth. "I'm sure to be in for it now."

They were escorted through the castle and asked to wait.

The king and queen's private rooms were tastefully decorated. There was a large stone wall covered with tapestries, similar to the ones throughout the rest of the castle. The furniture was of deep purple velvet material. There were chairs and sofas scattered around a big fireplace structured in the centre of the room.

King Morvand and Queen Paulina arrived a few minutes later. Queen Paulina put her arms around Elizabeth and embraced her.

"Thank you for saving my son," she said into Elizabeth's ear.

Paulina turned to Grandma and bowed her head slightly. Grandma made a small curtsy in return.

King Morvand motioned for all of them to sit.

Elizabeth sat in one of the easy chairs, and put her hand up to her neck.

"I forgot about the necklace! Why does it feel so uncomfortable all of a sudden?" she thought.

"Is it getting hot in here?" she asked.

"There is no fire burning. Are you not feeling well?" asked the King.

"I'm just a little… warm," replied Elizabeth, adjusting the necklace.

A servant entered the room with a tray of tea and sandwiches.

King Morvand knew of the traditions up in the Human Realm. Whenever he could, he would provide tea and sandwiches for Grandma. He secretly liked this tradition. The tea had a slightly nutty taste and the sandwiches always tasted so delicate; quite complimentary with the tea.

After Grandma poured tea for everyone, King Morvand stood and went behind the couch. He reached down and held up a bag.

"Do you recognize this, Elizabeth?" he asked.

"Yes! It's the bag Gideon and I took with us to Distardrian. Where did you get it?"

King Morvand returned to his seat and sat down with the bag, but did not open it.

"It appears that you were followed into Distardrian," said the King. "We all know Zoe followed you, but so did Bindyl."

Zoe was trying to find out what you and Gideon were doing out of sheer jealousy. Bindyl however, was trying to protect you both from afar.

When Zoe saw you bury the bag, she decided to dig it up and follow you.

Bindyl, suspecting foul play on her part, took the bag from her before the elviron captured her. We thank our blessings for that.

It seems that Bindyl could not put the bag back where you had hidden it, because you and Gideon got there before him. So he decided to go back and retrieve Zoe from the elviron castle.

He made a friend on his journey. This friend of Bindyl's helped him rescue both you and Gideon, after he had safely brought Zoe back here. I am sure he will introduce you later."

"Where is Bindyl?" Elizabeth asked.

"We have just found out that Bindyl's uncle Brondly was brutally murdered in his home a few days ago. Bindyl didn't say anything to us at the time, as there was too much going on here," the King said. "He has reported the murder to the sheriff's office and they are investigating it. I have told him to stay home for a few days. I think it best, until Brondly's remains have been seen to."

"How horrible!" said Grandma. "Do the authorities have any clues as to who killed him."

"Unfortunately, no," said the King. "But I have spoken with them and they have assured me, if they find anything, they will let me know."

Elizabeth took the necklace off and gave it to him. The king opened the bag and put the necklace with the rest of the Grymlons.

"So now we have all of them. That means we can start making preparations for the journey to Avebury," said Elizabeth.

"It will take a few days for Gideon and Zoe to get their strength back," said the King. "Besides, we have decided to do things a little differently this time. Bindyl will be travelling with you and perhaps Zoe too.

Rose and I have already discussed the situation and she whole heartedly agrees with the new plan."

"Zoe?" Elizabeth blurted out. "She almost got us all killed! She almost got herself killed! Now you want her to go with us? Are you mad?"

Her hand flew up to her mouth.

"Oh, I am so sorry your majesty. I didn't mean...," she quickly added.

"It is quite all right Elizabeth," the King said, waving his hand, dismissively. "I would feel the same way if I were you. Although, it seems that Zoe is very much changed by her experience.

She is grateful to have her life back and wants to be of help in any way she can. If you don't want her to go with you, I will not allow it. The decision must be yours, but please consider that she may be of help to you."

"Zoe is of noble birth. This makes her part of the warrior clan. All nobles are of the warrior clan and are required to learn fighting skills. Think it over for a few days and let me know what you decide.

In the meantime, I suggest that you rest too. Your journey will be a dangerous one. I will not lie to you about that. You will need every ounce of strength you have, if you are to be successful in your venture."

"I'm glad Gideon and Bindyl are going with me," said Elizabeth, "but Zoe? I'll have to think about that. What if Zoe decides she wants to change sides at the last minute?"

"Just think it over before you decide," said the King.

"I need time to talk to Zoe, get a feel for her and see if she really wants to help," said Elizabeth. "I also want to talk to Gideon. He and Zoe are betrothed, but they don't seem to get along too awfully well."

"The last thing I want is for them to be bickering and fighting all the way to Avebury. That could make the trip not only miserable, but possibly dangerous.

When will Gran take us to Avebury, so that we can renew the Grymlons?"

King Morvand raised and eyebrow and turned to Grandma.

"Did I say something wrong?" she asked.

"Why would Lady Rose go with you?" asked King Morvand. "This is your quest, not hers. She has not been the keeper of the Grymlons for years."

"Isn't Gran going to drive us to Avebury? How else are we going to get there?" Elizabeth asked.

"The Grymlons cannot be transported to Avebury by travelling through the Human Realm. If you travel up there, the orbs will lose their magical powers for good."

"I forgot to tell Elizabeth how she would be getting to Avebury!" thought Grandma, returning the king's gaze.

"You did not tell her how she was going to transport the Grymlons?" asked the King, who was obviously getting upset.

"In all the confusion and trouble, I forgot. I apologize," said Grandma.

"Will someone please tell me what's going on?" Elizabeth asked.

"You must go on foot to your destination." King Morvand explained. "It is tradition. All hundred-year protectors of the Grymlons have travelled through Kimadrian, on to Distardrian, through the badlands, then up through the Heel Stone at Stonehenge to Avebury. It is a quest that must be made by a champion for the Grymlons. You are not an elf, yet you have elven blood running in your veins. If any thing or anyone other than you carries the Grymlons, anywhere but down here, they may lose their power. They may even die."

"Your grandmother will get a book with the information you will need, and give it to you. You must read it, study the information in it, and you must do it soon.

It will take about a week for Zoe and Gideon to recover from their ordeals. That should be sufficient time for you to get the information you need."

As the King, and Queen Paulina stood to leave, the king turned to Elizabeth.

He took her hand and patted it, as though to console her.

"Please come and see me, Elizabeth, as soon as you have studied the book," he said. "Then we can talk more."

He turned to Grandma.

"Lady Rose, you and I will talk now. I must make sure that nothing else is forgotten. Elizabeth, you may wait here if you wish. Your grandmother will be with me for about an hour."

He headed towards the door.

"I'm going to visit Zoe and Gideon until you are finished with your meeting," Elizabeth said.

"I will meet you a little later," Grandma said, following the king.

"If you will excuse me, I have other business to attend to," said Queen Paulina.

Elizabeth curtsied, as the queen left for another part of the castle.

Grandma followed King Morvand into his office and sat in one of the chairs by his desk. He closed the door and turned to face her.

"How could you forget to tell Elizabeth that she has to travel on foot through the Realm to get to Avebury?" he asked.

"In all the excitement, I forgot," replied Grandma. "I apologize, your majesty. I'll make sure she reads and understands all of what is to be done to get to Avebury."

"Would you like me to go through 'The Book of Journeys' with her?" asked the King.

"No, I can do it. I trained my daughter before she died. I think I can manage with my granddaughter."

"I suggest Elizabeth stay down here for the time being. At least until I am sure she has received all of the required instruction," said the King.

"If you wish, your majesty," replied Grandma.

"I do wish. Now, Rose, let's go over the information Elizabeth has yet to learn."

An hour later Grandma Rose found Elizabeth.

"You will have to stay here for a while," Grandma told her.

"Why?" asked Elizabeth.

"Because the king is afraid I'll forget something important and you'll fail," replied Grandma.

"I don't mind. I like it down here," said Elizabeth.

"I am going up to the Human Realm," said Grandma. "I will have to arrange for you to be out of school for a while. I'll pick up some things for us. The king and I have agreed that Gideon and Bindyl receive some of the teaching normally given only to the guardian of the Grymlons. Zoe too, if you decide to take her."

"We will see about Zoe," said Elizabeth.

Chapter Fifty Five

Grandma sat outside the Headmaster's office, waiting to be called.

After a few minutes, Mr. Jones, the Head Master opened his office door.

"Mrs Humphries, if you would step this way," he said, with a smile.

"Thank you," said Grandma, getting up from her seat and walking into the office.

She sat down in one of the two chairs facing the Headmaster's desk.

Mr. Jones wore a black suit with the school tie. His thick white hair was swept to one side. He looked like the old style gentleman you would expect to be running a country school.

"What may I do for you today Mrs Humphries? I trust that everything is well with Elizabeth?"

"I have some very good news," said Grandma. "Elizabeth is walking. She has managed to overcome the paralysis in her legs."

"That is wonderful news," said Mr. Jones. "It is the best news I have heard in a long time."

"It most certainly is," said Grandma. "As you know, she has not been to school for the past few days. Unfortunately, she will have to be away a bit longer. She has responded well, but will have to undergo some physio therapy for a few weeks to help her regain her strength. So she will not be attending school for a while."

"We can send some work home for her to catch up," suggested Mr. Jones.

"That would be a splendid idea," said Grandma.

"I will see to it straight away. I will have my secretary put the work together and send it to you by post. That way, you won't have to wait around here for the teachers to prepare the necessary papers."

"I do appreciate your understanding," said Grandma.

"Not at all," said Mr. Jones. "In fact, I will mention that Elizabeth is now walking at the school assembly tomorrow morning. Please send her our best regards and tell her we hope to see her back at school soon."

"I most certainly will," replied Grandma, standing to leave.

Mr. Jones walked around the side of his desk. He opened the door and showed her out.

As she drove out of the school grounds, Grandma felt a little guilty for lying to the Headmaster.

"At least some of it was the truth," she thought. "The bit about Elizabeth regaining the use of her legs, anyway."

Chapter Fifty Six

Elizabeth, accompanied by Bindyl, spent the next two weeks learning some of the elven ways. It was decided that she would learn some self defence techniques called the 'Tammas Sheaal', an ancient form of elven martial arts and weapons training.

Bindyl was very adept at this art, so he took over her self defence instruction.

When Zoe and Gideon were a little stronger, they joined Elizabeth and helped with her training.

Grandma and Elizabeth had lived in Oaklade all of their lives, and Oaklade was a small town. Grandma knew that if they spent too much time away from home, people would start looking for them. She spent her days between the Elven Realm, teaching Elizabeth from 'The Book of Journeys', and spending time at the cottage.

Zoe, Bindyl, Gideon and Elizabeth were practicing their sword fencing skills when Zoe pulled Elizabeth to one side.

"I have been talking to my parents about you," she said. "We were wondering if you would like to come over to the house and have supper with us?"

"I would like that," said Elizabeth.

"Would you be available to come over tonight?" asked Zoe.

"I don't have any other plans," said Elizabeth.

"If you would like to come over at about 7:00 p.m. I'll send a carriage for you," said Zoe.

"I'll look forward to it," Elizabeth replied.

"I will see you tomorrow," Zoe said, turning to Gideon and Bindyl.

The two elves watched as Zoe left through the archway that led to the outside gate.

"Be careful Elizabeth. You don't want to get poisoned now," said Gideon, nudging Bindyl, trying not to laugh.

"Don't listen to him Elizabeth," Bindyl said, with a grin. "Zoe's mother has an excellent chef."

"You two are just jealous because she didn't invite you," she said, walking towards the doorway to the castle's apartments.

The two elves laughed.

"Have a pleasant evening," shouted Gideon, as Elizabeth started up the steps.

"I will," she replied, and left them to their snickering.

Chapter Fifty Seven

The Mindar's carriage arrived to pick Elizabeth up at precisely 7:00 p.m.

It raced away from the castle and continued across the countryside.

Twenty minutes later, the carriage came to an entrance with iron gates. Elizabeth looked out of the window, as they continued along a narrow road with immaculately landscaped lawns on either side.

They eventually pulled up to an enormous stone house. Elizabeth was helped out of the carriage by the driver. She went to the front door and pulled on a rope with a bell attached to it. She was greeted by a young female elf dressed in a maids uniform.

"Please come in my lady," said the maid, curtsying to Elizabeth as she entered.

She was shown to the drawing room, where Zoe's mother and father were waiting.

"Elizabeth!" said Zoe's mother, standing to greet her. "How are you? I hope all is well with your grandmother,"

"Everything is well with my family," Elizabeth replied, politely.

An elf servant entered the room.

"Dinner is served," he announced, with a bow.

"I hope you like the food our cook has prepared for you," said Zoe's mother.

"I'm sure I will," said Elizabeth.

After dinner a maid brought some elven tea..

"It is a very pleasant evening," said Zoe. "Would you like to go for a walk in the gardens before you go home, Elizabeth?"

She stood, grateful to be doing something other than drink tea. "That would be nice."

"We are going to retire for the night," said Zoe's father. "We will see you another day I hope."

"Thank you for the lovely evening," said Elizabeth.

"Not at all," said Zoe's mother. "You must come and visit again soon."

"Yes, I would enjoy that," said Elizabeth.

Zoe led the way to the gardens at the back of the house. As they were walking, she turned and looked at Elizabeth. "I cannot forgive myself for being so mean and nasty to you."

They sat by the pathway on a stone carved garden seat.

"It's in the past," said Elizabeth.

"I owe you my life," said Zoe. "I honestly think that if it had been me and I had been given the opportunity to save you. I may have let you die."

"I don't care what you would have done, Zoe. I chose to do what was necessary. Besides, if I had let you die, I would have to go on this quest without you or Gideon, so my motives weren't entirely selfless. I am curious though, and I don't mean to intrude on your family, but what happened to your brother."

Elizabeth saw Zoe turn pale.

"I'm sorry, she said. "I shouldn't have asked. It's none of my business."

"No, no. Its okay, Zoe said. "Tevyn was taken during the night a few weeks ago. We are still amazed that someone managed to kidnap him. The sheriff looked into it, but they don't seem to have any answers. No one has asked for ransom money, in fact, no one has made any demands on us at all. It's a mystery."

Gideon never mentioned that your brother had been taken," said Elizabeth.

"The Sheriff asked that no one be given any information about Tevyn. The king and queen have been very supportive of us since it happened."

"Zoe, if you don't want to do this, with all that's going on with your family. I would completely understand."

"From this moment, I pledge that I will give my life for you if I have to," Zoe stated, solemnly.

"Don't get carried away, Zoe. I think I can take care of myself."

"Elizabeth. I will help you in any way that I can."

"Thanks," said Elizabeth. "I'm going to be getting back to the castle now. The king has said that I can go home to Willow View tomorrow. I still have some studying to do before we leave."

"Am I going with you to Avebury, Elizabeth? Do you trust me enough to let me help you?"

Elizabeth smiled at her. "I wouldn't dream of even trying to make this journey without you."

Zoe smiled back. "I will call your carriage for you."

She walked Elizabeth to the front entrance.

As Elizabeth stepped up into the carriage, she looked out at Zoe standing on the doorstep.

"See you in a bit?" she said.

"You can count on it," said Zoe.

The carriage carried Elizabeth out of the Mindar estate and back to the castle.

Chapter Fifty Eight

Grandma was shown to the king's office in his private apartments. A few minutes later, King Morvand arrived.

I apologize for being late, Rose," he said, taking a seat at his desk. "Would you like some tea?"

"I would love a cuppa," replied Grandma.

The king called his servant into the room. He ordered tea and biscuits.

"Has Elizabeth thought anymore about taking Zoe with her on her quest?" the King asked.

"I don't think Elizabeth feels comfortable about Zoe going with them. She has gone up to the cottage. She needed a break from all the studying." replied Grandma.

"I am aware of that, Rose. Elizabeth made her feelings regarding Zoe very clear the last time we spoke. But Zoe could be of help to them. Didn't Elizabeth have supper with the Mindar's last night? That has to be a good sign. Zoe seems to have had quite a change of heart these past few days."

"Has she? Has she really? Or is she trying to save face in front of us?" said Grandma.

"Do not be so critical of her. Give the young one a chance to redeem herself," said the King.

Grandma shrugged. "Have the druids been informed of Elizabeth's upcoming journey?" she asked, changing the subject.

"They have. All has been arranged," replied the King. "Elizabeth will get as much help as we can give her, but some of this will be in her own hands."

"I am afraid for my granddaughter," said Grandma, quietly.

"Don't be, Rose. I have a strong feeling about Elizabeth. I cannot quite tell you why, but I think everything is about to change. I think she is about to play a large role in our future."

"I'm going up to the cottage," said Grandma. "I'll see you when I get back."

"Very well," said the King.

Chapter Fifty Nine

The sun was shining when Grandma came out of the Willow tree.
"Another beautiful day," she thought.

She walked towards the bridge, and noticed Elizabeth just around the corner with her back resting up against the trunk of the Willow tree.

Elizabeth turned and looked at her.

"She looks so much like her mother," thought Grandma.

"You will need to come into the house soon," she said.

"I know," answered Elizabeth.

"There is a lot still to get done, Elizabeth."

"I just want to watch the river for a while," said Elizabeth.

Grandma turned, and stepped over the bridge. She crossed over the river, and looked back at Elizabeth before going through the gate. "Don't be too long out here," she called.

"I'll be there in just a minute," Elizabeth shouted back.

"I'll make us a cup of tea," Grandma shouted, as she turned towards the path to the back of the cottage.

"It won't hurt to let her stay there for just a while," thought Grandma. "She will soon face a long and dangerous journey. I just hope she's strong enough."

Grandma stepped through the back door, and into the kitchen. She made her way down the hall to her bedroom. She moved the bed and opened the secret door, as she had done several times these past few days.

She picked out some additional books that King Morvand had instructed Elizabeth to read, before she began her trip to Avebury.

"Elizabeth won't have much time to take in so much information," thought Grandma, "but she's a bright girl. She should be able to study and learn quickly."

Grandma went back into her bedroom and closed the door, once again concealing the room. She returned to the kitchen, put the books on the table and made a pot of tea.

While the water was on the boil, she thumbed through a couple of the books. Some of them had been opened not long ago, when Audrey had been studying them. There were still a couple of them, Audrey not gotten around to reading yet.

As memories flooded back into Grandma Rose's mind, her eyes filled with tears.

"I mustn't dwell," she said to herself. "Too much to do."

Grandma opened a book with the title 'Wings and Fire'. Elizabeth's mother had not reached this stage of her training when she died. This would have been the very last thing that would have been done and the book would have been studied extensively.

Another of the books was an Atlas. Only the guardian of the Grymlons, who made the journey to Avebury, would need to study these two books.

Grandma wiped the dust off the Atlas and opened it. The maps had been drawn by hand and were hundreds of years old. Some of the writings in the book were Elvish and some were in English.

Both Grandma Rose and Elizabeth's mother could read Elvish. It was part of their training.

"I'll help her through the bits she can't read," thought Grandma. "Elizabeth had been able to read 'The Taminatin' as though she had been reading Elvish all her life. So she may be able to read these books without much effort. I'm not going to ponder too much on that incident either! I'll think about that and what the future may hold, when I see Elizabeth safely back from her journey."

Grandma placed the book on top of the others, made tea, and sat down to drink it.

She was thumbing through one of the books when she heard a noise coming from above.

"What was that? There is nothing up there but old furniture and boxes of stuff, unused in many a year… There it is again!"

Grandma looked up at the ceiling, trying to sense where the sound was coming from.

"Rats, it must be rats. I'll go up and have a look. I might have to call an exterminator."

Grandma picked up a torch that was on the kitchen counter and walked into the hallway. She pulled down the folding ladder from the ceiling and climbed up into the attic.

She stepped through the darkness towards a string hanging from the light bulb.

"There it is again! That scratching sound," she thought.

She pulled the string, but the light didn't turn on. She tried again, still darkness. "The light bulb must have blown."

Grandma slowly moved around in a circle, pointing the torch into the darkness as she went. She stopped suddenly, moving the torch quickly back to the corner… nothing.

She was about to walk back to the opening when someone grabbed her from behind. She tried to scream, but something damp and cold closed over her mouth. Grandma felt and heard nothing more.

Chapter Sixty

The Ogre was strong. It picked up Grandma as though she were a child. It carried her down through the opening of the attic and out of the back door, then skirted around the edge of the garden to the Beech tree in the corner. It disappeared with Grandma, unconscious and hanging limply over its shoulder.

Chapter Sixty One

Elizabeth sat looking out onto the water. It shimmered and danced in the sunlight. She glanced over to the cottage.

"It's so beautiful," she thought.

An unexpected bolt of sadness shot through her.

"I miss you mummy!" she thought, fighting back tears.

She looked up at the Willow tree's branches.

"There used to be an old tyre attached to a long piece of rope hanging from that tree. I wonder when Gran cut it down?"

Elizabeth could see her brother Jesse, his legs moving backwards and forwards to keep the tyre moving. She could see him as clear as day, even hear him.

It was hot and he was wearing only a pair of swimming shorts.

"Wheeeee! Elizabeth, look at me!" he shouted to her, then singing. "I'm the king of the castle."

Unable to hold back the tears any longer, she began to cry, sobbing bitter tears for her Jesse. After a minute or two she wiped her eyes, stood and crossed the bridge.

As Elizabeth neared the house, she felt a sudden dread. Fear, like a hot poker, shot through her body.

"Something's wrong!"

She began to jog along the pathway to the house.

The back door of the cottage was open slightly when she reached it.

"Gran?" she called, as she entered the back of the house.

The kitchen table had been pushed aside. A saucer, with its cup lying sideways rested on the edge of the table. The teapot was on its side, dripping tea onto the kitchen floor. The newly dusted Atlas sat open on the table.

"GRAN, WHERE ARE YOU?" Elizabeth shouted, knowing as she called out, that she would get no answer.

She ran into the hall, and stopped when she saw the attic steps pulled down.

"I must try to stay calm," she thought. "If I panic, I won't be able to think straight. I must find out what happened here!"

She stepped up into the attic with her heart in her mouth. As she peered into the darkness, she began to sweat. Finding nothing, she went back down the steps and closed the opening.

Elizabeth looked into the bedrooms, the living room, the dining room, then back to the kitchen.

Under the kitchen table she noticed a small brown pouch. She picked it up and turned it over in her hands. A faint smell wafted to her nostrils. She sniffed the pouch, and immediately felt dizzy. She found a plastic bag and sealed the pouch into it.

Elizabeth washed her hands and ran to her bedroom. She changed into a pair of jeans and a tank top, covered by a sweater.

Hurrying back through the house, she grabbed the bag with the smelly pouch. She picked up the books she was supposed to study, closing and locking the back door on her way out.

She was on her way to the Willow tree when she suddenly changed direction and headed for the Beech tree. "If you can hear me," she said, gently touching the bark of the tree. "You had better hope I never find a way in."

Elizabeth stepped back onto the path. Anger welled up inside of her, and as she passed the garden seat, she smacked it with her fist. The wooden seat shook.

"That won't get your grandma back," a voice said, softly.

Elizabeth stopped.

"If that voice came from an elviron it will surely die, and very slowly," she thought.

"Where are you? Come out from where ever you are and show yourself! I don't have time for games!"

Charlie the cat came out from under the garden seat and looked up at her.

"Well, don't get mad at me. I didn't take your grandma!" the little cat said, tilting her head to one side.

Elizabeth rolled her eyes. "When did you learn to talk? No, wait! Let me guess. You have always been able to talk, right?"

Charlie hung her head, looking up at Elizabeth with a guilty expression cats aren't supposed to have.

"Well, yes," she answered. "I was sent here when your mother and father died as company for you. King Morvand thought you may need something to comfort you. We cats are really good at that sort of thing."

Elizabeth sat on the garden seat and looked down at the little cat.

"You arrived just after the accident. You haven't left my side ever since. Can all cats talk in the Elven Realm?"

"No," replied Charlie.

"How about dogs?" Elizabeth asked.

"No," Charlie replied again.

"Then how come you can talk?"

"I was raised by Vandrayven," answered Charlie. "He charmed me when I was a kitten, so that he would have a companion he could talk to."

"He gave you up, so that you could be with me?" said Elizabeth.

"No. I go wherever I choose," said Charlie. "I was asked if I would like to come here. So I volunteered. I was not forced to go anywhere. Besides, I never intended to stay this long."

"Why did you?" asked Elizabeth.

"Just as I was thinking about leaving and going home, things started to get... well... interesting. So I decided to stay a little bit longer."

"Did you see who took my grandmother?" asked Elizabeth.

"Yes, it was an Ogre," said Charlie.

"Ogre's don't exist," Elizabeth said, irritated at her answer.

"You are spending your time with elves and you are having a conversation with a cat, but there are no such things as Ogres?"

Elizabeth smiled at Charlie's comment.

"Where did the Ogre come from?" she asked.

"Some Ogre's are servants to the elviron. Nasty things. They like to eat cats. That's why I was hiding under the seat.

"Why would they take my grandma? I'm the one they want," asked Elizabeth.

"You have a quest," replied Charlie. "They want the Grymlons. You give them the Grymlons. I assume they will tell you that they will return your grandma. Of course, they won't. They will only keep her alive until she is of no use to them anymore."

"How do they know that I am the one?" asked Elizabeth.

"They killed your family. You are the next female in line for the job," Charlie replied, immediately regretting her answer.

Elizabeth felt her arms go numb. "They... what? Did my Gran and King Morvand know the elviron killed my parents and my brother?"

Charlie sat down, she looked towards the Beech tree, avoiding Elizabeth's gaze.

"Yes," she replied.

"They knew all the time, but they didn't tell me?

"Yes," said Charlie. "The elviron knew you would be inexperienced in the elven ways. They knew that even if you tried to replace your mother, the chances were that your training would be inadequate. I think they have taken your grandmother so that it would cause you even more stress. This would make it easier for you to give them what they want. They think you are weak."

Elizabeth stood. She looked towards the Willow tree, then glanced down at Charlie, and started to walk along the garden path to the tree.

She turned. "Are you coming?"

Charlie caught up to her, following her through the gate and over the bridge. As the tree opened and they went inside, Elizabeth turned to the cat.

"What is your real name?" she asked.

"Vandrayven calls me Tut-tut," Charlie replied.

"Why?" asked Elizabeth.

"Because it took me a little while to realize where I had to go, you know, when I was a kitten," Charlie replied, shyly. "I didn't know that I had to use the litter box. So every time he cleaned up my mess, he would wiggle his finger at me and say "tut-tut, you naughty little cat, and it stuck. I like Charlie much better, so please keep calling me that."

Elizabeth laughed. She bent down and tickled her under the chin. Charlie purred, loudly.

"If you like the name Charlie, then Charlie it shall be," she said.

When the carriage reached the castle, Charlie jumped out and turned to Elizabeth.

"I'm going to go down and visit Vandrayven," she said.

"Okay, see you later," said Elizabeth, as she watched Charlie scamper off.

"And I need to find the king," she thought

Chapter Sixty Two

The conversation stopped when Elizabeth entered the room. All of them turned at once and looked at her.

"Why are you all looking at me like that?" asked Elizabeth.

It was Gideon who spoke first.

"Elizabeth, we have a note here from King Kalidryd. He says that he has your grandma and will not give her up unless we hand over the Grymlons."

"They took her while I was outside by the river. They kidnapped her from the cottage. I found this on the kitchen floor."

Elizabeth threw the plastic bag onto the table. Gideon picked it up and opened it. He sniffed the pouch, turning his head away, quickly.

"What is it?" asked Zoe.

"Potrious Root," replied Gideon. "Grandma Rose was drugged."

"An Ogre took her," said Elizabeth.

"How do you know that?" asked Bindyl.

"I have just discovered that I have been living with a talking cat. Charlie saw the Ogre run off with my Gran."

"Did you know that Charlie could talk, Gideon?" Elizabeth asked.

"Yes, she has been my lookout for quite some time now."

"Why didn't you tell me?"

"I am sorry, Elizabeth. It didn't seem important at the time. Besides, everything happened so fast I forgot about Charlie."

"What are we going to do?" asked Elizabeth.

King Morvand put his arm around her. "We cannot give up the Grymlons. If we do, the elviron will find a way to renew them and all will be lost."

"We will get your grandma back, Elizabeth," Gideon said.

"I'm glad that you brought the books with you," said the King, "Even if we were to give them the Grymlons, they would still kill your grandmother. She will be kept alive as long as we have them. Take them to Avebury, Elizabeth. Make them powerful again. You must study the rest of the books, especially the Atlas. I will go through it today and mark the pages you need to research. Please come by for it this evening. Try to study it tonight and tomorrow. Memorize as much as you can."

"I feel so torn," thought Elizabeth. "Time is running out." She looked around at the others in the room.

"We have to leave by tomorrow at the latest," she thought. "I have to trust the elves to save Grandma. Should I confront the king about my family? No, I think I'll wait, wait and see what happens. I've waited this long. A few more days won't hurt. There will be plenty of time to ask questions when I get back."

"Who goes with me to Avebury?" asked Elizabeth.

"We all go," said Gideon, "With your approval of course?"

"We'll leave tomorrow night. We'll sleep by day, like before," she said.

Gideon and Bindyl looked at each other and smiled. Gideon put his arm around Bindyl's shoulders and they both looked at Elizabeth.

"What do you think, Bindyl? Should we introduce Elizabeth to our new friend?" said Gideon.

"I think now would be an excellent time to do that," replied Bindyl.

"Bindyl made a friend while he was in Distardrian. Would you like to meet him, Elizabeth?" asked Gideon.

"What kind of a friend would anyone possibly want to make in that dreadful place?" she thought, looking at the two of them.

She smiled. "Okay,"

Gideon bowed dramatically towards the door that led to the gardens at the back of the castle's private rooms. It was getting dark, and harder to see into the huge expanse of pathways, greenery and flowers. The pathways were long and fairly narrow. They stretched out for about a quarter of a mile in both directions.

Once everyone was outside, Bindyl got down on his knees and said something to the ground.

"What are you doing?" Elizabeth asked.

"You'll see," said Bindyl, looking up at the darkening sky.

Elizabeth looked up into the coming night. What she saw took her breath away.

"It's a flying horse," she thought. "He's galloping through the air!"

The horse landed next to Bindyl and put his head down. He said something and Bindyl answered. The horse approached Elizabeth, who was standing completely still with her mouth open.

"Good evening. My name is Pennarius and I am honoured to meet you."

"He is the most handsome stallion I have ever seen. He must be at least eighteen hands high!" Elizabeth thought.

She watched wide eyed as he shook his black head, flowing out his golden mane, and saw a set of small wings just behind each hoof.

Bindyl stepped up beside Elizabeth and touched her elbow.

"Close your mouth," he said.

Elizabeth stared. "What?" she whispered, absent mindedly.

"Elizabeth, close your mouth!" Bindyl said, louder this time.

Elizabeth was suddenly aware that she was staring at this magnificent creature.

"I'm so sorry. Where are my manners! I am very pleased to meet you too. What are you?" she asked.

"I am a Pennar," said Pennarius.

"You are... well, you are... beautiful," she said.

"Thank you," said Pennarius.

Bindyl whispered something in Pennarius ear. The horse let out what resembled a low laugh and turned to Elizabeth.

"A laughing horse! Now I'm sure I'm dreaming," she thought.

"Could I interest you in perhaps having a ride on my back?" he asked.

"Yes! Oh, yes please," she answered.

Bindyl held his hand up and motioned for one of the servants to come forward. The elf servant handed him a bridle.

"This has all been planned," thought Elizabeth.

Bindyl put the bridle onto Pennarius' head. It was crafted from hand tooled black leather, and was covered with gold leaf markings to match the stallion's mane and tail.

Pennarius knelt down. Elizabeth reached her leg over him and sat on his back. He stood, gently rising into the air. He hovered just a few feet off the ground, until Elizabeth could get the feel of the weightlessness.

She looked down and saw King Morvand, waving. "Don't be too long, Elizabeth. There is much to do before night comes tomorrow."

'So he has met this magnificent creature too," she thought, waving back.

"Are you ready?" asked Pennarius.

"Yes!"

Up and up they went, until the lights of the castle and the town were tiny white specks below them.

"I used to love to ride a normal horse before my wheelchair, but this... there are no words for this!" she thought, as the hairs on her arms stood up.

"Where do you come from Pennarius? Do you live in Distardrian?" asked Elizabeth.

"No." he answered, "I live in the badlands with my herd."

"There are more of you?" she asked.

"There are many of us. I have many sons and daughters, aunts, uncles, brothers and sisters," he replied.

"Do you think if I make it back from our journey, that perhaps I could meet them?" she asked.

"Elizabeth, I would be honoured to introduce you to them. We will plan on it."

Pennarius made a wide turn, heading back to the castle.

Just for a second, Elizabeth thought, "Ride off into the darkness! Take me far, far away and drop me somewhere. Make me disappear so I don't have to go on this journey tomorrow."

When they landed, Gideon and Bindyl were waiting for them. Zoe had gone home to get some rest. Tomorrow would be a day of preparation, and tomorrow night they would be on their way.

"Thank you," said Elizabeth.

"It has been my pleasure," said Pennarius.

Bindyl removed the bridle. He stepped back as Pennarius shook his head, happy to be free of the leather.

"Stay safe Pennarius," said Bindyl.

"You, too, my friend," replied Pennarius.

Then he was off. With his front legs up, he jumped, as though running on air. The fabulous creature disappeared into the darkness of the night.

"Well that was amazing. Is there anything else I need to know about?" she said to Bindyl.

He smiled. "No. I think that's it for now."

"I must say good night. I have a lot of studying to do, and I don't know if I'll be able to concentrate now." said Elizabeth.

Gideon escorted her to King Morvand's rooms to get 'The Book of Journeys' and the Atlas.

"I'll see you in the morning, Elizabeth," Gideon told her, walking down the hall to his rooms.

"I'll study tonight," she thought, heading to her own rooms. "Then I'll rest for the journey."

***

Down in the darkest dungeon, in the bowels of the castle at Distardrian, Grandma Rose lay on a dirty stone floor. She was grimy, cold and felt very afraid.

Exhaustion had finally overcome her. But before she fell asleep, she thought of Elizabeth.

"I wonder if she will be lucky enough to somehow discover the traitor, who has infiltrated their valiant little group. If not, soon they will be leaving, and they will be taking with them a conspirator who could doom them all."

Chapter Sixty Three

Elizabeth sat at her desk. She ordered supper and began to study.

The book told of a druid who comes to guide the guardian when they reach the badlands.

"Gran told me that mum had taken months to study the book from cover to cover, and that I'll be the youngest guardian of the Grymlons ever to attempt to take them and renew them," Elizabeth thought.

She studied into the night and finally fell asleep with her head on a book.

Elizabeth dreamt she was walking through a forest and Charlie was with her, but Charlie was no longer a cat, she was a mountain lion.

In front of Charlie was a small dragon with scales that shone gold and silver in the moonlight, lighting the way. There was also someone else with them, a tall man in white robes.

Suddenly, Charlie turned and growled at something, then pounced!

Elizabeth woke with a start.

A knock at her door pulled her mind to the surface, dimming her dream.

"Who is it?"

"King Morvand has requested that you join him for breakfast in the library," the servant said through the door.

Elizabeth wiped the sleep from her eyes. She opened the door to the servant standing in front of her, waiting for an answer.

"What time is it?"

"7:00 a.m. Can I get you anything, Miss?" asked the servant.

"No thank you. Please tell the king that I will be down in a few minutes."

"Very well, my lady," said the servant.

He turned and walked down the hallway as she closed the door.

"I must have studied myself to sleep," she said, yawning.

She headed for the bathroom to get ready for the day.

***

Bathed, dressed and still trying to shake the dream, Elizabeth went down to the library.

Gideon was talking with his father when she arrived.

"Good morning, Elizabeth," they said, at the same time.

Elizabeth returned the greeting.

As she sat down, a servant approached her.

"Will you be eating breakfast this morning my lady," he asked.

"Yes please," she replied.

"Did you manage to read the book?" Gideon asked.

"Yes, but it doesn't really explain what happens to the Grymlons."

"We are not sure either, but we think if they all go up for more than a few days, they lose their power," said King Morvand.

"I'm curious," said Elizabeth. "Who took up the elviron's Grymlons? It just says that the second set of Grymlons were stolen and taken up to the Human Realm, where they vanished. It doesn't say who took them up there or why."

King Morvand and Gideon exchanged glances.

"We will discuss the matter when you return home," said the King. "You will probably have a lot of questions when you get back. I promise you I will try to answer all of them. Did you read 'The Book of Journeys'?"

"I did," she said.

"There will be references to certain things and places in there that you and Gideon will need to see," said the King, sitting down beside Gideon. "You will all want to plan a safe route."

Elizabeth left to get the book.

After she had left the room, Gideon turned to his father.

"When are you going to tell Elizabeth the truth about the other set of Grymlons, father?"

"She is already overloaded with information because of the situation," King Morvand replied. "She may get captured by the elviron, so the less she knows the better. Besides, 'The Book of Elven Prophecy' says that the chosen one will find a solution to the problems of the elves. If Elizabeth is the one, we will teach her everything we can, when she gets back."

"What if she gets killed out there?" said Gideon.

"Then she is not the one we have all been waiting for and it won't matter will it? But let's not speak of this now. We will talk again when you come home."

Servants entered the room with trays of food for breakfast. They put food out the on tables that had been laid out with plates and cutlery.

Zoe and Bindyl came in. They both bowed to the king. He nodded in acknowledgment.

"Would you two like some breakfast?" he asked them.

"I have already eaten, but a cup of elven tea would be nice," said Zoe.

"I'm starving," said Bindyl, heading towards the breakfast foods.

Elizabeth returned with the book. She sat with Gideon and studied the maps within it, while Bindyl ate.

After a while, Gideon helped himself to some toast and honey. He noticed a servant, he had not seen before. He took his plate and joined the king.

"Is that a new servant father? I haven't seen him around the castle before."

King Morvand turned to look where Gideon was pointing. "Yes, his name is Palik. When we had to let Brondly go because of his a… well never mind about that, mustn't speak ill of the dead. We promoted one of the guards to Brondly's old position. Then we promoted one of the servants to a guard. So we had to replace the servant. This one comes highly recommended."

Gideon could not stop looking at Palik. "He's just a little too close to us. It's as though he's trying to hear our conversation".

After Gideon and the others had finished with breakfast, Gideon told all the servants that they were dismissed. The servants picked up the breakfast things and cleared the table.

Palik approached the king.

"Would you like me to stay, Your Majesty. In case anyone needs something?"

"No, no," said the King. "You can leave with the rest of the staff."

The servants filed out of the room and Bindyl closed the doors.

"Father, don't you find it a bit strange that a servant would want to try and stay in the room?"

The king shook his head. "I think he was just trying to make a good impression because he is new. Stop being so suspicious, Gideon."

It took three hours to discuss most of what would be required on their journey.

By early afternoon everything had been arranged.

"I suggest that you all go to your rooms and get some rest. We will meet back here at 10:00 p.m.," said the King.

Chapter Sixty Four

Elizabeth felt rested in the morning. I sleep much better down here," she thought, stretching. "I had the same odd dream again about Charlie and the dragon."

She turned on her side to see Charlie on the floor, looking up at her.

"What do you want, Charlie? How did you get in here?"

"I jumped in through the window over there. It was open," Charlie replied.

"We are three floors up! How did you get up here?"

"I'm a cat. I like to climb. As to why I am here, Vandrayven wants me to go with you. There is a note in my collar. Please take it. It's digging into my neck."

Charlie jumped onto the bed, and Elizabeth removed a piece of paper that was wrapped around her collar.

It read.

"Elizabeth, please take Charlie with you on your journey. I know she is small, but she can be mighty. I bestowed her with some talents when she was a kitten that may be useful to you, if you get into any danger. Please try to be safe and if possible, return her to me unharmed. Good luck, Vandrayven."

"It says here that you have some talents. What are they?" asked Elizabeth.

Charlie moved closer, until she was sitting in front of Elizabeth. In the blink of an eye, the little cat turned into a mountain lion. Before Elizabeth could do or say anything, she changed back.

"Well, what do you think? Do I make a handsome mountain lion?" asked Charlie.

Elizabeth tried to sound calm. "Very nice, but do you have the heart of a lion?"

"Yes," Charlie replied.

"Then you shall come with us young 'Charlie the brave'."

"You had better get dressed, Elizabeth. They will all be waiting for us," Charlie said.

"You run along. I'll meet you with the others in a few minutes," said Elizabeth. "Oh, and you had better talk to Gideon about food and water for you. We hadn't intended on taking any animals with us."

"It has already been arranged. Vandrayven took care of it while I was up here with you," said Charlie.

"Go Charlie, I will be there in a minute," she said, opening the door, so that the cat could leave.

Chapter Sixty Five

After supper, everyone went to the portrait room.

"If I could have your attention for just a moment," said Gideon. "We need to designate chores for everyone. Bindyl, you can look for food, Charlie can help you. She can sniff out berries and roots. Mind you, Charlie, you can hunt for yourself, but you are not to bring any live food into the camp. If you can't find fresh food, we have packed some for you."

"Zoe, you're a pretty good cook, so if you wouldn't mind putting together some of your famous impromptu meals.

Elizabeth, if you could do the dishes it would help. I will put together the food items and make sure we have enough. Is everyone agreeable to that?"

"How much food are we taking with us?" asked Zoe.

"We should have enough to get us there and back," replied Gideon, "but it wouldn't hurt to pick and replenish our supplies as we go."

"I've never washed dishes without soap before," said Elizabeth.

"I'll show you how," said Bindyl.

"Elizabeth. Let's go up and get the Grymlons," said the King.

King Morvand accompanied her up to the tower. She picked them off their resting place one by one. "Wow! I feel as though something is recharging my batteries," she thought, as she put them in the bag.

By the time they returned to the portrait room, Vandrayven had joined them.

"I came just in case any of you thought you might need something from me before you go," he said.

"I can't think of anything, unless you can transport us there with magic," said Gideon.

"I would if I could," said Vandrayven.

King Morvand went to the table with the supplies on it, to check just one more time that the group had all that they needed for their trip. Gideon joined his father and led him away from the table.

"Please tell mother that I love her. I will be back soon, and I promise to take care of Elizabeth."

King Morvand nodded, and embraced his only son.

"Remember, your mother and I love you very much," he said quietly into Gideon's ear.

Gideon nodded, unable to reply.

King Morvand put his arm around Elizabeth's shoulder.

"I will be investigating the disappearance of your grandmother. Do not stop on your way to try and find her. We will take care of that while you are gone. Please trust us to do this for you, Elizabeth. You must attend to the task set before you or we will all pay dearly."

"I trust you, your majesty," Elizabeth said.

Vandrayven, who was sat by the large chiselled stone fireplace, motioned with his long boney hand for Elizabeth to join him.

She took a seat opposite him. "I agree with your mother. I suspect when Verina was born, the elviron were trying to bring forth their own saviour for their realm," he said. "The book that gives information on the child who will be of two worlds, does not say which realm will produce him or her.

There had been a rumour of sorts some years ago, of the elviron king trying to produce a half human female heir, but we dismissed them."

"Take caution, Elizabeth. If the elviron think they may have produced the chosen one, she will have been trained for years in the ways of magic."

"There can't be two chosen ones can there?" Elizabeth asked.

"No," said Vandrayven, "only one. It may be you, but I could be wrong and it may be her. I am sorry Elizabeth, I wish I knew more."

"I think I can handle her," said Elizabeth. "I bested her once. I can do it again."

"She will be prepared for you next time," said Vandrayven.

"And I will be prepared for her," said Elizabeth.

Gideon touched her on the shoulder. "Time to go."

The four of them picked up their back-packs. By the time they reached the north side of the castle, it was dark.

"We need to be well into our journey by midnight," said Gideon.

King Morvand watched from a window in the royal quarters, as the group walked out of the castle, towards Distardrian. Only when they were tiny specs in the distance, did he turn with a heavy heart to join his queen.

Chapter Sixty Six

"We're almost there. Can I have some of that beer now?" asked Holmon.

"No! The king said we had to go straight to the castle. No dawdling. Princess Verina has arranged for someone to meet us, and I for one don't want to get on the wrong side of her! I said we would have a drink when we got there," said Prymm.

Holmon gave Prymm a little sideways dig in the ribs. "Aw, come on. A little sip won't hurt. We can almost see the castle from here."

"Oh, all right, but just a sip," said Prymm.

Holmon and Prymm continued on towards the castle, sipping their beer.

"Which way is north," Prymm slurred, after a while.

"How should I know? I followed you all the way here. Never would have known how to get here by myself," Holmon slurred, with a giggle.

"You're an idiot Holmon."

"Yeah, I know," said Holmon, laughing.

"I think it's this way. Yes, see? There's the castle," said Prymm, pointing to the towers ahead.

Prymm and Holmon held each other up until they reached the castle wall.

"I'm getting a bit sleepy. Think I'll take a little nap," slurred Holmon, leaning against the wall and sliding down it.

"Good idea," slurred Prymm, dropping to his knees and toppling over onto the grass.

Chapter Sixty Seven

Palik watched the group leave.

"I didn't get as much information as I wanted," he thought. "At least I know who is in the group. Now they have gone, I need to find my two escorts to take me to Distardrian."

Palik crept out of the castle and made it to the north wall without being seen.

"Where could they be? They should have arrived by now. I'll keep walking along the wall. If they are here, I'll bump into them eventually."

The walls of the castle at Kimadrian spanned about four square miles. Unfortunately, Palik turned in the wrong direction. By the time he found the guards, Elizabeth and the others were long gone.

"What are you two doing here?" asked Palik. "The girl and the elves have been gone for hours. They're probably at the Distardrian border by now!"

"We were supposed to meet you here," said Holmon.

"Yeah, you're late," said Prymm.

"You were supposed to meet me at the north side of the castle," said Palik.

"Yeah, so?" said Prymm.

"This is the west side of the castle you idiots."

"Really?" asked Holmon, stifling a laugh.

"Oy! Don't be calling us idiots. We just have a bad sense of direction that's all, don't we Holmon."

"Yeah," said Holmon.

They both began to giggle uncontrollably.

"You're drunk!" said Palik.

"So what?" Prymm said, between giggles.

"If we don't leave now and we get caught. You won't be laughing then," said Palik.

He pulled both of them to their feet and dragged them along. He hoped he could get them away from the castle before anyone saw them.

Chapter Sixty Eight

It was time to stop and rest until nightfall. Bindyl built a fire. Zoe prepared a meal while Gideon stood guard.

When the meal was cooked, Elizabeth took a plate of food to Gideon. She took her own plate and sat with him to eat.

Bindyl sat down by the fire and Zoe sat down beside him with food for them both.

She handed Bindyl his plate.

"Thank you," he said, taking it.

"It's not castle food, but I think it's edible," she said.

Bindyl took a bite. "Mmm, it's rather nice. I knew it was the right decision to make you the cook."

Zoe took a bite of her food and looked over at Gideon and Elizabeth. "Do you think she is who they say she is?"

"I don't know. She looks like a normal human girl to me," replied Bindyl.

"She is sort of pretty, but nothing special," said Zoe, watching Elizabeth eat. "There doesn't seem to be anything spectacular about her. You know, like you would expect from someone who is supposed to be chosen."

"Are you jealous of her?" asked Bindyl.

"Certainly not!" replied Zoe.

"Then why do you stare at her so much? Are you afraid that she might steal Gideon from you?"

"Gideon is betrothed to me. Even if he fell madly in love with her, he wouldn't be able to do anything about it," Zoe replied.

"I know you don't love him," said Bindyl.

"How do you know that?" asked Zoe.

"I know," said Bindyl.

They locked eyes. For an instant they looked into each other's soul. Then the moment was gone. They turned away from each other at the same time. Bindyl got up and walked to the edge of the camp. Zoe brushed off her plate and put it in her backpack.

When everyone had eaten, Elizabeth cleaned up while the others made sure that they left no trace of being there.

They each took turns to go on watch for two hours at a time until night set in.

When it was dark enough, they continued on their journey. A few hours later, they passed the castle at Distardrian.

Chapter Sixty Nine

King Kalidryd and his daughter, Verina were in a heated discussion, completely unaware there was a party of three elves, a cat and a human, passing within half a mile of them.

"I want to go now. I want to be there when they get to the Obelisk," said Verina, pacing back and forth.

"Have a little patience," said the King. You should not run without thought into a situation. I don't think they have left yet. We sent two guards to wait outside of the castle, and have a spy inside who will meet up with them.

As soon as the girl and the elf prince leave, they are to follow them. I have arranged for the guards to send word to me when they get close to us. I was very specific. I told the two of them to wait at the north end of the castle. When they arrive, they will be met by your informant who is working inside. The informant will let the guards know when the girl is on her way here. Wait one more night. If I do not hear from the guards by tomorrow morning, you must be on your way."

"Let me kill the old witch down in the dungeon before I go," Verina sneered.

"Verina," King Kalidryd sighed, "she is the only thing we have to bargain with to get the orbs. Your attempt to steal the Grymlons has failed, but the girl is weak. With all that she has been through, she just may have had enough by now. Perhaps she will give up the orbs for her grandmother. The woman is all that she has left. You have killed the rest of her family.

After we get the orbs, you can do what you like with the girl and her grandmother. Until then, I want the old woman alive."

"What if the rumours are true?" asked Verina in a whiny voice. "What if the girl is the chosen one? You said yourself that she was very powerful. She put you to sleep didn't she? She got the necklace from you didn't she? We both know that the necklace was probably one of the Grymlons."

"The magician at Kimadrian is very strong. He may have given her enough power to get into my bedchamber that night," King Kalidryd said.

"But what if she is?" asked Verina. "I will be the one who has to try to get the Grymlons from her. What if she is the one of the prophecy and not me? The human girl was only supposed to be… well… human. We can't both renew the Grymlons. This could get a little more dangerous than I anticipated."

"You are very powerful," said King Kalidryd. "Use your knowledge. Use the teachings that you have studied all these years. This girl should be nothing to worry about."

He turned and left the room.

"I want those Grymlons and she is going to get them for me!" thought the King, walking along the corridor.

"If it costs her life, well, I have other daughters and they don't look quite so… human."

Around the time the king was on his way up to his bedchamber, Elizabeth and the others travelled on into the night, towards the badlands.

They continued on into the daylight hours. The closer they got to the badlands, the lighter it became. The elviron magician's influence on the difference between light and darkness began to fade.

"According to 'The Book of Journeys', there is not much activity around here," said Gideon. "If everyone is agreeable, I think we should keep going. If we walk during the daylight, it will cut some time off our journey."

Everyone agreed.

They continued for three more hours and finally stopped. All of them were exhausted, and decided to wait until dark before continuing with their journey.

"I'm going to look for some berries and try to find some water," said Bindyl.

Gideon made a fire and Zoe began preparing a meal for everyone.

"It's a bit strange around here," Zoe said, looking across the wide expanse ahead of them.

"Not much is known about this area," said Gideon. "No one wants to come this far, not even the elviron."

After their meal, Gideon settled down for the first watch of the day. The rest of the group put down blankets to rest.

Elizabeth tried to sleep. "I can't rest. I miss you, Gran," she thought.

She imagined Grandma Rose in the dungeons where she and Gideon had found Zoe and shuddered.

"I promise you, Gran. If anything happens to you, Verina will pay along with wall the other elviron," Elizabeth thought, as she drifted into a light sleep.

Gideon sat on a rock, looking out towards the border of the badlands.

"I miss my warm comfortable bed. And I miss Cook's Fennis Root Pie," he whispered into the night.

He turned, jumping to his feet as he heard a noise behind him, instinctively drawing his dagger.

"Hey! It's just me!" Zoe stood still with her hands up and her palms facing outward. "See? No weapons."

"Sorry. You should have said something. I could have hurt you," said Gideon.

He turned away from Zoe, sitting down again. She sat down beside him.

"What do you think is out there waiting for us, Gideon?" she asked.

"I don't know, but I don't think it is going to be easy. I wish we had more help," he replied.

"How long do you think it will take to get there?" she said.

"A day or two. If there are no unforeseen setbacks waiting for us."

"I want you to know that if we get out of this all in one piece. I am going to ask my parents to release you from the betrothal," Zoe said, looking into Gideon's eyes. "I don't think they will refuse. They both know that there is no love lost between you and I."

"I'm not good enough for you now?" he said with a smile.

"Gideon, don't be a brat, I know you don't care for me. Besides, I think I might have fallen for someone else," she said, looking down at her feet so she wouldn't have to look at him.

"That person wouldn't be Bindyl would it?" asked Gideon.

Zoe looked surprised. "How did you know?"

"I've seen the way you look at each other. You do know he feels the same way about you, don't you?" said Gideon.

Zoe grinned. "I was hoping he would."

"Well, he does," said Gideon.

"Did he say something to you?" Zoe prodded.

"No, but he looks at you when he thinks no one else is looking, and I have never seen that look in his eyes before. He wouldn't say anything, he is too honourable. I wouldn't stand in your way if I was sure that you would both be happy. Oh, and thanks for releasing me from our agreement. Although, I somehow don't think we would have wed. Honestly now, do you?"

Zoe laughed. "No, I don't think we would have."

She stood and brushed the dust off her pants.

"I'll be back in an hour. It's my turn for watch, after you," she said, turning to leave.

Gideon turned his eyes back to the badlands, and shiver ran through him.

"I feel as though someone just walked over my grave," he thought, wrapping his arms around himself.

Bindyl came to see him near the end of his watch.

"How goes it?" he asked.

"All is peaceful, but I had a visitor a little while ago."

"Someone we know I hope," Bindyl joked.

"It was Zoe," replied Gideon.

"Oh, I'm sorry. Was it very bad?" said Bindyl.

"Actually, we talked about you."

"Really? How come I was the topic of conversation?" asked Bindyl.

"Zoe is in love with you, Bindyl."

"Oh," was all Bindyl could muster, feeling his face flush.

"She has asked to be released from our betrothal, if her parents agree."

"Oh?" Bindyl said again.

"She was sort of hoping you felt the same way about her, as she feels about you."

"How would you feel, if I felt that way?" asked Bindyl.

"I would be delighted. I would also be relieved that she was no longer bound to me."

"I have loved her all my life," Bindyl admitted. "I never said anything because she became betrothed to you before I could make my feelings known."

Gideon turned to his friend and put his arm around him.

"Why don't you go and find her. Tell her you have spoken to me and tell her how you feel."

Bindyl looked into the eyes of his lifelong friend. "Are you sure?"

Gideon returned his gaze. "Absolutely."

Bindyl stood. "Thank you."

Gideon chuckled. "Don't thank me, my friend. I don't envy you. She can be a real pain."

"I know, but I love her anyway," said Bindyl, "I will see you in a little while."

Gideon nodded and watched Bindyl walk away.

"I hope it works out for them," he thought, turning back to the badlands once again, waiting for his watch to be over.

Chapter Seventy

They were back on their journey by dusk, stepping farther into the badlands and away from Distardrian.

Elizabeth looked behind her.

"This is the strangest place I've ever seen," she commented to Zoe. "Distardrian looks inviting off to what we're walking into."

Zoe glanced around. "I couldn't agree more."

Elizabeth noticed that the land was mostly sand and dirt, but there were strange spiral mounds that came up from the earth every now and then. It looked as if something had surfaced here and there from below.

She quickly turned her head towards the rest of the group and tried not to think of what may be out there, watching them.

A couple of miles into the badlands, the terrain changed slightly and the temperature dropped. There were now patches of trees here and there. The horizon, instead of being completely flat, became somewhat hilly.

"Its getting dark, and I'm getting cold," said Zoe.

"Me too," said Elizabeth.

"Let's stop and put on some warmer clothes," said Gideon.

They pulled jackets and hats out of their backpacks and put them on. They were about to continue their journey, when suddenly Charlie became alert, circling around them.

Elizabeth touched Gideon's arm and nodded towards Charlie. He looked up and frowned. "What's wrong, Charlie?"

"Can you smell something?" Charlie asked.

"Yes," said Gideon, "like burning."

Bindyl sniffed the air. "I can smell it too."

Charlie backed up, her hackles rose and she hissed. In an instant, she became a mountain lion. Her hiss turned into a throaty growl as she peered into the darkness.

Bindyl looked up and immediately drew his dagger. Gideon pulled his dagger almost at the same time. He motioned to Elizabeth and Zoe to stand either side of them, facing out.

Gideon grabbed a bottle of blue coloured sand from his pack.

"Vandrayven warned me about some of the things in this region. He said this stuff would protect us."

Gideon poured out the contents of the bottle, making a hasty circle with the dust in the dirt. He motioned for everyone to step into it. They backed up until they were all inside the circle facing outward, shoulder to shoulder.

"Be alert everyone! And don't step over the dust," he said.

Something caught Zoe's eye to the side of her. She looked down, and saw a small wisp of white smoke spiral upwards from the ground. Zoe looked to either side of her, but the others did not seem to notice it. The smoke moved upward and outward, becoming denser as it grew. Out of the smoke walked her little brother, Tevyn! He came towards her, crying, with his little hands outstretched.

"Help me!" he pleaded.

Zoe took moved towards him. She stepped out of the ring of before the others could stop her.

Something wrapped around her ankle and pulled her to the ground. She was being dragged into the night by an unseen entity. Bindyl grabbed one of her arms and Gideon grabbed the other. But something was pulling her with so much force, they had to let go or Zoe's arms would have come out of their sockets.

"Help me!" Zoe screamed.

Bindyl started out of the circle.

"Zoe!" he shouted, but Gideon pulled him back.

She disappeared under the ground. It was as though the earth had just opened up and swallowed her. Bindyl got down on his knees. He began frantically digging with his bare hands.

Gideon and Elizabeth looked at each other, then at Bindyl. "This is useless," Elizabeth said, as she watched small white wisps of smoke twisting out of the ground. "Whatever it was that took Zoe is coming for us too."

"I can smell burning all around us," said Gideon.

"We have to try and get Zoe out of the ground!" said Bindyl.

Charlie was turning in circles, growling at the growing number of smoky twirls rising from the dirt.

They heard wings flapping from above. Gideon looked up.

Four pennars were hovering just above their heads. One of them was Pennarius. He dropped down lower, the other pennars followed.

"Quickly, each one of you get on our backs!" he shouted.

Charlie didn't need to be told twice. She pounced up on one of the pennars. The others did the same. Charlie barely had time to change back into a cat, before they were off into the night.

Bindyl looked back.

"We have deserted her," he shouted into the night.

The pennars took them to a wooded area. As they flew closer, Pennarius shouted to Bindyl who was on his back, "HOLD ON TIGHT, WE HAVE TO DROP DOWN AND MOVE FORWARD VERY QUICKLY!"

"OK!" Bindyl shouted back.

They dropped down then shot forward, as though they had been propelled from a cannon.

Bindyl held on as tightly as he could. He managed to look over his shoulder and saw Charlie hanging on by all fours. Her ears were pinned back so hard, it looked like someone had glued them to her head.

As the pennars sped along, Bindyl looked from side to side. He could see strange looking creatures with large claws, trying to strike at them as they flew. One of the creature's claws came so close he felt a breeze from the swipe as they flew past.

The pennars finally landed in a clearing. Everyone dismounted. As they did so, other pennars came out from the trees. They were followed by people with wings.

"Fairies!" Elizabeth said, as her pennar walked toward one of them.

The fairy put his hand up to the pennar as they came together. The pennar nuzzled the fairy affectionately.

Bindyl jumped down from the back of Pennarius. As he and Pennarius began walking towards the camp, Pennarius stopped him.

"Bindyl, your face is bleeding," he said.

Bindyl put his hand up to the right side of his face, it felt wet. "I felt something brush past my face when we dropped down into the forest. It looked like some sort of animal's claw."

"That was a draghorn," said Pennarius. "They are carnivores. They live in the forest and love to eat my kind. We do not use that route very often. But when we do, they are always waiting for us. You would have made a tasty meal. You were very lucky.

It looks like one of them almost got you. We must clean that wound for you, and do it quickly. Draghorns carry nasty bacteria in their claws."

When they reached the clearing, they were met by two fairies.

"Where are we?" asked Bindyl.

"This is the Province of Shanseen. It is one of the few green areas in the badlands. Most of the badlands is desert," Pennarius replied.

"Did anyone ever tell you that you look just like fairies?" Bindyl said, holding up his finger, as if to make a point.

He staggered slightly and giggled, then caught himself. Bindyl suddenly felt as though he had drank a little too much elven ale.

"That's because we are fairies," answered the young blond male, who had a surprisingly strong hold on his arm.

Bindyl went down to the ground as though he had been struck.

Pennarius stepped up beside him. The fairies lifted Bindyl onto his back.

"Quickly, we must clean his wound. He is already showing signs of infection," said Pennarius.

They hurried into the heart of the camp.

Charlie jumped down from the pennar who had carried her. "Thank you for rescuing us. What's your name?" Charlie said.

"My name is Sirarry. You can talk?"

"Why yes," answered Charlie.

The pennar shook his head. His golden mane waved about his neck.

"A cat that can talk! Now I've heard it all," Sirarry said, as he headed towards the camp.

"Oh, and talking horses are normal?" Charlie smirked, mimicking him as she followed behind him.

Sirarry turned. "Watch your tongue young feline, or the draghorns might take it from you!" he said, continuing into the camp.

"What's a draghorn?" she asked.

Sirarry ignored her question.

Charlie ran past him and went to look for the others. She slowed to a walk when she entered a clearing and saw dozens of pennars.

Mingling among them were just as many fairies, some flying, others walking in between the pennar. The fairies were coming and going among neat little cottages with thatched roofs. Attached to most of them were buildings, resembling a stable. Many of the fairies shared homes with the pennar.

"I miss my garden by the river. No benches to hide under around here," Charlie thought, as she entered the camp. "I'll go and find Elizabeth. She always makes me feel better."

Chapter Seventy One

"Thank you," Gideon said, jumping down from the pennar that had carried him.

"My name is Kedra," she said. "If you need me, ask one of the fairies. I'd be happy to help you if I can."

He looked around for the others, when he noticed Bindyl lying on the ground with the fairies doing something to him. He hurried over to them.

"What is wrong with him?" Gideon asked.

"He was struck by a draghorn," answered the blond male who had helped Bindyl as he fell.

He was trying to get Bindyl to swallow some green liquid.

"Were those the things that were striking out at us on the way here?" asked Gideon.

"Yes," answered the blond fairy.

"My father told me of wars between the elves and the draghorn. They were banished from Kimadrian hundreds of years ago. Is he going to be all right? He looks awfully pale."

"Yes. He will need to rest while the herbs work into his blood, but he should be fine in a few hours," the fairy answered.

Gideon knelt and took Bindyl's hand.

"That's a nasty scrape on the side of your face, my friend. I thought you had learned to duck a little better than that," said Gideon, trying to be cheerful.

Bindyl laughed, closed his eyes and passed out.

Gideon looked at the fairy. "Is this normal?"

"He will be fine," the fairy said. "The bacteria from a Draghorn's claws impairs brain and muscle function. To an unpracticed eye, it might seem as though the victim was merely drunk. To the practiced eye, it is cause for great concern. The bacteria could cause a heart attack, or a stroke and even brain damage, if it were not treated quickly."

The fairy looked down at Bindyl. "He will sleep for a while. It will be good for him to do so. It will give the medicine a chance to work."

"Thank you for your help. My name is Gideon."

"My pleasure. My name is Paris."

"Well, Paris," said Gideon. "It seems that we will have to wait it out here for a while. I hope you don't mind. We will be leaving as soon as Bindyl is able to travel. We don't want to lose him. We have already lost one of our group."

"What happened?" asked Paris.

"We were on our way through the badlands, when something dragged our friend Zoe underground," replied Gideon. "We would have been dragged under too, but the pennars arrived just in time."

"Your friend has been taken by the gromtoks. I would not hold out much hope for her," said Paris.

"What are gromtoks?" asked Gideon.

"They live up in the mountains of Managroon, to the east of us," answered Paris. "They can move around underground. The gromtoks have the ability to make you see what is not really there. They take an image from your mind and then you see it in front of you. That's how they get you. Before you know it, you are their slave.

They dig tunnels into the mountains to find ore. They use slaves to mine it for them. The gromtoks capture anything that can work. They work whoever they have, until their victims die of exhaustion."

"Does this mean she could still be alive?" asked Gideon.

"I would bet on it. At least for a while," replied Paris, "but your chances of even finding her, let alone rescuing her, are pretty remote. We have lost fairies to them in the past. The gromtoks prefer the elviron, but they will take what they can."

"If Zoe is still alive, then we must try to find her. I thank you for all that you have done for us," said Gideon.

"Not at all," replied Paris. "We have heard a great deal about you and your friends from Pennarius. He has entertained us around the campfire with many stories, but the children love the stories about the elves the most I think."

"My father told me before we left that we would meet the fairies," said Gideon. "He also told me that very few elves have ever seen you."

"Both the fairies and the pennar try to keep to ourselves. Besides, no one comes to the badlands too much," said Paris.

"Why do you live here?" Gideon asked.

"It is close to the entrance to the Human Realm," replied Paris. "We help the hundred year guardian on their journey to the entrance to the Human Realm."

"You have seen the ritual?" asked Gideon.

"Some of us have," replied Paris. "It is very easy to be in the Human Realm when the solstice begins. It seems no matter how unusual you look, you can fit in. On some occasions we have gone up with the guardian, but two fairies will wait at the entrance this time around. You will be met up at the entrance by a druid. It is tradition that we are present at the cave in the badlands when the entrance to the Human Realm is opened."

"I was unaware the fairies helped with the Grymlons. I feel honoured that you and your kind will be assisting us," said Gideon.

"It is our honour to do so," Paris replied. "I must go now. Do not worry about your friend. The twins, Anna and Lebrue will be with him until he wakes up. Please feel free to move about the camp and meet everyone."

Gideon returned to the main compound and looked for Elizabeth. He found her talking with Pennarius. As he got closer to them, they stopped their conversation and both looked his way.

"Elizabeth, did you know about the fairies?" Gideon asked.

"Yes," she said, "it was in The Book of Journeys. The guardian of the Grymlons usually makes this journey only with one elf guard, but the fairies guide them to the opening of the Human Realm. I didn't know about the pennar until I met Pennarius. My Gran never told me about them, neither did King Morvand."

Pennarius explained. "The guardian of the Grymlons does not usually come to our little village. The fairies normally meet with the guardian at the entrance of the badlands. They escort the guardian and her guard to the entrance of the Human Realm. The fairies were a little apprehensive about meeting the elves, so we went out to find you. Just in time it would seem."

"I am sorry about your friend. Elizabeth has just been telling me what happened."

Gideon touched Elizabeth on the elbow.

"We have to talk. Paris told me that Zoe was taken by gromtoks and is probably still alive," he told her.

Pennarius snorted and began pawing the ground. "You cannot go after her! The gromtoks are evil. Even the elviron are afraid of them. They are totally merciless. Your friend cannot be helped."

Gideon was shocked. "Pennarius, we have to try to help her. We can't just leave her there!"

"You must," Pennarius said, "even if you rescue her, the gromtoks will hunt her down. They will kill her rather than give her up. They will kill you, too, for taking her from them."

"What are gromtoks?" Elizabeth asked.

Gideon squeezed Elizabeth's arm. She picked up on his meaning and put her hand on Pennarius' neck to reassure him.

"I think we all need to rest. We'll stay here until Bindyl is well, if that is all right with you?" she said.

"I will have the fairies prepare some food and a place for you to rest. I will see you both in the morning," Pennarius said, and walked away.

Gideon watched as Pennarius disappeared into the clearing.

"What has him so scared? Do you think these gromtoks are really that bad?"

"I don't know, but I intend to find out," Elizabeth replied.

"What are you going to do?" asked Gideon.

"I'm not sure yet," said Elizabeth. "Let's go and see how Bindyl is doing."

Gideon found Paris and he led them to one of the shelters.

"We would all like to stay with Bindyl if you don't mind," said Gideon.

"There is plenty of room for all of you," said Paris. "Bindyl is lucky to have so many loyal friends. I bid you good night. I will see you in the morning."

Gideon put his blanket down beside Bindyl. Elizabeth put her blanket on the floor and settled down with Charlie curled up at her feet.

Chapter Seventy Two

Elizabeth waited until everyone in the shelter was asleep. She got up and quietly left the shelter. Gideon, who had been watching her, got up and followed her out.

"I had a feeling you were up to something. Where are you going, Elizabeth?" he asked, catching up to her.

"Stop following me, I'll be back as soon as I can. Take care of Bindyl and Charlie."

"We do this dangerous stuff together, remember?"

Elizabeth turned. "Not this time, my good friend."

She waved her hand and softly said, "Gideon. I want you to go and make sure Bindyl and Charlie are okay. Don't do anything else. Do you understand?"

Gideon's eyes glazed over. "I must take care of Bindyl and Charlie."

"Yes," said Elizabeth, "go now, and take care of them."

Gideon walked away. An elf with only one purpose: to do as he was asked.

When she reached the edge of the compound, Elizabeth took a deep breath, closed her eyes and began to chant in Elvish.

Gideon returned to the shelter to check on Bindyl.

Charlie looked up sleepily when she heard him enter the hut.

"Where is Elizabeth?" she asked.

"Elizabeth? Who is Elizabeth?" said Gideon.

Charlie was just about to answer, when suddenly she had no idea who Elizabeth was, or why she had asked about this person. They both looked at each other for a few seconds.

Gideon sat by Bindyl and pulled his blanket up over him.

"We will have to wait for Bindyl to get better," he said. "We will just sit here and wait, but what are we supposed to do after Bindyl gets well? Not to worry. It is time to rest now. We'll just wait…"

With the spell now complete, Elizabeth opened her eyes.

"I have no idea how I just did that?" she said, looking into the clearing. Everyone was going about the business of settling down for the night. She hoped the spell had worked. It would stop anyone from following her and they would not go anywhere until she returned. She entered the camp, moving among the fairies and the pennar. Everyone ignored her.

"Yes, good, it's worked," she thought. "I will need help, but a pennar can't do it. They are much too nervous about the gromtoks."

Elizabeth made her way to the edge of the forest and chanted another spell. A perichron flew into view, and landed directly in front of her.

"I hope you aren't hungry," she said. "I don't want to be your next meal."

"Humans don't taste very nice," the perichron pushed into her head.

"I'm sorry about the perichron who died. I had no choice," Elizabeth said in her mind, to the huge bird.

"The perichron you killed was a murderer of humans. We are not a murderous race, but there are few of us left," the perichron pushed back.

"I need help to get my friend back. Can you take me to Managroon?"

The perichron circled around her. Elizabeth stood perfectly still. He sniffed at her, hesitating for a brief moment before crouching down so that she could get on his back. He took off almost before Elizabeth had managed to sit.

"This is a bit rougher than a pennar. These feathers are sticking into me," she thought.

"Would you like me to land?" the perichron pushed into her head.

"Uh, no, sorry. I didn't mean to be ill mannered," Elizabeth replied.

He ignored her, heading for the Mountains of Managroon.

Chapter Seventy Three

When the elviron guards and the elf spy reached the castle in Distardrian, they were brought before Verina.

"We missed them," said Prymm.

"How?" asked Verina.

"We uh, went to the wrong side of the castle," said Holmon.

"So you don't know your north from your south?" asked Verina, pacing back and forth.

"They were drunk when I found them," said Palik.

"Drunk?" said Verina.

"Yes, your majesty," replied Palik.

"How long have they been gone?" asked Verina.

"Two days," said Palik.

For a moment, Verina stood completely still, staring at the two elviron and the elf in front of her.

Suddenly, she flew into a rage. The two elviron and the elf watched her in terrified fascination, as she stomped around the room screaming and shouting.

Verina realized what she was doing and stopped. She stood motionless for a few moments, staring at the three of them.

"Come with me," she said, calm now.

They followed her to the gates outside of the castle.

A small crowd gathered, curious about the presence of the princess outside of the castle walls.

"Prymm," she said with a smile. "You stand here. That's right, stand by the side of the gate and face away from the castle."

He did as he was asked.

"Now Holmon, you go and stand on the other side of the gate and you also face away from the castle," Verina said, still smiling.

He also did as he was asked.

"You, what's your name?" she asked the elf spy.

"Palik," replied the elf.

"Palik, I want you to go and stand next to Prymm," she said.

"Why?" he asked.

A gasp escaped from the crowd of elviron who were watching.

"Because I asked you to," replied Verina.

"I don't want to," said Palik, suspecting something unpleasant was about to happen.

Verina lifted her right index finger and pointed it at the elf. She said something under her breath, then moved her finger. As she did so, Palik involuntarily moved towards her until she had him positioned next to Prymm.

The three of them watched Verina, paralysed with fear.

She stood between them, then in full view of all of the elviron watching: she cast a spell, turning all three to stone.

"They will watch for enemies now, and they will do it for all time," said Verina. "If any of you think that you are out of my reach," she shouted, looking around her at all who were present. "THINK AGAIN!"

She was about to return to the castle, then stopped, backed up and made a circling gesture with both hands. Someone in the crowd screamed as the statues of the two elviron and the elf shattered, leaving only broken bits of stone strewn everywhere.

When Verina heard the scream she smiled and continued through the castle gates.

"Taking into consideration the time it took them to get here. They have about a day's head start. I can catch them if I move fast," she thought.

Verina found her father. "I need to leave now. Those guards you sent got drunk and missed the elves."

King Kalidryd said nothing. He only stared at his daughter. Verina stared back.

"Have the servants prepare some food and water. I will take a servant with me. Try to find me an elviron who is not a total idiot," she sneered.

King Kalidryd cringed.

"I'm beginning to think you were a mistake," he thought. "You are becoming powerful, wilful and an utter brat!"

Verina went down into the depths of the castle to talk to Drewmanus, wizard to the king.

"I want some power. That little human witch is not going to best me," she told the wizard.

Drewmanus gave her what he hoped she would need.

"It wouldn't break my heart if you met with an unfortunate accident," thought the wizard, as he watched her leave his laboratory.

King Kalidryd waited by the entrance to the castle. He had intended to wish is daughter well, but she walked past him, and seemed to hardly notice he was there.

With a hurried wave, she grabbed the elviron servant by the back of the neck, shoved him forward and out of the castle grounds. Verina was gone before King Kalidryd could say a word. He turned and went back into the castle.

Drewmanus was waiting for him in his private chambers. King Kalidryd sat down with a heavy sigh.

"Will she succeed, do you think?" Drewmanus asked.

King Kalidryd looked down at the floor. "Perhaps," he answered, "but it may not be a bad thing if we have to wait another hundred years. Verina could get much too powerful if she managed to get her hands on the Grymlons, and that might be bad... for both of us."

Chapter Seventy Four

Elizabeth held on tight. She crouched low, so that the wind in her face did not take her breath away. After a while, the sun began to rise. Off in the distance, she could see the snow capped mountains of Managroon.

A large camp set against the mountainside came into view ahead of them. As they flew over it, she looked down, trying to see what was below. The perichron had climbed too high for her to make out whether the dark specs were two legged or more.

"I will land on the other side of the hill, behind the camp," the perichron pushed into her head.

"Thank you. I appreciate your help," Elizabeth thought back.

The landing was incredibly smooth. Once on the ground, she climbed down from the perichron.

"I'll be calling for you to take me back to the forest. I may have another with me. Will you be able to carry two of us?" she asked.

The perichron nodded, then turned and flew away.

Elizabeth sat down on a cluster of rocks.

"I came here with no plan. That was foolish," she thought. "I have to rescue Zoe and get back in time to get the Grymlons to Avebury, but now what do I do?"

She stood and began walking towards the compound. When she came closer, she hid between some rocks. They were at high altitude and it had been snowing, and she shivered, feeling the cold. She peered between the rocks to get a good view of the camp. There were dozens of creatures in the compound. There were elves, both young and old. There were elviron, some humans and a few pennar. All of the human types were looked unwashed and were dressed in rags.

"I can't see Zoe anywhere, but there are so many of them," she thought.

Elizabeth ripped at her clothes, grabbed a handful of the dusty ground and rubbed it onto her face, arms and legs. She mashed more dirt into her hair, took a deep breath, entered into the camp and tried to blend in.

Slaves were coming in and out of the darkness of a large hole in the side of the mountain. Some of them were carrying boulders almost their own size.

Creatures resembling the pennar were hooked up to a harness, pulling the larger, heavier rocks. They were being relentlessly whipped by the gromtok guards, who were overseeing them. Most of the two-legged slaves were picking up heavy rocks that had been mined out of the hillside. More slaves were pounding the larger rocks into smaller pieces.

Some were putting the rocks onto moving belts that led to a pool of water. The rocks were dropped into the water where they were tumbled out and transported to a shed.

Elizabeth circled the camp, but could not find Zoe. One of the guards who had been patrolling the compound stopped when he saw her. It was the first time that Elizabeth had paid any attention to what they looked like.

When one of them looked directly at her, Elizabeth saw that thick short dark brown hair covered his body. He had short but sturdy arms and hands with very long fingers. His legs were short and thin. The gromtok walked with a stooped gait as he headed towards her. He had front teeth like a mole.

"He looks like a giant rat!" she thought.

He mouthed something at her.

"What?" she asked.

He came within arms length of her, and without warning, reached out and swiped her across the head, knocking her to the ground.

"Well, that definitely isn't a warm welcome!" she muttered, rubbing the side of her head.

The gromtok grabbed her by the hair and began dragging her across the compound. Trying not to panic, Elizabeth let her body go limp. As the gromtok pulled her along, she began to utter words.

"Paition, Parition, Hibernation."

She kept repeating them until the gromtok turned around and looked down at her. He stopped, cocked his head to one side, listening intently. He let go of her hair and bent over, trying to hear what she was saying.

"He smells like sweaty feet," Elizabeth thought, catching a whiff of him.

She got up slowly, still saying the words. Then she waved her hand and the gromtok keeled over, fast asleep. She looked around, hoping no one had seen her.

One of the horse-like creatures was standing off to one side, watching what was going on.

The creature only had one eye in the middle of its head. It had incisors that came down below its bottom lip. The teeth reminded her of the pictures she had seen in history books, of sabre tooth tigers. The creature looked to the left and right of him. When he was certain no one else was paying attention, he approached her.

"How did you do that?"

Elizabeth sighed.

"If I had a penny for every time someone asked me how I do this stuff, I would be rich."

She looked up at the creature. "I'm looking for someone in this camp. Can you help me?"

Elizabeth suspected that the creature was not very old.

"I believe that I asked first," he insisted.

"It was magic," Elizabeth replied.

"Are you a powerful witch?" he asked.

"I'm not a witch," answered Elizabeth.

"I could alert the gromtoks," the young creature said.

"Why would you want to do that? I may be able to get you out of here."

The young creature hung his head low, looking dejected. "No one escapes from here."

"I'm going to get out of here, and if you help me, I'll take you with me," said Elizabeth, looking directly into his one large eye.

"I saw you sneak into the compound. Why are you here?" he asked.

"I just told you. I'm here to save a friend of mine. She is an elf. Her name is Zoe. Have you seen her? What are you by the way?"

"I am an Onu. Do you know how many different kinds of beings there are in this camp?"

"Be patient," she thought, sighing again.

"I'll find her. Do you have a name?" asked Elizabeth.

"My name is Onarian."

"Are you familiar with the pennar?"

"We are related to the pennar, but they don't eat meat. The onu are omnivores," replied Onarian.

"What kind of meat do you like?" she asked, feeling a little uncomfortable.

"Just about anything, but don't worry, I won't eat you. Not unless I get very, very hungry."

"I don't think that's funny," said Elizabeth.

"We should get away from that gromtok. Is he dead?" Onarian asked.

Elizabeth looked down at the gromtok, who had curled up into a tight ball. "No, just sleeping."

I will help you find her friend. Follow me," he said, beginning to walk away.

"How long has she been here?" Onarian asked.

"About a day," Elizabeth said, looking around her at the other occupants.

"Then she will be in with the newcomers," said Onarian. "The gromtoks always put the new ones in a different section of the compound. They break them in gently. They last longer that way."

"That's nice," Elizabeth said, thinking that she didn't much care for the creature.

As they continued through the camp, Elizabeth noticed all kinds of creatures. Apart from the pennar and the onu, there were a few fairies, but their wings had been cut off. Some sort of creature covered with so much hair, its features could not be seen.

None of them looked at Elizabeth or Onarian as they moved among them.

Daylight was coming, and the gromtoks had begun herding all the elviron together and heading them towards a large outbuilding. Elizabeth could see that a few were beginning to smoulder a bit.

"No creature should ever be a slave. Not even the disgusting elviron," she thought.

The other slaves went about their business as though nothing else mattered.

Suddenly, Elizabeth noticed Zoe.

"There she is!" she shouted.

Elizabeth was about to walk over to her when the onu stepped in front of her.

"Don't do that! Don't shout like that, or I will eat you just to shut you up!"

Elizabeth realized that she was drawing attention to herself. She had been so surprised to find Zoe so quickly, she had forgotten where she was.

Three gromtoks were walking towards them.

"We are dead," Onarian said.

He started to panic, prancing sideways as he spoke.

"They have seen you. We are going to die slow painful deaths."

The onu stopped prancing and stood still. He seemed resigned to the fact that he had been discovered and was going to take his punishment.

"No one is going to hurt me, nor anyone around me," Elizabeth said angrily.

She waited until the gromtoks had almost reached them, and stomped down hard with her right foot. The ground shook. The gromtoks stopped for a few seconds, looking down. When the shaking stopped they started towards her and Onarian again.

"ENOUGH!" she shouted, as she looked at them and pointed her finger.

"GALLENSHEY DISTRONTY!" she said, her face crimson with anger.

The gromtoks began to smoulder. They tried to pat themselves down to stop the smoke, but began to burn. A couple of them began to scream. The third tried to burrow into the ground, but half way in it stopped. It turned to Elizabeth as it went up in a puff of smoke. The other two were now engulfed in flames.

"ZOE! QUICKLY, COME HERE," Elizabeth shouted.

Zoe squinted, trying to see who it was. When she realized it was Elizabeth, she ran towards her as fast as her legs could carry her.

"Oh great, there are gromtoks everywhere now. How will we get out of here?" she said.

The words were hardly out of her mouth, when she looked down and could not believe her luck. The onu, who was obviously scared, was quite unconsciously hovering just above the ground.

"You have wings on your legs, just like the pennar! Can you carry both of us and fly out of here?" Elizabeth asked him.

"I... I think I could, but we will never make it!" replied Onarian.

"If we don't try, we are dead anyway, aren't we?"

The onu nodded and knelt down. Elizabeth pushed Zoe up onto his back, jumping up behind her.

"GO!" she shouted.

The onu began to fly upward. The gromtoks tried to rush them, but they were too late to grab Onarian. He kicked out with his back legs and hit one of them squarely in the chest. The gromtok hit the ground hard.

One of the gromtoks threw something up towards them. Elizabeth turned just in time a round brown blob land on Onarian's rump. At first it sat on his back like a flat furry puddle.

"What just landed on me?" Onarian asked.

Elizabeth ignored him, as she watched it burrow into his skin.

Another one hit Zoe in the thigh. She tried to brush it off, but it stuck to her. Another was heading towards Elizabeth, but as it reached her, she swatted it away.

"Get us out of here!" she shouted to him.

She grabbed the furry blob on his rump, trying to pull it off, but it wouldn't move.

"Don't do that! It hurts!" Onarian shouted back at Elizabeth.

They were high in the air now.

"Which way should I go?" he shouted, as he flew upward.

"Towards the west, until you see the forest at Shanseen,' she shouted. "We need to get to the badlands."

Elizabeth looked around at the furry thing in time to see the last of it burrowing inside of Onarian's rump.

"Oh no," she said.

"What did you say?" asked Onarian.

"I said go, go!" she shouted back.

Onward they flew. It was obvious after only minutes, that Onarian could not carry both of them. He began to drop and weave around. He finally landed.

Zoe and Elizabeth jumped down from his back.

Zoe sat on the ground, still in shock.

"I am sorry, I just can't carry both of you," he said, turning to look at his back end. "My rump itches so very badly!"

"It's all right Onarian. I can call a perichron. He can fly one of us," Elizabeth said, as she turned to call for the bird.

"A perichron! I hate those things," Onarian said, as he walked in front of Elizabeth to stop her.

Elizabeth looked up at the onu.

"You know, you have this very annoying thing that you do. Don't keep stepping in front of me!" she said, staring into Onarian's eye.

He backed up and turned, biting at his rump.

Elizabeth called the perichron.

Onarian paced back and forth constantly while they waited.

"Stop that Onarian. It's very annoying!" said Elizabeth.

"I can't, my rump itches. I think it is going to drive me mad!" he said, trying to bite the spot where the creature had disappeared.

Zoe stood. She hadn't said much since they had been rescued. "I think the gromtoks have infected us. I have one of those things on my leg, or rather inside the top of my leg now. My leg itches as well."

Elizabeth inspected Zoe's leg. The thing had burrowed underneath the skin, just above the side of her knee. When Elizabeth looked closer, she could see a little spike sticking up from the bulge just above the skin. She reached out to touch it and it snaked out, as if to hit her.

"What is it?" asked Zoe.

"I don't know," Elizabeth replied, walking over to Onarian.

"Keep still, and let me look at your backside," she said, touching his rump.

He crouched down so she could see. The thing on his back seemed to have grown a little. It too had a spike just above the skin.

She looked to the west. Up high, she could just make out the outline of a perichron.

The three of them watched, as the bird came closer.

When the perichron landed, Elizabeth approached him. But before she could explain the situation, Onarian spun around and attacked him.

The perichron took off, turned around and headed straight towards Onarian! Before it reached the ground it levelled off, circling the onu, pecking at him. Onarian hovered above the ground looking for somewhere to bite into the perichron.

Elizabeth watched the scene for about five seconds.

"STOP IT!"

They both hovered in the air, looking at her.

"If you must fight, please do it later. We need the help of both of you.

If you can't put your differences behind you for a while, Zoe and I will just wait here, and you have killed one another, I'll call for more help. So if you want to fight, be my guest."

Elizabeth sat down, folded her arms and waited. Zoe, unsure of what to do, sat beside her.

The perichron and the onu looked at each other. Then landed on the ground, side by side.

"That's better," Elizabeth said. "Now, could we please be on our way? We need to get to Shanseen as soon as possible."

Elizabeth got up onto the perichron and Zoe climbed onto Onarian. The perichron led the way, Onarian followed close behind.

Chapter Seventy Five

They landed about a quarter of a mile from the pennar camp.

The perichron took off again as soon as Elizabeth's feet hit the ground. As he climbed, he turned around and nodded to the Onarian in a gesture of respect. Onarian hesitated for a moment then bowed back.

Elizabeth watched them and smiled. "There may be hope for everyone yet."

"Wait with Onarian until I return," she said, turning to Zoe. "I have some explaining to do before anyone sees you."

"Time to try to undo the spell I cast," Elizabeth thought.

She went into the woods and stood at the edge of the clearing. She took a deep breath and chanted a spell. After a few minutes she purposefully walked into the camp and was greeted by Charlie, who rubbed up against her leg.

"Where is Bindyl?" Elizabeth asked.

Charlie walked in front of her. "He is in the shelter. I think he is awake now. Why are you so dirty?"

When Elizabeth entered the shelter, Bindyl was sitting up with Gideon by his side.

"Elizabeth, we have to go back for Zoe," Bindyl said, trying to get up.

Gideon put a hand on his shoulder and shoved him back down.

"Don't be an idiot, Bindyl. We will try to find her when you are stronger," he said, looking at Elizabeth and rolling his eyes.

Bindyl tried to get up again, but Gideon looked at him and pointed his finger as a warning.

"We must have all fallen asleep," Gideon said, "is it morning?"

Bindyl turned to Elizabeth, as though looking for an ally.

"No one has to go anywhere. I have already rescued her," she said.

Gideon and Bindyl looked at each other.

"How?" asked Bindyl.

"Elizabeth, what have you been doing?" asked Gideon, "You're filthy! And your clothes are all torn."

She looked down, brushing off some of the dirt.

"I'll explain later," she said. "Zoe and the onu have something that has burrowed under their skin and it needs to come out. Where is Paris?"

"An onu? Don't see them every day," Gideon said.

"We need to find Paris," she said again.

Gideon and Charlie followed her as the walked through the camp. Anna kept an eye on Bindyl to make sure that he stayed put.

Elizabeth found Paris at his shelter.

"Good morning," he said. "I hope you slept well."

"Elizabeth didn't sleep at all. She went to get Zoe from the gromtoks," Gideon said.

"Zoe is waiting at the edge of the woods with an onu," Elizabeth told him.

"How did they get there?" asked Paris.

"I cast a spell so that none of you would miss me," she explained, "then I called a perichron. He took me to the gromtok camp. The onu, who was also a slave, helped us escape. Before we could get away, the gromtoks threw these odd little furry things at us. One of them landed on the onu and the other landed on Zoe's leg. They threw one at me, but missed.

"We have to act fast," he said. "Both of them have screngers under their skin. They are parasites, and they will eat away at your friends. Screngers send out a high frequency whine that the gromtoks can hear for many miles. We have to stop the signal so the gromtoks don't come to the camp, or they will hunt your friends down. If they can't find them, they will wait for the screngers to do their work. Eventually, there will be no trace of your friend or the onu. The screngers will devour them completely."

"How are we going to tell Bindyl about Zoe? He thinks she's been saved," Gideon said, turning a little pale.

"He's right," thought Elizabeth "Bindyl had been frantic about losing Zoe."

"Can we get them out?" she asked Paris.

Paris shook his head. "I am sorry, Elizabeth. We have never been able to extract one of those things without the host dying. We should go and get the two of them. We will make them as comfortable as possible, but we can do nothing else."

"Then the gromtoks will find us?" Elizabeth asked. 'I did all this for nothing?"

"No," said Paris, "we can cover the creatures with a liquid we drain from a plant that grows around here. It stops the creatures from whining. We don't know how it works, but it seems to keep them quiet. It also stops the itching."

"There has to be a way. There's always a way," said Elizabeth.

Paris shook his head. He sent some of the fairies to get Zoe and the onu. Charlie went with them in case they needed some help.

When they reached the two newcomers, the onu looked up and saw Charlie.

"Tut-tut!" he shouted to her.

Charlie immediately answered with a delighted scream.

They ran towards each other. Charlie morphed into her mountain lion form and jumped up on the onu's back. They scampered around like a couple of kids for a minute or two.

When they had calmed down a little, Charlie put herself back into her cat form. Onarian bent down and nuzzled Charlie on the head.

"Will you come and see me later?" asked Onarian.

"Try and keep me away! But you have to go and see Paris first," replied Charlie.

A fairy led Onarian away.

Charlie ran over to Zoe, rubbing against her legs.

"I'm glad you're back, Zoe," she told her, as they headed towards the camp together.

"How do you know that onu?" asked Zoe.

"When I was a kitten," Charlie explained, "Vandrayven and I would go into the badlands together for days. Vandrayven and Oklandu, the leader of the onu camp had been friends for many years. Onarian was a colt back then. While Vandrayven and the head of the onu herd sat around the camp talking and exchanging stories, Onarian and I would play.

We visited the onu's camp just a few months ago, so Onarian must have been captured quite recently."

Charlie suddenly remembered that Onarian was going to die because of the parasite under his skin. She also knew neither Onarian, or Zoe were aware of this fact yet. She stopped talking. The excitement of seeing Onarian again quickly faded into a deep sadness inside of her.

Zoe touched Charlie's back. "Are you all right, Charlie?" she asked. "You suddenly look sad."

"I'm all right. I think I'm just a little tired," Charlie answered, not looking up at her.

They walked the rest of the way in silence. Zoe wondering why the sudden change in the little cat's mood. She absent- mindedly touched her leg at the spot where the parasite lay. The creature under her skin jumped slightly.

"I've come this far," Zoe said to herself. "I hope someone can get this thing out of me."

Charlie waited until no one was looking, then she headed away from the camp.

"If I'm lucky, no one will miss me for a while. They will think I've gone hunting for food," she thought.

Chapter Seventy Six

"Where is Bindyl?" Zoe asked the fairy escorting her, as they entered the clearing.

"I will take you to him," the fairy replied.

Bindyl, insisting he was feeling better, was outside of the shelter stretching his legs when he saw Zoe. For just a moment, they both stood and looked at each other. Zoe broke the spell by walking to him. They embraced and cried, relieved to see each other. The two of them went to a tree and sat down.

"I thought I would never see you again," said Zoe, touching Bindyl's face.

"If the pennar had not rescued us, we would have been in that camp with you," said Bindyl.

"What happened to your face?" asked Zoe.

"I'll tell you later," replied Bindyl.

Paris came over holding a small pot containing green paste.

"Hold still, while I put this on your leg and bind it," he told Zoe.

"What's wrong with your leg?" Bindyl asked.

"Something burrowed inside of it," she replied.

"What?" asked Bindyl.

"What is it?" Zoe asked Paris.

"Screnger," answered Paris, "now stop talking and sit still."

Paris spread the paste over the area where the creature lay underneath Zoe's skin. When he was sure all of the creature had been covered, he bound it tightly with a bandage.

Zoe looked up at Paris.

"The itching has stopped," she said.

Paris nodded. He walked away from the two elves before Bindyl could ask what a screnger was.

***

Zoe and Bindyl ate and spent time with Elizabeth and Gideon until well into the evening hours.

Finally, Gideon stood.

"I'm tired. I'm going to retire for the night," he said, excusing himself.

"Me too," said Elizabeth, "has anyone seen Charlie?"

No one had.

"She must have gone hunting. See you all in the morning," said Elizabeth.

Paris came and escorted Zoe to a place where she could sleep.

Chapter Seventy Seven

Six of the gromtoks had picked up the screngers signal. They were burrowing under the ground, heading west, and digging tirelessly, when suddenly the signal stopped.

The gromtoks branched out under the ground, trying to find the signal again, but it was gone. They came back together, bickered angrily at each other for a minute or two, then headed back to the slave compound.

Chapter Seventy Eight

All were sleeping peacefully at the pennar camp, as the sun began to peep over the horizon. The only ones awake were a few guards who stood watch.

The quietness of the morning sun was pierced by a blood-curdling scream.

Everyone woke instantly. Bindyl instinctively jumped up and ran through the camp looking for Zoe. He found her staggering towards him. The leg the creature had burrowed into was huge from her ankle to her thigh and it was moving under her skin.

Elizabeth walked up behind Bindyl, and stepped around him.

Zoe looked up when she saw her. "She's terrified!" Elizabeth thought.

She put a hand on Zoe's shoulder, and looked into her eyes.

"Sleep," she said, waving her other hand from side to side. Gideon, who was standing behind Zoe, caught her as she closed her eyes and fell backwards.

"Thank you," Bindyl said, trying to hold back tears. "What is happening to her?"

The pennar and the fairies formed a little crowd around them. Pennarius appeared in the crowd with Paris by his side.

Paris turned and addressed the gathering.

"As you can see, one of our guests is in distress. I know you are all concerned. We will keep you informed. Now please go about your business."

The crowd broke up, leaving Paris and Pennarius to take care of the crisis. The pennar and the fairies knew from experience, that the next few days would be difficult for Zoe and Onarian.

Pennarius turned and left the scene. He headed to where Onarian was, and found the young onu still asleep.

The screnger on his rump had also been busy. There was swelling all across the back of Onarian's tail and down one of his legs. Pennarius turned quietly and returned to Zoe.

When he returned, Elizabeth and Gideon were standing off to the side.

"I can do this!" Elizabeth was arguing with Gideon.

"If you fail, they will both die," Gideon said. "Even if you succeed, how much of them will be left? The screngers are eating them, Elizabeth! The two of them will have to spend the rest of their lives with half of them missing. You will have that on your conscience for the rest of your life!"

"If I had thought about that when I worked on you, you would be dead by now!" Elizabeth shot back. "If I can take a chance on you, why won't you let me do this for Zoe and Onarian?"

"She's right," he thought. "If she had not made that very daring move, Zoe and I would be dead by now."

Elizabeth turned away him. He followed her as she headed towards Zoe, who was lying on a blanket, still sleeping. Anna and Lebrue had sat down beside her.

Gideon followed her.

Elizabeth turned to Paris.

"Please take her into one of the shelters and make her as comfortable as possible."

"Would you two go and find some fairies to help me with Onarian?" she asked Anna and Lebrue. "Take two pennar with you to hold him on the ground until I come to you. Don't try to touch him near the screnger. No matter how much he begs you, don't let him get up. Mind what I say now, Onarian likes to whine and he's good at it."

Anna and Lebrue both nodded and left.

Three fairies carried Zoe into one of the shelters. These pleasant little buildings were warm and inviting. There was just enough room to have the essentials that one would need to stay safe and dry.

One of the fairies closed down the shutters and lit some candles so that Elizabeth could see.

"I'll need something to put the screnger in," she said.

A fairy left. He returned a few minutes later, carrying a bucket with a lid.

Elizabeth stood over Zoe and took a deep breath.

"I think I might be sick if, I touch that disgusting thing on her leg," she thought. "I just hope I don't throw up on her!"

Elizabeth put her hand above the spot where the screnger had originally settled inside of Zoe's leg, but did not touch her skin. Her hand hovered over the wound. The screnger jumped.

Elizabeth ignored the movement. Her hand hung over Zoe's skin for a moment, then she pressed it against Zoe's leg. As soon as her hand came in contact with the screnger, it jumped again. It began to move vigorously under Zoe's skin, bunching up, as though trying to protect itself. Elizabeth kept her hand on the same spot. Little spines came out of Zoe's leg, piercing Elizabeth's hand. The spines continued up through her hand, snaking around it and grabbing onto her wrist. Her hand bled, but she did not move it. A small hole appeared in Zoe's leg. Elizabeth almost gagged when she heard a slurping sound, as the long bloody form of the screnger slithered through the hole, using Elizabeth's hand as an anchor.

With a sudden movement, Elizabeth pulled upward. The screnger hung onto her hand. She pointed her index finger at it with her free hand.

The screnger began to smoke, then burst into flames. Elizabeth swiped her hand downward. The screnger let go of her and landed in the bucket. Lebrue slammed the lid down tightly. Anna went to Zoe. What was left of her leg was bleeding profusely. Anna put pressure on it with a clean rag.

Elizabeth knelt over Zoe and closed her eyes. She whispered something under her breath. With her palms facing down, she made a gesture, as though she were straightening something out over Zoe's body.

"You can lift the rag now," she told Anna.

Zoe's leg stopped bleeding. The wound closed, leaving her leg fully restored and healed within seconds. Elizabeth turned away from the sleeping Zoe and left the shelter.

She made her way over to Onarian, who by now was very awake. He was protesting loudly, struggling to get free of the ties the fairies had placed on him while sleeping.

"Stop wiggling, Onarian," she said, kneeling down beside him. "I can't help you if you don't keep still."

"What makes you think that you can help me? Don't touch me! And don't use that Hocus Pocus stuff on me!"

One of the fairies had removed the bandage from his rump.

"Oh! It burns!" Onarian shouted.

Suddenly he heard a familiar voice.

"DO AS THE GIRL SAYS, YOUNG ONARIAN, OR YOU WILL FEEL MY DISPLEASURE!"

Onarian stopped struggling and looked around to see where the voice came from.

"Father?" he said, craning his neck around one of the fairies holding him down.

Oklandu, the head of the onu heard, walked out from a clump of trees to the right of Onarian.

When Oklandu laid eyes on his son, he tried very hard to control his emotions. Charlie came up and stood beside him.

"Sorry Onarian," Charlie said, "but when I met you again, I knew that you may be dying. I had to try and find your dad. I turned into my mountain lion form and ran for hours, until I got to the onu community. I was so tired when I got there, but when I finally caught my breath, I told him that you were alive."

"Yes, at first when Charlie told me you were alive, I thought it was some sort of cruel joke," said Onarian. But Charlie was insistent. She said that it may be the last time I would see you because of the screnger. Well, when I realized she was telling the truth I couldn't get here fast enough. I picked Charlie up, threw her on my back and we flew here. When I arrived, Paris told me what had happened. So here I am."

"Oh father," was all Onarian could say between sobs.

"Can I do anything to help?" Oklandu asked, looking at Elizabeth.

"You can help hold him down. He won't let me put him to sleep, so I think this is going to hurt," she replied, looking up at Onarian's father.

His hair was golden with a white mane and tale. He was at least seventeen hands high. He had one large deep blue eye in the middle of his face, and long sabre teeth hanging down past his lower lip.

"He's beautiful," Elizabeth thought, "Scary, but beautiful."

Oklandu knelt down, putting his weight onto Onarian's shoulders, and Onarian let out a groan.

Elizabeth did the same thing with Onarian as she had done with Zoe, except they needed a larger receptacle for Onarian's screnger.

When the screnger was pulled from Onarian's rump, Elizabeth ran her hand over the wound, it closed and the flesh regenerated itself as quickly as Zoe's.

Onarian had passed out.

"You can get up now," said Elizabeth.

The fairy sitting on Onarian stood. Oklandu also stood and stepped to on side.

He turned, looking down at Elizabeth. "Thank you."

Paris watched Elizabeth as she walked away from the young onu. He found himself feeling both delighted and afraid.

"Gideon, who is Elizabeth? I mean really," he asked.

"I'm not sure," said Gideon. "We will have to wait and see what happens. If she is the Elf-Human that everyone has been waiting for, this could be very good, or this could be very bad."

"I most certainly agree," said Paris.

Elizabeth found an empty shelter and stretched out on the floor. She was asleep in seconds.

Chapter Seventy Nine

Everyone was rested by morning. Zoe and Onarian were as good as new. They were both back on their feet within hours. It was as though the screngers never existed.

"How are you feeling?" Gideon asked her.

"Never better," Zoe replied.

"I for one, am very relieved to see her up and around," said Bindyl.

Onarian's father was ready to leave. He and Onarian were going home. Elizabeth, Gideon, Zoe and Bindyl put supplies together, to continue their journey.

"I have to go now Charlie," said Onarian.

"Let's stay in contact this time. I'll let Vandrayven know about what happened to you," said Charlie.

"I would like that very much," said Onarian.

"Give Vandrayven my regards," said Oklandu.

"I'm sure he would like to see you," said Charlie.

"We will see what we can arrange," said Oklandu. "Where is Elizabeth?"

She stepped forward. Oklandu put his head over her shoulder and pulled her to his chest. He held her there for a few seconds. When he finally released her, she watched a large tear slip from his eyelid and down the front of his nose.

"I thought my son was gone forever," he said. "We have lost many onu to the gromtoks. Onarian was lucky that he still had his wings. If you had not been brave enough to rescue Zoe, he would still be in that dreadful camp. We owe you a debt, Elizabeth Ghenestone. I will not forget you."

Onarian ran to her and licked her face. She cringed, smacking him on the shoulder.

"Get off me you big nag!" she said, pushing him away.

He turned and caught up with his father. When they reached the edge of the clearing, they flew away.

Elizabeth turned and saw Gideon smiling.

"What are you looking at?" she asked.

"You have become quite fond of that whiny onu. Go on, admit it," he said, with a laugh.

Elizabeth grinned. "I suppose I have. Come on, we need to get going."

They went to find Zoe and Bindyl. It was time to travel through the badlands to the Human Realm.

Paris joined them "The two fairies, Anna and Lebrue are twins," he said. "Anna is mute. She communicates with Lebrue using her mind. Lebrue is her interpreter and communication to the outside world. They will both be going with you."

Paris accompanied them to the edge of the forest. "I wouldn't worry too much about meeting any unpleasant characters. It wouldn't hurt to keep your eyes open, but there is not much around the badlands," he told them.

"That's a relief," said Gideon. "It would be nice if the rest of the journey passed with no more snags."

Paris shook the hand of Gideon and Bindyl and kissed the hands of Zoe and Elizabeth. The travellers walked out of the wooded area and headed towards the desert.

"The pennars rescue has cut at least a day from our journey. It will be dark in a few hours, but if we move at a good pace, we could make the entrance by dusk," said Lebrue.

Chapter Eighty

It was beginning to get dark when Elizabeth noticed a faint glow off in the distance.

"Do you see it, Gideon?" she said.

"Yes," he replied, turning to Anna and Lebrue.

Gideon pointed to the light. "What is it?"

"It is the entrance to the Human Realm," said Lebrue. "It is always lit. The nomadic druids protect it."

The group headed towards the light and eventually came to a cave. Lebrue motioned for them to stop. He went inside and came out a minute or so later, with a man whose head was covered with a black cowl and his hands were crossed in front of him.

Lebrue introduced him.

"This is Ghyrone. He is the guardian of the entrance. He wishes to meet Elizabeth."

Elizabeth stepped forward and stood in front of Ghyrone. He pulled cowl from his head.

"He has the face of an angel," she thought.

"Hello Elizabeth, it is nice to meet you," Ghyrone said, in a low musical voice.

He held out his hands and Elizabeth took them into hers. They stood this way for a few seconds, then Ghyrone put his hands up to Elizabeth's face. He touched her eyes, her nose her lips and her forehead, turned to Lebrue and nodded.

"He has given you permission to pass through the entrance," said Lebrue.

"Why did he feel my face like that?" she asked.

"He is blind," Lebrue answered.

She touched her face where Ghyrone's hand had passed over her cheek. "But he looked straight at me!"

"It's time to proceed," Lebrue said to Ghyrone.

"Yes, we must get this young group on their way," Ghyrone replied.

They all followed Ghyrone and Lebrue to the cave entrance, except Anna, she was to stay outside as a look out.

Ghyrone stood to one side of the entrance. They filed past him one at a time. As Zoe passed by him, he held out his arm and stopped her from moving forward, and turned to Lebrue.

Lebrue hurried over to see what the problem was. There was a hushed conversation between he and Ghyrone, while the others waited just inside the cave entrance.

Lebrue approached to them. "Ghyrone senses something in Zoe. He says that she is not suited to go with you."

"What does he mean by that?" asked Elizabeth.

"He will not stop you if you decide to take Zoe," answered Lebrue, "but he does not want her to go any further. He does not say why. Only that it would be unwise of you to let her accompany you on your journey."

Bindyl stepped forward, taking Zoe's hand.

"We stay together," he said, "we have all trained for this. We need her, Elizabeth."

"I agree," said Elizabeth.

She turned to Ghyrone. He took her hand and led her away from the others.

"What is the problem with Zoe?" Elizabeth asked.

"I am not allowed to say," Ghyrone replied. "I can only advise you that she is not suitable for your quest."

"Is she in any danger?" asked Elizabeth.

"Of course she is. You all are," Ghyrone replied.

"That's not what I mean," said Elizabeth.

"I know," replied Ghyrone.

"Just a small clue perhaps?" asked Elizabeth.

"If you take Zoe, you may fail in your quest. But if you insist on taking her with you, I cannot stop you," replied Ghyrone.

"She comes with us," said Elizabeth.

"Very well," replied Ghyrone.

Elizabeth rejoined the rest of the group.

"What was that all about?" Gideon asked her.

"He wouldn't say," said Elizabeth. "He's afraid that somehow Zoe may cause us to fail, but he is going to allow her to come. So let's get going."

Ghyrone turned right inside of the cave and the others followed. A few yards along, there was an entrance with a large iron gate. Ghyrone held out his hand and touched the lock. A key appeared. He turned it in the lock and the gate swung open.

"Please enter here and continue up until you come to another gate," he said, ushering them into the tunnel.

When they were all inside, he locked the gate behind them.

"Good luck. I will be waiting for you when you return," Ghyrone said, walking away.

Gideon looked up the tunnel. "Well, come on, we need to get moving."

Gideon's voice spurred everyone into action.

They began walking upwards. A few minutes later, they reached another gate, beyond it, a well-lit cave.

Gideon turned to Elizabeth. "I don't suppose you have a key in with that other stuff you are carrying?"

"I would be opening the gate if I had, Elizabeth said, looking down her nose at him.

"Then how are we supposed to get through this gate?" Gideon asked, standing with his back to the bars.

The others were facing Gideon, but they were looking past him. Gideon turned around and jumped.

Standing at the other side of the gate was a tall slim man dressed in white. His iron grey hair stopped at his shoulders, and was topped with golden tiara. Hanging from his neck and across his chest was a breastplate that rested on full length robes.

Elizabeth recognized the breastplate from one of the pictures that she had seen while doing her research. The name of the breastplate was the Jodain Morain: the breastplate of judgement. Around his waist was a girdle made of pure gold with a crystal set in the middle of it.

The man standing before them was an Arch Druid.

Sitting by his side was a small winged dragon. The dragon's scales shone silver and gold. It stood beside the druid, staring at the group. The dragon seemed particularly fascinated by Charlie.

Elizabeth stepped forward.

"My name is Elizabeth and this is Zoe, Bindyl, Gideon and Charlie the cat," she announced, pointing to the others.

The druid bowed politely, the little dragon also bowed.

"My name is Thalios. I am the descendent of the Arch Druid, Pantheos. I will be escorting you to Avebury. This is my companion Keslyn."

The little dragon bowed again. Elizabeth bowed back. As she did so, the little dragon looked her in the eyes. Elizabeth stared into the most beautiful violet coloured eyes and felt an odd sensation. It was as though something was pushing inside her head.

"Hello," Keslyn said.

"Hello to you too," Elizabeth answered.

Gideon turned to her. "Who are you talking to?"

"Keslyn. Can't you hear her?" Elizabeth replied.

Thalios looked down at Keslyn. "She likes you," he told Elizabeth. "She does not communicate with everyone in that manner. You should be very flattered."

"Are we supposed to open the gate somehow?" Gideon asked.

Thalios stepped forward. "My apologies. I was not expecting so many of you. I was so busy looking at you, I forgot to let you out!" he said, producing a key and unlocking the gate.

They filed out of the cave through the open door.

"Please sit and rest for a few minutes," said Thalios. "If you need to eat, feel free to do so. Our journey will take a few hours. We will travel through Savernake forest, then on to Avebury. We should reach the forest before the sun comes up. It will be safer if we hide in the forest and rest there through the day. We will wait until nightfall, before we travel the rest of the way.

We must get to Avebury before the sun comes up the day after tomorrow. The solstice will be at approximately 4:00 a.m. You must place the Grymlons on the stone before the sun comes over the horizon or they will not be renewed."

Gideon noticed that Elizabeth had turned a bit pale.

"Are you all right?" he asked.

"I'm just well… scared," she said.

Thalios sat down beside her.

"It would be foolish of you to feel anything but scared," he told her. "You have been given a task of enormous responsibility and danger, but look around you. You have more help than any other guardian of the Grymlons has ever had."

Something touched Elizabeth's hand. She looked down and sitting beside her was Keslyn. She looked into Keslyn's eyes.

"Beautiful eyes. They have such kindness in them," thought Elizabeth.

Keslyn rubbed against Elizabeth's hand. Elizabeth felt a rush of happiness and strength run through her. Every hair on her body stood up. To her surprise Keslyn's scales were soft to the touch.

Thalios smiled. "I have never seen her befriend anyone like this before."

"Thank you Keslyn. I think I'm going to need all the help I can get," said Elizabeth.

Thalios stood. "We should be on our way if we are to reach Savernake forest before daylight. Please follow me."

He led them around the corner to some steps that rose up. Then turned to the group.

"Gideon, Zoe and Bindyl, please grow to human size," he said, walking up the steps with Keslyn. "We will make better time and we will look a little more normal. I will find you some human clothes so that you will not draw too much attention to yourselves."

They followed closely behind him. Thalios walked up twenty steps, coming to an abrupt dead end. They all looked up, seeing only darkness. Thalios lifted his staff and slammed it down on the top step. An opening slowly appeared above them. It grew larger until they could see the stars.

More steps magically appeared. Thalios climbed upwards, motioning to the rest of them to follow him. When they all stood on the grass, the opening closed behind them.

It was dark, but the stars were bright enough for them to notice the stone that rose several feet into the air next to them.

They were now standing next to the Heel Stone at Stonehenge.

The group turned. They stood for a moment in silence, staring at the imposing ruins, now fenced in from all sides. Thalios stepped in front of them, got down on one knee and bowed his head to the stones. He stood, pointing his staff to the north.

Thalios made an opening in the fence for them to get to the road. "We will go that way," he said, pointing his staff. "We have to stay off the road. We cannot be seen by any passers by, and there will be many people around here waiting for the solstice. I will lead you across the countryside. It will be quicker and safer that way."

They headed north, led by Thalios and his little companion, Keslyn.

Chapter Eighty One

Verina approached the cave and circled around to the right, creeping along the wall.

"Stay behind me and try to be quiet," she told her servant.

Gyrone went to the entrance of the cave.

"Hello?" he said to the outside. "Anyone there? Please make yourself known to me."

Verina was inches away from him, but he couldn't sense her presence. She reached forward and grabbed him by the throat.

Ghyrone struggled, but could not remove Verina's hands. She cut off his supply of air until he passed out.

When he neared death, Verina put her hand over his heart and slowly pushed her palm into his chest. A soft blue light appeared around her fingers. Her hand stayed motionless until the light grew dim.

Ghyrone was now dead and Verina had his essence in her hand. She let go of him, and he slumped to the ground.

The essence sitting on Verina's hand was at first a small ball of black mist. It slowly turned into a dim blue haze, until it was a bright light dancing on her palm.

She ripped it apart and handed half to her servant. They stuffed the light into their mouths and stood for a moment enjoying the experience.

"Come on," Verina said, "let's get going. We have some catching up to do."

When Verina reached the gate, she hesitated for just a second, before turning into her shadow form and walking through the bars as though they weren't there. Her servant followed.

Verina and her servant made their way up to the next gate, passing through it in the same manner as before.

They climbed up the steps, and Verina grew to human size, motioning for her servant to do the same.

When the steps ended, still in their shadow form, the two of them moved up through the earth to the Heel Stone. Verina stood for a moment to get her bearings.

"This way," she said, pointing the way for her servant, "and don't dawdle."

Chapter Eight Two

Thalios and his band of followers made good time. They reached the Savernake forest about a half an hour after the sun came up. He led them into the trees.

"I suggest we make camp here. We will rest until the evening hours, then move on."

The group put out their camping gear and set about making themselves comfortable for a few hours.

Thalios sat beside Elizabeth.

"It's not for me to question," he said, "but why do you have King Morvand's son and the other two elves with you? I have always escorted the hundred year guardian alone until now."

Elizabeth eyed him. "Always? How old are you, Thalios?"

"Older than you can comprehend," he said.

"I'm not the original hundred year guardian, my mother was," Elizabeth explained. "She was killed in a car accident two years ago."

"I'm very sorry to hear that," said Thalios.

"I think the king had considered finding someone else," she explained, "but when one of the Grymlons was stolen by an elviron, the king decided that I was to be the guardian."

"Why were you not prepared for this journey when your mother died? Two years would have been more than enough time to train you," said Thalios.

"I was too young. My fifteenth birthday was only last month, and besides, I was in a wheelchair for a while," she replied.

"You are better now I hope?" asked Thalios.

"Yes, thanks. The king decided that Gideon and the others should come with me, since my training had been so rushed."

"I agree," said Thalios.

"When we went to the castle in Kimadrian to get the Grymlon

back, we were attacked by a strange looking girl," Elizabeth told him. "My mother came to me in a dream and told me that she was an experiment, some sort of magical mix of human and elviron. Do you know anything about her, Thalios?"

Thalios frowned. "We will need to be very careful. This elviron girl could be powerful. Our Order has heard stories of such a child being born, but we never really thought that the elviron would succeed. The girl must not be allowed to get her hands on the Grymlons."

"I promise to do my best," said Elizabeth, "but she has had so much more training than me."

"Your best is all we can ask," said Thalios.

Even though it was sunny, the forest was dense. The shade from the thickness of the trees chilled them. The group gathered around a fire that kept them warm.

Thalios entered into the circle and stood next to the fire. He looked at Elizabeth, slowly turning his head, taking in the expressions on their faces, until he had the attention of all.

"You think your journey is almost over," he said, "but it is only just beginning. If you are successful enough to get the Grymlons regenerated, you still have to get them back to Kimadrian safely. The Grymlons will be as bright as a beacon when they have their full magical power. You will be at the mercy of all who may wish to challenge you. Some of you may not make it home. I can only guide you to your destination. I am here to assist Elizabeth with the Grymlons. When they have been regenerated, I will take you back through the entrance at Stonehenge. My Order is not permitted to interfere with the elves in any way."

"You will need all your strength and courage over the next few days. Tomorrow will be the most important day for all of you. Tomorrow is the summer solstice, the only day that the Grymlons can be regenerated.

My task will be finished when we have passed back through the entrance at the Heel Stone. I have great faith that you will be able to carry out this most daunting task.

Please, all of you try to get some rest. I am going to find some clothes for you elves. We will be back as soon as we can."

Thalios turned and motioned for Keslyn to follow him.

"I'll take first watch. I don't think I can sleep anyway," Gideon said, getting to his feet.

No one spoke.

He jumped up into a tree and settled onto one of the branches.

The rest of them made their beds on the forest floor, for the daytime hours.

Around six in the evening, Elizabeth looked over at Bindyl, who was keeping watch. He turned and looked at her. She motioned that she was going to go for a walk. He nodded and turned back to his lookout position.

She walked out to the edge of the forest, looked north to Avebury, scanning the countryside around her.

"I never realized how beautiful it was around here," she thought. "The fields and the rolling hills, still unspoiled after thousands of years. I can see for miles!"

Elizabeth felt as though someone was watching her from the edge of the forest.

She turned.

"Is someone there?" she said.

A young doe appeared. It looked directly at her, and her surprise the doe approached her. She reached out and touched the deer on the head. It pushed gently against Elizabeth's hand.

She went back into the safety and cover of the trees. The doe began to follow then suddenly stopped. Elizabeth turned to see Thalios standing behind her with Keslyn at his side.

"You have a gift," he said.

The doe disappeared into the trees.

"I think after all this is over, that you and I will meet again," he said.

"How would you know that?" she asked.

"You are the one. You are the one who will change everything," he said.

"You sound so sure, but what about the elviron girl?" said Elizabeth.

He handed her a bag. "We will see, Elizabeth Ghenestone. I obtained these clothes for the elves from some friends close by. I hope they fit," he said, as he turned and walked back into the forest.

"Where are you going?" she called after him.

Thalios either did not hear her or he chose not to answer. He disappeared into the trees. Elizabeth shrugged her shoulders and made her way back to the camp.

Gideon was awake and talking to Bindyl when she returned.

"Did you enjoy your walk?" he asked.

"Yes, I didn't realize how far into the forest we had come."

She looked into Gideon's eyes.

"You have the most amazing green eyes," she thought.

Realizing that she was staring, Elizabeth dropped her gaze and handed him the bag of clothes.

Gideon sat down by the fire, pulled the clothes out of the bag and began rifling through them. He gave some to Bindyl, who went to try them on.

Elizabeth also took a seat by the fire. She looked over at Zoe who was still sleeping. Charlie was curled up in a ball by her chest.

"Do you think she is going to be strong enough to be of any help?" she asked Gideon.

"I know she wants very badly to repay you for saving her life," he answered. "Bindyl is very grateful to you too. He loves Zoe very much."

Elizabeth let out a quiet laugh. "I wonder if he knows what he's in for?"

"All I know is that she wants to be with him and not me. That suits me just fine," Gideon replied.

They both laughed.

Gideon turned, as they heard a noise behind them.

Thalios was entering the camp with Keslyn.

"I could hear you two laughing back in the trees. It's good to hear laughter," he said with a smile.

It was 7:30 p.m. by the time everyone was awake and everything was organized. The elves looked almost normal in the clothes Thalios found for them.

"Be ready to leave by 11:00 p.m.," he told them. "I have to leave for a while. There is an important matter that Keslyn and I need to attend to before we can escort you further. Please try to stay out of sight."

He and Keslyn walked back into the forest, leaving a few hours before they could be on their way.

They sat around a newly lit fire. Zoe made some elven tea, and handed out some bread and cheese.

"Where does he keep going?" said Elizabeth. "He wanders off into the woods, then reappears from out of nowhere."

"We have learned not to question what the druids do," said Gideon. "They have an innate ability to be where they are needed. And we thank them for that."

"Well I've never met a druid up close before. Thalios gives me the creeps," said Zoe.

"He is our guide until we get back down to the badlands. I suggest you keep your opinions to yourself," said Gideon.

"I think he is rather a noble figure," said Elizabeth.

"You would, being a human," said Bindyl.

"What's that suppose to mean?" asked Elizabeth.

"All Bindyl meant was," Zoe chipped in. "We don't have many druids in the elven realm. You probably see them all the time up there."

"Actually, we don't see many of them at all, except on the solstice. They don't dress up in those robes all the time."

"Then why is Thalios dressed like that every time we see him?" said Zoe.

"He belongs to a secret order of well… full time druids, if you like. Unless you actually knew a druid in the Human Realm, you wouldn't now one if you saw one." Elizabeth replied.

"You are an odd lot," said Gideon. "But odd in a good way, Liz," he added quickly.

Just after 10:30 p.m., Thalios and Keslyn returned. Thalios looked a little tired, and so did Keslyn.

"The dragon looks a little different, don't you think?" Elizabeth said to Zoe.

Zoe glanced at Keslyn and shrugged. "She looks the same to me."

"We will be leaving soon," said Thalios. "I suggest you eat a light meal before we begin our journey. I'm not sure when we will get the chance to eat again."

Zoe prepared some berries. With them, she served a kind of pie she had brought with her that tasted of cheese and apples.

After they had eaten, they put out the fire and made everything tidy, careful to leave no trace of a camp.

Thalios called them all together.

"It is time to be on our way," he said, looking around at everyone. "All of you must keep your eyes and ears alert for any danger. I will lead the way. Please try to stay close. It is very dark out there, and it will be easy to get lost. We must try to be quiet. There will be many people around this area for the solstice.

Chapter Eighty Three

It was late in the evening when they finally exited the forest and headed in a north-westerly direction.

Their journey was slow going, but uneventful. At almost 3:00 a.m. they approached Avebury.

Following the road to the town of West Kennet, they veered north and entered the Avebury circles from Kennet Avenue. The first of the stones came into view, followed by many more, forming two lines straight ahead. As Thalios led Elizabeth and the others through the avenue of stones, the shapes in the dark began to give out a low humming sound. Elizabeth heard the Grymlons humming in return from inside of the back pack.

Thalios led them into the south circle.

In the surrounding fields, some people who had arrived for the solstice were sleeping. A few still moved around in the darkness.

"It's time to get to work, Elizabeth," said Thalios. "The rest of you must leave the circle. You may wait along the edge, but do not try to come in until after Elizabeth has regenerated the Grymlons."

Thalios turned and said something to Keslyn and she flew off into the night. Elizabeth entered the centre of the large stones, followed by Thalios.

"Step forward until you see a plinth about three feet high in the ground," said Thalios.

"Yes, that's where the obelisk was, isn't it?" asked Elizabeth.

"You are correct," replied Thalios. "You know what to do from there."

Elizabeth stepped up to the plinth. She put down the bag holding the Grymlons and held up her hands to the sky. Turning her face upwards, she said,

"As the sun rises to greet us.

Let all who gather here sleep.
Protect the chosen travellers.
From the eyes of those who seek.
As the morning meets the rising sun.
Let the ritual be done."

"Good," said Thalios. "Now everyone around us will sleep and
you can regenerate the Grymlons without being interrupted.

Elizabeth knelt down, opening the backpack. The Grymlons rose
out of it, circling in the air, moving over the plinth. As they moved, she
said some words in Elvish. The Grymlons lost their disguise and
turned into orbs once more.

Elizabeth stood back. The Grymlons rose higher, hovering fifteen
feet in the air. A rumbling sound shook the ground. The earth around
the plinth began to crack, and the plinth toppled to one side, pushed by
an enormous rock. The rock stopped about two feet below the orbs.

The obelisk had returned to regenerate the Grymlons.

The shape of a cross appeared on the side of it. The Grymlons
formed a line and descended onto it.

Colour ran through them, swirling, changing and moving all of the
time. A blue circle of light radiated from the obelisk, knocking
Elizabeth over as it rushed passed. The light stopped the other side of
the stones. The blue light hung in the air like a large protective hoop.

Gideon tried to step through the stones to help Elizabeth get up,
but was pushed back by the light. He landed on his backside three feet
away from the others.

Bindyl looked at Gideon and laughed, but stopped abruptly when
he saw Gideon pointing towards the circle. As Bindyl turned to look,
fear stabbed his heart.

Standing inside of the ring was an elviron girl. By her side was an
elviron male. The male was crouched in a submissive position, fearfully
watching the events unfold.

Bindyl instinctively turned to make sure that Zoe was behind him,
but she was gone. He looked back into the circle and saw her standing
behind Verina.

Verina stepped forward and Zoe followed her, walking beside
Verina's servant. As per Verina's instructions, Zoe had followed
Elizabeth into the circle, knowing that the Grymlons would protect
themselves by forming a ring around the stones.

"Elizabeth," Verina said. "So here we are at last. You should have
killed me when you had the chance. Zoe has been keeping me

informed ever since you reached the badlands."

Elizabeth turned to Zoe, dumbfounded. "I have saved your life not once, but twice, and you betray us?"

Zoe dropped her eyes.

Elizabeth turned to Verina. "How did you know it was me at the castle in Distardrian? I was wearing a magical disguise. And how has Zoe been keeping you informed? She has been with us the whole time."

"The answer to your first question," said Verina. "When we met at the castle in Distardrian, you seemed to be doing way too much magic to be just an elf. I cast a spell to see your true face. I have been studying the prophesy about the chosen one. My father thought it might have been me. He also knew about your bloodline and had to consider that it might be you. And here you are again."

"To answer your second question. Zoe has been leaving notes and signs behind all along. She will be well rewarded for her help.

Now I believe that the Grymlons will be mine, but first you will finish regenerating them."

Elizabeth looked past Verina to Zoe, who kept her eyes down.

"You will pay for this, Zoe, and as for you, you disgusting excuse for... what the heck are you anyway? Are you human or elviron? It doesn't matter. If you truly are the chosen one, then regenerate them yourself. My family are the guardians to the Grymlons. If you're not chosen to be a guardian, the Gymlons will take your essence as they regenerate. Do you really want to take that chance? I won't regenerate the Grymlons for you. I would rather they die than hand them over to you."

Elizabeth put an arm out to pull one of the Grymlons free from the cross.

"Oh, I think you will. I have your grandmother. I will kill her if you don't do as I want," said Verina, grabbing Zoe and pulling her to the front.

Elizabeth withdrew her hand from the Grymlons. She watched helplessly as Verina put her arm around Zoe's waist and placed a knife to her throat. Zoe looked at Elizabeth for the first time. Elizabeth could see she was petrified.

Elizabeth and Verina became locked in a gaze. "Don't do it Verina. If you kill Zoe, you'll pay for her life with your own."

Verina smiled at Elizabeth, raised the knife into the air and plunged it deep into Zoe's chest.

Bindyl screamed and tried to jump at the blue light surrounding the ring of stones. He was pushed back in the same manner as Gideon.

Verina let go of Zoe, who fell to the ground like a rag doll.

Thalios stepped forward and pointed his staff at Verina.

Verina put out her hand and pushed through the air. Thalios dropped his staff and grabbed at his throat, as though invisible hands were choking him. He fell to the ground, struggling with an unseen force.

Elizabeth stepped in front of him and put up her hand. Verina stepped back a few paces, grabbing her own throat, but soon stepped forward again.

"You'll have to have more than that to get the job done, you stupid human," she sneered.

The sound of wings flapping could be heard from above them. It was Keslyn. She had been waiting, in case Elizabeth needed help.

Verina looked up, swiping her hand into the air. A bolt of green light shot towards Keslyn, who deftly slipped to the side. The bolt of light shot off into the night. Keslyn looked down upon Elizabeth and pushed a thought into her head. Elizabeth listened, careful not to look up.

Elizabeth stood perfectly still. With her hands by her sides, she looked over at the Grymlons. A thin blue line appeared from the middle Grymlon and headed towards her. Elizabeth opened her mouth and inhaled the blue line until it stopped. She turned and looked at Verina.

The same blue light from the circle outside of the stones was now in Elizabeth's eyes. When Verina saw this, she felt a hint of panic rise inside of her. Elizabeth raised her hands upward with her palms flat, as though pushing up the air on either side of her.

Keslyn flew back into view. She shot fire from her nostrils. The fire wrapped itself around Elizabeth's outstretched palms, snaking out towards Verina. The fire surrounded Verina, wrapping around her like a rope. Elizabeth walked towards Verina, who was involuntarily moving forward, towards her.

"You can't do this! I am the chosen one!" said Verina, in disbelief.

The two continued to come together until they were only inches apart. Elizabeth put her hand through the fire and into Verina's chest. As the fire around Verina faded, a red light appeared inside of her chest. Elizabeth wrapped her fingers around it and with one swift movement, pulled out the light as Verina's lifeless body dropped to the ground.

Elizabeth now stood with the dark essence of Verina in her hand. She gently caressed the red light, moving it around in her fingers. She squeezed it and a scream pierced the air.

A faint red glow began to span the horizon. Dawn was coming. The blue ring around the stones began to dim slightly.

Verina's servant cowered beside one of the stones, waiting for his chance to escape.

Two robed figures appeared from the west end of the circle. Still holding Verina's essence in her hand, Elizabeth looked their way. "This is new," she said under her breath.

When they reached her, one of them stepped forward and held out his hand.

"I believe you have something of ours," he said.

Elizabeth looked down at the small light floating just above her hand.

"Everything inside of me wants to put this up to my lips and swallow it!" she thought, desperately trying to resist the temptation.

The figure in the dark cowl spoke to her softly. "You have a job to do. This creature is ours now."

With all of her willpower, Elizabeth handed the essence to the robed figure. He took the red light and rejoined his companion. They returned back the way they had come, but did not leave. Instead, they waited at the edge of the stones.

Keslyn reappeared. She shot a bolt of fire from her nostrils at Verina's remains. Her body burst into flames. A few seconds later, all that remained was dust. A slight breeze rolled what was left away to nothing.

"Hurry, Elizabeth!" Thalios called, still sitting on the grass. "Quickly, take my staff. The light is coming up over the horizon, soon it will be too late!"

Elizabeth ran to him. She grabbed his staff and ran back towards the Grymlons. She stood in front of the rock, facing the cross and slammed the staff down!

She chanted a spell as the Grymlons raised up and moved clockwise around the top of the obelisk. The orbs moved faster and faster until they were a multi coloured blur. The sun came over the horizon, hitting the orbs with a blinding flash of light. Then they just stopped - suspended in the air.

For a few seconds, everything was still. Then the ground shook, as the obelisk fell back into the earth. The plinth, as though being moved by unseen hands, rose off the ground and placed itself upright where the obelisk had been. The orbs floated down and rested gently where they had been placed.

Thalios came up behind Elizabeth and took his staff from her.

She stood for a moment, trying to absorb everything, when she heard a groaning behind her. It was Zoe. Elizabeth ran to her, knelt down and lifted Zoe's head. "She's bleeding to death!" she thought, cradling Zoe's head.

"Elizabeth, I'm sorry. Verina has my brother," Zoe said. "When she captured me at the castle in Distardrian, she knew that you would bring me back. She knew who you were all the time. She said that if I did what she wanted, she would give me back by brother. Please forgive me."

"I'm not going to let her die, not after all I've been through to keep her alive," Elizabeth thought, taking her hand.

Elizabeth closed her eyes and in her mind focussed on Zoe's wound. She put her hand over the site and waited to see if anything would come to her, to help the healing. Nothing came.

Thalios waved his staff in a circle. The blue ring faded from the stones.

Bindyl ran to Zoe and knelt down, cradling her head in his lap.

He looked up at Elizabeth. "You have to help her."

"I don't think I can this time," she said.

"Why not?" asked Bindyl.

"Well, for one thing. The other times I saved Zoe, they weren't around," Elizabeth said, nodding towards the two robed figures who had taken Verina's essence.

"Don't let them near her!" said Bindyl.

"I wondered why they hadn't left. I don't think I can stop them," said Elizabeth.

"They took Verina! What if they're… You know, from down there," said Bindyl, pointing at the ground.

"Well, why don't we ask them, Bindyl," she said.

Elizabeth approached the robed figures and talked with them while Bindyl waited with Zoe.

After a short conversation, she headed back to Bindyl and knelt down with him. "Zoe did what she had to, to try and save her brother. Those robed figures, they are called messengers. It's their job to transport elves to either the good place or the bad place. "They are here to take her, but they say she is going to a good place.

Bindyl looked over at them. "Are you sure, Elizabeth?"

"Yes," she replied.

The two robed figures began walking towards them, and Bindyl cradled Zoe's head protectively.

"Elizabeth, please try once more," he said, desperately.

Elizabeth knelt down and took Zoe's hand. She closed her eyes and concentrated on healing Zoe's wound.

"No!" she heard Bindyl say.

Elizabeth felt a hand on her shoulder. When she looked up, one of the robed figures was standing behind her shaking his head.

"Not this time," he said.

Elizabeth nodded. She gently turned Zoe's face towards her.

"I will find your brother and take him to your parents," she said. "I promise they shall have him back."

Zoe nodded and closed her eyes.

Crying, Bindyl looked down on his Zoe.

"Why?" he blurted out.

Zoe opened her eyes and looked into Bindyl's. "I love my brother. I had to try to save him. When I discovered he was at the castle, I stopped thinking about myself and how I was going to get back at Gideon for making me angry. My brother became more important than me."

Bindyl held her, he looked down at her, watching her life fade.

"Please help her," he pleaded.

Elizabeth looked up at the robed figure, and he shook his head again.

"I can't Bindyl. They won't let me," she said.

Zoe took hold of Bindyl's hand. "You have to let me go."

Elizabeth got to her feet and turned to the robed figures.

"Can you give them a few minutes to say goodbye?" she asked.

One of them nodded, and they returned to the edge of the stone circle.

Elizabeth went to the Grymlons. She bent down to pick them up. To her surprise, they rose and hovered in front of her. She held up the bag and one by one, they dropped into it.

A few minutes later, Bindyl stood. He walked towards Gideon who had been standing a few feet away. The life had finally gone from Zoe's body. Gideon put his arm around him. At Gideon's touch,

Bindyl crumpled into his friend's arms.

Elizabeth helped Thalios, who had sat back down on the grass to catch his breath.

"Are you all right?" she asked him.

"I'm a bit sore, but I have no serious injuries," he said, holding his lower back. "We have to leave. We need to get the Grymlons away from here as quickly as possible."

Elizabeth looked over at Bindyl and Gideon. "I know," she answered, "but they need just a little time. We can give them that can't we?"

"Yes," said Thalios, "we can give them that."

Elizabeth looked back at Zoe.

"You disgusting little monster!" she shouted, as she broke into a run towards Zoe's body.

Verina's servant had reappeared. It seemed the temptation of another essence was just too much, and he was leaning over Zoe, about to put his hand on her chest. Elizabeth stopped when the robed figures chased away the elviron and lifted her up. Thalios hurried over to them and said something. They placed her back on the ground.

Thalios called Bindyl back to Zoe's body.

"Zoe is going to be taken to her resting place. Why don't you go to her and say goodbye?" he said.

Bindyl knelt down and kissed her.

"I love you Zoe. I will always love you. I promise when my time comes I will find you. Please wait for me," he said, tears streaming down his face.

He stood back, watching as the robed figures lifted her. They walked out of stones, becoming more and more transparent, until finally they disappeared.

Bindyl looked on as they vanished, continuing to stare where they had been.

"It's time to go," Gideon said quietly, stepping up beside him.

"But what if there's been a mistake? Perhaps if we wait a few minutes, they might bring her back," said Bindyl.

"Bindyl, there has been no mistake. We have to leave," said Gideon.

Thalios approached Elizabeth, and looked over to where Bindyl was standing.

"We must leave. We need to get back to the forest as soon as we can," he insisted

Elizabeth nodded. She went to Bindyl and put her arm around him. Gideon joined her, putting his arm around Bindyl's shoulder from the other side.

"Bindyl, she's gone," Elizabeth said. "We have to go now."

The three of them left the stone ring.

"We can rest and shelter at a nearby farmhouse," Thalios said. "The people there are friends of the druids and familiar with the elves. We must hurry. The Grymlons will be giving off a powerful signal now that they have been regenerated."

He motioned for them to follow him.

Elizabeth turned towards the stones.

"It is done," she said, bowing to the circle.

The people camping and sleeping in adjacent fields began to wake.

With great sadness, the druid, the little cat, the elves and the young girl with the Grymlons, made their way out of the circles of Avebury.

Chapter Eight Four

The Cotswold stone house was old, but in good condition. As they approached the gate in the middle of a high stone wall, they were greeted by an elderly woman with grey hair. She wore an apron with a flowery pattern. Her name was Carrie Westbury. She had helped the elves for many years. Carrie and George Westbury were both ninety-five years old, but looked a lot younger: a gift from the elves for their help over the years.

"Follow me. You must all be hungry," she said, as she led the way through the cobbled stone courtyard.

"Do I smell freshly baked bread?" said Elizabeth.

"I just baked a few loaves this mornin' for toast and sandwiches," Carrie Westbury replied.

They passed a cow shed on the left, a horse barn and chicken coop to the right.

In the middle of the cobble stone yard stood a now obsolete hand operated water pump.

Carrie Westbury directed them up two stone steps and in through the back door to a large kitchen. In the centre of the room was a farmhouse table. On it, were half a dozen different jams and jellies in various glass jars, and a large jar of pure honey. Two racks full of toast sat on the middle of the table, made from home made bread. Bacon, sausages and scrambled eggs had been placed next to the toast.

"Who would like a cup of tea on this fine summer mornin'?" Carrie Westbury asked her guests.

Gideon shot his hand into the air, nodding his head vigorously.

"With four sugars please," he said, grinning.

The others said yes please, to the tea.

Carrie Westbury raised an eyebrow at Gideon.

"My, you 'ave a sweet tooth, but then you elves mostly do," she said to herself, as she turned to the stove.

Everyone sat down at the kitchen table. Keslyn and Charlie sat on the floor at the end.

"Well, dig in. I didn't make all this breakfast for my hubby and me, ya know," Carrie said.

She turned from the stove and walked to the back door of the kitchen. She opened the door.

"GEORGE! BREAKFAST IS READY AND OUR GUESTS ARE HERE," she shouted into the yard.

A faint voice could be heard from inside the cowshed, answering the call.

"George will be in to meet you all in just a bit. He's finishin' with the milkin'," Carrie informed, them as she sat down at the edge of the table.

She poured tea into tea cups for everyone.

Gideon helped himself to toast and honey. Bindyl had no appetite, but sipped his tea. Elizabeth and Thalios tucked into the eggs and bacon.

When George Westbury came in, he put his cap down on the counter to the left of him. He took his wellington boots off and put them outside of the back door. Then he went to the kitchen sink, washed his hands and dried them.

He went to Thalios, knelt down in front of him and bowed his head. Thalios said something in another language and George answered him in the same language. Thalios said something else and George repeated his words. Both Gideon and Bindyl bowed their heads, repeating the same words as Thalios and George.

George Westbury turned to the group. "Well, it's nice to meet you all. I see mother has put a good breakfast on the table as usual."

He sat down and helped himself to the eggs bacon and sausages.

"I take it that the job was well done then?" George asked, looking up as he ate.

Thalios looked around the table, waiting for someone to answer.

Elizabeth looked up from her food.

"Oh… ah. Yes. It, it went well, at least I think it did," she said, looking at Thalios.

"We had casualties, but the mission was accomplished," Thalios informed him.

Bindyl pushed his cup and saucer away from him. Gideon put his hand on his friend's shoulder and gave him a reassuring rub on the back.

Bindyl stood. "If you would excuse me," he said, leaving the table.

He walked outside, and Gideon started to follow.

"Sit down, Gideon," said Thalios. "He will need time, and he will need to be alone to collect his thoughts. These things you cannot help him with."

Gideon pushed his plate away. Suddenly, he did not feel quite so hungry either.

"What happened?" asked George, watching Bindyl walk across the yard.

"Would anyone like more tea?" asked Carrie.

The answer was yes, from everyone. She went to the stove and put the water on to boil.

"I will explain," said Thalios.

Chapter Eight Five

Bindyl stepped into the horse barn. "I think my heart is breaking, it hurts so much," he thought.

He sat at the far end of the barn and began to cry. "We could have had such a life together. Now I'm alone once more. My uncle killed, and now Zoe. Both at the hands of the elviron. When will it all stop?"

Bindyl wiped his eyes with the back of his hand and went over to the horse stall closest to him. Inside was a little white welsh mountain pony. The nameplate on the front of the stable door said 'Toby'.

When Toby saw Bindyl, he stuck his nose out of the opening in the stable door and nudged him on the arm. Bindyl rubbed the little pony's ears. Touching the animal made him feel better.

"Goodbye little pony," Bindyl said, after a minute or two of petting him.

He was about to leave the barn when he heard a sound in the loft. He looked up, but couldn't see anything. He started through the door when he heard the noise again. Looking up, he peered into the darkness above.

"There's someone up there, behind those bales of hay," he thought.

Bindyl climbed up the ladder, peering along the loft's narrow walkway. He turned and saw a string hanging from a light bulb. He pulled on it and as the light turned on, he heard a muffled yelp.

Bindyl stepped along the walkway, following the sound. Crouching down behind a bale of hay was the elviron who had been with Verina.

"What have we here?" Rage filled Bindyl's body. He shook with pure anger, as he leaned down, grabbing the elviron by the neck.

The elviron screamed as Bindyl dragged him to the opening in the loft floor and threw him down to the ground below.

The elviron scrambled towards the door.

"Oh no you don't!" said Bindyl, as he followed him through the opening, he grabbed the creature before it had the chance to make its getaway.

The door to the kitchen was open. The sound of chattering voices could be heard coming from inside. Conversation stopped when they heard the scream.

All of them stood at once and headed towards the back door. George Westbury was the first to step outside. When he looked towards the horse barn, he saw Bindyl dragging the elviron across the yard.

"Oh my, what now?" he said, putting his hands in his pockets.

Elizabeth moved around him, so that she could see what all the noise was about. She watched as Bindyl dragged the elviron to the water pump. The sun was up and smoke was twirling from several places on the elviron's body.

Bindyl seemed oblivious to the rest of the group, who were staring at him and his captive. The elviron struggled, but Bindyl held him still, waiting for the sunlight to do its job.

Elizabeth began to walk over to him, but George Westbury put a hand on her arm.

"It's too late, miss. You can't save the poor wretch now," he said, nodding at the spectacle before them.

The elviron was in flames. Within seconds, all that was left of it were a few ashes strewn here and there around the pump.

Everyone looked on in shock. Bindyl glared back at them, his face chalk white. He turned, walked through the gate and strode off across the fields.

"What if someone sees him? He's dressed like a human, but he doesn't look like one," said Gideon.

"It's mid-summers day," said Thalios. "Do you know how many strange looking people are out there on this day?

This is the one day of the year, when this peaceful, beautiful area is strewn with people from all walks of life.

People trying to ponder the origins of all the strange and wonderful things around here. I suspect that some of them are less than sane. Some dress so strangely, I wonder if half of England may go slightly mad on this day. No, Bindyl will not stand out in any crowd, not today."

"Thalios is right," said George. "On the solstice, we've seen many people dressed in some very strange clothes, doin' some very strange things around 'ere."

Thalios put his arm around Gideon's shoulder. "He will come back when he is ready. Today has been incredibly hard for him. Give him time."

"Things will never be the same now," Gideon said. "My once carefree friend with the wonderful sense of humour, has turned into a cold blooded killer, right before my eyes. No. Things will never be the same."

Chapter Eighty Six

"It felt good to kill that elviron," Bindyl thought, as he walked. "It feels a bit like the score has evened out just a little. How will I explain myself to the druid and the others? If they have a problem with it? Well so be it. What is done, is done."

He found a stone wall and sat for a while. He let the same sun that had killed the elviron, wash over him until he felt clean. When he felt better, he made his way back towards the farm.

Chapter Eighty Seven

It was almost noon by the time Bindyl entered the kitchen of the farmhouse.

Elizabeth, Gideon and Thalios were talking with George Westbury when he returned.

Carrie Westbury put her hand on his arm.

"Would you like a cup of tea?"

Bindyl sat down at the table with the others. "Yes please."

"Are you all right?" Elizabeth asked.

"I hate all the elviron," said Bindyl. "If I had not killed him, he would have killed at least one of us, if not all of us. Why did he come here?"

Carrie Westbury put a cup of hot tea down in front of him, and he took a sip.

"They are quick and this is the only farm around this area," said Thalios. "This is the only place he would have been able to hide safely until the night hours."

"We could have learned a lot from him about Verina," Gideon said.

"What good would that have done after the fact?" said Bindyl. "It was too late for him to give information to us. He had lost his mistress. All he wanted to do was feed and go home."

"It's done now," said George Westbury. "No good cryin' over spilt milk. I suggest you all eat a bit of lunch and get some rest. You have a long walk back to Stonehenge."

George left the table and went into the parlour. He sat in his favourite chair, filled his pipe with tobacco and enjoyed a smoke.

Carrie Westbury had put out blankets and pillows in the living room for everyone, so that their guests could sleep if they wanted to. She had also put out clean towels and soap in the bathroom, in case anyone wanted to take a bath or a shower.

Elizabeth took advantage of the bathing opportunity. She closed the bathroom door and turned both bath faucets wide open. When the bathtub was half full, she undressed and slid down into the water.

"It feels good to take a bath. It feels like weeks since I bathed," she thought.

She put a towel behind her head and closed her eyes. After about ten minutes she washed, then dried and dressed.

"I think I'll take a bit of a nap," she thought, making her way into the living room.

Elizabeth found a place on the floor where Carrie had put a blanket and pillow. She made herself comfortable and fell asleep.

***

Zoe was laid out on the table, as still as stone. Elizabeth reached out and touched her face. Zoe opened her eyes. Elizabeth gasped and jumped back as Zoe sat up, turning towards her.

"Beware Elizabeth, there is danger ahead," Zoe said. "The entrance to the cave in the badlands is unprotected now. You should be careful."

"Who? Do what?" was all Elizabeth could say. "Why am I having this awful dream?"

Elizabeth tried to run, but her feet would not move. When she tried to lift her feet, it felt as though they were glued to the floor. As she struggled to move, the light in the room began to fade, until it was almost dark. Sure there was something behind her, Elizabeth screamed.

"Elizabeth, Elizabeth, wake up!"

Elizabeth opened her eyes. Gideon was shaking her by the shoulders.

She sat up, trying to catch her breath.

"You must have been having a nightmare. You were screaming in your sleep," Gideon said, gently touching the side of her face.

Elizabeth turned to see everyone standing in the doorway of the living room. Keslyn shoved her way between Thalios and George Westbury and ran to her. She pushed against Elizabeth's hand until it touched the little dragon's face. Elizabeth immediately felt a rush of joy run through her, then calmness.

"Thank you Keslyn. I needed that!" she pushed back, stroking Keslyn's head.

The little dragon nodded and returned to her master.

"Why don't you get up young Miss. I'll make you a cup of tea," said Carrie.

Chapter Eighty Eight

The rest of the day was spent discovering things around the farm, playing with the animals and talking to George Westbury. As it turned out, George had some amusing stories to tell about the druids.

At 11:30 p.m. it was time to prepare for their journey to the Savernake forest.

Elizabeth and the others gathered up their belongings. While she was putting all her things together, she picked up the backpack with the Grymlons inside.

"It feels light, as though it's empty," she thought.

She opened the backpack to look inside, and a light blazed out of it, making the whole room glow.

"Close that bag!" Thalios shouted, rushing towards her. "You are sending an invitation to all who want those orbs to come and get them."

"Sorry!" she said, startled by his sternness, zipping up the backpack.

"Do not open that bag again until you are inside the castle at Kimadrian!" Thalios said.

"Yes, yes. I get it!" Elizabeth answered.

"The journey back to Kimadrian is going to be an even more nerve wracking experience than the journey here," Gideon whispered to Bindyl.

He nodded in agreement, as they turned and left the room.

Just before midnight, George and Carrie Westbury waited by the back gate. Carrie Westbury gave Elizabeth a hug. She gave Bindyl an even bigger hug. She made as if to hug Gideon, but he quickly grabbed her hand before she could put her arms around him and shook it vigorously. George Westbury shook hands with all the males in the group. Then he put his hand out and clasped Elizabeth's hand in his.

"Be careful, miss. Your job's not done yet."

"I will," Elizabeth replied.

She reached up and kissed him on the cheek, she did the same to Carrie.

George and Carrie Westbury stood by the gate and waved goodbye to them, as they made their way homeward.

A few minutes into their journey, Keslyn came up beside Elizabeth and walked with her. Elizabeth turned to Thalios, and he smiled and nodded to let her know it as okay. She looked down at Keslyn, who seemed quite content to be her walking companion.

They travelled slowly, their minds and hearts heavy. When they reached the forest, the group stopped for a rest, and then continued until they were almost to the other side.

The sun had been up for a while when they made camp.

"We are all very tired," said Thalios. "I suggest we eat, then rest for the daytime hours. I will take the first watch, as I need to leave for a while.

When it was Gideon's turn to watch the camp, Thalios woke him.

"I have to go now. I'll be back in a bit," he said.

Bindyl was sitting in a tree guarding the camp, when Thalios and Keslyn returned. He noticed that Thalios looked worried.

"Is anything wrong, Thalios?" he asked.

"Wake the others and have them gather around the campfire," said Thalios.

Bindyl jumped down from the tree and woke everyone.

Thalios stood by the fire. "While I was attending to my duties, I ran into Malion, a nomadic druid who travels the countryside," he told them. "Malion decided to pay Ghyrone a visit. For him to be able to get down below, Ghyrone has to grant him access. Malion told me that he could get no further than the Heel Stone. Try as he might, he could not contact Ghyrone. Malion finally gave up and decided to track me down. He warned me that I may find it difficult to get you back down to the badlands."

"Will we be able to get back down to the badlands, if Ghyrone isn't there?" Gideon asked.

"As a member of the druidic Council, I can go just about where ever I choose," said Thalios. "Even if something has happened to Ghyrone, I have the power to get us below.

"We must get to the Heel Stone as soon as possible," Elizabeth said.

"I agree," said Thalios. "It's not quite dusk, but I think we should risk setting out now. We should be able to get to the Heel Stone by dark,"

"We should change into our elven clothing now it will save time," said Gideon.

"Good idea. You and Bindyl change. Elizabeth and I will clean up," said Thalios.

A few minutes later, they set out across the fields towards Stonehenge. As twilight began, they came to a road and crossed to the other side. They were climbing under a fence to cut across the fields, when the sound of a police siren was heard. Just one blast, enough to get their attention and make them turn around.

Thalios moved to the front of the group, as the officer got out of his police car.

Constable Goodley wiped his brow as he approached this strange band of people.

"Not another group of weirdos," he thought as he neared them. "If I 'ave to deal with one more group of creepy, odd, strange idiots. I think I just might shoot myself!"

He stepped up, confronting them. "All right, what 'ave we got 'ere. Just where do you people think you're goin? Did you know this is private property?" he asked, rocking on his heels with his hands behind his back.

Thalios stepped forward. "I am an Arch Druid, officer, and I have been given permission to take these young folk across the fields to Stonehenge."

The officer looked him up and down, then turned his gaze to the others.

"Do you know 'ow many "druids" I 'ave come across this last twenty-four hours," the constable said, making quotational bunny ears with his fingers, "and do you know 'ow many of 'em 'ave actually been druids? I know most of the druids around 'ere, sir. I was born and bred 'ere. I don't remember seein' your face. Besides, I would think that if you were a real druid, you would know the summer solstice is over." He smiled at Keslyn.

"Nice dragon though, very realistic."

"Well... I... I..." Thalios stammered, trying to find the right words to make the police officer go away.

"I thought so," said Officer Goodley.

At the Constable's comment, Elizabeth stepped forward. As she waved her hand, she looked at the police officer.

"Sleep," she said, looking into his eyes.

He obeyed, as they all did when she did this. In fact, he closed his eyes and dropped like a stone in the middle of the road.

"Oh my heavens! Quickly!" said Thalios. "Help me get him off the road and into his car."

Gideon and Bindyl rushed forward and helped to pick the police officer up. They put him in driver seat of his police car, propping him up so he wouldn't attract attention.

They made a hasty retreat back to the edge of the field. As they were hurrying away, Gideon looked back at the police car.

"How long will he sleep?" he asked. "Have you wondered how long these people sleep if you don't tell them when to wake up?"

"I don't know, I haven't researched that too much yet, haven't had the time. But he looked awfully peaceful didn't he?" she said, with a grin.

They both laughed.

Thalios was also smiling as he walked ahead of the others with Charlie and Keslyn.

They made their way across the fields, and saw many people on their way home from the Summer Solstice. Some by car and some on foot. Most of them ready to go back to being normal for another year.

Chapter Eighty Nine

At 11:00 p.m., Stonehenge came into view in the murky darkness.

There were no more visitors. Most of the rubbish and other bits and pieces that contributed to the solstice celebrations had already been cleaned up by the local council workers.

Thalios made an opening in the fence. The group made their way to the Heel Stone and waited, as Thalios used his staff to summon the opening in the ground.

"Hurry! We must not be seen," he said.

Elizabeth went down first, followed by Charlie. Gideon and Bindyl were hot on their heels.

Thalios took a quick look around to make sure that no one was watching, then he and Keslyn hurried down the steps. He quickly closed the opening. Thalios picked up a torch and lit it. He stood in front of the gate and produced the key. He opened the iron gate that stood at the entrance to the tunnel. They hurried through, Thalios following behind them.

"I'm not supposed to go any farther, but I must make sure Ghyrone is unharmed," he said, locking the gate behind him. "I may be worrying for nothing, but I'll go with you, just in case."

When they reached the gate to the entrance of the cave in the badlands, Elizabeth called out Lebrue's name.

The twins, Anna and Lebrue were standing inside the entrance. They were looking out, watching something.

Lebrue jumped so high into the air, he had to use his wings to steady himself.

"Are you trying to give me a heart attack?" he said, as he turned towards her with his hand on his chest.

"Sorry, but we need to get out of here. Where is Ghyrone?"

Lebrue cast his eyes down, turning his gaze to the corner of the cave.

"Over there," he said, pointing to a bundle of brown cloth on the cave floor.

"We can't see from here. Is he all right?" asked Thalios.

"No," replied Lebrue, "he's dead. He was that way when we returned here."

Elizabeth felt a chill run through her. "Lebrue, do you know how to get us out of here?"

Lebrue shook his head.

"We arrived back here two hours ago. I checked to see if Ghyrone was breathing, but he was dead."

Thalios stepped to the front of the group. "Stand back all of you."

He began chanting words in the same language he used back at the farmhouse.

"What is that language?" Elizabeth wispered to Gideon.

"You do not recognize you own langauge?" he said, "it's Old English."

"Well, taking into consideration, it hasn't been taught in the mainstream school system for well… ever! No, I didn't recognize it." She wispered back.

Ghyrone's body moved slightly. Anna ran to Lebrue and stood behind him. Thalios slammed down his staff and said the words again, only much louder and more forcefully.

This time Ghyrone's body shook. With tremendous effort he stood, and struggled to the gate. His face was as white as chalk.

Thalios uttered more words as Ghyrone moved unsteadily towards the bars. He touched the lock on the gate. As he did so, the door swung open.

Thalios rushed through the gate followed by Elizabeth and the others. He gently touched Ghyrone on the shoulder.

"Go to your resting place my son, and thank you for waiting for our return," Thalios told him.

Ghyrone slumped into Thalios' arms, and Thalios let out a loud cry, falling to his knees beside Ghyrone's body.

Thalios held both his arms high and looked to the ceiling.

"Come, my brothers of the past," he shouted. "Honour this druid whose time has come. Take him in your arms and lift him to his resting place."

The others had to cover their eyes from the glare, as the room filled with a bright light. The body of Ghyrone rose off the ground. It continued upwards, until hands came down from the ceiling and held him, pulling him. Ghyrone's body hesitated for a couple of seconds when it reached the ceiling, then was gone.

"You called him your son. What did you mean?" asked Elizabeth.

With tears streaming down his face, Thalios explained.

"Ghyrone was my son. He could have moved on, but he chose to stay in his body, until we arrived so that he could let us out of the tunnel. That was what I meant when I told you that I would have the power to get us out of here. I knew that if Ghyrone had been killed, his essence would stay here until I arrived.

He knew I would have the power to get him to the gate."

"Oh Thalios, I don't know what to say," said Elizabeth.

Lebrue returned to the cave entrance and was once more looking outside.

"We have a rather large problem outside," he said.

Thalios looked out of the cave entrance. "Oh no!"

Elizabeth joined them. "Why are they out there?" she asked.

"What is it?" asked Gideon.

When he looked outside, his mouth dropped open and his face went white.

Bindyl started to join the others at the entrance, but when he saw Gideon's face, he stopped. "What's out there? Come on, someone tell me."

None of them answered him.

Bindyl finally plucked up the courage to look outside. Without thinking, he touched the side of his face where the scar from the claw of the draghorn had caught him.

Gideon turned to Elizabeth.

"There must be over a hundred draghorns out there," he said.

"Yes," said Lebrue, "we didn't know there were so many."

Anna put her arms around Lebrue. He returned the embrace.

"What do you think they want?" Bindyl asked.

Elizabeth looked around her. "Is there another way out of here, Lebrue?"

The twin shook his head. "The only way out, is to go back the way you came and you cannot take the Grymlons back up there."

"Then we will find out what they want," said Thalios, moving a little farther back into the cave.

"They want the Grymlons of course," Elizabeth said, following him.

Thalios shook his head. "The draghorns have no use for the Grymlons. They are immune to magic. No, they are here for something else."

It was then that Thalios noticed Keslyn was missing.

"Yes! That's it!" he said. "Quickly, we must find Keslyn. She is hiding somewhere. Look around, find her, we need her."

Elizabeth looked towards the gateway of the tunnel. She went to the bars and saw Keslyn standing a little way up the tunnel. In all the confusion, no one had noticed that she had not followed them into the cave. Elizabeth looked through the bars and directly into Keslyn's eyes.

"Keslyn, tell me what's going on," Elizabeth pushed into her head.

"They want my baby," she pushed back.

"Baby! What baby?" Elizabeth said.

"The baby I left up in the Human Realm," Keslyn replied.

The sadness in Keslyn's voice almost made Elizabeth cry.

She turned to Thalios. "What baby? What is she talking about?"

Thalios motioned for Elizabeth to come closer.

"Keslyn has laid an egg. It has a very special little dragon inside of it. It has been hidden to keep it safe," he said quietly.

"Where is it?" she asked.

"I cannot tell you," he replied. "We have to keep the egg out of sight. Keslyn gave birth on the eve of the summer solstice, which means that everything came together just right. The regeneration of the Grymlons, the summer solstice and you. All of the signs seem to have come together.

Keslyn may have given birth to a most powerful dragon. The draghorns want the baby to rule as their king or queen. They too have been waiting for their special leader. Keslyn, like any good mother, does not want to give up her baby to those flesh eating savages."

"I still don't quite understand. Why are they waiting here? How did they know to wait at this entrance?" she asked.

Thalios looked back at Keslyn.

"The draghorns are waiting for you and Keslyn. If they find out she has laid the egg. They will assume that you have it," he replied.

"Me! Why me?" said Elizabeth.

"The draghorns must have been watching the events unfold," Thalios replied. "They think that you may be the all powerful Elf/Human all have been waiting for. If the draghorns win the egg from you in battle, they get their prize. A leader to make them powerful again."

"But I don't have it," said Elizabeth.

"That's right," said Thalios. "The draghorns won't go up to the Human Realm, but they must have had one of their scouts watching this entrance. They know that the Grymlons have to be regenerated at this time. They must have waited it out to see who went up and who came back down."

Elizabeth and Thalios moved away from the bars, so they would be out of earshot of Keslyn. Charlie pushed her little feline form through the bars of the entrance to the tunnel, and sat down beside her frightened little friend.

"We have to get her out of there, and we have to get rid of the draghorns somehow," said Elizabeth.

Bindyl began pacing back and forth.

"We could kill her!" he said.

Everyone looked at him in horror.

"Just kidding!" he added, quickly. "I like the little dragon."

"Keep your morbid sense of humour to yourself, Bindyl," said Gideon. "What has come over you?"

Bindyl shrugged his shoulders, turning away from everyone.

An idea formed in Elizabeth's mind. "We could make the draghorns think that she's dead."

"Draghorns communicate telepathically the same way dragons do," said Thalios. "If we tell them that she is dead, they will want to see her body. If Keslyn is not dead, they will be able to get into her mind and they will know that we are lying."

"We do not want to upset them," Bindyl said, touching his face again. "It gets very uncomfortable when they get mad!"

Elizabeth returned to the gate.

"Keslyn," she said. "Keslyn, come here. I want to talk to you."

Keslyn shook her head.

"She's not going to come to you Elizabeth, she's too afraid," said Gideon.

"I wonder if I were to think about…"

Elizabeth stood completely still, closed her eyes and concentrated.

The others heard Charlie growl from inside the cave. She had changed into her mountain lion form and was staring at Elizabeth, as though she was going to attack her.

"LOOK!" Bindyl said, pointing to Elizabeth.

They watched as Elizabeth's body grew transparent: just like an elviron. When she was almost invisible, Elizabeth passed through the closed gate.

Gideon and Bindyl rushed to the gate, followed by Thalios and Lebrue.

Elizabeth continued towards Keslyn. The little dragon's hackles rose, and she spat a warning shot of fire. Elizabeth stopped, and moved back into solid form.

"It's okay Keslyn, I'm not going to hurt you," she said, holding out her hands.

Keslyn sat down. Elizabeth knelt beside her. They looked into each others eyes, and had a soundless conversation.

The others went back into the main cavern.

Bindyl began pacing back and forth again. "Only the elviron have the ability to turn to shadow form, and they have to eat another's essence to do it!"

Thalios motioned for the two elves and the two fairies to sit with him.

"It says in the prophecies that the Elf/Human will have the ability to do everything that an elf or a human can do," he whispered. "We know that Elizabeth has elf in her from down her family line. Well, the elviron are a type of elf too."

"That's too powerful for anyone! And I thought that the elviron could only do that shimmer thing after they had been turned," Gideon said, a little too loud.

"I think Elizabeth probably has the power to do anything an elf, elviron or human can do, and much more," said Thalios.

"Hush," said Bindyl, "she will hear you."

After a few minutes, Elizabeth and Keslyn walked down to the entrance of the tunnel. Elizabeth turned back into the newly acquired shadow form and touched Keslyn's front claw. The physical contact with Keslyn, allowed both of them to pass through the bars.

On the other side, Elizabeth let go of Keslyn's claw and Keslyn turned back into solid form. Elizabeth did the same. Charlie moved back into her cat form, squeezing through the bars behind them.

"Thalios, I need to talk to you, alone if you please," Elizabeth said, looking at the others.

"Of course, but we cannot step outside, nor can the others. So where would you like to have this conversation?" he asked.

"I don't think I want you to go anywhere with her!" Gideon said, looking at Elizabeth in a way she had never seen before.

"I won't hurt him, Gideon. I just want to talk to him about Keslyn and a plan we have to get us all out of here."

Gideon eyed her suspiciously. "If you have anything to say, then say it in front of all of us. That is, if you have nothing to hide."

"What is wrong with all of you?" asked Elizabeth, "I'm trying to help you. Why are you all thinking that I am going to harm you now?"

"They're looking at me that way because I've just turned into a shadow like an elviron!" Elizabeth thought.

"Okay. I admit turning into shadow form like an elviron is well… a… new. I just thought about it happening and it did, but I promise you I am no elviron. I hate them as much as you do. They have my Gran, remember?"

"It is all right, Elizabeth," said Thalios, "We can share whatever plan you may have with the others, but you must be quick. We need to get the Grymlons to safety."

Keslyn and Thalios stood at the edge of the entrance, engaging in a silent conversation of their own, while Elizabeth outlined her plan.

"I would like to try and take Keslyn's essence from her body. So in effect, she will seem to be dead, the same way Zoe's essence was taken from her body by Verina," Elizabeth explained.

"How?" asked Gideon.

"The same way I took your essence," Elizabeth replied.

"You were reading a spell from a book," said Bindyl.

"Yes," said Elizabeth.

"You don't have that book with you," said Gideon.

"I don't need 'The Taminatin'. I remember how to do the spell."

"From the way you explained what happened to Zoe and I, there are two obvious problems with this plan," said Gideon. "One being, that if Keslyn's essence stays out of her body for too long, she will really and truly die. The other being, that in order for Keslyn's essence to go back into her body, she will have to perform a selfless act."

"You'll all have to trust me," said Elizabeth. "When Keslyn's essence has been released, I want you all to make a big show of being distressed by her death. The draghorns won't be able to sense Keslyn if they push into her head, because her essence will be gone. That should put and end to our problem."

The others turned when they heard Thalios shout "No!" to something Keslyn said.

"You have to trust Elizabeth. I do," Keslyn pushed into Thalios' head.

"Are you sure?" Thalios pushed back.

"I will do anything to save my baby," replied Keslyn.

"Very well. If anyone can do it, Elizabeth can," said Thalios. "Let's make sure that the draghorns are here because of your egg. No sense in putting your life in danger for nothing. I will go out and confront them. They are flesh eaters, but they have some respect for the druids. They know we nurture the dragons and their knowledge."

Chapter Ninety

Thalios left the safety of the cave, and six draghorns ran forward, surrounding him. They hissed and pawed at him, but did not touch him.

Thalios stood still as they circled around him. Suddenly the draghorns stopped, standing bolt upright, as though at attention. The circle parted directly in front of Thalios and a black draghorn walked into the centre.

Thalios bowed to him and he bowed back.

"I am the Arch Druid, Thalios."

"I am Zorgar of the Draghorns."

As they acknowledged each other, the surrounding draghorns hissed and pawed the ground again. Zorgar turned and silence ensued.

Zorgar pushed his thoughts into the mind of Thalios.

"We have come for the female dragon. The one who will lay the sacred egg."

Thalios noticed that the draghorn's voice sounded surprisingly soft and well spoken, inside his head.

"The dragon is dead. She died before the egg could be saved," Thalios thought back at Zorgar.

At this, chaos broke out. The draghorns began letting out odd little screams and snorting. They flew around, snapping and clawing at each other.

Zorgar reeled around on his hind legs, snorting loudly. The others settled down, but were still agitated.

"You know of course, that you will have to prove this," Zorgar pushed into Thalios' head.

"How would you like me to do that?" Thalios pushed back.

"We want to see the body of the dragon."

"I will return," Thalios pushed, and returned to the cave.

"Elizabeth, do what you must to Keslyn. The draghorns want to see her body. Please be quick. It's bedlam out there!"

He went to Keslyn and knelt down beside her.

"I'm sorry Keslyn. I wish there were another way."

She brushed up against Thalios, looking up into his eyes.

"I trust Elizabeth. I will be back with you before you know it," she said.

Thalios nodded and looked away, not letting her see him wipe a tear from his eye.

"I'm ready," Keslyn pushed into Elizabeth's head. "Let's do it now, before I get too scared."

"Lie down and be comfortable," Elizabeth said.

Keslyn made herself comfortable on the floor of the cave and closed her eyes. Elizabeth put her hand on Keslyn's back and started to chant the spell. A few minutes later, a small spiral of smoke rose out of Keslyn's body. It swirled around, rising upward. The smoke hung in the air for a moment, edging towards the gate. The swirling smoke moved through the bars, disappearing up into the dark recess of the tunnel.

All that was left was the lifeless body of the little dragon, lying at Elizabeth's feet.

Thalios picked up Keslyn's body and left the cave.

Zorgar approached him. Thalios stood and waited. Zorgar walked around him in a circle. Thalios felt him pushing at Keslyn's mind. Zorgar pushed so hard, he almost knocked Thalios down.

Zorgar turned to the rest of the draghorns. "The dragon is dead," he announced.

In an instant one of the draghorns ran towards Thalios, pushing him to the ground. As Keslyn fell from his grasp, two draghorns grabbed her and ran.

Zorgar ran after the draghorns who had seized her, but he was too late. Thalios watched in horror as they flew away with her.

"I am sorry," said Zorgar. "I will bring her back for you so that you can give her the appropriate burial."

He turned and flew away. The rest of the draghorns followed behind him.

The others saw what had happened and ran outside.

"We have to get her back!" Elizabeth said. "I promised her I wouldn't let her down. What will we do Thalios?"

"We will get her back," he answered with determination in his voice.

"This I've got to see," said Gideon, standing behind Elizabeth. "Do you know how dangerous those things are?"

Thalios turned, glaring at Gideon.

"I am well aware of how dangerous they are, and I don't need you to tell me! They fooled me! I just may have lost my companion of many years! I don't need you to state the obvious. Believe me when I say, one way or another we will get her back!"

Gideon put up both hands, as if to ward off a blow and backed away.

"All we can do is follow them and try to find Keslyn's body," said Elizabeth.

"I know where their lair is," said Lebrue.

Anna was holding onto Lebrue shaking her head vigorously.

"Stop it Anna, I have to. Keslyn will die if we don't get her back," Lebrue said, pushing his sister away.

Anna dropped her hands and bowed her head, and went back into the cave.

"Thanks Lebrue," said Elizabeth. "If we can't find another way we will consider your help."

They followed Anna into the cave.

"Lebrue, can you give us directions to the draghorn lair?" asked Thalios.

"It's quite a distance from here, but I can draw you a map," said Lebrue.

"Why don't you draw a map in the sand? Gideon and Bindyl can memorize it," suggested Thalios.

"Oh no. I'm not going any where near that draghorn lair," said Bindyl.

"You can show me," Gideon said, turning to Lebrue. I'll go… by myself if I have to,"

Lebrue and Gideon sat down, and outlined a map in the dirt.

Elizabeth prepared some food.

"Come on all of you," she said. "We still have to eat."

No one was hungry. They were picking over their plates when Charlie sprang to her feet, hissing at something outside.

Thalios went to the entrance, and looked out. Staring back at him out of the darkness, was Zorgar.

Thalios turned to Charlie. "It's all right. Go back into the cave. I will handle this."

"He's discovered our plan," he thought.

Thalios shielded his thoughts. "What are you doing here?"

"I have come to make a bargain with you," Zorgar pushed into his head. "Let me come in, so we can talk about it."

Thalios turned to the others. "He wants to come in."

"No! It's a trick. He'll kill us all," Bindyl shouted.

"Oh shut up, Bindyl," said Gideon, "Don't be so dramatic. If he was going to kill us, he would have done so by now."

Bindyl was beside himself. He drew his knife and ran towards Zorgar. Elizabeth stepped in front of him and waved her hand and Bindyl dropped like a rock.

"Thanks," said Gideon.

"My pleasure," said Elizabeth.

Gideon pulled Bindyl over to the side of the cave and made him comfortable.

"Come in," said Thalios, "and we will talk."

Zorgar was so large, he had to crouch down to get through the entrance. Once inside, he settled on all fours.

"What do you want?" Thalios asked.

Zorgar snorted at the ground, he looked around, pushing into all their heads except Thalios.

"I don't believe you when you say that there is no egg. I think the little dragon laid the egg before she died and you are all protecting it."

There was silence.

Zorgar pushed into their heads again.

"I have been ruling the draghorns for one hundred and fifty years. I do not wish to give up my position to a belief in something that may or may not exist. It is for this reason I am here. I will return the dragon's body, but in return, you must destroy the egg."

Elizabeth stood to speak, but Thalios held up his hand.

He turned his attention back to Zorgar.

"It is possible of course, that Keslyn laid her egg somewhere," he said, "but if she did, these people would not even know where to start looking."

Zorgar looked around at the others, pushing into their minds one by one.

"They do not know where an egg was laid, but what about you

druid?" pushed Zorgar. "If I were to enter your mind, would you reveal the whereabouts of an egg?"

Thalios looked directly into Zorgar's eyes.

"Enter my mind, but beware of what you see," he warned.

Zorgar sat for a moment. "If I look too deeply into the mind of the druid I might not like what I see," he thought, "this druid is with a mystical order, not without their own dubious ways of taking care of a troublesome situation."

He turned away.

"Oh thank the stars!" thought Thalios.

He decided to put on a show for the draghorn leader, hoping he would leave.

"Keslyn has been by my side for many years," Thalios said, hanging his head, weeping. "She was looking forward to laying her egg and being a mother to her baby dragon. I have lost my companion. I am overwhelmed with grief."

He put the back of his hand up to his forehead and turned away from Zorgar.

The draghorn leader looked at him disdainfully.

"You are weak and pitiful, but I will also mourn for your loss. I will return the dragon to you."

Zorgar backed out of the cave. He turned and rose. Beating his massive wings, he disappeared into the night.

Thalios turned to the sound of clapping, coming from Elizabeth and Gideon.

"Bravo, Thalios. What an actor you are!" said Elizabeth.

"Wake up!" she said, pointing to Bindyl.

Bindyl slowly opened his eyes. Then he sprang to his feet, looking around him.

"Where is he?" asked Bindyl.

"Who?" said Gideon, looking behind him.

"The draghorn. Where is he?"

"Put away your dagger Bindyl. He's gone," Gideon said.

"But I was running towards him with my dagger drawn. I..!" Then it occurred to him that Elizabeth had waved her hand just before it went dark.

"Elizabeth! What did you do?" he said, walking towards her.

"Now wait a minute Bindyl, let me explain." She said, backing away.

"Bindyl, don't be hasty," said Gideon, stepping in front of him.

"Elizabeth was trying to protect you. If you had attacked that draghorn, he would have killed you with one strike."

"I know being angry at you is useless," Bindyl said, "I also suspect that you could do horrible things to me if you wanted to. Just, please don't put me back to sleep. I suppose I should thank you really. It was a bit silly of me to lose my temper like that."

"I don't want anything to happen to you," said Elizabeth. You're my friend. I want to keep you safe.

"We need to get Keslyn back safely," said Thalios. "That means we have to wait here until the black draghorn returns with her."

Elizabeth sat with the others around a fire Gideon had lit.

Anna had fallen asleep with her head on her brother's lap. Bindyl sat watching the fire, when a wisp of smoke began swirling around his head. He swatted at it, and it dissipated, but then it came back. He swatted at the smoke again, cursing.

Elizabeth looked up as she heard him swear.

"Bindyl stop that," she said, watching the smoke.

"Why?" he asked. "It's just the smoke from the fire."

Elizabeth watched the swirling smoke as it headed for Bindyl again.

"No, it's Keslyn," she said.

"Why is she hanging around me?" Bindyl asked, rolling his eyes.

"How would I know," Elizabeth replied. "Perhaps she's paying you back for the comment you made about killing her. She might be haunting you now."

Bindyl looked up and around him.

"All right, I'm sorry I said that, Keslyn. I was just joking. Come on Keslyn, leave me alone!" he said, putting his arms over his head.

The smoke backed away and disappeared.

"Thanks," said Bindyl, looking around to make sure she had gone.

Elizabeth laughed and Bindyl smiled back at her.

"I suggest we all try to get some sleep," said Thalios. "It may be morning before, Zorgar delivers Keslyn's body back to us."

"I'm going to take a walk outside," said Gideon.

"I'll come with you," said Elizabeth. "I'm tired of being cooped up in this cave. Do you want to come Bindyl?"

"Oh, no thank you. I think I'll stay here where it's safe."

"Don't go too far," Thalios said.

"We won't," said Gideon, as they went out of the cave, into the darkness.

They walked together, enjoying the night air.

"How long will Keslyn be able to stay out of her body?" Gideon asked.

"I'm not sure, but we need to get her back soon," Elizabeth replied.

"You needed that magical book when you save Zoe and me. Are sure you don't need it now?" he asked.

"Nope, but I'm getting a little concerned that we may not get her back in time."

Gideon stopped.

"Elizabeth, we could just go and get her."

"How do we do that?" she asked, stopping to face him.

"You could call a pennar and we could fly to the directions that Lebrue gave me," he said. "The draghorns won't be expecting us. We could get Keslyn's body back in the dark of night and fly back here before anyone knew what we were doing."

"We'll take Keslyn. She will probably be able to find her body for us," said Elizabeth.

"Good idea! Come on Liz. Let's go and wait for everyone to fall asleep. Then we'll scoop up Keslyn and be on our way."

When they returned to the cave, everyone had put down blankets and made themselves comfortable. Elizabeth motioned for Gideon to lie down behind her.

"What are you going to do?" he whispered.

"Shush!" she replied.

She waved her hands around her and quietly said, "sleep for two hours."

"Elizabeth!" said Gideon. "You don't play fair!"

She went over to Charlie, who was sleeping peacefully.

"Wake," she said.

Charlie opened her eyes and looked at Elizabeth.

"Gideon and I are going to get Keslyn," she told her. "You have to stay here. I need you to protect the others. We'll be back before they wake up, if all goes well."

Charlie settled back down.

"Keslyn?" Elizabeth called.

A wisp of iridescent smoke appeared and wafted towards them. Elizabeth motioned for Keslyn to follow her and Gideon outside.

Once they were a few feet away from the cave entrance, Elizabeth knelt down to the ground, but she did not call a pennar.

"Oklandu I need you. Try to be quiet when you reach me." she whispered into the ground.

Twenty minutes later, Oklandu appeared. He landed noiselessly beside Elizabeth.

"We need to rescue Keslyn from the draghorns," Elizabeth explained. "I think with your help, we can sneak into their camp and get her out."

"I will help you in any way I can. I owe you a great debt," Oklandu said.

"I have seen a map of the draghorns liar," Gideon told him.

"No need," said Oklandu, "Their liar is a great distance from here and I am familiar with it. I suspect they are camped out not far from here."

Gideon and Elizabeth climbed onto Oklandu's back. Elizabeth held open one of the pockets of her jacket. Keslyn's smoky form disappeared into it.

Oklandu rose, flying into the night.

The others in the cave slept peacefully, with Charlie keeping one eye open, as usual.

Chapter Ninety One

Oklandu put them down by some rocks two miles into the badlands. Elizabeth jumped down and let Keslyn's essence out of her pocket.

"Where to Keslyn?" she asked.

"I feel my body is close by," Keslyn pushed into Elizabeth's head. "It is hidden by some rocks about a half a mile from here."

"Keslyn says that her body is very close," Elizabeth said, turning to Gideon and Oklandu. "She says it is hidden in a large rock formation."

"I think I know where she means. There are not many large rock formations around here," said Oklandu.

"Can you search for the rocks that she is describing without being seen?" Elizabeth asked.

Oklandu returned a few minutes later. "The draghorns have made camp nearby and Keslyn's body is there."

"We will need to move quickly," said Elizabeth. "Gideon can you stay here and take care of Keslyn?"

"I want to go with you," he protested.

"You should stay here. If anything happens to me, Oklandu will be able to get you back to warn the others."

"That makes sense I suppose," said Gideon. "Don't forget Elizabeth, the draghorns are not affected by magic."

"I'll be careful. Keslyn, stay with Gideon until we get back." Keslyn's essence floated towards Gideon.

As Oklandu rose off the ground, Gideon looked up. "Take care of her."

"With my life," said Oklandu, as they flew away.

A few minutes later, they landed a little way from the camp.

"You wait here. If I call you, please come quickly," Elizabeth whispered.

She approached the campsite, creeping around the edge, taking care not to be seen. She saw Keslyn's body lying off to the side of a group of sleeping draghorns.

"There is no one guarding her body. I think the fact that the draghorns are not affected by magic has made them a little over confident," thought Elizabeth.

She crept over to Keslyn's body, picked it up and slowly, but quietly crept back out of the camp.

Elizabeth shrugged Keslyn's dead weight upwards to get a better hold. "My goodness, Keslyn," she said, beginning to struggle. "You're heavier than you look!"

When she was far enough away, she called to the ground and Oklandu dropped down out of the air.

"That was fast!" Elizabeth whispered.

"I was hovering above you, waiting for you to call me."

They flew back to Gideon and picked him up.

The draghorns never stirred, except Zorgar, who had been feigning sleep. "Now I won't have to lie to my herd," he thought, putting his head back down on his enormous front claws.

Chapter Ninety Two

Bindyl and Zoe were together. They were strolling arm in arm around the castle grounds.

"I feel so happy," he thought, looking into the face of his love.

Suddenly, Zoe began to frown. She looked down at her dress, as blood appeared around the bodice.

She looked up at Bindyl.

"Why didn't you help me?" she said, touching the blood on her chest.

Bindyl caught her as she fell.

"I'm so sorry. Don't leave me!" he pleaded.

Bindyl woke up with a start. He put his hands up to his face and quietly wept.

"If only this pain would go away, just for a while," he thought.

He wiped away his tears and looked for his friend, who was... gone? Elizabeth's spot was empty too.

"What are those two up to now?"

Bindyl jumped up from his blanket. "Get up Thalios! Elizabeth and Gideon, they're gone!"

Thalios sat up trying to wake, just as Gideon and Elizabeth ran into the cave with the lifeless body of Keslyn in Gideon's arms. He put her down and released Keslyn's essence out of the pouch on his belt.

Thalios stood up and leaned on his staff.

"What have you two done?" he asked, sleepily.

"We have taken Keslyn's body back," Elizabeth said. "We are running out of time. I must act quickly, then you must both go back up to the Human Realm where you belong and stay there."

"We cannot go back until the next keeper of the entrance arrives," said Thalios, looking down at Keslyn's lifeless little body.

"We can't worry about that now. We need to get Keslyn back," said Elizabeth.

"I'm a bit confused," said Gideon. "Doesn't Keslyn have to perform a selfless act to get her body back?"

"Yes," answered Elizabeth.

She smiled at Gideon and with one swift movement, grabbed the dagger from his belt, turned and stabbed Thalios in the heart.

He fell to the ground, holding his chest.

Anna, who had been awakened by the noise, let out a strange sound. Lebrue grabbed her.

Charlie, not knowing what was happening, instantly turned into her mountain lion form. She ran and stood by Elizabeth's side.

"No matter what is going on, I have sworn to protect Elizabeth," she growled. "I misjudged her once. I will not do so again."

Gideon lunged forward, making a grab at Elizabeth, but she held up her hand and looked straight into his eyes. Gideon stopped dead in his tracks, unable to move.

Bindyl, who was standing behind her, lunged at her. Without turning around, she moved her other hand behind her and held it up.

"Don't!" she shouted at them. "Thalios and I had already arranged this. We knew if we discussed it with you two, you would argue about it and we don't have the time. Let me do my job and get Keslyn back into her body."

Gideon looked at Bindyl, and both of them stepped back.

"Put Keslyn next to Thalios and please be quick," said Elizabeth.

Gideon picked up Keslyn and laid her next to her beloved master.

Elizabeth stood at their feet and closed her eyes. The temperature in the cave dropped about thirty degrees in seconds. She raised her hands, palms up. She opened her eyes and looked down at the two bodies lying before her. She cast the spell from 'The Taminatin'. Repeating it, as she turned her head upwards. Keslyn's essence grew and swirled in the air. Another wisp of smoke appeared, swirling around Elizabeth's head.

Keslyn's essence dived into Thalios, then out again. The essence above Elizabeth's head moved to Keslyn's body, disappeared into it, then came out and went into Thalios.

Keslyn's essence returned into her own body, and both the swirling wisps of smoke stayed where they had landed.

Elizabeth closed her eyes and slumped to the ground. Gideon ran to her.

The two fairies still clung to one another, looking with disbelief at what had just happened.

Gideon knelt down and propped Elizabeth up in his arms. She opened her eyes.

"Did it work?"

"Yes," he replied.

Thalios sat up. He looked down, putting his hand over where Elizabeth had stabbed him. The blood was still there, but no wound.

Keslyn, still lying on the floor of the cave, opened her eyes and stretched. She stood and walked to Elizabeth, nudging her arm with her snout.

"Are you unwell, Elizabeth?" Keslyn pushed into her head.

"No, Keslyn. I am a little tired. I'll be fine in just a minute."

Thalios stepped outside to get some fresh air. Keslyn followed him.

It took a few minutes for Elizabeth to recover from her ordeal. Bindyl boiled some water over a fire and made some elven tea for her. He knew Elizabeth had developed quite a liking for its flowery taste, since visiting the Elven Realm.

Bindyl handed her a small mug. She took it, sipping the warm liquid. She looked at him and smiled. He smiled back, then turned and went to the fire.

Daylight was coming and they needed to be gone, but they could not leave Thalios and Keslyn unprotected.

Thalios came back into the cave with Keslyn.

"How are you feeling Elizabeth?" he asked.

"I am feeling great," she replied.

"I am glad to see everyone is well. Can someone please open this gate?" a voice came from the tunnel.

Elizabeth spun around.

Thalios turned, looking through the bars.

Malion, what are you doing here?" he asked.

"I have been chosen as the new guardian to the entrance," Malion replied.

Thalios rushed over to the bars. "Well, come on out of there and let me congratulate you!"

Thalios touched the door. A key appeared in his hand. He put it into the lock and turned it, opening the gate so that Malion could enter. When he entered the cave, Thalios took the key out of the lock. It shimmered for a second, then it was gone.

As Malion came out of the tunnel, he and Thalios looked at each other, both beginning to speak at once. They laughed, embraced, then turned and looked at the rest of the group.

"May I introduce to you, the new keeper and guardian of the cave: the Judicial Druid, Malion," announced Thalios.

Everyone applauded.

Malion bowed regally.

"Come," said Thalios, "we have much to tell you."

Thalios and Malion sat down with the others, and they told him their story.

Chapter Ninety Three

Malion listened with great interest to what had transpired.

"I agree with Elizabeth," Malion told Thalios. "You and Keslyn must leave immediately."

"What if the draghorns come back here?" Elizabeth said, "I'll bet they're pretty angry that we took Keslyn."

"The draghorns won't harm me," said Malion. "I am a druid. The draghorns aren't afraid of much, but they are cautious of druids. If they do come back and find Thalios and Keslyn gone. I doubt they will do anything.

The draghorns have no desire to go up to the Human Realm. They will know that I am the guardian of the gate. They will not harm me even if they think I know something. If the entrance is unguarded, humans may find their way down here. The draghorns do not want that."

"Malion is right," said Thalios.

When it was time for Thalios and Keslyn to leave and go back to the Human Realm, Elizabeth felt sad.

"I have become rather fond of you, Keslyn," she told the little dragon.

"And I you," Keslyn pushed into her head.

"I have one more task to perform before I go up to the Human Realm," said Thalios. "You must all leave the cave for a few minutes."

Everyone filed outside except for Malion and Thalios.

"I wonder why the draghorns have not come looking for Keslyn's body?" Gideon asked.

"Perhaps they know it would be too late to do anything about it now," Elizabeth answered, wondering herself, why they hadn't had any backlash from their little venture the night before.

Thalios emerged from the cave.

"It's time for Keslyn and I to be going. If you want to say goodbye to Malion, now is the time to do it," said Thalios.

They followed Thalios back into the cave. Malion took hold of his arm and Thalios led him to the gate.

"Malion are you all right?" Gideon asked.

"I am splendid, thank you," Malion answered.

"Then why are you holding onto Thalios like that?" he asked.

"Malion is now blind, just as Ghyrone was," explained Thalios. "I have to perform a ritual on the guardian of the cave to make this happen. He is this way so that his other senses become more intense. He is holding on to me because he needs time to adjust to his blindness. Soon, he will be able to distinguish between good and evil without taking it for granted, by just observing with his eyes."

"It is a great honour for me to have this position in the druid priesthood," Malion told them. "I will be happy and content in my calling. Have no fear, I am well looked after and well protected. Anna and Lebrue will come here now and then, to make sure I am all right."

"It didn't seem as though Ghyrone was very well protected," Elizabeth said, quietly.

"Ghyrone was attacked by Verina, who had more magical power than any other elviron in the entire history of the Elviron Realm," said Thalios. "Ghyrone had never come across anyone like her. He did not have the tools to protect himself or the gate. We will take steps to make sure, it does not happen again. Before I go Elizabeth, I want you to put your arms around Malion and embrace him."

"Why?" Elizabeth asked.

"Please, just do as I ask," said Thalios.

Elizabeth walked to Malion and embraced him. As she did so, Malion caught his breath.

"What a curious feeling of both bone chilling fear and heart soaring happiness, at the same time," he thought.

When they stepped away from each other, Malion turned towards Thalios and nodded.

"I felt as though my energy was being drained. What just happened?" Elizabeth asked.

"Don't be concerned," said Thalios. "Malion was sensing who you are. You may be the most powerful person there is as far as magic goes. He will know the power when he is near it, whether it is good or bad."

"I'm not like Verina," said Elizabeth.

"You are more like Verina than you think," said Thalios. "You are what the elviron hoped Verina would become. Now Malion knows and recognizes that power. He will not meet the same fate as Ghyrone."

Malion opened the gate for Thalios and Keslyn to start back up the tunnel to the Heel Stone.

"Goodbye, but only for now," Keslyn pushed into Elizabeth's head.

"What do you mean?" asked Elizabeth.

Keslyn winked at her and scampered up the tunnel.

Thalios took Elizabeth's hand in his.

"Be careful Elizabeth. Use your power wisely."

Thalios turned to the others and waved goodbye. They waved back.

Chapter Ninety Four

Elizabeth, Gideon and Bindyl packed their things to begin their journey home.

"We'll use some of the daylight hours to walk," said Gideon, "stop to rest for a while, then use the night to continue our journey."

"I think that's a good idea," said Elizabeth.

"Me too," said Bindyl.

Malion followed them to the cave entrance.

"Goodbye Malion," said Elizabeth.

"Goodbye to you all. Don't worry about me. I have been given a great privilege."

Elizabeth looked back a few minutes into their journey. Malion had disappeared inside of the cave.

The two fairies, Anna and Lebrue, went with them until they were close to the pennar camp.

"We will be leaving you now," said Lebrue.

"Thanks for all your help," said Elizabeth.

Lebrue embraced her. So did Anna.

"Have a safe journey home," said Lebrue.

"You too," said Gideon.

The twins flew home.

That left Elizabeth, Gideon, Bindyl and Charlie to complete the journey. Each walking with their own thoughts. Each mourning Zoe silently in their own way.

"Shall we stop and have a bite to eat?" asked Bindyl, when evening came.

"I'm hungry," said Elizabeth.

"Me too," said Gideon.

"I'll be lookout, so you can get some rest," said Charlie, morphing into her mountain lion form.

Elizabeth put some food together for a meal.

"I'll carry you in my backpack when it's time to leave. So you can get some rest," Gideon told Charlie.

"I would like that," she said.

***

They broke camp at dusk and continued on their way. Charlie slept peacefully snuggled in the bottom of Gideon's backpack. The journey continued with no unpleasant occurrences.

As daylight began, they came close to the castle at Distardrian.

"Why don't we use our old shelter to rest for a while," suggested Gideon.

"I'll be lookout if I can sleep in your backpack again," said Charlie.

"I'm agreeable to that," said Gideon.

Charlie patrolled the camp for a while. She was about to rest her legs, when she heard a noise. She sprang up, ready to pounce in the direction of the sound.

"Calm down Charlie, it's just me," Elizabeth whispered.

Charlie sat down in front of her. "What are you doing Elizabeth? You are supposed to be sleeping."

"I'm going to get my Gran."

"What about the Grymlons? Aren't you supposed to be guarding them? Shouldn't they come first?"

"Charlie, I could put you to sleep right now, but the others would be unprotected. I have hidden the Grymlons. Please Charlie, let me go to her. If she is still alive, I can get her out of there."

Charlie sat for a few seconds, then she moved aside to let Elizabeth go past her.

"Please be quick, and try to stay alive!" Charlie whispered, watching Elizabeth walk away.

Elizabeth kept going, but raised her hand up to let Charlie know she had heard.

Chapter Ninety Five

Elizabeth entered the castle using the same entrance as before.

"If Grandma is still here. There's a good chance she'll be in one of the dungeons," she thought.

She looked inside the dingy cells, but only one was occupied by an elviron prisoner.

Elizabeth rapped on the door and the elviron came to the grating at eye-level.

He peered out at her.

"Have you seen a human down here?" she asked.

The elviron stared at her and shook his head.

"Please let Grandma still be alive!" she thought.

As she turned the corner and headed for the steps, an elviron walked down towards the dungeons. He stopped when he saw her.

"She's not here," he said.

Elizabeth noticed this elviron wore slightly better clothing than the other elviron she had seen.

"He looks familiar," she thought. Then she remembered who he was, it was King Kalidryd.

"I'm not going to harm you," he said. "I know my daughter is dead. I know because you're here. She was becoming a little too dangerous to have around, but still."

King Kalidryd eyed Elizabeth. "I let your grandmother go yesterday, when I realized that Verina was not coming back. If she had been successful, she would have been here by now. I decided to let your grandmother go in the hope that you would not completely destroy me and my realm. I know I cannot hope to win any battles with you. Go, get out of here and go home to your precious grandma."

The king began to walk back up the steps, but stopped and hesitated. "If you would wait here for a minute, I have something for you," he said. "No it is not a trap. Just… please wait here. I will be straight back," he added, as he turned and walked up the steps.

"What could he possibly have that I would want," she thought, after a few minutes.

Elizabeth was about to leave, when she heard footsteps. King Kalidryd came back down the steps dragging a dishevelled elven boy with dark hair. When he reached the bottom, he pulled the child in front of him by the arm.

"Here take this with you," said the King. "Verina was keeping the little brat to train him for her servant, but now that she is gone, he is just another mouth to feed. He is too young for me to take his essence."

Elizabeth noticed the boy had a resemblance to Zoe. "Is this little boy Zoe's brother?" she asked, trying not to cringe.

"I believe so," replied the King.

Elizabeth took the little boy by the arm am led him away. The king turned, walking back up the steps without another word.

She and the boy made their way back to Gideon and the others. When they entered the camp, Gideon was waiting for her.

"Where have you been? You fool. You could have been killed!" he exclaimed.

Elizabeth tried to think of something to say, but laughed instead.

"I know it would be highly unlikely that you would have been harmed, but you never know," said Gideon. "Where is your grandma?"

"The elviron let her go," Elizabeth said.

Gideon looked down at the child with Elizabeth and his mouth dropped open.

"Tevyn!"

"King Kalidryd gave him to me," Elizabeth said. "He told me Verina had been keeping him at the castle."

"Do you know who this is?" he asked.

"Yes, this is Zoe's brother. We haven't been introduced yet though," she said, looking down at him.

The elf boy looked up at her with a blank stare.

Elizabeth got down on her knees, so she was face to face with him.

"Nice to meet you Tevyn," she said, looking into his eyes.

As Elizabeth said the boy's name, he looked up at Gideon.

"At least he still knows his name," said Gideon.

He knelt down beside the boy.

"Do you remember me Tevyn?" Gideon asked.

The boy only stared.

Elizabeth touched Gideon's arm. "We have to get him back to Kimadrian. He looks as though he is badly in need of some food and he definitely needs a bath. He smells awful."

Gideon took Tevyn's hand. He sat him down and handed the boy some berries and cheese.

"Tevyn, slow down!" Gideon said, holding on to Teyvn's arm. "You'll choke if you eat like that."

After the boy had eaten, Gideon led him to where he had been sleeping. He put the child down on his blanket, lying down beside him to keep him warm.

"I'm going back to sleep. See you in about two hours," Gideon said. The boy snuggled under the blankets, grateful for the warmth.

Elizabeth turned to Charlie. "When did Gideon wake up?"

Charlie sat by Elizabeth's side. "He woke up about half an hour ago. He wanted to go and find you, but I told him if you had found your grandma, you would probably be back soon. So he decided to wait a while. He was a lot more worried about you than he let you know."

Elizabeth stroked Charlie's head. "I'm going to rest for a while. Can you be lookout for a bit longer, Charlie?"

Charlie stood. "I can sleep in Gideon's backpack," she said, stretching. She walked out towards the edge of the camp.

Elizabeth stretched out on her blanket.

"I hope Gran is all right," she thought, before she fell asleep.

When night came they packed up their things. Elizabeth retrieved the Grymlons from their hiding place and they headed for home.

The journey continued to be uneventful until they were two miles into Kimadrian.

As they were passing through a wooded area, Gideon stopped.

"What's wrong?" asked Elizabeth.

Gideon put his finger to his lips. Everyone stood still. Both Gideon and Bindyl pulled their daggers. Elizabeth did the same.

Two elves came from behind a clump of trees.

"Your Highness?" said one of them.

"Mendry is that you?" Gideon said, peering into the elf's face.

"Yes Sir!" replied Mendry, smiling and saluting at the same time.

"What are you doing here?" asked Gideon.

"One moment please, Your Highness," said Mendry. He turned and whistled. Half a dozen elf guards came out of the trees.

"We have come to escort you and the others home," he said.

"Well let's go!" said Gideon.

Chapter Ninety Six

King Morvand was waiting when they entered the castle gates. He embraced Gideon.

"It's good to see you, son," he said, with tears in his eyes.

"It's good to see you too father," Gideon replied, holding on to his father's shoulders.

The king shook Bindyl's hand and embraced him. "Well done!"

"Thank you, Your Majesty."

"Is my grandma here?" asked Elizabeth.

"Some of our guards picked her up this morning," the King replied.

"Is she in her rooms?" Elizabeth asked.

"She is. The doctor examined her. He found that all she needed was rest. Why don't you go up and let her know you are home."

Elizabeth raced up the steps. When she reached her Grandma's rooms she knocked.

"Come in," Elizabeth heard her say.

Grandma Rose raised her head when she heard the door open.

"I knew you would be safe," said Elizabeth, rushing to her bedside. "You're too tough to let the elviron hurt you."

Grandma Rose began to cry when Elizabeth put her arms around her.

"Verina told me Zoe was spying for her," Grandma said, through the tears. "I was so afraid that Verina would kill you."

She kissed Grandma Rose on the cheek. "Well, she didn't, Gran and I'm here now. Verina did kill Zoe though, and I couldn't help her this time."

"When the time came, Verina didn't have as much power as she thought," said Elizabeth. "I had a lot of help. Verina killed Zoe, but before Zoe died, she told me why she did it."

"I am so sorry Zoe is dead, but what possible reason could she have had to betray you after you saved her life?" asked Grandma.

"Verina had Zoe's brother. She promised Zoe that she would give her brother back if she helped her," Elizabeth answered.

"Where is Zoe's brother now?" asked Grandma.

"When we reached the castle in Distardrian, I went in to try to rescue you, but King Kalidryd had already let you go," Elizabeth explained. He gave Zoe's brother to me, hoping I wouldn't take revenge on him for Verina's failure."

"What a wise king he has become," said Grandma.

"I'll believe that when I see it," said Elizabeth. "You get some rest now, Gran. I'll come back and see you in a little bit."

"I am very tired," said Grandma, lying back down.

Elizabeth kissed her on the cheek again, and pulled the covers up to her chin. She left and made her way to the king's private chambers.

"Do you have them with you?" the King asked, when Elizabeth found him.

"They have never left my side," said Elizabeth, patting the backpack. "Well, that is, except when I went to the castle in Distardrian to try and get my grandma."

"Yes, Gideon told me about that," said the King. "very foolish, Elizabeth. Although, I gather you came out of the castle with someone just as precious."

"Yes," said Elizabeth, "Zoe's brother."

"He is being cleaned up and his parents are being sent for," said the King.

"I can't imagine how Zoe's parents are going to feel. They lost her once, and now they have to be told that she is gone for good," said Elizabeth.

"When Tevyn was taken, they were beside themselves," the king explained. "We thought he had been kidnapped by elven thugs for a ransom. We were waiting for some sort of demand. The Mindar's asked us to keep Tevyn disappearance a secret, in case it endangered his life further. They will be glad to have him back."

King Morvand and Elizabeth made their way up to the tower where the Grymlons lived.

The King pressed on the points of the circle to unlock the door.

"It's time for you to learn the combination of this door," he said, as they entered.

Elizabeth placed a Grymlon on each of the tables. One by one they rose, spun in the air for a few seconds and came to rest on the little pedestals.

"They know they are home," Elizabeth said.

King Morvand put his arm around her shoulder.

"It is good to know that all is well in my Kingdom again and it's all thanks to you."

Chapter Ninety Seven

Elizabeth walked down into the dimness of Vandrayven's chambers.

When he saw her, he could not hide his delight. He rushed over, robes swishing and hugged her.

"Thanks for bringing Charlie back safely," he said, as they sat in his living area.

"We couldn't have done it without her. She was very brave," Elizabeth said.

"I am happy that everyone is home and safe," said Vandrayven.

"I need to rest, but I will come back and see you later. Perhaps you can teach me some of your magic," said Elizabeth.

"I believe we have a lot of work to do in that department young lady. You have years ahead of you as the protector to the Grymlons."

Elizabeth found her way to her rooms and bathed. She had just dressed when there was a knock at the door. She opened it, to find Gideon.

"Come in," she said.

He sat in the chair by the fireplace.

"There is a huge party going on down in the ballroom. I have been asked to come and get you," he told her. "Come on Elizabeth, let's go downstairs and have some fun."

He took her hand and they went down to the party.

When Elizabeth and Gideon entered into the room, all the elves and other creatures, who had been invited to the party cheered. Gideon bowed to the whole room, then he whisked her off over to where the food was. They filled a couple of plates and sat down to eat.

After a few minutes, a half a dozen elves entered carrying instruments. They set up at the end of the room and began playing music. Everyone danced and had an excellent time.

At the end of the evening, Gideon walked Elizabeth up to her rooms. He kissed her hand, bowed and left.

***

Elizabeth dressed for bed. When she went to her bedroom, Charlie was lying on her pillow.

"How did you get in here?" she asked.

"The window is open. Can I sleep with you tonight?" she asked.

Elizabeth smiled, glad to have her little friend close by.

"Of course you can, but no snoring! And get down the other end of the bed."

Elizabeth stretched out on her bed with Charlie curled up at her feet. They both fell into a deep, comfortable sleep.

Chapter Ninety Eight

The next few days were spent getting everything back to normal.

Gideon, Bindyl and Elizabeth attended a memorial service for Zoe.

When the service was over, Elizabeth turned to leave with the others, but Zoe's mother called her back.

"We want to thank you for bringing Tevyn home," she said.

"I'm sorry for your loss," said Elizabeth.

"At least we still have one of our children," said Zoe's mother, trying to hold back tears.

"I tried to save her," said Elizabeth.

"We know you did, Bindyl told us everything."

The two of them embraced, then parted. Elizabeth caught up with the others.

When Grandma Rose felt well enough, she was invited to tea with the king.

"How are Zoe's parents doing?" asked Grandma.

"It is a very sad time for them, Rose. They have lost their daughter for good this time. They have been given back their son and they know that it was partly because of Zoe that Tevyn was still alive.

It is good that they can remember Zoe died doing something honourable."

"We will be going back up to the cottage soon," said Grandma.

"Yes, it will be good for the both of you to get back to normal again, but please, stay a few days," said the King. "Paulina so enjoys your company and I have elves watching the cottage."

"Very well, Your Majesty," Grandma replied. "It won't hurt to spend a day or two more here. I enjoy the queen's company too.

Chapter Ninety Nine

It was early in the morning when Elizabeth was awakened by one of the guards.

"The king respectfully requests your presence in the breakfast room, immediately," the guard informed her.

Elizabeth dressed and hurried downstairs.

When she arrived, breakfast had been laid out on tables on the back wall, but no servants were standing ready to serve it.

Bindyl was looking out of the window. Gideon stood next to him. They were staring at something outside.

"What's going on?" she asked.

"Why don't you go and see for yourself," said the King.

As she approached the two elves, Elizabeth noticed that Bindyl's face was chalk white.

"Oh no," she thought. "I've seen that look before."

When she looked out of the window, there were about a hundred draghorns hovering above the castle grounds.

Four of them were holding Zorgar up in the air.

"I can't make out if he's unconscious or dead," thought Elizabeth.

She turned to the king. "What do they want?"

"They are asking for you," said the King.

"Me? Why!"

"They think there is an egg," said Gideon, turning to her. "They think that Zorgar deceived them, so that he could continue to be their leader. The thing is, they are right aren't they, Elizabeth?"

Elizabeth stared out of the window, ignoring Gideon's remark.

"I have to do something," she thought.

She began walking towards the door that led to the gardens, but Gideon stepped in front of her.

"Gideon, please get out of the way," she said.

Gideon stood firm, as he folded his arms and shook his head. Elizabeth waved her hand in front of her, and Gideon flew through the air. He made a perfect landing on softest part of a couch nearby.

"Sorry!" she whispered, as she opened the door and walked out.

The courtyard was surrounded by a square wall, approximately eight feet high. When the draghorns saw Elizabeth, they landed on it.

She stood in the middle of the courtyard.

"If you want to talk to me. COME DOWN HERE! AND BRING YOUR LEADER DOWN WITH YOU!" Elizabeth shouted in her mind.

Most of the draghorns heads snapped back at the loudness of her request.

Some stayed on the wall, but many of them flew down and landed in front of her.

Two of the draghorns were being pushed forward by two more hovering behind them.

The draghorns holding Zorgar, flew down to the side of her, dropping him to the ground with a vicious snarl.

"Why have you come here?" Elizabeth pushed with her mind.

A bit of a scuffle ensued, as the draghorns tried to decide who was going to be the speaker.

Eventually, the larger of the two draghorns who had landed in front of her stepped forward.

"We were deceived!" the draghorn hissed into Elizabeth's head.

"You were not!" she pushed back.

The larger draghorn stepped closer to her.

"There is an egg. Zorgar is concealing this from us because he wants to remain our leader," the draghorn hissed.

Elizabeth stepped forward, looking straight into the draghorn's eyes.

"There is no egg," she pushed into its head. "Zorgar will make a good leader. He is fair and just. He will lead you with honesty."

"If we don't get the egg, we will kill all of you," the speaker for the draghorns pushed back at Elizabeth's mind.

"DO NOT THREATEN ME! If you kill all of us and there is an egg, you'll never find it, you fool!" she pushed back.

"Then so be it!" said the larger draghorn, backing up.

He hissed, as he pushed fire through his nostrils, aiming it directly at Elizabeth's face. She quickly raised her hand in a defensive gesture.

To her surprise, the draghorn's fire stopped in mid air, as though it had been paused in time.

Elizabeth put her hands over her ears, when a collective gasp from all the draghorns invaded her head.

The draghorn that had dealt the fiery blast was fighting to get away from the paused blaze. Some of it was still up his nose and appeared to be stuck.

Another draghorn came from behind her with its claws outstretched to attack. Elizabeth saw him out of the corner of her eye. She moved to one side and pointed her finger at the flames frozen up the other draghorn's nose, then pointed her finger to the attacking draghorn. The flames jumped to life, burning the attacking draghorn's outstretched claws. It yelped, as it pulled back two blackened stumps.

King Morvand looked on in awe.

Gideon turned to his father. "Am I seeing things?"

"Draghorns are supposed to be impervious to any magic," said the King. "She is the one. Elizabeth Ghenestone is the mixture of elf and human that we have been waiting for all these years."

The draghorns, now unsure of what was happening, backed away. The draghorn that had fired the flames at Elizabeth, saw his opportunity to fly out of the way and rejoined the others. The draghorn with the burnt claws followed him.

"Wait!" Elizabeth called to them. "STOP!"

They all halted, hovering in mid air and looked down at her.

"Please, come back down. Let's all come to some agreement," she said.

The two draghorns who had been negotiating with Elizabeth looked at each other. A few draghorns were fighting among themselves. Some of them tried to communicate with Elizabeth. She held her head. All the voices together were too much.

"STOP IT, ALL OF YOU!" she pushed into their heads.

The draghorns hovered in the air.

Off to the side, Zorgar had regained consciousness.

"ALL OF YOU COME DOWN INTO THE COURTYARD!" she pushed the message out at all of them.

A few actually fell to the ground, dazed by the sound in their heads.

When all of them had landed, Elizabeth went to Zorgar, and knelt down beside him. "Come with me."

He struggled to his feet, standing behind her.

"As you have just witnessed," Elizabeth pushed into their heads. "You are no longer protected against magic. Times are changing and you must change with them, if you wish to survive.

Zorgar is your leader. Any of his offspring will lead you in the future, only when he decides to hand over the power."

"He will lead you well. He is strong and honourable. Follow him, and I promise you, if he is an unjust leader,.you can come to see me to try to solve any problems. He will form a council of twelve of your best draghorns, and no more fighting!

You cannot live together peacefully, if you continually bicker and squabble amongst yourselves. And mark you well! I will be in contact with Zorgar, to keep an eye on all of you."

"This is your chance to be a good leader," Elizabeth said, turning to Zorgar.

Zorgar stepped forward.

"Come, let us go home. We will do as the witch says. We will form a council."

He rose into the air. The rest of the draghorns rose up and formed a crowd behind him.

"You!" Elizabeth pushed at the draghorn with burnt claws. "Come down here."

The draghorn looked at his singed claws and shook his head.

"I can heal you," Elizabeth pushed.

He hovered for a second or two then landed in front of her.

"Hold out your claws."

The draghorn held out his paws, turning his head to one side, so as not to watch what she was about to do.

Elizabeth touched one of his paws with her index finger. As she did so, all the fur and the talons were returned to normal. She did the same with the other one.

"Thank you," the draghorn pushed into her head.

"My pleasure," Elizabeth answered, realizing that the draghorn was a female.

Elizabeth looked up and noticed a couple of the draghorn's sniping at each other. They suddenly caught themselves, both looking down at her. She wagged her finger from side to side, shaking her head as she did so. Both of the draghorns hung their heads and looked away.

The procession of draghorns flew away. There were so many of them, they darkened the sky for a minute or two. Then it was quiet around the castle again. In fact it was too quiet.

Elizabeth turned to see everyone standing outside, speechless. They followed her into the breakfast room and looked on as made her way to the breakfast table and built a plate of food.

"Delegation, it seems, makes Elizabeth Ghenestone very hungry," thought the king.

Chapter One Hundred

"Everything is changing," Gideon said, to his father as they returned to the breakfast area.

"This is only the beginning," said King Morvand. "There are many things that are said to happen in the future if the prophecy is fulfilled, and it looks like it will be."

"I'm curious father? Just when will all of this happen? I mean, if the prophecy was true?"

"I'm not sure about that," the King responded. "The book that tells of the coming of the human/elf with magical powers is hundreds of years old. It could not predict when this would happen. I suppose we will just have to wait and see how this turns out. There are one or two events that we may have some control over, though."

"What are they," Gideon asked.

"We will talk later," the King said, as Elizabeth approached him.

"My grandma and I would like to go home now," she said calmly.

"Of course," the King said.

Gideon called the servants back into the room. The king asked one of them to approach.

"Help Lady Elizabeth and Lady Rose pack to leave," he instructed.

"I have matters of importance to attend to, so I will say goodbye to you now," he told Elizabeth and Grandma Rose.

He turned to Gideon. "It's time for you to get involved with matters of the Realm. You and I have much work to do."

"Yes father. Goodbye Elizabeth. Goodbye Grandma Rose," Gideon said, as he turned to leave with his father.

Elizabeth and Grandma curtsied.

A couple of hours later, Gideon found Grandma Rose at the castle entrance attending to her luggage. A carriage was waiting to be loaded to take her and Elizabeth home.

"I have a question for you Lady Rose," Gideon said, looking around to see where Elizabeth was.

"I will answer it if I can," Grandma said.

"Could I please visit Elizabeth?" he asked, shyly.

"You can visit Elizabeth anytime you like," replied Grandma.

"No, Lady Rose. I mean officially visit Elizabeth. You know, court her."

Grandma Rose stopped moving luggage around and looked at him. "Are you sure you want to do this, Gideon?"

Gideon looked through the doors, watching Elizabeth, who was in the great hall putting the suitcases together for the guards.

"Lady Rose, I am as sure as I could ever be," he replied, as he watched her giving instructions to the guards.

Grandma Rose followed his gaze. "Is this at your father's command, or is it your wish?"

"Both. I never realized how much I feel for her. My father has just made it easy for me to be with her. With your permission of course.

"I will explain everything to her," said Grandma. "I'll send a messenger to you in a couple of weeks. It has to be entirely her decision. For now though, Elizabeth needs time to get back to normal."

"I absolutely understand," said Gideon.

He bowed to Grandma Rose. "I should get back to the king and let him know that you and I have talked."

Gideon took one last look at Elizabeth. As he did so, she turned and noticed him. Gideon nodded to her politely, and went back into the castle.

Grandma Rose was helped into the carriage by a castle guard. Elizabeth stepped in after her.

Chapter One Hundred and One

Grandma and Elizabeth entered the kitchen at Willow View Cottage, happy to be home.

"It feels as though we have been gone from here for a lifetime," said Grandma, putting the kettle on for tea.

"It is good to be home," said Elizabeth.

There was a knock at the back door.

"It's Andre," said Elizabeth, looking out of the kitchen window.

"I'll let him in. You sit. He doesn't know you can walk yet," said Grandma.

Grandma opened the back door. "Hello, Andre. How are you?"

"Where have you two been?" he asked, as he stepped into the kitchen. "I've been coming here at different times of the day for the past week. Did you go on a trip?"

Grandma Rose and Elizabeth looked at each other and laughed.

"Yes Andre," Elizabeth answered. "We've been on a great adventure."

"I didn't mean to be nosy. I just wondered where you were. That's all," he said, sitting at the kitchen table.

"Would you like a cuppa?" asked Grandma.

"Yes please," he replied.

Grandma Rose looked at Elizabeth, who picked up on her grandma's thought.

She giggled slightly.

"What's so funny?" Andre asked, looking from Elizabeth to Grandma.

"Elizabeth has something to show you," said Grandma.

Elizabeth stood and walked to the kitchen sink, then turned with a big grin.

"Wow! How long?" he asked.

"About a week or so," Elizabeth replied.

"But how?" he said, wide eyed.

"A little physio and a lot of hard work," said Grandma, before Elizabeth could answer.

Andre stood and put his arm around her.

"I'm so very happy for you," he whispered in her ear.

"Sit down, Andre. Your tea is going to get cold," said Grandma.

He sat back down. Grandma put a cup of tea in front of him. He picked up a chocolate biscuit, broke it in half and dunked it in his tea. Elizabeth looked at him and smiled.

"It feels good to be home," she thought.

Chapter One Hundred and Two

Two weeks later, Elizabeth and Grandma were in the garden drinking iced lemonade. It was a warm evening, and the river was calm.

Every now and then, people would walk along the riverbank. Some would stop and wave at Elizabeth and Grandma. They would wave back.

"Gran," Elizabeth said.

"Yes?" asked Grandma.

"I want you to tell me what happened the night mum, dad and Jesse were killed."

"I don't want to talk about it just now," said Grandma.

"You keep avoiding the subject, Gran. I think I have the right to know how they died."

Grandma Rose sipped her lemonade. "I agree, but we have been through enough. Especially you. I don't think now is the time to discuss what happened to your mum and dad, and Jesse. Sometime in the future, you and I will sit down with King Morvand and we will discuss it. For now though, I don't feel the time is right."

"But I want to know now," said Elizabeth.

"All in good time," said Grandma. "You'll have to be patient and trust me. Now I don't want to discuss the matter any further."

Grandma got up from her chair. "I'm going in the house. I'm tired, so I think I'll have an early night."

Elizabeth watched her grandma disappear into the cottage. She stood, walked down the pathway towards the Willow tree. When she reached the gate, she leaned against it, staring at the river.

"I'll find out what happened eventually, Gran. You can't keep it from me forever."

Chapter One Hundred and Three

The month of July arrived, and school was over for the summer.

Elizabeth decided after breakfast one morning, to go into the garden and lie on the grass.

"I haven't done this in a while. I'd forgotten how nice it feels," she thought, picking at the blades of grass. "It feels comfortable and safe."

She turned over onto her back, and looked up at the sky.

"Up until now, I've been so busy catching up with school, I haven't had the chance to think about what's happened," she thought.

Elizabeth closed her eyes and just for a moment, she allowed herself to think of her mother, father and brother. The pain hit her immediately, and the tears came quickly.

Elizabeth Ghenestone turned over face down on the grass, put her head on her arms and sobbed. When the tears finally subsided, she fell into a light sleep with the sunlight bathing her back.

"You're not dead are you?" a familiar voice came from the side of her head.

Elizabeth looked up. Charlie was sitting beside her.

"Did I look dead?" Elizabeth asked, faking the disdain in her voice.

"You were lying very still," said Charlie.

"What are you doing here?" asked Elizabeth.

"I missed you," said Charlie. "Oh, I like being in the Elven Realm, but Vandrayven is always so busy. Besides, the mice are bigger here. Can I stay for a while?"

Charlie looked directly into Elizabeth's eyes and Elizabeth saw love. Pure, no questions asked, love.

"Charlie, you can stay as long as you like," Elizabeth said, as she stroked the back of the little cat's head.

"Thank you," Charlie purred, lying down beside her.

For a while, the teenage girl who had fought and won the battle against evil and the little cat who could talk, relaxed on the grass together, soaking up the summer sun.

***

A few days later, Elizabeth and her Grandma Rose were lounging on the back lawn after supper.

"Elizabeth, you are now fifteen years old," said Grandma Rose.

"Yes I am," replied Elizabeth.

"In the Elven Realm, when a girl reaches the age of fourteen or fifteen and she is royalty," said Grandma, "it is customary for her to be courted by an arranged beau.

This happens early, because the courtship is meant to go on for many years, until the couple are in their early twenties at least. After that time, the couple are expected to marry. All of this is very proper."

"Any relationship between a boy and a girl is closely watched. A chaperone is employed to oversee any time spent between the two young people, until the time they marry."

"Grandma, I have no idea what you are talking about."

"I'm telling you this," Grandma continued, "because Gideon has asked to court you. This decision would not have been reached lightly. Believe me, after what happened with Zoe, I think Gideon is very sure of who he wants to be with.

He has asked me to ask you if he can come and visit, to perhaps see if you may feel the same way."

Elizabeth's heart leapt in her chest. "Why do we have to have a chaperone?"

"I know it sounds ridiculous. You and Gideon spent days alone together, but he was betrothed to Zoe then," replied Grandma.

"So it was all right for us to be alone, as long as he was not courting me?" said Elizabeth.

"It all has to do with tradition, which is sometimes outdated and serves no real practical purpose," replied Grandma. "Even so, if you choose to be courted by Gideon, you will officially be his betrothed. A whole new set of rules come into play when that happens."

Elizabeth and Grandma Rose stared in silence at each other.

"Well?" asked Grandma Rose.

"Yes," Elizabeth answered.

Grandma Rose cocked her head to one side.

"Yes to what?" she asked.

"Yes, he can come and visit," answered Elizabeth.

"Then it's settled," said Grandma. "I'll send a messenger to let him know and we will make arrangements for you both. The way things are done in the Elven Realm will have to change. There has never been an elven queen who is also the guardian of the Grymlons."

Grandma got up from the table and walked down the path to the bridge.

As Elizabeth watched Grandma Rose head towards the Willow tree, she felt a sort of excitement she had never experienced before.

"I know that's years away, but to be a queen? How exciting!"

Grandma Rose stood for a few minutes talking to one of the guards. When the guard disappeared into the tree, Grandma returned to the cottage.

"Well, that's out of the way. Come on in the house. I'll make us a cup of tea."

Elizabeth followed her grandma into the house. She put out the cups and saucers, while Grandma put a pot of water on to boil.

"It feels as though this was meant to be," thought Elizabeth. "Gideon feels like the next step in my life. Yes, that's how it feels, like destiny!"

Chapter One Hundred and Four

When Gideon arrived at the cottage for tea, he had an old elf woman with him.

Grandma Rose and Elizabeth came out of the back door to greet them. Gideon smiled at Elizabeth. He turned and looked behind him, then looked back at Elizabeth and rolled his eyes.

Grandma Rose couldn't help but grin.

"Lady Rose, Elizabeth, I would like to introduce Golda. She will be our Chaperone," said Gideon.

"I am very pleased to meet you, Golda. Would you like a cup of tea?" asked Grandma.

"I would enjoy a cup of tea, thank you," Golda replied.

Grandma Rose opened the back door, and everyone followed her inside.

"Elizabeth, please show Gideon and Golda into the living room, while I make some tea."

Elizabeth led them down the hallway.

Grandma had put a table in the middle of the room with sandwiches, some chocolate biscuits and a homemade sponge cake with raspberry jam filling.

Golda and Gideon sat by the table.

"If you will excuse me," said Elizabeth. "I'm going to go and help my grandma with the tea things."

She left the living room and hurried down the hall.

"Is something wrong?" asked Grandma, as Elizabeth entered the kitchen.

"Gran, it all feels so, well, awkward."

"It will only feel that way for a few minutes," said Grandma. "Once we all have a nice cup of tea and a biscuit or two, we can all talk and break the ice."

"I hope so!" said Elizabeth.

"Come on," said Grandma, "help me with these trays."

Elizabeth picked up the tray with the cups and saucers. Grandma grabbed the tray with the teapot, sugar and milk. They made their way down the hall to the living room.

Grandma took a seat. "How do you like your tea, Golda?"

"Milk and one sugar, please."

"I'll have milk and four sugars please," said Gideon.

"Just milk for me please, Gran."

Grandma poured tea for everyone.

"What would you like to eat, Golda?" asked Elizabeth.

"A piece of that cake would be nice, please."

"Me too, please," said Gideon.

Everyone had cake.

Grandma and Golda quickly engaged in conversation.

"I knew your daughter," said Golda.

"You knew my Audrey?"

"Yes, I worked with her on some of her tuition with the king, when she was at the castle. Nice girl, always very polite."

"I miss her so much," said Grandma.

"There, there," said Golda, patting Grandma Rose's hand.

"You may have lost your daughter, but you still have a beautiful granddaughter."

Gideon sat watching the conversation. He looked at Elizabeth now and then, but didn't say anything to her.

"He's shy!" thought Elizabeth. "I suppose I should try and get some conversation going with him, or this will be a horrible visit."

"Oh my!" said Grandma, looking at Elizabeth, "I have forgotten the lemon. I don't like milk in my tea."

"I'll get it for you, Gran," Elizabeth said, standing.

"I'll come with you," said Gideon.

Golda stood to follow him.

"Oh I think those two will be safe in the kitchen. Don't you?" said Grandma.

"Don't be too long," said Golda, sitting back down.

"We won't," said Gideon, following Elizabeth out of the room.

When the two of them reached the kitchen, Elizabeth took a lemon out of the fridge and began to slice it.

"I have had tea here many times," said Gideon, "I don't remember Lady Rose having lemon in her tea?"

"She doesn't," said Elizabeth, giggling.

"Oh... now I understand," he said, "bit embarrassing, all this, isn't it."

"Does it get better?" Elizabeth asked.

Gideon looked her in the eye and smiled. "We'll make it better."

Elizabeth felt heat rise in her chest and suddenly felt shy. She put the sliced lemon on a small plate and the two of them went back to the living room.

Before everyone knew it, it was time for Gideon and Golda to be going.

Gideon stood, took Elizabeth by the hand, kissed it, bowed and turned to leave. Golda followed closely behind him.

Grandma Rose and Elizabeth escorted the Golda and Gideon to the gate at the end of the garden and waved goodbye. After the two elves had disappeared into the Willow tree, Elizabeth and Grandma returned to the kitchen and cleaned up the tea things.

Elizabeth was putting the chocolate biscuits into an airtight container, when there was a knock at the front door.

"I'll go," she said, putting down the biscuit tin.

Elizabeth went to the front door and opened it. There was no one there. She looked down. On the top step was an envelope. She picked it up and read the front. It was addressed to her.

She looked again, but saw no one, so she closed the door and took the envelope back to the kitchen.

"Who was it?" asked Grandma.

"There was no one at the door, but someone left this envelope for me," Elizabeth replied.

"Well open it," Grandma said, "it might be something important."

Elizabeth slid her finger along the top edge of the envelope and pulled out a piece of pale blue paper with gold inlay around the edge.

"It's from Thalios," Elizabeth said.

"Well read it," said Grandma.

"2nd, July.

My dearest Elizabeth,

I am sorry to be so secretive, but I need to see you. I have something for you. I cannot bring it to you. You must come and get it. You will understand more when you see it.

I will be at the Avebury end of the Savernake Forest two days from now. There is an entrance to the forest, with a high stone wall attached to a wooden gate located by the roadside. I would like you to meet me there. Please only bring your grandmother. I will assume that she will be able to drive you. I will be there at around 6:00 a.m., please try to be prompt.

Your friend always,
Thalios.

That's it. That's all it says," said Elizabeth.

"Would you stay here and clean up the rest of the kitchen for me, please?" Grandma said. "I have to go and find something."

"Find what?" asked Elizabeth.

"I'm not sure yet," Grandma said.

Grandma Rose headed down the hall to her bedroom and opened the secret room behind her bed. She turned on the light and looked around her.

"There it is," she said, picking up 'The Evengaere'.

Grandma thumbed through it, until she came to a page with a picture. The picture was of things to come. Of things not yet true in time.

Grandma Rose smiled. She put the book back where she had found it, turned off the light and closed up the room, and returned to the kitchen.

"Did you find what you were looking for?" asked Elizabeth.

"Oh yes," replied Grandma.

"Well?" said Elizabeth.

"I can't say anything yet, but if what I suspect is true, you are in for a very pleasant surprise."

"Well, if you're not going to tell me what all this is about, I'm going to go to bed early. I want to go to the stables in the morning," Elizabeth said.

"I think it would be a good idea for me to get an early night too," said Grandma.

Elizabeth went to her room. She tried to read a book, but the letter from Thalios kept popping into her head.

She eventually fell asleep with the ever faithful Charlie curled at her feet.

Chapter One Hundred and Five

Elizabeth called ahead and spoke to Mavis, her riding teacher.

"I was hoping you would change your mind and try to ride with us again," Mavis said.

"I'm not in a wheelchair anymore," Elizabeth informed her.

"I know, Andre told me, that's wonderful news!"

"I was wondering, Mavis, since I haven't ridden a horse for a while, if you would give me a couple of lessons? Just until my legs are strong again."

"I would be delighted. Why don't you come to the stables today? I have an hour free this morning," Mavis replied.

"I'll head over now," said Elizabeth.

"I look forward to seeing you. Emily, Ben and Louise will be here. So will Lynda and Karen," said Mavis.

"Good, I'll see you in a few minutes."

Elizabeth hung up the phone, went to her room and rummaged around in her closet for her riding clothes.

She tried on her jodhpurs, delighted that they still fit. She pulled a hat box from the shelf of her closet and tried on her riding helmet.

"I look exactly the same as I did a couple of years ago," she thought, looking at herself in a full length mirror on the wall.

Elizabeth walked down the hall to the kitchen, where Grandma was sat drinking a cup of tea and reading a book.

"Going riding?" she asked, noticing how Elizabeth was dressed.

"I called Mavis. She said if I go over there now, she'll give me a lesson and I can meet up with everyone."

"Would you like me to drive you?" said Grandma.

"No thanks Gran, I'll walk."

"Be careful," said Grandma.

"I will," replied Elizabeth, heading for the back door.

She walked along the back pathway, through the gate, over the bridge and past the Willow tree. Then she turned right and made her way along the riverbank until she came to a gate. She climbed over it, turned left and continued along the road until she came to the Levell's farm.

When Elizabeth reached the tack room, everyone was waiting for her, including Andre.

"Surprise!" they all shouted, as she opened door.

"We bought you something said Andre," handing her a wrapped box.

Elizabeth stood, looking at everyone.

"Well open it," said Lynda.

Elizabeth unwrapped the box. Inside, were a pair of string riding gloves.

"Thank you!" she said, trying them on. "They fit perfectly."

"Come on, you lot," said Mavis. "Time for your lesson. Elizabeth, I want you to ride Arthur."

"Thanks Mavis. I really like him."

"Well go and saddle him up and let's get busy," said Mavis, walking out of the tack room.

After the lesson, Elizabeth dismounted from her horse.

"Oh my" she said, rubbing her backside. "I'm already getting sore!"

"I'll put Arthur away for you," said Andre.

"I can unsaddle him," said Elizabeth.

"Tell you what," said Andre. "I'll unsaddle your horse today. You unsaddle my horse after our next lesson."

"Deal," she said, feeling the soreness begin to travel from her groin, down into her legs.

Grandma Rose was waiting for Elizabeth by the office door of the stables.

"What are you doing here, Gran?"

"I thought you might be tired, so I thought I would come and pick you up."

"Thanks. I am a bit tired, and saddle sore," she said, rubbing her backside, "but I had a lot of fun! It felt good to ride a horse again."

When they reached the cottage, Elizabeth changed her clothes.

"I'm going to go to the Elven Realm and meet with the king," said Grandma.

"Nothing serious, I hope," said Elizabeth.

"No," said Grandma, "just the usual matters that need to be taken care of."

"I think I'm going to relax and read a book, while you're gone," said Elizabeth.

Elizabeth watched as Grandma Rose walked across the bridge and disappeared into the Willow tree.

She went back into the house, picked a book from the bookcase, and returned to the garden.

"Another beautiful day," she thought, sitting on a lawn chair by the living room window.

As she read, Elizabeth became drowsy. After a few minutes, she fell into a light sleep.

***

Elizabeth was holding an egg, and not just any egg. It was about the size of a basketball. Her grandmother was standing in front of her.

Grandma Rose put her hand on the egg.

"That egg will not fit in the saucepan. We will need a smaller egg for breakfast," she told Elizabeth.

Elizabeth woke with a start. Gideon was knelt down on one knee, peering at her. He had his hand on her arm, and he was grinning.

"What's so funny?" she asked.

"You were mumbling something about a giant egg. You have dangerous dreams, Elizabeth. Be careful. Remember what happened when you dreamt that it snowed?"

Elizabeth dismissed his remark. "What are you doing here, Gideon?" Where is Golda?"

Gideon laughed again.

"I sneaked out. I thought you and I could have some fun while your grandma is with my father."

Elizabeth stood. "What kind of fun?"

"Can we go to your stables and ride horses do you think?" he asked. "Vandrayven gave me this potion to take. He said that if I swallow it, I will look more human. You know, like when he made you look like an elf."

"No," she said.

"No?" he said.

"Gideon, go home. When we have been seeing each other for a while, it might be all right to do that, but for now, we have to follow the rules."

Gideon hung his head, dropping his shoulders in mock shame. Before Elizabeth could stop him, he turned and kissed her on the cheek. He jumped to his feet and ran down the pathway, laughing as he did so. He turned and waved to her, as he disappeared into the branches of the Willow tree.

Elizabeth put her hand up to her cheek and rubbed it. She smiled and went back into the house. As she entered the kitchen she turned and saw something moving under the table.

A meckit ran at her.

"PYRIDUS ASKEMYU," she shouted, pointing at it.

The creature stopped. Elizabeth heard a popping sound as it burst into flames.

"They sound like popcorn!" she said to herself. "And now there's a mess on the floor."

She swept the remains of the meckit into a plastic kitchen bag.

"I know where you came from," she thought, holding up the bag. "King Kalidryd is going to get a little visit, and he can have you back."

She left the house and went down the path to the Willow tree.

Chapter One Hundred and Six

Elizabeth reached the gates at Humadria, and two elven guards ushered her through.

"Can I get you a carriage, my lady?" asked one of the guards.

"No thank you," she replied.

Elizabeth set out on foot across the countryside. A mile from the gate, she knelt down and called to Pennarius.

A few minutes later, she saw his outline in the sky.

He landed gracefully beside her.

"It is good to see you again, Elizabeth."

Elizabeth looked at him.

"He is magnificent!" she thought.

"I am always happy to see you, Pennarius," she said, patting his shoulder.

"This used to be a meckit," she said, holding up the bag, showing it to him.

"It doesn't look much like a meckit anymore!" said Pennarius.

"I think it came from the King Kalidryd. Would you take me there, so I can deliver the meckit to him?"

"It would be my pleasure," said Pennarius.

He knelt down so Elizabeth could get on his back, and they headed towards Distardrian.

A few minutes later, the elviron castle came into view. Pennarius put her down.

"I will wait by those trees," he said.

"Thanks Pennarius, I shouldn't be long," Elizabeth said, walking towards the castle entrance.

With the bag of meckit remains in her hand, Elizabeth entered through the front gates of the castle.

The elviron guards ran from her, as she approached them.

Elizabeth opened the massive door to the castle's interior.

An elviron servant saw her and started to run.

"Stop!" she commanded.

The servant stopped in his tracks.

"Come here," she said.

The servant and turned, unable to resist, he walked to her.

"Take me to the king."

The elviron servant turned and climbed the stairway. Elizabeth followed.

When they reached the top of the stairs, they walked to the end of the passageway. In front of them was a large door. The servant opened the door and went through. The king stood and was about to say something to the servant when he saw Elizabeth.

At first he made to run, but then stopped. He turned around and sat back down.

"Why are you here?" he asked.

Elizabeth held up the meckit remains. She opened the bag, emptying it onto the dusty floor.

The king looked down at the grey dust. "What is that?"

"This was what I think you call a meckit. I say this because it is now dust," Elizabeth replied.

The king recoiled with fear and disgust.

"Don't send anymore of these horrible little things. In fact, don't send anything else after me, or anyone that I am related to, am in contact with, or may come into contact with in the future. If you do," she pointed to what was left of the meckit. "I will do this to you. Do you understand?"

The king stared back at her, nodding.

"Good," she said.

Elizabeth turned away from him and headed towards the door. The king rose out of his chair and threw and threw a knife. Elizabeth, not turning around, put her hand into the air and caught it.

She turned and threw it back. The knife whizzed past the king's left ear, embedding itself in the back of his chair with a dull thud.

Elizabeth made her way unhindered until she was outside of the castle walls. She returned to the wooded area, where Pennarius was grazing.

"All is well?" he asked, as she approached.

"Yes, it is," she replied.

Pennarius returned Elizabeth to where he had picked her up.

"Thanks again," she said, sliding off his back.

"Anytime," Pennarius replied.

Elizabeth watched as he flew off into the distance, then made her way home.

***

When Elizabeth arrived at the cottage, Grandma Rose had returned and was preparing the evening meal.

"Where have you been?" she asked. "I thought you were going to have a relaxing day?"

Elizabeth explained what had happened.

"That was a foolish and impetuous thing to do," said Grandma,

"If I hadn't killed the meckit, it would have killed me," said Elizabeth.

"That's not what I mean and you know it," said Grandma.

"The elviron king was really scared," Elizabeth said, stifling a giggle.

"Oh, you think scaring someone is funny?" asked Grandma, trying to keep a straight face.

"No!" said Elizabeth. "It's just that... well, he had it coming."

"Eat your supper," said Grandma, ignoring Elizabeth's remark. "I'm going to have an early night. We'll need to leave early tomorrow."

"Why?" asked Elizabeth.

"Druid's get up early," replied Grandma.

"Gran?" asked Elizabeth.

"You will see," Grandma replied.

Chapter One Hundred and Seven

Grandma Rose woke Elizabeth at 4:30 a.m. the next morning. They ate breakfast and headed towards Avebury.

Elizabeth sat in the car, watching the fields as they drove into the countryside.

"Do you know why we are meeting Thalios?" she asked.

Grandma Rose kept her eyes on the road. "We will have to see won't we."

The rest of the journey was made in silence, as they both imagined in their own minds what it could possibly be.

They arrived at the wall with the gate, and Grandma parked the car. Elizabeth got out and looked around.

"It's a bit chilly out here," Elizabeth said, putting on her jacket.

Grandma Rose went to the back seat of the car and pulled out a blanket.

"I don't need a blanket, Gran."

Grandma bundled the blanket under her arm. "But I might."

Elizabeth opened the gate, and they walked through, closing it behind them. They had been walking for about a minute, when Thalios appeared and started to walk with them.

"One day, he is going to tell me how he does that," thought Elizabeth.

"Where is Keslyn?" asked Grandma Rose.

"We are going to meet with her in the woods up ahead," Thalios answered.

"Why am I here Thalios?" Elizabeth asked.

Thalios looked down at her. "All in good time. You will see."

They continue on for five more minutes, until they came to a dense part of the woods. They approached a little cave hidden in the side of a small rock face.

Thalios bent down.

"Keslyn? Elizabeth and Lady Rose are with me," he called.

They all heard a little whistling sound, as Keslyn answered. Thalios motioned for Grandma Rose and Elizabeth to follow him. They crouched down, crawling through into the darkness. A few feet in, they came to a small cavern.

Thalios produced to torch and turned it on.

Against the back of the wall was what resembled a large birds nest. Keslyn was lying down beside it.

"It's nice to see you again. I've been waiting for you," she pushed into Elizabeth's head.

"It's nice to see you too, Keslyn. What's going on?" Elizabeth pushed back.

Thalios looked into the nest, then he and Keslyn both looked at Elizabeth.

"Come here Elizabeth and see what is inside," said Thalios.

Elizabeth stepped forward, peering into the ring of moss and branches. In the middle of the nest was an egg about the size of a football. It was predominantly black, with blues, purples, greens and reds running all over it.

"Is this the egg that Keslyn told me about?" she asked, looking at Thalios.

Thalios nodded and smiled. He waved his hand, gesturing for Grandma Rose and Elizabeth to sit.

"Keslyn has given birth to a new dragon," Thalios informed them. "She wants you to be its companion. All dragons give their offspring to another to take care of. Eventually, the dragon will not only become your companion, but your guardian. This is a great honour. Dragons mostly give their offspring to us druids to care for, but in this instance, Keslyn has chosen you.

If you agree to take the dragon, you must guard it with your life. This is a commitment of a lifetime. Your life will be extended by many years, the elves will see to that. If you bond with the baby dragon you will both be connected forever."

Elizabeth bent down and touched Keslyn.

"I would be honoured," she pushed into the little dragon's head.

Keslyn rubbed her head against Elizabeth's hand. Grandma Rose started to cry, as she handed the blanket to Elizabeth.

"Wrap it well," said Grandma. "We have to get it back to the car."

"You knew, that's why you brought the blanket," said Elizabeth.

"Yes, it is in the prophecy," said Grandma. "It says that the elf/human with the elven powers will have a dragon as her companion. The prophecy is almost complete. I have already informed the king. So they will be expecting to see the baby dragon soon."

"Almost?" Elizabeth asked.

Grandma Rose looked at Thalios, then back to Elizabeth.

"That discussion is for another time. Let's get this egg back to our house and take care of it," said Grandma.

Keslyn touched Elizabeth with her claw.

"Take care of my baby," she pushed into Elizabeth's head.

"I promise I'll protect him or her with my life," she answered.

Chapter One Hundred and Eight

A week later, at 2:30 a.m., Keslyn and Thalios arrived at Willow View Cottage. Half an hour later, a baby dragon was introduced to the world.

It was a boy, and Keslyn was there to nudge him out of his egg, towards Elizabeth. He waggled to her and climbed up into her arms.

"What shall I call him?" said Elizabeth, cradling the baby.

"You have to be the one to name him," said Thalios.

"Merlyn, I'll call him Merlyn," said Elizabeth.

"Very appropriate under the circumstances," commented Thalios.

"It's time to go," Keslyn pushed into Elizabeth's head. "Can I say goodbye to him?"

Elizabeth gently put the baby dragon on the floor. Keslyn brushed her face against his.

"Thank you," Keslyn pushed into Elizabeth's head.

"Oh, no. Thank you," Elizabeth replied.

Epilogue

Elizabeth, with the help of Gideon and their chaperone Golda, began the task of bringing up a dragon.

Gideon was delighted with the little creature and visited often to play with him. Elizabeth took him down to the Elven Realm and showed him to Vandrayven. He cast a spell on little Merlyn to make him invisible if needed, to protect him in the Human Realm.

Charlie thought that a baby dragon for a playmate was just fantastic. They frequently played until they both dropped from exhaustion.

Grandma Rose decided to permanently employ a tutor for Elizabeth. It became a little difficult to explain away some of the times that Elizabeth could not attend school.

Time passed quickly.

The next five years passed with no incident. Elizabeth's relationship with Gideon grew. The time was coming for the two of them to make preparations for their wedding.

Elizabeth was in the garden one morning, sipping her lemonade and enjoying the sunshine, when she noticed an elven guard coming towards her.

"I wonder what he wants?" she thought, getting up from her chair.

But that is another story.

Acknowledgments

I would like to thank the following people for their contributions:
GlenBledsoe for your advice on writing,
Dr. Tony Valley for patiently reading my books before they were books,
My editor, Lee Shaw for believing in my work, and
My beta readers, Amanda Clark, Beth Negrey, and Kelly Ingram.

A special thanks to Jean and June of Wroughton, UK for allowing me on their property.

Author's Bio

Jacqueline Nydam was born in the United Kingdom. She now lives in Oregon. Jacqueline loves to spend her spare time riding horses with her husband, and taking long walks with their dogs.

She occasionally returns home to the U.K. to visit her family and friends.

Designer's Bio

Jack Tuckwell lives and works in Wiltshire, UK. Currently working for himself under the name Alarm Eighteen, he is producing a range of graphic and typographic artwork, illustrations, 3D spatial design and commissioned paintings. www.alarmeighteen.co.uk

Coming in 2014

The Mirronstep

The Grymlons are dying and the secrets to saving them are lost in time. Elizabeth must find a legendary mirror that will let her search the past in a quest to save the Gymlons and the world that will be irrevocably changed upon their death.

www.ingramcontent.com/pod-product-compliance
Lightning Source LLC
Chambersburg PA
CBHW020240200626
46816CB00001BA/58